By Rhys Ford

I0691647

Clockwork Tangerine
With Poppy Dennison: Creature Feature 2
Dim Sum Asylum
Grand Adventures (Dreamspinner Anthology)
Murder and Mayhem
There's This Guy

COLE MCGINNIS MYSTERIES
Dirty Kiss
Dirty Secret
Dirty Laundry
Dirty Deeds
Down and Dirty
Dirty Heart
Dirty Bites

HALF MOON BAY
Fish Stick Fridays
Hanging the Stars

HELLSINGER
Fish and Ghosts
Duck Duck Ghost

SINNERS SERIES
Sinner's Gin
Whiskey and Wry
The Devil's Brew
Tequila Mockingbird
Sloe Ride
Absinthe of Malice

Published by DREAMSPINNER PRESS
www.dreamspinnerpress.com

FISH AND GHOSTS

RHYS FORD

REAMSPINNER
PRESS

Published by
DREAMSPINNER PRESS

5032 Capital Circle SW, Suite 2, PMB# 279, Tallahassee, FL 32305-7886 USA
www.dreamspinnerpress.com

Fish and Ghosts
© 2013 Rhys Ford.

Cover Art
© 2017 Anne Cain.
annecain.art@gmail.com
Cover content is for illustrative purposes only and any person depicted on the cover is a model.

ISBN: 978-1-62798-417-1
Digital ISBN: 978-1-62798-416-4
Published December 2013
v. 1.1

Printed in the United States of America
∞
This paper meets the requirements of
ANSI/NISO Z39.48-1992 (Permanence of Paper).

This book is for Jenn. She really, really loves this book and licked it first. So it's hers. Kind of like that last chocolate donut.

Acknowledgments

As ALWAYS, any book with my name on it goes to the Five; Jenn, Penn, Lea, and Tamm—as well as my beloved younger sisters, Ree, Ren, and Lisa. Couldn't have gotten here from there without you.

To the Dreamspinner staff, I send you all a huge thank-you—Elizabeth North, Lynn, Julianne, Mara, Ginnifer, Grace, Julili, lyric, and everyone else there. Thank you. Thank you. With cookies too.

And once again, my Beta readers and the Dirty Ford Guinea Pigs—Reetoditee "Didi" Mazumdar, Bianca "Bubbles" Janian, Tiffany "Coffee Bunneh" Tran, Lisa "Java Goddess" Horan, Linda E., Piper Vaughn, Amy Peterson, Aniko, Camiele White, CC Hunt, Christy Duke, Crissy Morris, DarienMoya, Giselle Key, Stellar Princess Fantastica Heather Cook (thank you for your name), Jess B., Leigh A.D. Logan, Lea Walker, Lisa "Lakerkat" L., Marna Riser, Nikyta Jerkins, Sadonna, Sey, Sue N., Verena M., VJ Summers, Whitney Watkins.

Lastly, to the things that go bump in the night. Thank you for keeping me company when I couldn't sleep.

Prologue

"SMELL THAT?" Wolf Kincaid paused at a narrow doorway, his broad shoulders wedged up against the creaking wooden frame. "Effervescent in nature, a whiff of dirt."

He was speaking of the wispy mist blanketing the battered floor, its swirls created by the uneven knotty planks as much as by the two men walking down the hall. Around Wolf, the plantation house creaked with noise and echoes, tidbits of sound reaching back to tantalize the men sent to document its haunted history.

Built during the early days of Louisiana's settlement, Willow Hills Plantation was once a hub of Southern activity, providing the surrounding area with food and, during bleaker times, an avenue for escaped slaves to begin a new life in the North. Stripped down nearly to its frame by its aging tenants, Willow Hills had been resurrected from its near death as a bed-and-breakfast. Positioned as the last stop of an Underground Railroad tour, the plantation soon earned a reputation of being a great place to eat as well as a home to restless spirits.

It was the latter part of its reputation that Wolf Kincaid came to tear apart.

"Hey, Wolf, want me to get an air sample?" Matt peeked out from behind his shoulder-mount camera, its illuminated trim splashing up enough of a glow for them to see in the plantation's dark halls. "Or is it an ambient leak from outside? Swamp gas?"

"*Some* kind of gas," Wolf muttered. "Nah, I know what it is. Don't bother."

No, he wasn't going to feel bad about taking out the Willow Hills ghosts.

And if he had a chance, he'd go back in time and kick the shit out of its builders too. At a little over six feet, he should have had more space to walk around in the upper floors' hallways. Instead, he felt like Alice after she had too many frosted cakes. His elbows hurt from banging into the walls, and the household staff wouldn't have to dust for cobwebs because Wolf was pretty sure he'd walked through all of the ones in the attic storerooms. If he'd thought ahead, he could have taken a feather duster, done the job right, and charged the Willows for a deep cleaning as well as a spectral investigation.

Another step into yet another tiny room in the warren of servants' quarters and Wolf found himself face-to-face with an apparition.

As apparitions went, it was fairly strong. White pallor, groaning black mouth, and empty eye sockets, with trails of ebony bleeding out under the spirit's surrounding mottled skin. Her features were difficult to see, but the jut of her breasts straining against the thin lawn shirt she wore left Wolf with no doubt that he was staring through a woman.

Then she opened her mouth and a horrendous shriek rattled his eardrums and set fire to Wolf's nerves.

Somewhere behind him, Matt screamed, and from the thudding sounds that soon followed, Wolf guessed he'd toppled over, probably taking the camera with him. The woman flickered in and out, a blue-white veil of features and fabric. Without warning, she rushed them, advancing on Wolf with her hands stretched out in front of her like talons.

He ducked. It was instinct born of human nature, and he cursed himself for it nearly as soon as he curled his shoulders away from the ghost. An icy chill hit him, whooshing over his face and arms. Then another struck, a stronger blast of air, cold enough to peel goose bumps up from his skin. The screaming continued, a murderous shriek echoed at a lower volume by his cameraman.

Something wet struck his cheek, and Wolf turned, looking up at the angled ceiling, where clotting strands of something dark and viscous dripped slowly down on top of them. It smelled rank and of curdled metal. Dabbing at a moist spot on his cheek, Wolf tasted the thick fluid, recoiling at its sourness when it spread over his tongue.

"Blood," he murmured, holding up his wet finger for Matt to see. "Are you recording this?"

"I'm fucking freezing my nuts off, and I think I swallowed my tongue." The young man struggled to get to his feet, tugging his ill-fitting Hellsinger Investigations T-shirt down over his slightly rounded belly. "Did you fucking see that? Shit, tell me you got readings on that."

"Oh, I got something on it," Wolf replied with a grin. "Come on, Matty. See if you can keep up."

He left the younger man behind, edging past him, then launching into a full run down the tight staircase leading to the kitchens. His elbows took a beating. Obviously, his body had picked through his genetic soup and decided it preferred the enormous bulk of his Scottish ancestors above everything else and poured out his muscles and bones with a maniacal, enthusiastic glee.

While height and brawn were good in a fight, it made for shitty going while trying to run down a spiral staircase meant for tiny seventeenth-century women.

Somewhere behind him, Matt clomped along. He'd hired the young man for his filming and technical skills, not for going through an obstacle course, but Wolf didn't really care. Most of the time, Matt could keep up. This time, however, it wasn't as important as Wolf getting down to where he thought the apparition originated.

Because he needed to put an end to the haunting.

It was what he was paid to do. It was what he loved to do. Capturing that moment on film wasn't as important as just having that moment.

And Wolf Kincaid was famous for having those kinds of moments.

Booming thumps echoed in the rear of the house, percussive rounds loud enough to shatter the eerie silence that settled down after the ghost's shrieking. The walls around Wolf shook, and he ducked out of the way as a framed sampler fell off its hanger as he rounded the stairwell's landing.

Behind him, Matt followed, stomping and cursing at the tight fit. The young man would have a hard time of it. The camera was too big, too bulky to make the tight turns quickly if Matt insisted on keeping it fixed to his shoulder to film. Which was what he'd certainly do. It was what Wolf paid him to do, even as he was tumbling ass over teakettle down the stairs behind his boss.

The staircase let out into the servants' kitchen, a dank-smelling, closed-in room that, despite the staff's best efforts, seemed to cling to its grimy lower-class roots. Wolf slipped on a tile, his sneaker catching on a thick line of grout, the sandy mixture providing some traction against the overpolished ceramic floor.

Ahead, the noises grew louder, more ear-shearing rattles and booms. More shrieks followed, echoing first upstairs, then suddenly snapping to the bottom floor, louder and more profane than the ghostly banshee moans. Rounding the corner, Wolf found himself in a room directly beneath the staircase, a long, rectangular space the plantation used for storage.

A stein flew past Wolf's head, nearly clocking him on the temple. The heavy ceramic shattered against a wall behind him, and he felt a shard cut his cheek, the brief sting deepening into something heavy and wet on his skin. Another stein followed, then a plate wide enough to host a good-sized turkey.

"Fuck!" Matt exploded into a round of curses. From the sounds coming from behind him, Wolf guessed a piece of flying crockery had found its target in the cameraman or his equipment. "Poltergeists now?"

Wolf fumbled to find a light switch. His fingers found a bank of sliders on the wall next to the door, and the storeroom burst into view, two banks of overhead fluorescents throwing everything into a stark contrast of bright and shadow. Fully drenched in light, two women in period costume froze in place, one caught in the middle of throwing a metal steaming tray while the other's hands were tangled in audio-visual feed lines. The cables disappeared through a small hole in the ceiling tiles, and nearby, a tripod lay on its side on what looked like a camera case. Both women were bleached white from heavy layers of makeup, their eyes hollow and bleak from a coating of dense theatrical kohl.

Smug, Wolf gave both women a short, mocking bow, then sneered, "Hello, ladies."

Chapter 1

"THEY WERE pretending to be ghosts so people would go stay there?" Nahryn placed a steaming mug of black coffee in front of Wolf and settled into an empty wing chair next to his. "Why would someone do that?"

A bubbly young Armenian woman and Hellsinger's Girl Friday, Nahryn kept their office running at a finely tuned hum and, more importantly to Wolf, made certain he had a pot of Ka'u coffee to bolster him by the time he made it into their San Francisco office.

Even if sometimes her coffee was strong enough to bleach Wolf's dark-brown hair to white from its bitter shock.

"Because ghosts equal profit," Gidget pronounced from behind her teacup, her mascara-thick eyelashes fluttering the steam rising from her Earl Grey. "It was a pretty stupid rig too. Projection onto dry ice mists with leads feeding into speakers on the third floor. They're never going to get the pig's blood out of those ceiling beams."

Their technician and Matt's lover went for a more Rosie the Riveter look that morning, a piss-yellow bandana holding back a spill of flame-red curls from her pale face and her overalls creaking as she shifted in her chair, the heavy denim still so new it stank of dye. Glass cherries dangled from her lobes, a row of four in each ear, and they chimed when she moved her head. While they matched the printed cherries on her button-up shirt, Wolf thought it looked like she'd lost a fight with a fruit salad.

He'd tell Gidget that as soon as he told Nahryn about her coffee. One wrong, pissy word and Gidget could have his sensors bleeping a spectral hit on every pile of dog shit he walked by.

While he might get the hots for a long-legged man in jeans, he could commiserate with a straight man about the minefields of living with a woman. He spent days on end with two of them and still had to tread carefully with the best of them. Also—Wolf grinned into his coffee—he always had Matt to throw in as a sacrificial lamb whenever he needed an out.

"But that's lying," Nahryn insisted.

"It's what keeps us in business, Nah-nah," Wolf pointed out. "And since Willow Hills invoked our confidentiality clause and paid their invoice in full, we can't say anything about their two wayward docents. The powers that be didn't know, and now that they do, they want to make sure no one else does."

"So we can't even tell people they're lying?" Her big brown eyes were narrowing. "That's wrong too. The world sucks."

"People hire us to prove their ghosts are real or at least come up inconclusive." Turning on his tablet, Wolf tapped through his appointments. "Willow Hills gambled and lost. They didn't know they were playing loaded dice. It happens sometimes. A lot of people think they can pull one over an investigator—"

"But the equipment doesn't lie," Gidget crowed, resting her heels on the corner of the conference table.

"Nope. It usually doesn't." Wolf saluted her with his coffee mug. "Let's see what we've got on the books for today."

"You have an appointment with a Mrs. Walter Pryce the Third in half an hour. She called right as I was making coffee, so I didn't get a chance to put it down on the books yet." Nahryn scrolled through her own tablet, then stopped to wrangle her curly brown hair into a tie. "She wants to hire you to look into a haunting. She thinks it's bullshit."

"She actually say bullshit?" Wolf's eyebrows lifted. "People with *the Third* in their names don't usually trot out the word bullshit."

"No, she said implausible, but I was having problems spelling that so I just wrote down bullshit." Nahryn grinned at him. "I didn't think you'd mind."

"Nope, I don't," Wolf admitted. "Okay, I'm going to talk with Mrs. Pryce. Then, after that, I'll take all of you to 39 for some lunch."

"Crab?" Nahryn paused halfway out of her chair and did a little dance with her butt against the upholstery. "'Cause you know... *crab.*"

"For you, Nah-nah, we can get crab." He tweaked his Girl Friday's nose. "First Mrs. Pryce's boo-wigglies and someone get Matt on the phone. About time he got to work."

"MY NEPHEW is insane."

Wolf spared the woman a brief glance as he shuffled through the papers she'd brought with her. Mrs. Walter Pryce III was an older woman, one Born-to-the-Park, pinkie-lifting Junior Leaguer. Patting her swing of artfully done blonde hair, she took a moment to pause at the doorway of his pier-front office, her critical gaze taking in the space's blend of gentlemen's club furnishings and broad, sweeping view of the water. He almost didn't catch the curl in her lip or the slight flare of her nostril, but he did. The brittle smile that chased after the hint of disapproval slipped from her face. After tugging carefully at the hem of her cardigan, she then smoothed her black pencil skirt and held her head up as she let herself be led into Hellsinger's conference room.

Now, settled into a leather wing chair and armed with a porcelain teacup filled with a lavender-lemon blend, Mrs. Pryce seemed much more in control, especially after she'd shocked Wolf with her pronouncement. She nodded curtly at Wolf's glance, probably mistaking his curiosity for something else. Or maybe, Wolf thought, she didn't really care what he thought just so long as he took the assignment and delivered on the job.

"Rather than me reading through now, why don't you give me the highlights so I can decide if I'll take the case?" Wolf matched Mrs. Pryce's haughty sip of her tea with a sloppy slurp of his coffee.

"I didn't realize I was here to be auditioned." Another sip, and this time, the nostril flare remained too long on her face to be dismissed as a tic.

"I don't take every case presented to us," Wolf replied. "If I did, I'd never get any sleep. But please, tell me about your nephew… the insane one."

"Are you mocking me, Mr. Kincaid?"

"Not at all, Ms. Pryce." Wolf shook his head. A lot of people walked into Hellsinger either thinking they were crazy and hoping to find out they weren't or dancing on the razor's edge of needing a wraparound jacket and looking for someone to prove them sane. It was, however, the first time someone sat across of him and openly declared her prey nuts. "Please go on. I'm all ears."

"Tristan has always been a delicate boy." Her pinkie flexed slightly, hovering over the cup's handle as if she was afraid to let it touch the porcelain. "It all started when Great Uncle Mortimer Pryce died—"

"Mortimer?" Wolf nearly snorted coffee through his nose. "Really?"

"It's a family name," she replied smoothly. "My third son is named after him."

"God help him," he muttered to himself. "Sorry, continue. I didn't mean to interrupt."

"Tristan's parents were quite normal. Did the best they could for him, but of course, he always seemed to wander away. Even if he was right in front of you, he would... rather... appear to not be paying attention. Great Uncle Mortimer was fond of the boy and would have Tristan visit him over the summers. I personally didn't think his parents should have let him go to Hoxne Grange by himself. Mortimer was... a confirmed bachelor, if you know what I mean?" Her eyebrows somehow both lifted and scowled with disapproval, something Wolf had not thought possible before he'd met the woman.

He didn't answer, merely blinking with a muted ignorance of what she was implying. "There wasn't anyone for him to play with?"

"No, that is *not* what I meant," Mrs. Pryce said firmly. "Tristan was a young boy and at an impressionable age. Great Uncle Mortimer should not have had access to him. He filled the boy's mind with rubbish."

"What kind of rubbish?"

"That Hoxne Grange is haunted and that he somehow was its caretaker... the ghosts' caretaker." She shuddered, either with the foolishness or the growing bitterness of the cooling tea. "Mortimer was one thing. I mean, he was an older gentleman. Very set in his ways and the Grange is... well, it's a family legacy. The Pryce family had it built nearly a century and a half ago. It's on a fantastic property in Mill Valley. Great Uncle Mortimer inherited it when his father died. When he passed, he left everything to Tristan. It's been a touchy subject in the family since then."

"So Tristan getting the property wasn't expected?" Wolf began taking notes, diagramming out the Pryce family tree.

"No, my husband is the next eldest son in the Pryce family. Tristan's father was his youngest brother." She set her cup down, the saucer rattling beneath it. "It should have gone to him, but instead, Tristan is Mortimer's sole heir, and from what we can tell, he's continued the man's insane claims about the Grange being haunted."

"How long has he been its owner?"

"Since he was nineteen. Really, it was too big a burden to hand over to a teenager. He's almost twenty-eight." Mrs. Pryce's mouth flattened into a line, crinkling her pink lipstick. "Luckily, he kept most of the landscaping staff, and there is a daily housekeeping staff that comes in, so at least the estate isn't being run to the ground."

"So he's maintained it?"

"Thankfully, Mortimer set up a trust fund to dispense monies to Tristan until his twenty-eighth birthday. It truly is a blessing. Tristan's... an artist of sorts. A children's book writer, I think. Certainly not enough of an income to keep the Grange up." She lifted her shoulders in an elegant shrug. "On Tristan's birthday, he'll inherit the rest of the estate and have full control of its assets. The family is concerned that with Tristan's... peculiarities... he'll be taken advantage of. We'd like you to help us ensure this will not happen."

"What about Tristan's parents?" Wolf cocked his head, tapping the tip of his pencil on two empty boxes on his flow chart.

"Carol and Sandy... Alexander was his real name... they died in a small plane crash off of the coast of Italy about six months after Tristan inherited the estate." A frown crinkled her smooth brow, and she played with a button on her sweater. "Sandy was against Tristan living there. He thought Mortimer was setting his son up to continue playing his little ghost game. Of course, Tristan denies this. He fully believes the Grange hosts his little friends. He's turned the family home into an *inn*, Mr. Kincaid, and the majority of his guests are *not* real."

Wolf didn't have to guess at the Pryces' motivations. Mortimer's money and estate seemed to be their first priority, although he couldn't rule out the woman's concern for her nephew. A few taps on his tablet called up the Grange's visual from an overhead map. Constructed during the Gilded Age, the sprawling estate was built into a nest of hills, and from what Wolf could make out, clearly designed by someone with a love for the Renaissance Revival form. A photo of Hoxne Grange called up a view of its front drive and landscaped grounds. The place was huge—sprawling seemed to be too weak of a word for the winged W set among the redwood trees—and embellished with formal gardens.

"What do you want me to do? I'm not in the business of declaring people mentally incompetent," Wolf pointed out. "Even if I've got a sheepskin telling you I can."

"The family would like you to stay at the Grange and investigate Tristan's claims. Your agency is known to be fair. We'd just like you to show Tristan that his ghosts only exist in his mind. If you can do that, Mr. Kincaid, just show him that the Grange isn't a way station for phantoms, we will pay you anything you ask for. He needs to be shown reality, Mr. Kincaid, and I think you're just the man to do that."

HIS UNCLE was going to wear a hole in the library floor; Tristan was sure of it. The last half hour was ticked off by the squeak of his Italian loafers when he turned, a five-second interval bleeding off Tristan's morning. Checking the grandfather clock for what he thought might have been the hundredth time since Walter Pryce III came through his front door, Tristan waited for his uncle to wind up yet another argument meant to move him out of the Grange.

"Your aunt is speaking with the agency now—" Walter began another circuit, his meaty hands clasped around his back.

"Is she still counted as my aunt if she's your third wife?" Tristan huffed a breath up at his forehead, hoping to move a chunk of blond hair away from his eyes. If he used his fingers, he knew he'd get trapped in playing with his hair, and anything Walter said to him would be lost in the contemplation of how the sunlight changed the colors as it bled through the shafts. "I mean, Aunt Judith counts because she was first, right? Sharon maybe because she had Mortie, but Ashley? Is she my aunt too?"

"Tristan, please concentrate on what I'm saying to you." The man harrumphed, exhaling forcefully enough to make his lips flap. Tristan's fingers itched for a sketchbook, wanting to scribble out his impressions of a disgruntled walrus waddling back and forth on an ice floe. "We're hoping you'll see reason."

"Reason…." Tristan repeated softly. "By opening the Grange up to people who chase ghosts?"

"They are paranormal psychologists. Or at least the agency head is." Walter turned again, squeaking off another tick of time. "I know it would be terrible to discover that perhaps you've been encouraged to… um… what is the word I'm looking for?"

"Hallucinate?" he supplied for his uncle. "Sucking on guano from the bats in my belfry? Rowing with one oar?"

"You're not crazy!" His uncle frowned, caught in midstep, his large belly jiggling under his suit. "Look, boy, I'm fond of you. I want the best for you. Just let them come stay here for a bit and see what they can find. Is that too much to ask?"

Tristan stretched out his legs, rubbing at the cramp forming along his thigh. He'd not asked Mara to turn the heat on in the library that morning until Uncle Walter's sedan pulled up in front of the Grange. It had been an unexpected visit, and they'd both sworn under their breath when the man's driver let his short, soft-bellied uncle out of the car.

Well, he'd sworn. Mara merely muttered darkly and scurried off to turn the heat on before pulling together a coffee tray for his guest. He'd sworn enough for both of them. His elderly housekeeper, while a pleasant woman for the most part, liked to get her daily work done and out of the way so she could spend her afternoons watching the shows she'd recorded the night before. Since most of her day included making sure he kept himself fed, Tristan didn't care how she spent her days so long as the Grange was always guest ready. With fifteen bedrooms to keep up and two young women from the nearby town coming in to help her dust and mop, Mara kept the Grange primed and lemony-fresh, and she resented his uncle's sudden appearance on a tightly scheduled Tuesday morning.

Tristan wasn't too fond of Walter's arrival either. He had only ten more minutes before he had to be at the reception desk, and from the man's squeaky pacing, it didn't sound like Walter Pryce was going to leave until Tristan gave him some kind of concession.

"And if they find out I'm not crazy?" he offered up in exchange. "Suppose they hand you a report that I'm sane and the Grange is what Uncle Mortimer and I say it is? Will you leave me be then?"

The look of confusion on his uncle's face told Tristan the man had not considered that possibility. A few lip flaps and another squeaka-squeaka pass later, Walter Pryce grumbled, "If he comes back and says that there's something here, then yes, I'll acknowledge that there *might* be something to your claims. But the agency has to verify that there is some sort of activity here. If not, then I'm going to insist you stop this nonsense and come home."

"I am home, Uncle Walter," Tristan said softly. "I've lived here at the Grange for most of my adult life and spent nearly all of my summers here. If this isn't home, then where is that?"

"Then we'll come to you." The man's hand on his shoulder was meant to be reassuring, but Tristan felt it held a greater weight than his uncle's skin, bones, and flesh. "We'll come here to you at the Grange. It *is* the family home, after all."

He was able to hustle his uncle out with a few murmured assurances and then exhaled a sigh of relief when the door closed behind him. A few seconds later, the sedan's quiet engine rumbled away and Tristan was left with the silence of the Grange around him.

The snick-snick of a dog's nails on the foyer's parquet floors echoed up into the high ceiling, and Tristan grinned at the shaggy gray head poking out from around the side of the sweeping mahogany counter Mortimer Pryce had built to be the Grange's reception desk.

"Come on out, Boris." He whistled to the Irish wolfhound. "He's gone."

"That dog knows evil when he smells it." Mara appeared at Tristan's elbow, moving as silently as one of the hall's guests.

"He knows Uncle Walter doesn't like him." Bending over, Tristan scratched at the enormous dog's floppy ears, sending Boris into a wiggling dance of ecstasy. "The man's not evil, he's just... closed-minded."

"Well, ghosts or no, he's a menace." The woman's harrumph was less pronounced than Walter's, but it was still impressive. "Your ghosties are your business. This is your house. If you want to hold balls for faeries, it's your right, and damn anyone else who says something against it."

A dusting rag hung from her elbow crook, and a faint hint of the green-tea soap Tristan gave her for Christmas perfumed her soft white skin, its delicate scent fighting a losing battle against lemon polish and the arthritic salve Mara used for her aching knees. A softly curved woman, she came up to Tristan's shoulder and often was in and out of a room, leaving behind only plates of sandwiches and cookies as evidence she'd been there. Something clung to the frosted candy floss of Mara's silvery hair, and Tristan reached over to pluck it off.

It was a single diamond stud, and he handed it to her. "Did you find the other one?"

"No." She shook her head, closing his fingers over the stone. "You keep that one. Maybe even change that silly hoop you have in your ear. You look like a little boy playing pirate."

"Maybe." He'd never told Mara the hoop belonged to his mother, a sliver of gold some faceless official handed him over her remains. She would scold him about being morbid, not understanding the hoop made him feel close to the woman who'd given birth to him but never really understood the changeling she'd been saddled with. "Or maybe even a second hole?"

"All you need is a parrot instead of that dumb Sasquatch you've brought into this house." A deep belling roll began to sound off from the library, and Mara sniffed at the chilling air. "Well, that's time, then. I'll be off. You deal with... *that*. Don't get to talking too much. I'll be bringing you lunch at noon, and don't forget, the gardeners will be here this afternoon, so get that beast to his walk before then."

"Yes, Mara."

He was talking to her back by the time the final chime from the library's grandfather clock struck. Settling himself on the stool behind the old-fashioned reception desk, Tristan immediately regretted leaving his coffee behind. There was no telling how late his morning arrival would be, and he'd only had half a cup. He'd have to scare up another pot before he headed to his study on the third floor.

"If I'd really been thinking, I would have brought a sketchbook too," he informed Boris. The dog lolled his long pink tongue at him and began a leisurely scratch at a spot near his jowls. "Really, Uncle Walter showing up just screwed the whole morning."

He didn't have to wait long. A few minutes after he'd sat down, the Grange's front doors rattled and swung open. A brisk wind cut through the open portal, carrying in the scent of rain on its breath. As suddenly as it opened, the wide doors closed, whispering on their well-oiled hinges. From behind the desk, Boris whimpered, tucking himself into a huddle, and Tristan patted the dog's broad head.

A wet footprint appeared on the wooden floor about two feet into the foyer, then another, a sopping trail of steps marking someone's progress toward the reception area. Elongated shadows played beneath a large round table set in the middle of the circular area, and something brushed against a stray pink rose that drooped from the enormous flower display sitting in a mint-green urn on the table's top.

She came into view a step or two after she passed the table, a bedraggled woman dressed in a neatly patched plain dress. Clutching her case in front of her in a white-knuckled grip, she nodded carefully at Tristan, then plastered a tentative smile on her pleasant face, clearing her throat before she spoke.

"I've come about the cook's position, sir." Her melodic voice was stamped with the distinct grit of a Northern Londoner, and if Tristan looked carefully, he knew he would see the black grime of the Lower Hells stuck under her fingernails. The rest of her was neat and trim despite the wear on her clothes and the fatigue on her still young face. "I've got no references, as the Lady turned me out for what the Lord was doing, but...."

"I don't need your references. You'll do fine," Tristan reassured her. "Wages are forty pounds, and you'll be given tea, beer, and sugar, as well."

"That's too generous, sir." She blushed, a pink lightening up her pallor. "I'm not skilled for that—"

"We've only one cook position," he cut her off gently. "Kitchens are through that door and down the hall. Can you start now? I've nearly a full inn and need a dinner set up for the guests. Your rooms will be behind the kitchen."

"Yes, sir. I can start immediately." She dropped into a short curtsey, nearly losing her satchel. "My name's Heather. Heather Cook, sir. Thank you so much. I won't be letting you down."

"I know, Heather. I know," Tristan said, pointing to the door. "Welcome to Hoxne Grange. We're glad to have you here."

As soon as the words left his mouth, she whispered away, dropping out of sight in flecks of light until nothing remained of her but the wet footprints on the foyer's wooden floor. He was about to fetch a mop when Mara came out of the door he'd directed Heather to.

"So she's gone, then?" Mara asked, wheeling out a metal mop bucket in front of her.

"Yeah, she is." Tristan smiled, saddened by the young dead woman he'd spoken to.

"Well, then, it's done until next Tuesday," his housekeeper pronounced in a firm voice. "I'll clean this up, and you go on upstairs. There's coffee waiting for you and some brekkie. Maybe later on, you'll get a nap. I know how Tuesdays wear you down."

"Thank you, Mara." He kissed the froth of silvery-white curls at her temple. "I don't know what I'd do without you."

"You'd be mopping your own damned floors every Tuesday after you hire your dead cook again." She slapped at his arm. "Go on with you, and take that cowardly beast with you."

Chapter 2

"HOLY FUCKING shit, that's a mansion!"

Matt wasn't far off in his description of Hoxne Grange. The edifice—no other word really suited the place—rose up over a roll of hills, its solid, tall chimneys jutting above the redwood stands surrounding the landscaped portion of the estate. Made of gray brick, the structure dominated the greens around it, its solid three-storied W shape thrusting into the overcast sky and demanding their attention as Wolf's SUV cleared its wrought iron gates. Arched windows cut through the stern brick, their form echoed in the covered walkways connecting the building's wings. The ground ran to evergreen bushes in the front, sculpted into oval shapes to mimic the softening lines of the home's solid Gilded Age architecture.

It was a place where people were born not only with a silver spoon in their mouths but rather the entire silverware set and a teapot or two thrown in just for shits and giggles.

Wolf loved it on sight, even if he had an overwhelming urge to drive around to the back and knock on the servants' entrance to be let in.

"*That*, Matt, is considered a cottage," Wolf informed his tech. "Only thirty rooms or so. Depends on how you counted them. Some of these places run to over seventy."

"Who the hell can clean that shit?" Gidget whistled and counted off the chimneys. "Christ, they've got like, ten fireplaces."

"Might be more. The chimneys sometimes support two fireplaces on stacked floors," he replied. "Wouldn't want the family to get cold."

The long driveway circled to the front door, wrapping around a fountain embellished with an enormous trio of fish taken right off a pirate's treasure map. Blackened with age, the piscine sculptures spouted out delicate sprays of water into the marble bowl below. A side road led off the main driveway to the back of the house where Wolf assumed there was a garage, but glancing back at the equipment they'd piled into the car, he wasn't quite sure where they'd need to unload.

"Okay, kiddies." Pulling up to the main entrance, he put the SUV into park and unsnapped his seat belt. "Let's go find us some ghosts."

Up close, the Grange was even more intimidating. Twenty-four rooms or not, Wolf figured the architect probably had a different idea of bedroom space than he did. When he opened the front door to let Gidget and Matt in first, they both dropped their voices to an awed whisper, and his suspicions about spatial relativity were confirmed once he stepped over the threshold.

He was pretty certain the Grange's front hall could have swallowed up his apartment building and still left enough space to house a Chinese restaurant and possibly a few branches of Starbucks besides.

"Holy fucking shit." Matt turned to whisper at Wolf. "And *this* is a cottage?"

"So they say." He hated that he lowered his voice and cleared his throat, nodding to the pigeonhole and grand swerve piece someone had the good luck to scavenge from one of San Francisco's grand hotels. Certainly not something that came with the house, the nearly eight-foot counter and back piece held its own in the Grange's cavernous foyer.

As did the blond man talking to himself behind it.

An explosion of flowers coming out of something porcelain and expensive blocked the young man, but Wolf was able to catch a peek through the artfully arranged rainbow of spiked flowers and pink-hued roses. Messy was a word Wolf would have used if fucking gorgeous hadn't first come to mind. Even the messy was merely a casual disregard to the polish one would expect in a multi-million-dollar mansion rich people called a cottage.

The blond hair was a dirty mix of mica flecks, gold, and mink, running to darker hues underneath. Tousled around an aristocratic face, it framed high cheekbones Gidget would be sighing over if given the chance and an aquiline nose obviously unmarred by any sibling's stray fist. He looked up from what he was doing, and Wolf would have sworn his eyes went black with displeasure. His lightweight sweater nearly matched the foyer's seafoam-colored vase, but his face was a bit colder than the chill that seemed to sweep over Wolf as he stood waiting. From across the room, the man's eyes appeared to be a brown as rich as the desk he stood behind, but as they drew closer, Wolf caught a bit of amber and green in their depths.

He'd been right about the anger, though. The man Wolf assumed was Tristan Pryce tightened his mouth as they drew near, and his changeable sage-brown eyes narrowed slightly. The talking to himself continued, a rolling, plush rasp hammered with those damned silver spoons and something darker Wolf couldn't identify.

Behind him, Matt and Gidget wandered about the foyer, enraptured with its art and furniture, but Wolf only had eyes for the man in front of him.

"It's all right if you can't sign your name," the man purred at a spot to the left of him, nodding politely at nothing. "Many people spend their lives doing more important things than learning to write. Let me register you and get you a room."

It seemed like Auntie Mrs. Walter Pryce The Third definitely had a leg to stand on. Hell, she had enough legs to give a horny centipede a hard-on.

"James Rhodes?" He spelled out the last name, and that mouth turned wicked with a knowing smile. "We'll just say that's right, then. Where are you from?"

The man's head tilted, spilling out golden strands over his shoulder. Wolf cleared his throat, and the blond ignored him, pretending to listen intently to the space in front of him. Gidget came up behind Wolf, either bored or curious about the man talking to himself.

"What's he doing?" she whispered into Wolf's ear.

"I have no fucking clue," he admitted softly. "I think he's pretending to check someone in. It *is* an inn after all."

"So should I unload the stuff, or we're just calling it a crazy and heading home?"

"Unload." Wolf jerked his chin toward the owner. "He's wrapping that up, by the sounds of it. Supposedly, Mrs. Walter called ahead. Let's see if she's made this easier or harder for us."

"Enjoy your stay, Mr. Rhodes. Dinner will be served tonight promptly at seven in the large hall, and there should be dancing in the ballroom later. Your room is on the second floor to the right." The man closed the large book he'd been writing in and motioned to a birdcage elevator set between the two staircases leading up to the second floor. "If you need anything, please let me know, and welcome to Hoxne Grange."

Wolf strode across the lobby floor toward the blond, squaring his shoulders as he went. From the jut of the other man's jaw, Wolf knew he was going to be in for a battle, and the growl that greeted him did nothing to persuade him otherwise.

"I was with a guest." His raspy purr wasn't an affectation. Something gritty curled through the man's voice, turning it smoky and sensual. "I take it you are from the society my uncle's wife spoke about."

"Dr. Wolf Kincaid." Wolf didn't hold out his hand. The man didn't seem to expect it because he placed his hands into the pockets of his jeans. "I take it you're Tristan Pryce?"

"I am," he replied smoothly. "No doctor or anything. I barely got out of high school alive. Well, since you're here, I guess I better find someplace for you and your team to sleep. Just the three of you?"

"Yeah." Wolf made a show of looking around. "Not many people here."

"The Grange is nearly full. I wish you'd called before you headed over here. I would have told you we're low on space. Uncle Walter was *supposed* to tell you to call ahead."

The man barely glanced up at Wolf as he opened the register again, flipping through the pages. Its yellowed sheets were covered with names and addresses, with room numbers and dates filling in three right-hand columns. From what Wolf could see, the Grange got a lot of guests, although how much of it was real was anyone's guess. Nearly two-thirds in, Tristan stopped and studied the book, comparing its ledger to a floor layout he pulled out from under the countertop.

"I really only have a couple of rooms left, and they're on the small side. Two of you will have to double up." Pryce reached behind him, drawing out two vintage keys on leather fobs, and held them out for Wolf to take. "They're on the third floor. Please keep in mind that the door marked Do Not Enter means you and your staff are not allowed past that point. Those are my personal quarters. Mara—the housekeeper—lives in the carriage house, so don't wander over there. The servant quarters behind the kitchen belong to Cook, so I'll kindly ask you to please respect her privacy during your stay. Most of the hotel visitors won't notice you, but if you hear any noises or music, please keep in mind that they are the Grange's guests. Some will be leaving us in a day or so. If you plan to be here longer than a few days, I can move you to a larger room, but chances are, you'll be shuffled back to the third floor if someone else checks in. Do you understand me, Dr. Kincaid?"

"Third floor, doubling up. Your space is off limits. Mara is the housekeeper, and Cook lives behind the kitchens," Wolf repeated as he took the keys. "Dinner's at seven in the large dining room, and we're not to disturb your... guests. Spectral or otherwise. Providing, of course, you *have* otherwise."

"I know my aunt has probably told you I'm insane, but the Grange *is*... well, it is what it is. Yes, we sometimes have the living come here, but mostly our clientele are spirits about to leave this earth. I make no apologies for what I do or how the Grange works." Pryce shrugged, dismissing Mrs. Walter's accusation with a feline elegance Wolf couldn't pull off if he'd been possessed by Pussy Galore. "If you have an issue with that, the door is right behind you, Dr. Kincaid."

"No, no issue at all," Wolf replied. "You know your aunt and uncle sent me to document the Grange's... purpose."

"They want me locked up someplace that serves me strawberry Jell-O and pudding, and they hope your report will help them buckle me into a wraparound jacket. I'm not stupid, Dr. Kincaid." The green in his eyes turned emerald, and the air around Wolf grew icy cold. "*Or* crazy."

"We'll need someplace to set up." Wolf held up his hands in surrender. "I'm not taking sides here, Pryce. If there's paranormal activity here, then yes, I want to document it. If there isn't, then that's what I'll report to you and your relatives. Either way, my team and I are here as observers. Nothing more."

"You can set up in the ballroom." Pryce slapped a copy of the floor layout on the counter, sliding the paper toward Wolf. "Under the musicians' shell. There is power there for your equipment. It's either that or the basement, but that sometimes floods. I don't think you want to set up anything that plugs in down there since we're expecting storms."

"Ballroom should be fine," Wolf replied as Tristan was about to turn away. "Pryce, if you didn't want us here, why did you agree to it?"

"Because my family wouldn't leave me alone until I did *something* to make them shut up." Pryce's mouth relaxed, plumping out his lower lip, and his shoulders lowered slightly. "So you are the result."

"I promise, we'll try not to get in your way. It's what? Friday? We should be out of your hair... maybe Monday at the latest."

"I'm not worried about you getting in my way." The corner of Pryce's mouth lifted, quirking a dimple in his cheek. "Piss any of the guests off and they'll let you know about it. Oh, and one more thing, Dr. Kincaid."

"Yeah?" Wolf raised his eyebrows.

"Dining in the hall is only for spectral guests. Cook will be providing their meal, and I don't think you'll get much to eat there." Pryce turned around, tossing a wave over his shoulder. "You and your team will be having supper with me in the Blue Room. I'll tell you when it's ready. Usually after Mara's done bitching me out about needing more clean linens."

WOLF WAS surprised to find a curvy, matronly woman dressed in a gray servant's uniform waiting for them at the landing to the third floor. Her slightly rounded face was creased with only the faintest of crow's feet, but age lurked in her steady storm-gray gaze. A whiff of silvery-white hair curled up from her forehead, and her hands were where her years sat, knuckles thickened from hard work, her fingers callused and rough. A single gold band sat on her thumb, its width much too clunky for a woman, and he spied the flattened portion of a signet stamp at the curve of the joint. Sensible loafers covered her feet, and the dress's stark gray was broken up by a broad swath of white ribbon around her waist with a thinner trim of the same white satin at her collar and sleeves. Her hands were clasped in front, and from the looks of her, she appeared to have settled in patiently, waiting for him to arrive.

"You must be Mara." He smiled as charmingly as he could at the woman. Honey was tastier than vinegar, his mother often said, but personally he thought vinegar had more use. It cut through honey and washed away its cloying sweetness better than anything he knew. "I'm Wolf. I'm heading the team that's staying here."

"Aye, he told me." Her cunning gaze flicked to the empty birdcage cab behind him. "He told me there were more than one of you. Are the others still downstairs?"

"Yep. They're setting up our equipment." He kept up the charm, although the woman certainly didn't appear to be swayed by it. No nonsense and firm, Wolf guessed Mara the housekeeper was Tristan Pryce's fierce gatekeeper and would put up with no bullshit from anyone who crossed her path. Lugging out the suitcases Gidget brought with her, he hefted them to the side, then grabbed his duffel.

"Give me the fobs. I'll take you to your rooms." He held them out, and she examined the room numbers stamped into their surface. "Ah, the sheets are fresh in there. I changed them a day ago, but you'll be needing more towels. Most of the rooms up here are used for storage, but Tristan has his suite and studio up here on the right wing. You'll be across on the left wing. He told you two of you will probably have to double up."

"That's fine." Wolf hurriedly grabbed a couple of the suitcases, abandoning the others for another trip, as Mara turned around and trod away on silent loafers to the left wing. "Gidget and Matt are… engaged."

"We'll put them in the bigger room, then."

The woman was nearly a foot shorter than him, but her pace left Wolf nearly panting. He felt like a water buffalo fumbling behind her elegant glide, with Gidget's hard-bodied suitcases rattling and bumping into nearly everything along the hall. He'd nearly taken out a slender-legged half-moon table with a pink hatbox and then almost irreparably damaged a full-length Victorian mirror as he turned quickly about to steady the rocking table. The hallway was narrower than the ones downstairs, and Wolf surmised the third floor had once been servants' quarters, something quickly confirmed by Mara's curt nod.

"There's not much of an attic, and that's mostly filled with old furniture. We keep these rooms for last-minute guests, really. These used to be smaller, but the late Mr. Pryce removed many of the walls to open up the space. They have their own washrooms, so you'll not be having to share with each other."

The long hallway of the wing's L boasted only four doors, two set near the juncture of the wing to the main part of the house and two farther down. One of the tall arched windows Wolf had seen from the outside let a wash of pale afternoon light into the hallway, bringing up the gold thread in the cabbage rose runner under his feet. Motioning to the nearer doors, Mara said, "Those are for storage. Mostly linens. If you find yourself needing something, please help yourself. If you want fresh towels, put the used in the hamper, and I'll replace them when I make the beds in the morning."

"You don't need to wait on us," Wolf said softly. "We're here to work. We can make our own beds and take down the linens since you're so busy."

The woman gave him a look he couldn't interpret, then fit one of the keys into a lock and opened a door to the right of the hall. Swinging it open, she motioned Wolf to go inside. "If you're taking the smaller, this is yours, then. It's facing the side gardens rather than the front lawn, and the bathroom is a mite bigger. Both rooms have only one bed each, but they're big. It should be tall enough for the likes of you. You won't be dragging your feet over the edge."

After depositing the suitcases in front of the other door, Wolf walked into his room, and the love he had for old homes flared up anew.

The Grange's idea of a smaller room was a far cry from Wolf's. He'd grown up with a closet space for a bedroom in order to get some privacy, and ever since then, he'd sworn he'd live someplace where he'd have room to spread out his elbows and not hit a wall.

In the supposed smaller room, he was pretty certain he could do a cartwheel or two and still have enough room for a lively jig. An enormous canopy bed took up the far wall, a thick red duvet plumped up to support a bank of feather pillows. The room held two armoires, a sideboard, two wing chairs, and a window-seat nook filled with more pillows. An open door to the right offered him a clear view of a very modern bathroom, but the rest of the furnishings were mellowed from age and polish. A Persian rug was spread out under the furniture, leaving enough space around the edges for the burnished bronze heating vents set into the floor.

It was comforting, inviting, and luxurious.

Wolf began to wonder what he'd have to do to move in.

"Will this do?" Mara's soft murmur intruded on his room lust. "It's really all we have left. The other rooms are… occupied."

Wolf tore himself away from his plotting and crooked an eyebrow at the woman, recalling what he'd come to the Grange to do. "Do you believe that? That this place is a hotel for ghosts?"

"There are too many things in this world that I cannot explain away, Dr. Kincaid," Mara demurred. "And if Tristan says there are spirits who come here for three days before they go on to their rewards, who are we to say that he is wrong… or crazy."

"Does he see them? Speak with them?" Wolf frowned, thinking back on the slender, blond man he'd seen downstairs. "When we came in, he was supposedly checking someone in. Am I supposed to believe he was helping someone or just being rude to us because he doesn't want us here?"

"Well, you'll believe what you believe. If you are right, then Tristan harms no one. But if you are wrong and his family succeeds in taking the Grange from him, then you've helped consign every lost soul he *could* have helped to wander the earth forever." Mara clasped her hands in front of her again, bringing herself to a stillness Wolf found unnerving. "Now, if that is all, I'm off to my afternoon. We hope you will enjoy your stay here at Hoxne Grange."

"YOU COULD have seen them to their rooms, Tristan Pryce," Mara said as she shuffled into the carriage house's parlor. "Your uncle would be disappointed in you."

"I know." Tristan knew she was right. Uncle Mortimer had been gracious to anyone who crossed over the Grange's threshold. "I just… he made me angry."

And since he was being truthful, Tristan also had to admit Dr. Wolf Kincaid stirred up a whole range of emotions and sensations he wasn't quite ready to deal with. Up until the moment he'd seen the tall, scruffy scientist, his attraction to men had always been theoretical at best. Face-to-face with a square-jawed, laughing blue-eyed man who smelled of sunshine and cherries, all Tristan could think about was the man's large hands running under his shirt and exploring every inch of his skin.

He'd never really understood the attraction to the bad-boy type until Wolf Kincaid darkened his foyer. The jeans worn low on his hips were so thin in places, Tristan had no trouble seeing the man's thick thigh muscles moving below an enticing, heavy swoop slung to the left of Kincaid's fly. His dark-brown hair was probably more in need of a cut than Tristan's, something he'd not thought possible since he frequently forgot about the blond mess until he discovered he really couldn't see out of it anymore. On himself, it looked like a game of monotone Pick-Up Sticks gone wrong. On Wolf Kincaid, the rumpled strands made it appear he'd just rolled out of bed after a long night of steamy sex and oiled fingers.

Running away was the only option, but Tristan stayed as long as he could, gripping the edge of the reception desk so he wouldn't climb over the counter, wrap his legs around Kincaid's, and beg the man to split apart his virgin body with anything Wolf wanted to use on him.

"So they're here for a week, then?" Mara shot him a look that Tristan would feel burning into him long after he was put to the ground. He'd known Mara since before he could walk, and there were times when he was certain she could see right into his thoughts and pluck out his deepest shames.

Especially since his mind wandered over to the thought of Wolf's tongue and wondered how it would feel down the length of his spine. Blushing furiously, Tristan nodded. He was still angry at the quacks on his doorstep and even more pissed off at his uncle, but they'd left him alone for far too long. Uncle Mortimer had warned him that the family would try to meddle. He'd just hoped they would wait until he was long dead before they stuck their noses into something they didn't understand.

"Kincaid said Monday, but you know these kinds of people." He slumped down into the soft confines of a floral loveseat. Hellsinger Investigations wasn't the first ghost-sniffing curiosity they'd had come 'round, but they certainly were the only one sent by his own family. "They get one whiff of the Grange and we have to toss them out on their asses. Maybe I should get Dobermans. Big, trained, vicious Dobermans. That only speak German. And bite scientists."

"They'd be a damned sight better than that hairy slug you've got by your feet." Mara snorted as Boris rumbled and flipped over, his rear leg sticking straight up in the air. "He'd sooner bite his own tongue in his sleep than defend you."

"Yeah, but I got him for companionship," Tristan murmured, scratching the dog's ruffled belly with his bare toes. "I'd want the Dobermans to eat people."

"That kind of talk will land you in the crazy house for sure." Her fingers flew through a length of yarn, her metallic knitting needles winking at Tristan as she dove and wove the thread into something he'd never get to wear. "So should I poison them? Bad shellfish? Sour pork?"

"No, someone else will just take their place." His groan matched the dog's. "The damned doctor is good-looking too. Because I needed *that*."

"Language, dear." Mara corrected softly. "If you're going to swear, make it worth your while."

"Sorry, that fucking doctor," Tristan murmured.

"Better. Lacks the punch of a good curse, but you don't really have it in you." She sighed, tucking her knitting into her lap. "Have you ever thought that maybe you should go and have some fun in the city? Maybe find someone to help you here?"

"Right, because someone who can see and talk to ghosts is out there looking for a day job." He got his pinky toe stuck in a gnarl on Boris's flank, and Tristan spent a few moments untangling himself. "Hell, can you imagine what would have happened to me if Uncle M hadn't taken me in? I'd be drooling in a corner and weaving baskets out of my own leg hair."

"I've seen your legs, dearie." Mara glanced pointedly at Tristan's shins. "You're as bald as a baby bird. Have you gotten any tingles from the doctor? Does he… how do they say it? Pitch your cricket?"

"I think it's bat for my team. I'm not even sure if 'pitching my cricket' is a thing." He had to think about it, then decided he was right. "I don't *feel* the gay. Shit, I barely can tell *I'm* gay. How the hell am I supposed to figure out if someone else is? There should be a handshake or something. Worst fucking club ever."

"Better use of profanity." She nodded approvingly. "Very natural. Now, talk to me about the doctor and why he makes you pink up like a spanked piglet."

Chapter 3

HOXNE GRANGE was a bowl of supercharged Rice Krispies someone poured Pop Rocks on top of, then set the whole thing on fire.

As soon as Gidget plugged in their first electromagnetic reader, it lit up and sang "Yankee Doodle Dandy," then broke out into a cover of Sugarhill's "Rapper's Delight" as imagined by R2-D2.

And that was only the least sensitive of their equipment.

"Fuck me." It was rare Gidget was left speechless, but that tiny whimper of profanity took her nearly a minute to work out of her mouth. "I mean, really… fuck me."

More surprisingly was Matt's lack of his standard comeback: *I do*. Instead, Hellsinger's cameraman stood at the bank of unlit panels and monitors, his mouth slack and motionless as their EM began to pop off with another long litany of squeaks and squeals.

"Did you drop it?" Wolf pulled out the device's charger and reset the scanner. The EM did a repeat performance, and if it had chosen at that precise moment to get up and dance across the table singing "Hello My Baby," Wolf would not have been surprised.

"Did you really just ask me if I dropped a piece of equipment?" Gidget's pineapple earrings chimed their own angry dance as her head jerked around so she could glare at him. "Really? Out of *your* mouth?"

"I dropped *one* mobile EM reader, and you give me shit about it for the next ten years?" He lifted himself over one of the wide banquet tables they'd pulled over to the ballroom wall and began to fiddle with connectors.

"You lobbed it into the Mississippi." She sneered at Wolf before sliding under the table to plug in another surge protector.

"It caught on *fire*. Do you remember that?" he replied, peering down at the space between the table and the wall at his tech below.

"That's because you told that poltergeist to quit fucking around and come out," Matt interjected. "And that someone must have gotten it wrong about him being a war hero because he was the biggest pussy you'd ever seen."

"Alleged poltergeist," Wolf grumbled back.

"The EM reader caught. *On. Fire.*" Matt began to unpack his camera case, arranging the cables he'd need on one of the smaller tables nearby. "I'm pretty sure one day you're going to get us killed."

Gidget's voice rose up from under the table. "Just make sure we're married first so I can collect the life insurance."

"Ghosts… if they exist… cannot kill you." Wolf found the end of a power cord and plugged in their main spectral analysis machine. Luckily, since he was stretched out over its main chassis, it did not begin singing "The Battle Hymn of the Republic." "See? This one's fine. Something's got to be wrong—"

"It's not turned on," Matthew said, reaching under Wolf's belly to flick the machine's switch. The machine flared on, and while it wasn't exactly a battle hymn, it was close enough Wolf suspected a flight of winged women to swoop down on them. "Yep, apparently that one's broken too. Well, it's a really nice house, pity we've got to go."

"I'm not taking a damned step out of this place until I use up all of the bath salts and soak in the tub we've got upstairs." Gidget pushed herself out from under the table and dusted off her cargo pants. "Okay. Light us up, babe."

Matt ran his hands over the bank of equipment, turning knobs and pushing buttons until the console ran hot with green and red lights. The monitors flared blue, flickering white noise across their screens as the data streams began to feed into their displays. One by one, each device powered up, scanning their immediate surroundings and processing the variations against the control equations Wolf had programmed in.

The cacophony was enough to drive them all back a step, and Gidget's inventive profanity was buried beneath a rapid crescendo from one of the night-vision goggles on the table as it overloaded. The whine grew louder. Then the goggles popped, showering sparks over the table and onto the ballroom's marble floor. Smoke seeped out from under a misting shield, curling in a little plume followed by the eruption of a tiny flame, its fire spreading quickly to swallow up the goggles.

They all dove for one of their fire extinguishers, and Gidget came up with the nozzle primed, unloading a swath of suppressant over the engulfed goggles. The fire died with a sizzling whimper, and she laid down another spray over the goggle's remains before poking at the smoldering pile of plastic and electronics with a pencil she'd had tucked behind her ear.

"Fuck. Me." Gidget shook her head, continuing her litany.

"Tell me about it." Matt wiped at the sweat on his brow with a packing towel. "Imagine what would have happened if I'd actually turned *that* one on?"

IT TOOK Wolf nearly half an hour to hunt down the Grange's owner. It should have been a fairly easy thing to do, but in the echoing boom of the empty mansion, Wolf found himself backtracking through a warren of rooms on the first and second floors with a side trip back to the ballroom when he thought he heard someone calling his name.

And found Matt and Gidget sprawled over one of the banquet tables, half-naked but fully aroused.

"Jesus!" He turned around, blocking his eyes. A scurry of sounds, swearing, and shuffling went on behind him, but Wolf didn't dare look. "I *don't* need to see that."

"What the hell did you come back here for?" Gidget admonished him. From the sounds of things, someone was hopping around, either trying to put pants back on or looking for a shoe. "You're supposed to be gone. Like... *gone*!"

"Doesn't look gone," Matt muttered from somewhere behind Wolf. "Looks like he's standing in the doorway like he's my mom or something."

"Look, just... get the equipment set up, and I'll see if I can find Thursday Addams," Wolf grimaced when he heard more thumps. "And you two... try to *not* get us kicked out of this place."

Stalking out of the ballroom, Wolf turned a corner and nearly slammed into Mara. Skidding back a step, he pulled up short, and his heart began to thunder along with the beeping machines he'd left behind in the ballroom.

"Shit!" Wolf rubbed at his face, telling his heart to get a grip on itself. "Sorry. I'm... you scared the heck out of me."

"Don't apologize for your profanity, Dr. Kincaid." Mara pursed her lips in disapproval. "If the situation calls for a heartfelt curse, then so be it. I'm not some shrinking violet quivering because a man used a bad word. Now, is there something I can help you with? Or are you merely wandering around the Grange to get a feel for the old place?"

"I was looking for Pryce." His heart settled down. "I was hoping to get permission to set up cameras to record activity. Maybe get some history out of him. Unless you'd like to do that."

"You will definitely need to talk to him about the cameras. And as for Hoxne Grange's history, I'm sure you're referring to its more ethereal guests. You will *definitely* need to discuss that with Tristan. I have no opinion on the matter." She studied him, and Wolf shuffled his feet, feeling like a little boy caught with his hand in the cookie jar. "Just head up to the third floor and take a right instead of a left. You'll find him in his studio. He's just taken up some coffee. I'm sure he wouldn't begrudge you a cup if you take one up with you. There's some on the sideboard there."

"Thanks, Mara," he said softly. "I appreciate you looking after us."

Her loafers squeaked a little, and Wolf watched the woman disappear into the shadowy hall as she headed to the back of the house. After grabbing a heavy white coffee cup from a sideboard's tray, Wolf bounded up the stairs, intent on finding the blond, who'd left him nearly as unsettled as his house.

Unlike the wing Wolf shared with his two technicians, Tristan's wing was shut off by a solid oak door with a discreet engraved plaque informing a potential trespasser they were about to tread into someone's private space. Knocking might not get him past the door, not given the look Pryce gave him the last time he saw the man.

"Try the knob or knock?" Wolf put his hand on knob, then realized the door was partially open. "Okay, so that was easy enough. Onward to find Don Quixote."

This particular wing of Hoxne Grange was definitely set up for Tristan Pryce's tastes. Once past the foyer, Wolf found himself in the apartment's living space, and he took a moment to get a feel for the man he'd come to see. With not an antique in sight, the furnishings ran to more modern lines, clean Mission-style pieces with comfortable, bright cushions and soft, filmy curtains covering the building's long windows. Nearly every wall boasted at least two bookshelves filled with a curious blend of literature and photo books. It was a lived-in space, nothing like the polished staidness of the house beyond the apartment's front door, but it was the art on the walls that gave Wolf pause.

There was a lot of it.

And they were all of monsters.

Arranged more like a collection of large family portraits on a long wall, the pieces varied in size and style, but the content was consistently fantastical. A demon bunny with black wings and a katana held a small rodent, his fierce visage thoughtful as he listened to the creature, while next to him, a Wild Hunt poured out of books and decks of cards, engaged in a ferocious battle with a host of banshee and merrow. Some pieces were contemplative art, portraits, or a single study, while others were fully realized scenes. All were matted in hues to match the pieces' colors and enclosed in black steel frames.

But still… monsters.

"Fuck me." Wolf stole Gidget's favorite curse. "You really *are* Thursday Addams."

Somewhere in the apartment, the Gorillaz sang about a green world, and Wolf headed down a hall leading to the front of the house. The suite was enormous, taking up the entire length of the wing opposite the Hellsingers' guest rooms.

Unsure on where to find the Grange's owner, Wolf let the music and the smell of a good dark roast lead him on.

Tristan Pryce was sprawled back in a papasan chair, his slender, long legs folded up and crossed in front of him. Angled so he and the chair were diagonal to the window, the late afternoon light lingered over sheets of blank paper spread out on a low drafting table in front of him, its buttery glow turning Tristan's hair wheaten and gold. The man held a steaming mug, his index finger tapping at the cup's side while he stared out one of the room's arched windows. A ratty gray T-shirt hung on Tristan's torso, its folds swaddling his belly. His feet were bare, and his knees poked out from holes in his jeans. More white patches and threads dotted the denim, and from the distracted way Tristan plucked at a spot on his thigh, Wolf had a good idea how the holes got there.

The man was more Byron than brawler, so very much *not* Wolf's type, but his dick had other ideas. It stirred and thickened, his balls tightening up into the hollow of his thighs, and he stopped at the doorway, tugging at his crotch to give himself some relief.

Of course, that was the exact moment Tristan Pryce sensed someone else was in the room and turned around to look over his shoulder, catching Wolf in midsquirm.

He played it off. He'd had years of faking things. He could even be smooth at it, despite what his mother thought. Clearing his throat, Wolf held up the mug he'd brought from downstairs.

"Can I steal a cup of coffee?" He dangled the cup from his index finger, swinging it gently.

Tristan jerked his chin toward a sleek stainless steel coffeemaker sitting on a built-in counter, its glass carafe nearly full of a dark brew. The appliance was much more modern than the old, beat-up plastic model in the kitchenette, and from the array of sugar and individual creamers on the counter, a central piece to his owner's life. Wolf had to step over a large mound of brindle and gray fur to get to the coffeepot, and the dog grumbled good-naturedly, huffing out its massive jowls as he patted his head.

"Who's this?" He scritched the wolfhound's ears. The dog's back legs thumped in time to Wolf's ministrations, and he sighed contentedly when Wolf tugged gently at his ruff.

"That's Boris the Cowardly. If you want, there's crème brûlée creamer in the fridge." Tristan pointed toward a large cabinet next to the coffeemaker. "Top shelf inside the door."

"Thanks," Wolf murmured, crossing the room. His cock was doubling as a dowser, and Tristan seemed to be its idea of an artesian well, because he could have sworn its head remained firmly fixed on the blond as he fixed himself a cup.

"How did you know I had coffee up here?"

"Mara told me," he answered, stirring in a tablespoon of sugar. Debating the creamer, he opened the fridge, snagged the bottle, and popped it open to sniff at it.

"Mara?" The man sounded surprised, and Wolf glanced at him, curious. "Mara told you I was up here? With coffee?"

"Yeah, she was downstairs when I came out of the ballroom." He added a small dollop of the creamer, then put it back, stirring the coffee until it was blended. The room was furnished much like the front space, and he sat down on a puffy red couch near Tristan's papasan chair. "I was looking around for you, and she told me you were up here. The coffee was a bonus. I was about to hunt down the kitchens and see what I could find there."

"Huh." Tristan made a face Wolf couldn't quite identify. "Okay, then."

There were more monsters on the walls of what looked like Tristan's studio. Unlike the formality of the living room's art, the pieces on the studio's walls were sketches and character studies, mostly taped to the wall near Tristan's work space. A few finished pieces were hung opposite the windows, a lineup of fierce and cuddly creatures smiling out from their frames like grade school photos of the damned.

Wolf needed something to fidget with, anything to take his mind off of the man's chameleon-shifting gaze and his boneless, sexy sprawl. Spotting a red bouncy ball on a table next to the couch, he was about to pick it up when Tristan's curt voice stopped him.

"Don't. Once you pick it up, he'll never leave you alone," Tristan warned. "You'll be finding that ball in your bathtub if you're not careful."

"It's kind of too small for him." Wolf palmed the ball, checking its girth. "Aren't you afraid he'll swallow it?"

"Boris isn't the one you've got to worry about. Just… put it down."

Placing the ball back, Wolf looked around him. A sheep-warthog mutant plushie sat on the couch with Wolf, and he grabbed it, examining its bristly fuchsia fur tipped with orchid and the bright-blue horns that wrapped down around its plump cheeks. A pair of gold hoops dangled from the toy's left ear, and white tusks poked out from around its sliver of a mouth. Its yellow glass eyes stared malevolently back at Wolf from under coarse, beetled brows.

"That's Vernon," Tristan commented softly.

"Vernon?" Wolf tucked the… thing… back into its spot.

"He's Carl's monster." The man returned to tapping his mug.

"He?" Wolf eyed the stuffed creature. "He looks kind of… frilly?"

"It's his curse, or so he thinks." Something in the blond's changeable eyes told Wolf he was being judged and had not passed. "He's a boy monster with pink-and-purple fur, so he doesn't think he'll be a good imaginary friend for Carl because of how he looks. In their book, Vernon needs to understand he can be whoever he wants to be, as long as he's a good monster. That's all Carl needs, for his monster to be a solid, kind friend."

"So does he?" The judging eased, lightening the dark gold in Tristan's eyes to a sparkling amber. "Learn, I mean."

"After a bit." Tristan turned in his chair, fully facing Wolf. "But I don't think you came up here to talk about my monsters."

"I needed to talk to you about my team setting up cameras in the house. No nails or anything. Nothing mounted someplace we can't take off without damaging anything." Wolf explained how the pressure mounts would work in a corner of a hallway or room. "We want to have a good sweep of the place so we can record activity as we go along."

"Sure." Tristan nodded slowly. "That shouldn't be a problem. Anything else? Did you get settled into your rooms?"

"Yeah, Mara took me to them." Wolf caught the semiamused crease on Tristan's forehead. "She doesn't normally show people where they're sleeping? She's the housekeeper, right? She's staff, yeah?"

"Of sorts," Tristan murmured softly. "She doesn't really have anything to do with the guests, living or otherwise. Mara's more of a legacy employee. She was here with my Uncle Mortimer, and when he passed, she stayed on with me. It's her home as much as it is mine. There's a cleaning staff that takes care of most of the house, but she goes through and changes the sheets after a guest leaves."

"Even if they're... not real?" Wolf needled, wanting to see the man's reaction.

"Just because you're incorporeal, doesn't mean you want to sleep in another person's sheets," Tristan replied. "Usually Mara toddles around the Grange in the morning, then goes back to the carriage house to relax. Sometimes, if she's feeling bossy, she comes back over here to tell me it's time to cook dinner."

"She's not the cook?" If ever he needed to retire and still pull an income, it looked like being Hoxne Grange's housekeeper was the way to go. "Your aunt said we didn't have to worry about meals, but if I've got to get some food for my crew, let me know. I'll head back into the city."

"Trust me...." Tristan's sudden laughter was a bubbling wave of glee. "You do *not* want Mara cooking for us. She is disastrous in the kitchen. No, I'll cook. There's enough in the walk-in and fridge downstairs for a couple of days, but I put in an order. Groceries will be delivered tomorrow morning when the house staff is in. I don't mind cooking, but I hate putting stuff away."

Wolf smirked teasingly. "Lord of the manor and all that?"

"Only about putting away groceries." Tristan cocked his head. "And dusting. Oh, and lawn work. I leave that stuff to the professionals. Cooking, I can do. Any allergies? So I don't kill anyone you might need."

"I don't think so." Wolf turned his cup around in his hands. "Since I'm up here, mind if I ask you a few questions about the place? To get some background?"

"What kind of questions?" Any camaraderie they'd built up turned to ash under Tristan's hard, suspicious glare. "If I'm on medication? The answer to that is no."

"Actually, I was wondering how you got to be the Grange's owner instead of your Uncle Walter. Your aunt seemed to think it should have gone to him. Being the family house and everything. How do you feel about that?"

"She wouldn't last a day at the Grange," Tristan snorted. "Uncle Mortimer gave it to me because he knew I'd take care of it. Ashley would tear out the gardens and put in a tennis court or something."

"And that would be bad."

"Horribly bad." The blond raked his fingers through his hair, mussing its golden threads back into the darker strands. "Whether she… or you… believes it, Hoxne Grange *is* a farewell point for passing spirits. It's a final respite before they leave this world. Ashley would do enough damage to the Grange that she'd drive the ghosts off, maybe even trapping some forever. Uncle Mortimer would die all over again if that were to happen. I'm not going to let the Grange die because of someone's greed. It has a *purpose*. I'm merely its caretaker."

"You said three days. So they… the ghosts… stay for three days, and then what? Walk into the light?" Wolf wasn't sure what amazed him more, the monsters all over the walls or the man's delusional state. "Head to heaven. How do you know it's not hell?"

"God's a parent. What loving parent would create a place of eternal torment for their children?" Tristan shot back. Shifting in his chair, he freed his feet from underneath him and wiggled his toes. A silver ring encircled the fourth toe on his left foot, the metal gleaming as Tristan moved about. "And yeah, walk into… peace, I guess. I think that's the better word for it. Uncle Mortimer called it heaven, but I don't know. The Grange attracts all kinds, all religions. I don't want to put a name on what the souls find so long as they find some peace there."

"Very modern of you. So the Grange is very in tune with the changing times."

"The spirits who come here are from different eras." Tristan spoke carefully, as if teaching someone too slow to grasp a simple concept. "Heather, the cook, comes every Tuesday. She's probably from around the late nineteenth century. I think she died on the way to a lord's house to ask about a position there. My Uncle Mortimer thought maybe someone killed her because the lord got her pregnant, but we'll never really know."

"She breaks the three-day rule."

"She does. I don't know why. I wonder sometimes, but maybe because she'll never find peace? While she's here, she's happy, so maybe Hoxne Grange *is* her peace," Tristan murmured. "I talk to her sometimes. Heather likes visiting with the guests, and they all like her. She's quite nice and doesn't seem to mind when a Hindi merchant asks for something other than beef."

"But everyone else moves on?" Wolf wished he'd brought a recorder with him or even a pad to make notes on. "Have you seen one? Move on, I mean?"

"The guests do, yes. Cook's not a guest, maybe?" The blond shifted again, silver winking seductively from his foot. "And yeah, I've seen a few walk across the pond and disappear into the fog. I don't know where they go from there."

"How do you know when they've been… checked out?"

"Their names are crossed off on the registry, and Mara finds their rooms slept in but empty. Sometimes they leave something behind."

"And always on the third day?" Wolf made a mental note to research journey myths. If Tristan spent a lot of time with his Uncle Mortimer, the older man might have influenced his nephew's beliefs to include something tangible Wolf could disprove.

"Always." Tristan nodded. "Fish and guests stink after three days. I guess the same goes for ghosts."

"So what happens to the place when *you* go?" Wolf put down his cup, shifting closer to the edge of the couch. "Are you hoping to pass Hoxne Grange to one of your kids? How do you know who should get this place next? How did Mortimer know it was you he needed here?"

"Because I've been seeing the Grange's guests ever since I was a kid."

The smile was back on Tristan's face, but it was wistful, hinting at a sadness inside of him. He looked vulnerable, malleable enough to fold into Wolf's arms and let himself be driven senseless with hot kisses and exploratory fingers. Wolf pulled his thoughts away from the image of Tristan's pale body spread out over his room's dark-red duvet, his jeans raked down over his hips and his bared nipples a dark blush from Wolf's teeth. No, lusting after the crazy man living at Hoxne Grange wasn't what he needed in his life. Not by a long shot. Especially since the man obviously needed to secure himself a legacy of spawnlets in order for his delusions to survive his own death.

"And as for what is going to happen to Hoxne Grange? I don't know." Tristan's teeth worried at his plump lower lip. "Marriage is out. I don't like women. Not like that. So, unless another man can get me pregnant, I'm going to be in the same boat Uncle Mortimer paddled up the river without a paddle… hoping one of my relatives has a child as screwed up as I am."

Great, Wolf thought. Not only was he on the job with a hot crazy man who thought he talked to ghosts but the guy was gay and available. If Wolf ever wondered whether God had a sense of humor, he now had proof. Like the platypus wasn't enough evidence of that.

Chapter 4

THE TEAM'S dinner was a hurried shovel of roast beef sandwiches and chips washed down with coffee and Diet Coke. Fueled by Tristan's permission to set up cameras, Wolf declined a sit-down meal in exchange for something quick. Within half an hour, someone from the housekeeping staff set up a banquet-style platter of sourdough bread and rare thinly sliced beef, served with homegrown tomatoes and a horseradish mayonnaise Gidget loved so much she swore she'd knife anyone who stood between her and the jar. Armed with full bellies and an array of beeping machines, Hellsinger Investigations plowed through the house and laid down their ghost-imaging traps.

At three in the morning, the team checked their camera feeds and did a final walkthrough, then collapsed in their respective rooms, exhausted from the long day.

At three forty-five, the noises began.

There was no escalation. No simmering ease into the hammering knocks on the ceilings above them or the squeaking of service carts being wheeled through the hallway. The din began immediately, a raucous shriek of noise with no discernible origin.

A din that stopped immediately whenever Wolf, Gidget, or Matt opened the doors to their rooms.

"I'm going to head down and see what the monitors are picking up," Matt grumbled, rubbing at his eyes.

"I'll go down with you." Wolf grabbed a T-shirt and tugged it over his head. "There's got to be a trigger or something on the doors. This kind of activity is too concentrated... too concise. It's got scam peed all over it."

"But why?" Gidget mumbled, shuffling along behind them. Her nighttime apparel ran to a pajama set printed with smiling dinosaurs and a pair of fluffy shark slippers whose mouths opened and closed with each step. "He's not running an actual inn. There's nothing to gain here. Shit, he doesn't even want a reality show or something."

"Maybe that's it." Matt punched the lift button, and the birdcage cab rattled back up from the ground floor. "He wants to be on one of *those* shows. Make this the next Winchester."

"My question is, why isn't the elevator up on this floor?" Wolf tapped at the elaborately worked elevator screen blocking access to the empty shaft. "We were the last ones to use it. It should have stayed up here."

"So someone's down there?" Gidget yawned. "Fuck. I'd hate it to be him doing this shit. He's hot."

"I'm standing right here," her lover complained as he pulled the screen back when the cab settled in.

Gidget leaned over and rubbed at his slight potbelly. "I love my furry teddy bear, but I'm not blind. That Pryce guy is hot but way out of my league. And like Kincaid here, he worships the peen. I'd be more worried about Pryce lusting after you than you have to worry about me lusting after him."

"Screw this, you guys take that thing. I'll meet you downstairs." Wolf nodded at the steps. "Maybe we can catch who decided to start shit."

He beat the birdcage by a few seconds. As Wolf rounded the second-floor landing, he could hear Matt complaining about the rapid descent, a note of hysteria hitting his voice after Gidget suggested they were free-falling to the first floor. Leaving the pair to follow him, Wolf headed to the ballroom and flicked on its bank of lights.

Only to stand speechless with shock at the sight of the equipment they'd left on the tables.

"Holy shit." Matt's normally boisterous voice dropped to a low, shaky whisper. "God fucking damn it."

"Okay, we're screwed." Gidget gulped. "Kincaid, I'm going to ask for combat pay on this one because damn… we are *so* screwed."

All of their equipment was cleared from the table, and from looks of the cases and bins lined up against the wall. Every single bit of their gear'd been packed up and put away as if they'd not spent the entire afternoon setting up.

Rows of systematic, precise loops of cables lined the open blue bins the team used for site transport, their curls zip-tied and so tightly arranged, Wolf seriously wondered if he'd somehow stumbled down in a sleepwalking stupor and done it himself. A closer inspection of the cases confirmed Matt's grumbling terror. Everything they'd put up and connected was neatly in its cushioned case or stacked in the plastic containers they'd come in, including three floors worth of cameras and sound detectors.

"Fuck me sideways and call me a snake." Gidget ran her hands over an EM reader. "There wasn't enough damned time for someone to do this. I mean, come on… it took us all fucking night to get shit up!"

"Not if you've got the money to hire a bunch of people," Wolf growled. "You two start to unpack. If Pryce thinks he's dealing with some pack of amateurs, he's fucking mistaken."

"Wait, really?" Matt's slack eyes widened. "Come on, Kincaid, we're dead here."

"And what do you mean *you two*?" Gidget faced him, squaring her shoulders, hands on her hips. "Where the hell do you think you're going?"

"I'm going to beard the lion in his den," Wolf replied sharply. "Tristan Pryce isn't going to know what hit him."

THE POUNDING on the other side of the house had stopped long enough for Tristan to finally fall back asleep when it migrated over to his wing. Lying in the dark with the covers pulled up over his head, he groggily wondered if it would be worth it to haul himself out of bed and yell at Wolf and his crew when the hammering quieted, leaving behind a still silence.

Even buried under the covers, Tristan saw the lights come on in his room, and he groaned.

Now it looked like the ghosts were in on the dance. Flinging back the blankets, Tristan grumbled loudly at the ceiling. "Look, can you all just let me get some sleep?"

Unlike any other time when he'd shouted at the unknown, the lights remained on and he found himself staring a large, snarling ghost hunter dressed only in a tight white undershirt and a pair of black cotton board shorts. If he'd been handsome dressed in jeans and a sweatshirt, he was devastating when half-naked.

Tristan didn't think he'd survive if ever he saw the man nude.

Even under the man's fleece, Wolf's sensual power was evident in his muscular chest and arms. His thighs weren't bad either, thickly formed and clenched tight with strength, a light dusting of black hair coating them. The shadowy line Tristan saw when Kincaid's shirt slid up while he walked toward Tristan's bed promised more soft fur. If there was any question of Wolf Kincaid sporting underwear beneath those loose shorts, it was answered when the man placed his hands on the mattress and leaned over to bring his face close to Tristan's before he could speak.

Anything that came out of the man's full, sensual mouth was lost under the press of heavy flesh brushing against Tristan's bare thigh, the swing of Wolf's blood-warmed, cotton-encased cock searing a path onto Tristan's skin.

The whole experience was like a damned romance novel so badly written the person who bought it left it half-finished and in the sticky mess of a bus stop bathroom.

His nipples felt hot under his T-shirt, and a curious tightening was starting along his belly. A heat flushed through Tristan, thin fires creeping under his skin and spreading out until his fingers and toes tingled and burned. If he'd had time… and realized how fucking sexy Wolf Kincaid would look bent over him, Tristan would have shoved a pillow over his crotch so the man didn't see Tristan's cock beginning to thicken with lust.

He'd never been so close to wanting another man. The times he'd spent down in the city sliding into clubs and bars, hoping someone would see him… needing someone to show him exactly what the fuck his damned, contrary body wanted… left him with a sense he'd been wrong about preferring men. He'd slunk back to the woods to lick his wounds and ponder what drove him down the hills to seek out something to answer the questions he had inside him.

Because in the dead of the night, when he was surrounded by ghosts and the sounds of an old house settling down on her bones, Tristan anguished over the lonely coldness inside of him. Nothing seemed to affect it. Nothing he did or said chipped that core of chill away. Until the moment when Wolf Kincaid's mouth was nearly touching his and the man's ocean-tinted eyes were stormy with a passionate fury, Tristan often wondered if he was as dead as the spirits he'd opened his house to.

With that single accidental lean of a cock on his thigh—that man's cock—Tristan's chilled soul melted, and he was left exposed, vulnerable to Wolf's heat and wanting so much more.

"It's like I'm a damned teenaged girl," Tristan muttered under his breath. Or how he imagined one would act. He had about as much knowledge of women as he did about being gay. Rubbing his eyes, he tried to concentrate more on what was coming out of Wolf's mouth rather than the mouth itself. "I'm sorry, what? Can you repeat that?"

Wolf took a shuddering breath and looked away, composing himself before he spoke again. "If you didn't want us here, you could have just said no."

"I did say no." Tristan blinked, confused. "You came anyway. 'Sides, it was either you or someone else. *That's* why you woke me up?"

"I woke you up because your little gremlins packed away all of the stuff we spent the whole night setting up." Wolf's smile bordered on violent, and despite the heat Tristan felt a chill run down his spine. "How many people did you hire? Thirty? More? Because damn, they worked fast."

"I didn't hire anyone. What the hell are you talking about?"

"Not more than an hour after we went to bed, your crew not only took everything apart but packed it all up so we'd be ready to leave in the morning." The growl in Wolf's voice grew deeper. "Is this some kind of joke to you? I don't give a shit if you hate my guts, but fucking with my equipment? My crew? That's crossing a fucking line you don't want to cross."

A flickering realization of what Wolf was talking about finally sunk in past the erotic images Tristan's mind played at. Shaking his head, he replied, "It wasn't me. It probably was the ghosts. Maybe they don't want you here?"

"Really? Because they're really going to give a shit about being filmed?"

"It's kind of intrusive." Tristan shrugged. "And they get curious. Especially if they're from a time when there wasn't a lot of technology. Hell, you should see what they do to my studio sometimes."

"You expect me to swallow that?"

"I don't care what you expect," he sighed. "It's what happens here at Hoxne Grange. Just ask them to leave your stuff alone. They're pretty good about it once you tell them."

"Just leave my stuff alone?" It was less of a question and more of a mocking repeat, much like a five-year-old mimicking another. "So, what? I just go to the ballroom and what? Ask nicely? Light some candles? Burn some incense?"

"Probably just not being a dick would be enough," Tristan ground out from between his teeth. "Maybe a please?"

Wolf straightened, lifting his weight from the bed. Cool air rushed between them, and Tristan was thankful for the slight chill, hoping its touch would get his unruly cock under control. He waited for the other man to speak, but it seemed like Wolf was more interested in studying him, as if he were something strange the man came across on the sidewalk.

After a long few seconds, Wolf said, "You really believe that shit, don't you?"

"What? That please works?" Tristan nodded, confused. "Usually people like it when you're nice. Even dead people. Here, we can try it. Can you please get out so I can go back to sleep? I actually *do* have to get some work done tomorrow… today. Whatever."

Kincaid opened his mouth, then closed it again, all the while staring down at Tristan. Finally, throwing his hands up in the air, he turned on his heel and headed back to the bedroom door. Tristan groaned, burying his face in his pillow when Wolf's tight ass flexed as he walked.

"God, I just want to get some sleep," he mumbled into the feathers and fine cotton. "Why are you doing this to me? First the noise and now… him?"

"You know what?" Wolf's voice broke through Tristan's quiet, desperate prayers, and he pulled the pillow away from his face, only to realize Wolf had crossed back over to him. Staring up Wolf's long torso, Tristan inhaled sharply, accidentally sucking the tang of the man's skin into his lungs.

It was bad enough Wolf looked good enough to eat. Did he have to smell of lemon curd and male?

If he wasn't certain of it before, Tristan was now convinced. He'd done something to piss God off, and he'd been put in his own special circle of hell, trapped to care for ghosts and embroiled in a sexual ambiguity that could only be breached by a roughly gorgeous man who thought he was crazy.

His. Own. Circle. Of. Hell.

If it wasn't so torturous, Tristan thought he'd feel kind of pleased God went through all the trouble. But since Wolf Kincaid looked like he was expecting an answer or something, Tristan sighed, "Okay, what?"

"I'm going to play along with your game. Let's say this place is the fucking Grand Central Station for ghosts looking for a new life—"

"That analogy would probably work better if you said Ellis Island," Tristan cut in. He had to trust that Kincaid wasn't going to strangle him, but by the way he clenched his hands into tight fists, Tristan wasn't betting on it. "Sorry. Fine, Grand Central Station it is."

"I came here to see if there was any activity. Not to find out if you're crazy… although honestly, I think your relatives have got a good argument for it, especially after tonight."

Those large hands were unclenched again, and Tristan's mind wandered over to the possibility of the man's palms cupping his ass and squeezing.

His cock seemed to like that idea and once more poked its head up from its cotton-sheet prison.

"So between you and me, let's just see what I find, okay?" Kincaid cocked his head at Tristan. "No trying to convince me that some oogie-boogie packed up all my equipment or that there's a woman who comes by every Tuesday to get hired on as the maid—"

"She's the cook, and her name's—" Tristan corrected softly. Wolf's hard look quelled him into silence. "Sorry. Right. No convincing."

"And I won't say anything about your little game of checking people into this place." Wolf stuck his hand out for Tristan to shake. "Do we have a deal?"

Putting his hand in Wolf Kincaid's was going to be a huge mistake, but it was one Tristan wanted to make. Wolf's skin was rough in places, gnarled with calluses along his palm. When his fingers closed over Tristan's, his ass actually clenched at the idea of Wolf's long digits doing more than squeezing his hand.

The team from Hellsinger Investigations couldn't leave fast enough for him. Tristan didn't think his overheated body would be able to survive close contact with Wolf Kincaid for much longer than a few days. If he wasn't careful, he'd melt like a witch with water thrown on her, and his Uncle Walter would have the run of Hoxne Grange.

Mara would never forgive him and would probably drown his maybe-Aunt Ashley in the back garden's koi pond the first chance she got.

"Deal," Tristan agreed, biting back another groan when the tips of Wolf's fingers slid over the pulse point of his wrist when the man pulled away.

"By the way." Wolf nodded to the sleeping wolfhound curled up at the end of Tristan's king-size bed. "Nice watchdog you've got there. You might want to actually invest in an alarm system or something."

"We had one. Uncle Mortimer had it disconnected. The guests kept making it go off in the middle of the night."

"Yeah, crazy." The man shook his head.

"Thought we weren't going with the crazy thing?"

"I'm not here to prove you're crazy. Doesn't mean I can't think it." Wolf stopped at the bedroom's open door and leaned over to grab something off of the table Tristan normally tossed his keys and wallet on. Holding up the red ball he'd been told not to touch, Wolf threw it up in the air and caught it with a snapping grasp. "And to show you how much of the crazy I think you are, I'm taking this with me."

WOLF WAS dragging when he stumbled out of bed a few hours later. By the time he'd gotten back downstairs to the ballroom, Gidget and Matt had unpacked and hauled their equipment back out onto the tables. Telling the couple to go back to sleep, he'd followed them upstairs, intent on getting some rest before they set up all over again.

Except sleep seemed to be the furthest thing from his mind.

A long-legged, sleep-ruffled blond kept slipping into his dreams, and Wolf couldn't seem to shake off the idea of having a naked and moaning Tristan underneath him while he found out exactly how hot the man's blush could be.

"Come on, Wolfgang," he'd grumbled to himself in a bathroom mirror. "Tristan Pryce is *not* the kind of guy that makes you horny. Shit, his legs would snap apart like a wishbone the first time you lifted them up and pushed into him."

If only the promise of his firm, high ass didn't rub up against Wolf's lust like a friendly, purring cat.

He was still rubbing the grit from his lashes by the time they were ready to replace the cameras, and Gidget poked at his ribs, finding a tender bit of meat with her fingernail.

"Did you know this place doesn't have Wi-Fi?" She curled her lip up in disgust. "I asked Pryce about it, and he said the ghosts were bothered by the transmissions. He thinks maybe that's why the cameras got taken down, because of the wireless bounce through the halls."

"Sure, that doesn't sound nuts," Wolf muttered. "Did he tell you to ask the boo-wigglies to leave our stuff alone?"

"Yeah, so I stood in the middle of the ballroom and said please." Gidget shrugged, bending the straps of her overalls. "Seemed to work out okay. We turned everything on and nothing exploded. I took it as a win."

"Or whatever we overloaded yesterday burnt out and we're not feeding anything through it," Matt suggested. "But he seemed happy about the please. I asked the staff that came in to help if they knew about what happened to our stuff but... you know."

"They knew nothing, I take it," Wolf snorted. "Of course, he might have used another crew. What else do we need to do? Give me whatever you've got next on the checklist."

"How about if you take a break, boss?" Gidget handed Matt three of their remote viewers. "We'll set these up in the lobby and call it a day. Or better yet, how about if you interview our host? See if he sparkles or something?"

"You guys are going to need—" He started to contradict her; then Matt stepped in.

"Nope, got it covered. Pryce loaned us some of the house staff, so we powered through a lot of it. Third floor's already done and most of second. Just a few more to put back in and we can call it done until it's time to man the screens." Matt jerked his head toward the ballroom door, loading up his own arms with feeds. "An interview would be good. See if you can get something on the spectral reader on him. One of the maintenance guys said strange shit's always happening around Pryce. It'll be good if we can get that on film, right?"

"We'll want to get the staff too. Maybe for a few minutes before they leave for the day?" Wolf nodded. "Especially Mara."

"Which one is Mara?" Gidget sniffed at a cup of cold coffee, then sipped at it, making a face when it hit her tongue. "God, that's rough. Time for a new pot."

"Um, older woman. Kinda plump. Looks like she should be baking pies and cookies?" Wolf raised his hand up to his shoulder, guessing at the woman's height. "Probably could beat our asses with a wooden spoon if we pissed her off?"

"Haven't met her yet, but that's probably 'cause there's like thirty people who work here." Matt let Gidget hook yet another loop of cable over his arm. "Babe, this shit's heavy. We can take a cart."

"Then we'll have to bring it back," Gidget muttered. "And I'd rather just head upstairs when we're done so we can—"

"I don't want to hear this…." Wolf threw up his hands to protect himself.

"Get a nap in before we stay up all night," she finished, poking him again. "You've got a filthy, filthy mind, Kincaid. Onward, Ambrosius!"

Gidget hefted a camera case to her shoulder, and Matt shuffled behind her obediently before his head jerked up suddenly. Whining plaintively, he complained, "Why the hell do I have to be the dog?"

Surprisingly, Tristan was easy to find. Standing behind the Grange's antique reception desk, his eyes were hooded when he swept his gaze over Wolf. Once again, he was talking to himself, seemingly having a conversation with more than one invisible person and scribbling in the hotel's ledger. Wolf let Tristan wind himself down, taking the time to set up the feeds for the lobby, then checking his handheld's charge. By the time Tristan closed the ledger, Wolf was cooling his heels near a larkspur arrangement one of the staff placed on the central table.

He crossed the floor toward the reception desk, then slowed as Mara came out from the door connecting the foyer to the staff area. Wolf motioned for Mara to go first, holding his camera up for her to see. "I'm going to be a bit, so Mara doesn't have to stay. Hoping the lord of the manor will give me an interview."

"Mara usually is quick. It's nearly one. She's got stories to watch." Tristan's bemused grin did as much to warm Wolf's belly as the thought of his long legs wrapped around Wolf's hips.

"I'll be as fast as I can." The older woman preened, tucking a stray lock of gleaming pale hair behind her ear. Reaching into the pocket of her uniform, she pulled out a pocket watch, its mariner-style chain dangling through her fingers. "This was in the Sturas' room. I thought maybe you'd like to have it. It looks like they had a lovely visit."

"I thought they'd like the Rose Room." Tristan took the watch and placed it reverently on the countertop. "They both seemed to really like the idea of waking up to the gardens outside. I'll see if there's any family who might want it. If not, I'll give it a good home."

"May I see that?" Wolf held his hand out to Tristan. "The detailing is very reminiscent of Northern Italy."

"It might be," Mara said, picking up the watch and placing it in Wolf's palm. "The husband's family was from up North. I think the wife was Sicilian. Lovely couple. I'll leave you to it then, Tristan. I've an afternoon to catch before it slips away."

Wolf waited until the woman was gone before dangling the watch in front of Tristan's nose. "You know, she told me you leave these things for her to find. Don't you think you're going too far with this?"

"If by *this* you mean trying to find someone in the Stura family who might want the watch back, then no." Tristan shook his head, the smile gone from his face. "I don't leave anything for Mara or anyone else on the staff to find. And if something is discovered, we try to get it back to where it belongs if we know who left it. If not, then it either goes to someone who likes it or I put it into a keepsake box. I think they were local. He was waiting for her to join him before they went on together. I remember him saying that, so their family shouldn't be hard to find."

"How do you intend find the family with no Internet? Carrier pigeon?" Wolf pressed.

"I have Internet. We just don't have a wireless network." Tristan looked partially disgusted with him. "There should be a LAN connection by the desk in your room. Same with Gidget and Matt's space. There's also one in the library, the lower study, and in a couple of the rooms on the second floor."

If Tristan purchased the watch from a family member or an estate, he'd find out. Regardless of what he'd promised Tristan, if the man truly believed his own delusional reality, maybe his Uncle Walter would be able to get him some help.

"So then you don't mind if I take a crack at trying to find out who owned this?" Wolf studied the engraving on the inside of the watch. A man's name was scrawled there as well as a reminder that he was loved. There was no date, but Wolf was certain it was enough to go on.

"Knock yourself out." Tristan leaned in and closed Wolf's hand over the watch, the press of his fingers as hard and unyielding as his hazel eyes. "And while you're at it, see if you can find out who bought your soul too. Because unless Satan's got a receipt for it, you might want to get it back."

Chapter 5

DINNER WAS a mound of stroganoff and egg noodles Wolf had been determined to eat quickly so he could get back to work. Gidget and Matt had other ideas.

Instead, they lingered over the meal, sipping at a pour of red wines, then sighing over a lemon meringue pie Tristan admitted to buying from a home-style café nearby. Baking appeared to be outside of the artist's skills. If Wolf had to guess, Gidget was pretty sure that was the only thing Tristan couldn't do.

He'd hoped to get some sort of brotherly support on the subject from Matt, but the technician was fairly useless.

"Damn, my belly's happy," Matt groaned and patted his rounded abdomen. "I probably shouldn't have eaten that much, but it was soooooo good."

"We'll work it off later," Gidget said, winking at him.

"Hey, don't want to hear it." Wolf really should have given up protesting their overt flirting a few years ago. Neither one of them was discreet, and he'd learned more about straight sex from his two techs than he'd wanted to know. "Can we focus on what we're here to do?"

"Sure, boss." Matt leaned over to whisper into Gidget's ear, "Tristan told me we can raid the leftover pie later. I've got plans for that white frothy stuff, just so you know."

Wolf could come up with his own plans for the meringue, especially after watching Tristan sliding a pie-laden fork into his mouth, then closing his lips over the white crème, his eyes dark with pleasure as he sucked his utensil clean. He'd wanted to climb across the table, shove aside the delicate china and lead crystal glasses, and rip Tristan's clothes off his body so he could show Gidget and Matt exactly what butter-slick, rock-star marathon sex looked like.

Instead, he'd stabbed his pie and stared at Pryce's crème-dotted lips for the rest of the dinner.

Shoving aside any thought of a naked Tristan lying on his back with meringue speckled his blush-pink nipples, Wolf pointed at the banquet table set up as their mess. "Matt, go fire up the coffeemaker. It's going to be a long night."

The team decided against roaming the halls. Hoping their equipment would help pinpoint high spectral areas, they each settled into comfortable chairs Pryce offered for their use. By midnight, they'd seen very little and heard even less. Matt continued to pat at his belly and by one in the morning was dozily leaning his head on his lover's shoulder. Sighing in contentment, Gidget glanced over at their mess table, obviously debating something to eat.

"Pryce's heading outside," Matt declared from his place in front of the camera monitors. "Dude's hardcore. It was fricking ball-freezing cold when I went out for a smoke. Must be penguin-nut chilly now."

"That's pretty cold." Gidget unfolded from her chair and ambled over to the trays, lifting up covers and oohing over what she found. "I should go take him a sweater or something. Think he wants a Hellsinger hoodie?"

The last thing Wolf wanted in his head was the idea of Gidget chatting Tristan Pryce up while he shrugged on something to keep his slender body warm. Especially not something with Wolf's name on it.

"I'll do it. I've got to ask him a few more things about the place, anyway. You two stay here," Wolf muttered, grabbing one of their promo zippered jumpers. "And no fornicating."

"Never on the clock, boss," Matt assured him. "Once the cameras are on—"

"The eyes are on the screen," Gidget finished for him. "Maybe take some coffee with you. Looks like fog's rolling in too."

He knew how Tristan took his coffee. He'd watched the man stir in mostly equal amounts of sugar and cream, and apparently his brain somehow counted off the seconds it took for Pryce to whiten his brew. With the hoodie shoved under his arm, Wolf balanced two mugs of coffee and headed out to the back of the Grange.

The mansion was eerily quiet. A house its size should have sounds of people, murmurs of conversation, or music playing softly from one of its elegant rooms. Instead, Wolf walked through a dirge of silence, his footsteps muted by the plush carpets laid on the Grange's honeyed oak floors.

French doors led out to the Grange's back pavilion, a semicircle elevated patio overlooking the grounds below. The slope was a gentle one, cut through by a rough cobblestone path leading to the ponds and gardens surrounding the manor house. The tip of the carriage house's roof could be seen beyond a brace of juniper trees, its peaks echoing the Grange's larger turrets.

Gidget had been right about the fog. Thick misty banks were slowly rolling over the gardens' hedgerows and bushes. Wolf found his quarry leaning on the marble banister, his legs crossed at his ankles and his ass jutting out when he rested his weight on his elbows.

The moonlight bled the color out of the Grange's vibrant surroundings, turning the greenery to dots and lines of pitch against a rainbow of grays. Spots of red poked out of the monochromatic sea, tired heads of cabbage roses bobbing under the touch of the mist's creeping fingers. The silver light coming from the sparse clouds touched Tristan's body, pouring shadows into the dip of his spine and brightening a hand's width of skin above the waistband of his jeans, where his T-shirt was pulled up on his back.

It was the perfect spot to place a kiss. The shallow crease of Tristan's lower back begged for one, and Wolf's mouth watered when he thought of his teeth scoring red lines on that patch of pale skin. Then his throat closed up, dry and wanting, as he realized he could just as easily tug down the man's loose jeans and bite into the succulent rounded ass hidden below.

He was going to hate hiding the man's sensual lines under the swaddling fleece, but the wind chewed through Wolf's face with icy teeth, and Tristan was probably freezing, even if he wasn't paying much attention to anything but the dark swatch of a large pond stretched out in front of a small Gothic-style folly.

"Here," Wolf said, shoving the mug he'd brought at Tristan. "Got a hoodie for you to put on too. Gidget's worried you'll catch cold."

"Ah, thanks. Hold on, let me put that on first." Tristan's fingers brushed over Wolf's, and they were as cold to the touch as he'd imagined they would be. Wolf watched Tristan shrug on the fleece then zip it up. He patted at the Hellsinger logo on his chest, then took the cup from Wolf's clenched hand. "I didn't expect it to be this cold tonight. You'd think I was a tourist or something. I'm never prepared for the weather."

"Where's your furry companion?" Wolf looked around for the man's overly large dog.

"Inside, probably sleeping on my bed where it's warm." Tristan grinned. "I needed some air, and I like coming out here. The view's nice."

"You often come out here at night to stare at… nothing?" Wolf leaned on the railing, looking down at the gardens. "Not much to stare at in the dark."

"I'm waiting for the fireflies to come out." The man sighed as he cupped his hands and took a sip of coffee. "I used to think *I* drank too much of this stuff, but you guys got me beat."

"Comes with the territory. Most of what we do happens in the dead of the night." He tried to ignore the man settling in next to him, but Tristan's cooler skin gave him the shivers. Moving closer, Wolf told himself it was to help warm up the slender man, but the clench in his balls called him a liar.

"That's funny. Ghosts. Dead of the night," Tristan snorted. "You know, ghosts are around during the daytime too. Especially around here. No people."

"You think people are the reason the spookies don't come out during the day?"

"People are noisy."

"Loud." Wolf cocked an eyebrow at the man. "Ghosts like peace and quiet? They're the librarians of the supernatural?"

"No, not that the ghosts don't like sound. Well some kinds of sound, I guess." Tristan gave Wolf an unreadable look. "People make *subphysical* sound. Not by talking or anything, just by being around. Their heat, their bodies… everything thrums. They echo against things. Ghosts can hear that… feel that. They exist in that realm of sound and light… and consciousness. Live people bleed into that space, making their rude little reverberations. It's quieter when people are asleep. Ghosts can slip out and not be stolen into."

"So you think it's Hoxne Grange's quiet that draws your guests in?" Wolf mulled the man's theory over. It wasn't so much bullshit as some of the explanations he'd heard from other investigators. "Because people bleed into their existence?"

"Yep." Tristan nodded. "That's what I'm saying."

"Huh." He blinked, thinking on the matter. "Kind of makes sense. Never really thought about the why of ghosts' existence. Other than from a haunting aspect."

"Ghosts are… smaller echoes than the living. They have no form. It's harder to exist that way," the other man replied. "I know it sounds simplistic, but wouldn't it be hard to exist if someone's always pushing into where you are? Not having equal mass means you can't take up equal space."

"So you don't think they're just memories? Imprints? That's the popular theory."

"I've never been popular." Tristan's laugh was bitter. "Maybe that's how it works in other places. Here, they're… people."

"People you see walking around you? Talking? Having scones on the patio?" Wolf scoffed. "Convenient that there are always rooms for them. No overflow. No lost luggage."

"I didn't make the rules." The man shrugged off Wolf's skepticism. "I'm not sure who did. Maybe Uncle Mortimer? Hell, maybe even someone before him? All I know is what I've been taught. Open the doors, sign them in, hire Cook on Tuesday mornings, and be polite whenever one of them comes out of the silence to speak to me. I don't see them all the time. Sometimes the *only* time I see one is when they check in. Other times, I walk into the ballroom and they're all I see, but they don't see me."

"And you've never once wondered if they're really there?" Wolf probed gently.

"No, not after I came here." Tristan shook his head, a fall of gold-and-dun hair bleached out to floss and smoke. "Before, yeah. When I was a kid, I was afraid to fall asleep because there were see-through Chinese prostitutes being herded through my room by a large man with a gun. He would shoot one, maybe two. Every night. And she would die… she would take a long time to die, but I wouldn't always hear them screaming. Sometimes they just lay on the ground, kicking their feet and twisting around until they turned to smoke. Then the next time, new women… young girls, really. And I would go through it all over again."

"Did you tell your parents?" He could only imagine what a rational person would think if their son came to them with a tale of dying ghostly whores.

"I saw every psychiatrist ever to work in San Francisco." Tristan sighed. "No school for me. Tutors. Because I couldn't be trusted not to suddenly 'see' something and get crazy. After a while, I just didn't say anything anymore. Not about the prostitutes. Not about the cowboys riding up Stockton. Not even about the little boy getting thrown into the water by the pier. They thought it all went away. It didn't. I just shut up about it."

"Until Uncle Mortimer."

"Yeah, until… Hoxne Grange." His face grew wistful, and he took another sip at the cooling coffee. "Uncle Mortimer told my parents to leave me here during the summers. The summers became all the holidays. Then one day, I just never went home. The tutors came here, and I could be as crazy as I needed to be without anyone trying to measure me for a wraparound jacket."

"They still might," Wolf murmured and took the nudge to his ribs from Tristan's elbow with a grin. "Especially since you're out here looking for fireflies in San Francisco. They don't glow out here. That only happens east of the Rockies."

"What are you talking about?" Tristan frowned at him. "We have glowing fireflies. I've been watching them at the Grange since I was a little kid."

"I don't know what you're watching, but it sure as hell's not fireflies."

"They're here," Tristan insisted. "They're all sparkly, and they hover out there by the waters. We get a few that come in closer, but they're usually over there. They're little dots… like yellow-green with some white. Sometimes there're so many it looks like the stars have fallen down. And when they're in the fog, they light up the whole bank from underneath. It looks like one of the *leong*—the long dragons—during the Chinese New Year parade."

"Well, not like it's any more crazy than you're seeing ghosts." Wolf shrugged, then winced when Tristan punched his arm.

"I'm not crazy," the man muttered under his breath. "You watch. I'm warning you. They'll be here."

"Just like you've warned me about this ball?" Wolf pulled the small toy out of his pocket. "Tell you what. I'm going to throw it someplace you won't be able to find it in the dark. If it somehow comes back to me before morning, I *might* believe in your ghosts."

"Everything has strings for you, don't they, Kincaid?" Tristan's smile was a sad pull on his pretty face. "Throw it. Jack'll bring it back to you, and then you'll never get rid of him."

"Jack?"

"Yeah, the dog. He's been here for as long as I've been around." Another shrug but this time, the man's smile was nearly smug. "He's the only spectral dog I've ever seen here at the Grange. Horses, yeah, and a giraffe once, but they disappear with the guests. Oh, and there was a camel. Uncle Mortimer says he saw a couple of Tasmanian tigers, but I think he was pulling my leg. Jack's the only one who stays."

"And you know his name?" Wolf tested the ball's weight in his hand. It was hefty enough to take a good toss, and he scanned the gardens, wondering if his arm was good enough. It'd been years since he'd played ball, and the occasional pickup hoops game wasn't the same thing as tossing in something from outfield. "The dog. Not the camel. Or the giraffe. Does he talk? Or did you just hear it in your head?"

"It's just what I call him, asshole. Not like he's got a collar and a tag. I think he's a Jack Russell terrier. They call them something else now, I think. Parsons something or other. But I'm not changing his name now. He knows it. I think."

"You are a beautiful but strange young man, Tristan Pryce."

"So some people say." Tristan's eyes followed the ball as it arced through the air. It landed with a small splash in one of the smaller man-made ponds pooling in the garden's more informal walks. "Well, the strange part. Don't think anyone's ever called me beautiful."

"Well, there's no coming back from that one. And yeah, you're beautiful. Someone should have told you that sooner. Maybe you'd be out in the real world instead of living here with your imaginary friends," Wolf said before draining his coffee cup. "Don't go wading in there now."

"Wasn't planning on it. The water's too cold." Tristan leaned forward again, staring back out into the gardens. The stone balustrades were spaced wide enough for him to lodge a knee in between them but not much more. Wolf set his cup down on the patio floor and turned so he was up against Tristan's side. The man eyed him but didn't pull away. "What?"

"You're like Sleeping Beauty in this place. Waiting for a prince to climb the roses and battle the dragon to set you free?"

"I don't think there was a dragon in the original story." Tristan smirked. "And you've seen my studio. I'd sooner have the dragon than the prince. Besides, there's no such thing as a Prince Charming."

"And here I thought *I* was the cynic."

He wanted just a small taste. The man's mouth had haunted Wolf's mind since the first time he'd seen Tristan staring at him from across the Grange's reception desk. His hands itched to be buried in the man's unruly golden-tinted mane. It was a good length to be wrapped around his fingers so he could pull Tristan's mouth closer to him.

Which was exactly what Wolf Kincaid did.

The angle was awkward, but Wolf didn't care. His palms were cupped around Tristan's high cheekbones, and his mouth tasted of the man himself.

He was right about Tristan's hair. The strands were soft, silken, and long as they slid through Wolf's fingers, but they were nothing compared to the touch of Tristan's tongue against his.

Tristan's hands needed somewhere to be because they pulled and moved along Wolf's shoulders and chest until finally settling on his sides. They tangled tongues, their teeth lightly touching when Wolf pushed in deeper. He wanted to crawl into the man, exploring every recess and shadow inside of him until Wolf came out the other side of his lust drenched in Tristan's scent and feel.

Everything about Tristan Pryce was wrong… from his cracked mind to the ideas he'd packed in it, and Wolf should have run screaming as soon as he saw the lean blond lying in bed. He might have made his living taking on challenges other men fled from, but one as sinfully sweet as Tristan Pryce gave Wolf pause. The man had no idea how seductively innocent he was, and Wolf wanted to be the one to plunge through Tristan's icy personality to the fire he knew lurked deep within Tristan's body. Tristan vibrated with an intensity and longing Wolf's body begged to touch, even if he knew he might singe them both beyond recognition.

Damning any whispering alarms from his brain to tread lightly, Wolf was just about to pull Tristan against him when the man pulled away, leaving Wolf wanting more.

"You… didn't have to do that." Tristan took a step back from Wolf and lifted his fingers to his mouth. "I don't need a Prince Charming, Kincaid. Not even one to kiss me awake."

"I'm not very charming." Wolf was thankful the man didn't wipe the taste of him off his lips with the back of his hand. He could handle Tristan's need for space and air—they'd both been drowning in one another—but he didn't think he could take the man rubbing away the feel of his mouth. "And if anyone needs to be kissed awake, it's you, Pryce. It is *definitely* you. If you're not going to let me kiss you, at least come inside. It's fucking freezing out here."

"No, I—" Tristan shook his head but didn't finish the thought, leaving Wolf with a curious itch. "Besides, it's time to watch fireflies."

"Look, I've told you. Fireflies don't—"

"Then what's that?" Tristan pointed out to the lily speckled pond by the garden's folly. "Swamp gas? An electrical disturbance? Bad mushrooms at dinner?"

There were hundreds of them. Floating through the misty curls rolling around the garden and over the folly's large pond, Tristan's fireflies danced and swarmed, tiny glowing dots leaving behind chartreuse trails in the moisture-thick air. Wolf stood, transfixed by the sheer beauty of the luminescent sprinkles rising and falling in their own silent ballet. They peppered the landscape, curving into the low points in the garden before cresting over the hillocks and banks of flowers.

They swam about, sparkling through the fog and weaving about, putting on a private spectacle for the men standing on the Grange's grand pavilion balcony. Then in a whispering shush, the lights went out slowly, a few at a time at first, then entire waves of darkness ascending from the garden's shadows to swallow up the lost, fallen stars.

"I'll be damned," Wolf whispered, then turned, finding himself alone on the balcony, the memory of Tristan's hot body burned into his flesh. Picking up their discarded coffee mugs, Wolf shook his head and took one last look out at the grayscape of garden below. "Well, I'll be fucking damned."

"YOU WERE out there for a bit," Gidget remarked as Wolf walked in.

The coffeepot was full, and he headed toward it and poured some into one of the mugs. When it swirled up with a hint of cream, Wolf realized he'd filled Tristan's cup and stared down at it, wondering if the blond had locked his bedroom door in case the taste of him drove Wolf to seek more.

After adding sugar to the cup, he brought it to his mouth, instinctively searching for the spot Tristan had placed his lips, but he found nothing sweeter there than the grains he'd ladled in.

Composing himself, Wolf turned to his technicians and nodded at the monitors. "Anything pop up?"

"Yeah, a few things. Orbs, some light streaks." Matt grinned up at his boss as Wolf sat down next to him. "About half an hour ago, we heard a harpsichord playing in the corner. Gidget recorded it, and I got some readings. It blew out one of the scanners, but I think I can fix it."

"Processing the sound?" Wolf put his cup down on one of their overturned bins, then wheeled over to Gidget's equipment bank. "Could be a leak coming from the speakers? The place is wired for hosting balls, you know."

"Trying to isolate it now. I'm going to need a little bit of time." Her eyes never left the scrapes of light dancing up and down on her monitor. "It was pretty loud. Scared the hell out of me because it was so quiet and then boom… music. It *could* have been something ambient, but I don't know. Faded away pretty quick so I'm not sure I got enough of it. I didn't have anything keyed up for this room, so I had to use my MP3 player. Matt got more on the spectral."

"Great." Wolf patted her on the shoulder. "Quick thinking with the music player. Let's see what we can use. Maybe even identifying it. Too bad about the scanner. I'm going to have to charge Pryce's uncle double just for the damage to our equipment."

"Hey, speaking of equipment," Matt interrupted, jostling Wolf's chair with his foot. "Aren't you the one who's always yelling at us about putting wet things down next to our stuff?"

"Yeah." Wolf felt the blood leave his face when he turned to Matt.

"You're slipping, boss. A toaster in a bathtub would be a hell of a lot faster way to electrocute us, don't you think?" Holding up a red ball, its rubber surface slick with water and algae, Matt crowed, "Putting this manky wet ball on the table next to the power board sure as hell ain't gonna to do the trick."

Chapter 6

MARA'S COMFORTABLE tread on the dewy marble was the only warning Tristan had before she began to scold him. "You're going to catch your death of cold coming out here without a—"

"Can't. Wearing a jacket." Tristan stopped Mara in midrant, turning so she could see the hoodie he'd gotten from Kincaid. The fleece was warm, almost too warm, and any lingering scent Wolf might have gotten on it when they'd touched was long gone.

He knew. He'd tried sniffing the hoodie for any residual Wolf-ness but only got a whiff of newly printed ink and a nose full of fluff.

"Humph." They'd been going back and forth for years, her haranguing him to wear warmer clothes and Tristan honestly forgetting to grab something before he headed outside. "You're still going to catch your death."

"Then it's a good thing I'm already here, then, huh?" He leaned over to scratch at Boris's head, reaching under his chin to hit a spot that made the dog's leg thump in pleasure. Avoiding the line of drool beginning at the corner of the wolfhound's jowls, Tristan patted Boris's side, and the dog slumped down in a heap of boneless contentment. "Kincaid asked if they could stay longer. Something about his team getting readings but not full ones. He's got some more equipment arriving today. Apparently the Grange keeps breaking what he's already got."

"Well, it can be rough on things," Mara conceded. "Remember the poor elevator man? I thought he was going to have a nervous breakdown."

"Told him to put an out of order sign on the lift before he started working on it. Turning it off wasn't going to be much use." Tristan shook his head and leaned on the railing, not minding the damp stone under his arms. "Wasted an hour of my life getting his head out of that door. He should have listened."

"Some people never learn to listen. You know that." Mara stood next to him and sniffed at the air. "The roses got a good drenching last

night. Like the night you were out here with that Hellsinger man—
Kincaid. He asked to stay longer, right? I assume you told him yes?"

"Yeah, I did." Tristan scuffed his shoes on the marble, kicking a
few dry leaves off of the balcony. "Seemed important to him, and really,
the guests don't seem to mind. I'd better order more groceries, though.
We've got frozen, but I like fresh to cook with. Seems like we can grow
everything else, but asparagus hates it here."

"Your uncle probably cursed the grounds against it." Mara's chortle
brought a smile to Tristan's face. "He hated it so much. Vile demon
penises, he called them. Only bought it because you loved it."

"Uncle Mortimer did that a lot."

He missed the old man. Hoxne Grange was a special place he'd
shared with his grandfather's brother, and the senior Pryce had gone out
of his way to make sure Tristan knew he was safe and loved. Tristan
was devastated when he'd walked into the library and found his uncle
slumped over, soulless, lifeless, and cold in his favorite wing chair. It
was the first time in years Tristan was scared. He hadn't known if he
could go on without his mentor, and there were days when he'd wander
to the second floor just to listen for his uncle shuffling through the library
and mumbling to himself.

The silence was heartbreaking, but Tristan had seen the man off
with love and a promise to see him again. Even if the loss made Tristan
feel cold and empty inside.

Except now his house had voices, live voices that laughed and
quarreled and teased. He wasn't used to hearing *people*, and the Grange
felt different. He'd hesitate to say the place felt like it was more among
the living than the dead, especially since the manor was merely wood,
bricks, and plaster. It was hard to admit he *liked* having people in the
Grange, and he'd be damned if he ever admitted that seeing Wolf every
morning across the breakfast table made him feel more alive than he'd
ever felt before.

It'd been days since he'd kissed Wolf on the balcony, and Tristan
found himself staring off into nothingness when he should have been
working, reliving the feel of the man's lips on his own or the feel of Wolf's
tongue when it touched the roof of his mouth, ruffling his steady calm.

Much like the couple who chased one another through the garden,
their voices rising in a furious anger. Gidget spared Tristan a glance as
she passed him.

Tristan had to admit Gidget in full fury was something gorgeous to behold. He liked the young woman. She in some ways reminded him of Mara, with a twist of modern someone could only find in San Francisco's funky subcultures. With her shoulders left bare by her retro sun dress, Tristan could see the tattoos she'd put on her skin, inked three-quarter sleeves of birds, flowers, and whatever else took her fancy. The bright-orange-and-yellow plaid of her dress made her easy to find in the folly's greenery, especially when she stomped through the columned pavilion and passed by its pointed faux windows.

Matt didn't even look at him. Instead, the man hurried past, nearly slipping on the slick marble steps leading to the garden. Neither said anything to Tristan or Mara, focusing instead on one another.

"It's cheating!" Gidget whirled about at the bottom of the stairs, poking Matt in the chest.

"It's a game!" he shot back, grabbing the railing to keep on his feet. "It's *not* real. You're being—"

"Think about that before you finish that sentence, Olson," Gidget spat, turning around. "Or better yet, maybe you should think about other things you've finished. Kinda like us."

"It's a *fucking* game!" he protested, dogging her heels. Both were nearly at a full trot, with Gidget tramping through the garden as if she were on safari. Matt's plaintive cry for her to wait up seemed to be falling on deaf ears. If anything, she stepped up her pace, taking them nearly to the end of the long garden in a few moments.

"Ah, true love. It looks… fractious." Tristan looked through his lashes at Mara. "Explain to me why I'd want that? Because I've got a better relationship with Cook than they seem to have right now. And I really only see *her* on Tuesday mornings."

"Because the lows are fairly easy to wade through," she replied smoothly. "If the two of you work at it. And it makes the highs unbelievable when you're passionate. Besides, not only is Cook a ghost, she's also a woman. Wolf, however, is neither of those things."

"There's no two of us. Wolf and me," he grumbled. "You know what I mean. Fuck."

"You'll get there. What are those two doing down there? Couldn't they fight inside? It's cold out here. And it's going to rain." Mara craned her neck and pointed to Hellsinger's technicians as the couple walked around the large pond at the end of the gardens. "They're going to fall in if they're not careful. Then where will they be?"

"Wet, I guess." Tristan spotted Gidget and Matt among the low evergreens. They were close to the water's edge, and the ground there would be slippery after the rains. He'd fallen into that pond more than once, mostly on purpose but sometimes by a misstep. "Kind of looks like they're still arguing. I'm waiting for one of them to push the other in."

"I'll have to get more towels if they go in," she grumbled good-naturedly, then frowned. "It looks like they're doing more than having a disagreement."

It looked to be an epic battle, one bards would have penned lengthy songs about and added verses to as pub drinkers called for more. Too far away to hear anything specific, Tristan could only imagine the furious, sharpened words Gidget flung at the now-cowering Matt. He winced at one particular volley, his shoulders shaking and pulling back as he tucked his elbows in against his ribs as if staving off an attack.

"She's a sight to behold," Mara proclaimed. "Good form, really. Arms have nice gestures, and her legs are apart enough to steady her. Look how she's facing him, full force. Whatever he's done, it's pissed her right off."

"Best thing about being gay, then," Tristan murmured. "I don't think I'd survive that. Look at Uncle Walter and Ashley. She looks like someone who'd stab you while you're sleeping. With tiny little needles. Poisoned needles so it'll look like you fell into an orgy of lesbian black widows."

"Most men wouldn't survive that. Gay or no," the woman replied. "Really, Tristan? Black widows?"

"Best I could come up with. You knew what I meant. Praying mantises wouldn't have worked. Had to be black widows."

Gidget's voice grew louder, a banshee wail carrying over the bushes, and Tristan caught a snatch of an accusation. There seemed to be a question of infidelity, and she'd found something out but he couldn't tell what.

"I didn't see what shoes she had on. Hope she's not wearing those stilettos I saw her in the other day," Mara commented. "She could kill a man with those."

"They looked like switchblades." A small nibble of an idea bloomed into a larger awareness in Tristan's mind. "That's why they call them stilettos. Well, shit. I never knew."

"It's good you're pretty, Tristan." She patted his shoulder. "Or I'd worry that no man would want to marry you."

"Nice," he grumbled. "I don't think about women's shoes. Hell, I barely think about *my* shoes."

Matt's beseeching arguments seemed to only infuriate the woman more, and she stopped at the end of the steps, right on the edge of the garden path. Pulling at something on her finger, Gidget wrenched and twisted before finally coming up triumphant. Whatever she yanked off her finger—Tristan could only assume it was a ring—sparkled as it turned in midair, a flash of white and gold against its graying skies and lush evergreen backdrop.

The ring flew, winged by the woman's ire, then landed in the middle of the folly's pond, rippling out a small splash across its murky waters.

The water wasn't the only thing that rippled when the ring struck the pond. Something dark flowed up out of the disturbed waters, a malingering otherness that spread over the garden and smacked Tristan full in his face. Next to him, Boris whined, hunching over and tucking his head into the back of Tristan's legs, trying to bury his muzzle into Tristan's knees. Mara gasped and clenched the balcony's railing, her knuckles white as she tried to stay on her feet. Buckling, she held on, riding out the forceful undulations as the rings grew outward, spreading a thin, dusky veil over the grounds and the manor behind them.

Anything Matt or Gidget might have said after that was buried under the roar of thunder ripping out from the growling cloud banks above them and flickers of lightning spitting across the sky, pushing back the shadows for a brief instance before the grounds were consumed again. The storm moved in quickly, spreading its coal-dust front much faster than Tristan could imagine. In seconds, the rain began, its enormous drops hot and painful where it struck his skin.

"Get inside, Mara," he growled, bending over to hoist Boris to his feet. The dog whimpered and cowered, but he hefted him up, cradling Boris in his arms. "Get out of this."

They ran the short distance from the end of the wide pavilion to the house, but the rain had already done its damage. Soaked through, Tristan gently placed Boris on the floor as soon as he crossed the threshold, not trusting his balance on the polished wood.

"What the fuck was that?" He turned to Mara, not caring about the puddle he was making on the parquet. "What the hell just happened out there? What did we just see?"

"I don't know, Tristan love." Mara turned and stared out of the french doors at the rain and hail pounding the Grange's sturdy walls. "I really don't know."

IT WAS a bad time for the children to have a spat. Not that any time was a good one, but Wolf had just wrestled the crates a courier service dropped off for them and sent back what they'd broken during their stay at the Grange. Hefting five bins across the long haul to the ballroom made his shoulders ache, and what he'd really wanted to do was hunt Tristan down and demand why the man was avoiding him. He'd spent the last few days playing cat and mouse with the blond, only pinning him down long enough to ask if they could stay longer, but when Wolf tried to talk about their single kiss, Tristan was like smoke in the wind.

"You'd think *he* was a damned ghost here," Wolf muttered, shoving yet another crate under a table. "Where the fuck *are* those two?"

It was past their normal lunchtime break... and that *fucking kiss*.

"Goddammit." Wolf leaned his head back and pressed his hands against the small of his back, working out a kink. "Pryce, between your mouth and that damned ball, you keep fucking with my head. It's got to stop."

There was no denying the ball's reappearance. He'd thrown it away several times, even knotting it into a plastic bag and dropping it into the trash, but the damned thing reappeared when he'd least expect it. At six in the morning before they shut down for the night, he'd thrown it out his bedroom window. He'd grabbed a new pair of underwear to put on after his shower and found the ball floating in the tub—in a hot bubble bath he'd *not* drawn before he went hunting for his briefs.

Wolf had grabbed the ball from the water, tossed his underwear on the counter, drained the tub, and said fuck it to the bath. He'd shower in the morning.

Since his dreams were full of a lean, naked Tristan rolling about on dark satin sheets, his shower was an extremely cold one.

"You should just fuck him, Kincaid." He slumped down into a wing chair, flipping on the camera feeds to look for his crew. "Fuck him and get it over with."

Because having sex with the firm-assed young man was going to somehow stop the damned red ball from appearing under his feet whenever he left it someplace other than his pocket or on the nightstand.

He took the ball out of his jacket pocket, bouncing it against the ballroom's marble floor. It made a *snick* sound, then another as he tossed it against one of the silk-covered walls. It hit and neatly ricocheted off, bouncing right back into Wolf's open hand. There was some small, niggling sense of satisfaction in seeing a mark on the silk wallpaper, but that only lasted a few moments before he got to his feet to wipe it off.

"That fucking son of a bitch." Gidget slammed through the ballroom, stomping toward the equipment setup. Skidding to a stop, she stared at the stacked bins Wolf had dragged in. Bedraggled was the best word Wolf could use to describe his electronics technician. She was sopping wet, her once spotless sundress soaked down with a strawberry Jell-O stain from the temporary color she put in her hair. The puddles she left behind were pink-speckled, and Wolf sighed, wondering where he could find a mop in the Grange's massive kitchen.

"What happened?" He really didn't want to know, especially when Matt came through the open doors, hot on Gidget's heels and, if possible, even more drenched than his girlfriend. Gidget's face got hard when she spotted Matt, and her chest heaved as she took a long breath, obviously filling her lungs for a good scream. Wolf stepped between them, holding his hands up. "Stop. I'm only going to say this once. When the two of you hooked up, you promised that your relationship wouldn't impact the job. So I'm going to have to ask, is that what's going on now? Because if it is, then you both need to take a step back and deal with this because I'm not having it in front of me. Am I clear?"

"Yes, sir," Matt murmured. Gidget said nothing but nodded, dropping her eyes to the floor, abashed.

"I don't hear you, Gidge," Wolf pressed.

"Yeah, boss," she replied softly.

"Now, one of you go get a mop and clean up this floor. You tracked it in, you get rid of it." Wolf stabbed at the table behind them. "Then dry off and get that stuff hooked up. If you've got time to deal with whatever you've got going on between you, then good. If not, then make sure it's done by the time we sit our asses in those chairs tonight to do our jobs. Got it?"

They both nodded, eyeing one another over the ocean of pink-and-clear puddles they'd smeared over the ballroom. Matt cleared his throat. "Um, what are you going to be doing?"

"I'm going to find our host." Wolf squeezed the red ball in his hand. "He and I have a few things we need to work out."

THE DARKNESS was troubling. As Tristan stared out at the garden from his apartment, he watched shadows lengthen, a sheer impossibility considering the encroaching moonless night, but there they were, moving and writhing about the paths as if alive and seeking something to feed on. So far, the house seemed quiet, untouched by the fingerlings of darkness outside, but he wondered for how long and, more importantly, how the hell was he going to stop them?

Situated behind the kitchen and running along the length of the wing, his library was a hodgepodge of books, furniture, and artifacts culled from Uncle Mortimer's travels before he settled into Hoxne Grange. Picked out mostly from his uncle's hoard in the attic, Tristan found a soft comfort in the ancient, worn furniture, settling into a tapestry couch someone had dragged over from England during the house's glory days. It was a fantastical piece, long enough for him to stretch out on if he wanted, but mostly, he curled up into its corners and pulled pillows up around him, watching the world pass by him through the Grange's broad windows.

Now he wished he could pull at the filmy curtains and hide behind them, veiled from the shadows and the storm brewing just beyond the Grange's walls.

The howling winds drowned out any other sound, and he nearly swallowed his tongue when Wolf Kincaid appeared at the end of the couch. His satyric presence loomed over him, a wickedly handsome man squishing the hell out of Jack's red rubber ball.

Boris looked up from his place on the floor, rumbling a low hello before flopping back down into his nest of pillows. Stepping over the wolfhound's lanky body, Wolf navigated around the dog, then sat next to Tristan, his long legs crossed under him. His feet were bare, like Tristan's, but with a fine black down on the rises of his toes. It looked softer than the springier hair on Wolf's calves, but Tristan would need to touch both to make sure.

As if Wolf Kincaid would want Tristan's hands on him, especially after he'd pulled away from their kiss.

The feel of the man under his hands had been too much, and Tristan knew if he'd stayed ruched up against Wolf's body for a moment longer, he would have torn off their clothes and embarrassed himself. More than he usually did.

Instead, Wolf eyed him suspiciously and held the ball up under Tristan's nose, his fingers running over its curve. The smell of dog-spit rubber tickled Tristan's senses, and he nearly sneezed, catching a whiff of algae and something danker on the ball's surface. Rubbing at his face, Tristan drove the sensation out, waiting for Wolf to say something.

"Talk to me about Jack," he finally said.

"Jack?" Tristan eyed him again, this time with a bit more heat. "Really? You want to talk about the dog?"

"Dog first. Then us."

"I think I told you all I know about Jack. He's about maybe a foot and a half tall? Bluish, like the others. They really don't have a lot of color. I think he's got white fur. A couple of darker spots on his body and ears. They could be black or brown. Hard to say." Tristan pursed his lips thoughtfully, yanking on the man's chain. "Oh, and he's a *dog*."

"And he likes this ball?" Wolf waved the smelly thing under Tristan's nose again, and he pushed at Wolf's arm with a swipe of his hand.

"Yes. Don't make me smell it. It stinks. Worse than Boris's tennis balls."

"Okay," Wolf said, tucking the ball behind him. "Now we're going to talk about us. And this place."

"I'd rather talk about how many ways I could lose a fingernail, starting with hot pliers," Tristan muttered. "But sure, we can talk about *us*. What's there to say? You kissed me. I ran away while you were watching my hallucinations. End of story. I'd rather talk about whatever your team did to my place."

He got no further. The lights flickered. Then a bulb popped in a stained glass lamp by the door. Another followed, smoke rising from the cracked bulb, and Tristan sat up, startled at the black stain creeping over the library's windows. Boris whimpered and shoved himself as far against the couch as he could, and Tristan thought he might fight the dog for some place safe to hide.

"Tell me you see that, Kincaid." He got to his feet, nearly falling over Boris. An intense cold slipped over him, and the windows began to crinkle with a dusky-gray frost, curls of inky swirls folding over each other as it quickly covered the panes. "Tell me I'm crazy *now*."

"What the hell is that?" Wolf came up behind him, and the man's strong arms wrapped around Tristan's waist, cradling him from behind. The touch of the other man felt too good for Tristan to shove away, especially since his warmth chased off the icy prickling slipping over his skin.

Something felt… wrong. Tristan had no other word for it. The sick of it stained his senses, and he swallowed, trying to get the film's thick, oily taste off of his tongue. His fingers dug into Wolf's forearms, a tight grip hard enough to bruise flesh, but the other man said nothing, bearing whatever pain he might have felt.

"Something happened today," Tristan whispered softly. The chill was leaving him, a speck at a time, but it lingered, lurking just outside of the Grange's once-clear windows. "Gidget and Matt were arguing by the folly… and she took something off of her finger. When she threw it, it landed in the pond… the big pond where the fireflies gather… where I've seen some of the guests… the spirits… walk into when they leave.

"When the ring hit the water, it was like an explosion of… something. Nothing real. Not like how you count real, but there was something there. It churned up the waters. I could see the pond ripple out, much bigger and darker than the ring could have made." Tristan shuddered. "I saw it come up over the gardens. Then the storm hit, and we… Mara and I… ran inside. I thought maybe it would stay out there… whatever it is… go away after the rains are done. I never thought it would reach the house."

"Could be natural," Wolf pondered. "Something in the clouds. Stuff like that happens. Rains frogs in some place. Could be something as innocuous as spores caught up and dumped back down. Or ash. Stranger shit's happened."

Tristan was about to say something when the howling began. It started small, a shriek off in the distance, then grew louder until the windows rattled from the fury of the sound. The library door slammed, over and over, until the frame cracked with the force of the repeated impacts. Frightened, Boris somehow leveraged himself under one of the wingbacks, toppling the chair over, his tail high in the air, his long legs splayed out from under him.

"I think they broke something... something that held this all back from the Grange," Tristan murmured, his fear cut by the growing anger he felt at his home being invaded by something he couldn't quite see. "What the hell did they do?"

HE DIDN'T have an answer for Tristan. Not by a long shot. Wolf could definitely see the black tendrils spreading over the windows, and the door's suicide couldn't be explained away by wind. The banshee wails coursing through the manor rose and fell, roiling through the rooms. He could have explained it away by a faulty sound system or perhaps an ancient intercom buried beneath layers of plaster from a past remodel, but he'd not found any evidence of that when they'd set their cameras up. More importantly, the man he held in his arms was cold, a bluish tint beginning to form at the edges of Tristan's lips.

"Come on, we need to get you warm." Wolf nudged Tristan's motionless body. "This room is freezing."

Their breath frosted the air, plumes of mist heaving out of their mouths as Wolf half carried Tristan out. Not wanting to be left behind, Boris bolted out of the room ahead of them, nearly knocking the men off their feet. As soon as they cleared the library, the shrieking stopped and the apartment's temperature rose, hitting Wolf in the face like a wave of steam from a sauna. Shivering, Tristan stumbled, and Wolf held on tightly, easing the man into the apartment's living space. Settling Tristan down on a couch, he pulled a soft cashmere afghan over him, tucking it around Tristan's legs, then kissing him briefly on the mouth.

Boris was nowhere to be seen, so Wolf figured the hound had found a way to hide under Tristan's bed.

"I'm going to make you some tea, okay?" Wolf wondered if Tristan had something stronger somewhere in the cabinets, because his stomach clenched at the thought of going any longer without fortification.

As if reading his mind, Tristan stuttered through chattering teeth, "There's some Macallan in the sideboard."

Kissing the man's cold away seemed like a better idea, but he wanted them to have their senses about them. Since pushing Tristan up against the back of the couch to ravage him seemed like a more mind-altering experience than getting drunk, he'd settle for alcohol.

His cock disagreed, but his brain was firm on the subject. There had to be answers… sane answers other than Gidget tossing something into an old pond and opening up a mouth to hell.

Wolf found the whiskey, whistling at the bottle as he dusted it off. It was a simple tall vessel with a white label bordered in black and gold, but that white label bore an imprint of rare quality, and Wolf looked over at the man behind him. "You want me to crack open a twenty-five-year whiskey."

"A gift from my agent," Tristan murmured, his silky rasp wrapping its warmth around Wolf's dick. "For my monsters. I think it's fitting. I got that for my monsters. I'm going to drink it because of monsters."

"You've got a Macallan Cask Strength in here too. Let's pop that one instead. If I'm going to drink a whiskey that cost more than my first car, I want to enjoy it." Wolf blew out two tumblers and padded over to the couch, handing the other man the glasses so he could undo the bottle's top. After splashing some of the heady amber liquid into one glass, he took the other from Tristan and poured one for himself.

Toasting the blond next to him, Wolf raised his glass and said, "*Slàinte mhòr agad.*"

He would have said more, something witty and warm to take away the tremors coursing through Tristan's slender body, but he had the glass halfway to his mouth when he spotted a familiar red ball on the couch. Usually when the ball reappeared, it showed under his feet or in his bed, sometimes on a table or in his bathroom. This time, its appearance wasn't so much a shock as where it was.

This time, the ball was firmly in the jaws of a transparent, filmy-blue dog standing proudly on a couch cushion, its stub tail wagging so furiously, Wolf had a hard time seeing it through the blur. Moving closer until he straddled Tristan's legs, the rough-coated terrier dropped the ball and lolled his cornflower-blue tongue out, a cunning smile pulling up his doggy lips. The ball rolled across the cushion and came to rest against Tristan's covered leg, its pungent smell reaching Wolf's nose nearly as quickly as the dog's hot breath touched his face.

"Well, shit." Wolf gulped at the Scottish brew, burning his throat. "I guess that's Jack."

Chapter 7

THE BED was cold underneath him but ragingly hot on top when Wolf finally woke up. Worse, it seemed to have lost a few feet and grown a hard back he'd somehow gotten his elbow lodged into. Something smelled of wet dog, and there was a whirring sound he couldn't quite place. Then he turned his head and realized the whirring sound was coming from behind him… in the form of a sleek purple vacuum being run over hardwood floors.

His eyes weren't quite working, blurring everything around him whenever he tried to blink, and sitting up proved to be a huge mistake, especially when something in his head began to pound against the inside of his skull, perfectly in time with the whirring. The bed turned out to be a couch that while comfortable, certainly wasn't meant to be shared with a floppy-legged wolfhound that seemed slightly damp, either from the rain or perhaps from diving into a sewer, because the dog certainly had a special odor seeping up from his fur.

Beneath the whirring and now the snorfling grunts of a sleeping wolfhound, the storm railed at the manor, slamming into it with as much fury as Wolf's headache on his temples. Dislodging Boris was more difficult than he thought, and for a moment, Wolf debated just dying on the couch, his bones pressed down to dust beneath the heavy dog's weight.

"Isn't that how they tested for witches?" he mumbled, starting the cacophony in his head again. "Wait, that was just one witch. Corey?"

"Giles Corey. And he was an American," Mara supplied as she turned off the vacuum. "Most people who died by *peine forte et dure* were those who refused to enter a plea in Great Britain. But by the looks of that beast on you, it won't be long for you."

"It's not the dog. I feel like shit," Wolf grunted, shoving Boris behind him as he rolled off the couch. His stomach joined his head in complaining, and he clutched at his belly, wondering what the hell he did to deserve the assault. Even his bones ached, and he had a sneaking suspicion he'd swallowed either a pumice stone or cleaned the Grange's fireplaces with his tongue.

Coming face-to-face with an empty bottle of Macallan's brought it all back, including the sloppy kiss he gave Tristan before he collapsed into a deep-black unconscious sleep.

"Fuck." Wolf rubbed his forehead. Even his hair hurt. The bottle was definitely empty, and the dog snored on, content to have the couch to himself. "Where's Tristan?"

"Downstairs." Mara picked up an accent pillow, beating it back into shape, then tucking it back into a chair. "It's Tuesday. He's waiting for Cook to come in. Then I think he plans on working. You'll have to ask him."

"He's not…." Wolf bit the inside of his cheek to stop himself from whimpering as he stood up. It was one thing to show his frailty to the dog, but the sharp-eyed woman bustling about Tristan's apartment was something else.

"Hungover?" The woman fluffed another pillow, then grabbed the empty whiskey bottle from the table. "No, the boy's fine—not a headache or anything. You still a bit ossified?"

"Is that a fancy word for fucked up?" He glanced up at the woman as he bent over his own knees, catching his breath before standing up again.

"Yes. Yes it is."

"Then yes, I'm ossified, fossilized, and any other –ized you want to call me right now." The world tilted a little bit when he stood up straight, but his stomach seemed to stay in place. "I'm going to head for a shower."

"And then?" Mara turned, her shoes squeaking on the floor.

"Then I'm going downstairs to bell the cat," Wolf said, grabbing the red ball off of the low table in front of him. "And maybe a dog too."

A SHOWER made him feel more human—barely—but Wolf didn't trust himself with a sharp blade against his face, not even one set into a safety razor and primed with skin softening gel. The room across the hall from his was quiet, so either Gidget and Matt weren't inside or they'd killed one another and joined the Grange's spectral guests.

"Good, they can throw the ball for the damned dog." Jack hadn't made an appearance yet, but he wasn't holding his breath. Something had happened to either push him over the edge into seeing Tristan's delusions or he'd jumped onto the crazy train all by himself. "Fucking hell, my mother's going to laugh her goddamned ass off about this."

The ballroom doors were open, and he heard the soft murmur of voices coming from inside the cavernous space. Voices that not only seemed to be getting along but cooing excitedly over something.

"I liked it better when they were fighting." Wolf bit the bullet and headed into the ballroom, hoping both of his technicians were dressed and oohing over a kitten or something. Of course, he owed them an apology for not showing up last night. "I didn't even get laid or anything. Just fucking drunk."

What he found was much more thrilling than a kitten.

The ballroom's chandeliers were dimmed, the bank of monitors and analysis equipment casting an eerie glow over the tables and floor. Both Gidget and Matt were hunkered in front of the camera feed displays, tapping furiously at their keyboards and cackling between their gleeful mutters. Their boards were lit up, dancing with waves of green and yellow as the feeds and sensors picked up activity through the Grange.

Matt was the first one to spot him, and he grinned up at Wolf, motioning him over with a frantic wave. "Dude, you've got to come see this. It's been insane since last night. Readers are off the board."

His body sung with the chase, and Wolf was torn between diving into the team's results and hunting down Tristan to talk about what happened between them the night before. A few beeps and a flash of something on the screen in front of Gidget and Wolf decided a few minutes staring at the feeds wouldn't hurt anyone.

"Here, watch this one." Gidget got out of her chair, bouncing up on the balls of her feet. "I'm going to get some coffee. You want some coffee? We should have enough. Deidre... she's one of the morning staff... she set us up with an espresso machine. One of those packet jobbie things. We've been using it all night. Awesome stuff."

"Sure, an espresso would be nice." Wolf's head throbbed when he plopped into the chair Gidget vacated.

"Look at what I've got keyed up," Gidget called out. "There's some clear manifestations on the edges of the film. No faces or anything but still, forms! Or something!"

Wolf flicked the playback to the beginning of the patch Gidget started. Frowning, he tried to distinguish which of the manor's many hallways was being shown when the marker flashed up on the screen, labeling the feed's origin. The second-floor feed had been promising before, and the junction camera flickered and danced with static, then settled down to a strong, steady view of the birdcage lift landing.

The time markers flew by at double speed, advancing the video quickly. For a few minutes, the feed appeared normal. Then a white shape dashed across the screen, just beyond the camera's fixed lens. Curious, Wolf paced the film back in increments, slowing the form down until he could barely make out what looked like the curve of a shoulder and maybe an arm. The rest of the shape was sporadic, a lacy construct of light and shadows, but there was definitely something there.

"Did you run this through the infrared feeds?" He took the cup Gidget offered him when she shoved it over his shoulder.

"That's the fucked-up part." She dragged another chair up to the table. "They went offline every time we tried flaming them on. Matt even went upstairs with a handheld, but as soon as he got off the elevator, everything went dark."

"Yeah, we tried staking the area out a few times last night." Matt yawned, his eyes heavy with bruises and bags. "It was crap. Every time we came back downstairs, the screens lit up. Orbs. Dashes. Everything but faces and full forms. My legs hurt from going up and down those damned stairs."

"We thought maybe the birdcage thing was triggering something, so we parked it up on the third floor and ran up and down." Gidget pointed to another shape edging into the corner of her video. "See that one? It's shorter and moves quicker. I think it's a kid."

"No evidence," Wolf responded automatically. They'd been down that path more than once. Gidget or Matt would get excited, and he'd be the one to pull them back. Evidence was only evidence when there were firm readings, and so far, a few pixels on a screen weren't firm enough for him to call it a haunting.

Like the fucking dog that brought back a stinky red ball while he was busy getting drunk on Scottish whiskey and yearning for a pretty blond with soulful, changeable hazel eyes.

"Shit...." Take his own word for it? Ghosts were supposed to be people, not happy-faced terriers keen on a game of toss. "I've got to get readings. I just can't...."

Saying something to the pair wasn't going to do him any good. He had no proof. Only speculation and the curiosity of the black frost coating Tristan's library windows. Frowning, Wolf flicked through the feeds, hoping to find a view of the Grange's exterior.

"Let's set up more cameras," he finally pronounced. "Close up the holes. Assuming you guys are talking to each other again."

"Yeah." Matt sounded sheepish. "About that...."

"Tristan said you guys went pretty hot at each other in the garden. And not in a good way." Wolf pierced Gidget with a look. "Said you tossed something into that pond by the fake ruins."

"Shit, the ring," Matt murmured.

"Wait until it stops raining." Gidget moaned softly, burying her face in her hands. "I can't fucking believe I did that."

"I'm not saying this is true...," Wolf prefaced. "But Pryce said something happened when you tossed the ring into the pond. Did you guys feel anything? See anything?"

"I was pissed off." Gidget looked sheepish. "He...."

"I had sex with someone else," Matt explained, then held up his hands when Wolf turned to give him a filthy look. "It's not like that. Not *real* sex. In game—in a video game. Sorta. She's not even on that server."

"Dude, *cheating*." The anger might have left Gidget's voice, but the firmness remained. "Do not nookie another person's bits. Flesh or pixels."

"Get back to the ring." Wolf steered the conversation back to its original subject. "Did you *see* anything?"

"Storm hit right about then," Matt replied. Leaning back in his chair, the young man stared up at the ceiling, his eyes unfocused. "Um, there was a lot of thunder. And it was close—"

"You could feel it on your skin, you know?" Gidget interjected. "Like it was punching through the air at us."

"Yeah, it did." Matt looked down, staring at his boss. "The rain was just so fucking cold."

"And hard." Gidget looked toward the ballroom's curtained windows. "I don't think it's stopped, even. Maybe a little bit but not enough for me to go out there to look for Matt's grandma's ring."

"Great-grandmother," Matt corrected. "It was her wedding ring. From her first marriage. Some duke or something. He died, and then she married a couple of other guys afterward."

"What? Five more?" Gidget frowned, counting off on her fingers. "Yeah, I think it was six total, right?"

"She got married six times? Jesus, I can't get married *once*." Wolf shook off their inquiring looks. "Not that I want to. Just… shit. Six? How many ex-husbands can one woman have? What the hell did the family dinners look like?"

"Not ex-husbands." Matt grinned at Wolf. "Dead husbands. That's what Great-Grandma Winnie was known for. Killing off her husbands. They finally caught her before she killed off number seven. Turns out he was allergic to quinine. Got blisters and shit in his mouth when he drank some tea she gave him. Someone came over from Scotland Yard and leaned on her a bit, and she confessed to trying to kill him. Apparently she killed all of her husbands because you couldn't get divorced back then or something."

"So your great-grandmother was a serial killer?" Wolf rubbed at his eyes, feeling the tint of a migraine blooming behind his right orbital.

"Yep, pretty much." Matt nodded. "Loved her kids, though. Had three of them. None by the duke or we'd be sitting in some castle somewhere drinking oolong and sniffing about the riffraff. She had insurance out on all of them but put it in her kids' names. The courts couldn't take any of it back."

"And *you*…." Wolf stopped his rubbing and stared at Gidget. "You threw the ring of a known serial killer into a pond of a house we're investigating for spectral activity? A place pretty much known for *generations* as an inn for ghosts?"

"Yeah, kinda." Gidget grimaced. "We were going to get it back once the rain stopped. That pond's pretty fucking deep. It's more like a minilake. Really, someone could drown back in that shit."

"It's dark too. Can't even see the bottom," Matt murmured. "Even without the rain. 'Sides, I wasn't the one that tossed it in there. *That* was Gidge."

"Hey! I was pissed!" Gidget protested.

"Why would you even want a ring that was worn by a woman who offed her husbands?" Wolf asked, fearing the answer. "And why the hell would you give it to her, Matt?"

"I thought it would be cool, you know? I mean… her being a serial killer and everything. It's a pretty ring." Gidget crossed her arms over her chest. "It's a ruby. The family thinks it came from India."

"No one else in the family wanted it." Matt shrugged. "Gidge and I thought it was sweet… kind of in a macabre way, but sweet. It was from her first marriage. You know… her first love."

"And her first kill. Maybe. They didn't prove she did *him* in." Gidget smiled at her lover. "Not like she chopped the others up into meat pies."

"Jesus fucking Christ," Wolf sighed heavily. "It's like the two of you are trying to get us killed."

"Hey, wait a minute," Matt protested. "It's not like you believe in any of this shit. It's just a storm… and a damned ring! It's not like tossing the ring made anything happen. We don't even have any proof this is real, and you don't believe in ghosts, remember?"

Wolf stood up, sending the chair toppling onto its side, pissed off at the skeptical doubts that were no longer whispering in the back of his mind. Growling as he stalked out of the room to find Tristan, he shot back at them, "Well, I fucking do *now*."

THE FLOOR was wet. More importantly, there were damp footprints coming into the Grange, a large puddle and then footprints, just as moist as the ones before, leaving again.

Tristan couldn't quite believe it.

There was no Heather Cook. There was no inquiry of employment. There wasn't even a shy confession about having no references because the lady had turned her out.

Nothing. Just water, footprints, and silence.

He didn't even get a chance to *see* her.

Heather Cook, the Grange's spectral cook for at least two generations, did not come to ask for a job she'd always been given. Instead, she took measure of the place, and despite having no letters or good word from a spiteful woman whose husband's attention wandered over to a pretty Cockney girl who'd tried to better herself, Heather Cook got the fuck out of Dodge without a single word to the man waiting for her.

Tristan wanted to cry. In some way, he felt like he was losing parts of Uncle Mortimer all over again.

Or worse, parts of himself.

He jumped when he felt a hand on his shoulder, then steeled himself not to cry when Wolf gently turned him around. The compassionate look on the man's face broke him, and Tristan bit into his lower lip, hoping the pain would keep him from blubbering like a baby into Wolf's broad chest.

"Hey, what's wrong?" It was hard to ignore the sensual rub of Wolf's voice against the crumbling bits of his heart. Especially when the man's wide, rough hands scraped over his jaw, a tender, gentle touch Tristan didn't even realize he'd been missing until he felt it. "Pryce, talk to me. What's happened? I can see it in your face."

"She's not coming." He glanced over at the door, his gaze catching on the watery footprints marring the floor. "Well, she came, but she... didn't stay. Something's *wrong*, Kincaid. Something's horribly wrong."

"Yeah, I know." Wolf's mouth lowered, brushing on Tristan's cheek, and anything he might have said was now caught in his throat, stymied by the warmth of the man's body against his. "Come on, we need to talk."

"THEY THREW a murderer's ring into my pond?" Tristan stared out the window of his library, not quite believing what Wolf was saying. "And not just any murderer, but a woman who killed six of her husbands?"

"Five. The sixth... well, really he was the first... is disputed," Wolf murmured, refilling Tristan's wine glass. "He might have just died of natural causes."

He'd allowed Wolf to bring him upstairs to his apartment, wrapped himself in a mound of quilts, then curled into one of the old floppy cushioned couches in his library. The room's expanse of windows were now clear, the black frosted shadows either wiped clean by the torrential rain or perhaps even had crept into the manor, playing havoc with his peaceful existence.

Much like Wolf Kincaid was doing to his body and mind.

Kincaid put the bottle back down on the table he'd taken it from, stretching his long arm across Tristan's knees and in front of his face. If he'd wanted to, Tristan could have actually bitten the man, taking a bit of skin and flesh into his mouth until Wolf's blood ran down his chin. Not that he was actually bloodthirsty, but he was pretty pissed off about what Gidget and the rest of the Hellsinger team had brought to his front door.

Apparently not so pissed off that his cock didn't jerk up when Wolf brushed against him, because his groin began its own little dance club beneath his zipper as Kincaid looped an arm around Tristan's shoulders and pulled him close.

"Fucking dick," Tristan muttered at his traitorous piece of flesh. "I hope you fucking get bitten off by a barracuda someday. That'll show you."

"Who are you talking to?" Wolf looked around. "Someone here?"

A few days ago, Tristan would have crowed at hearing Wolf Kincaid, mighty ghost stalker extraordinaire, admit to the possibility of some other presence in the room. In the middle of a darkness eating his home, there was little joy he could find in the man's words.

"No one's here. Shit, even Boris is asleep on my bed," Tristan grumbled, resting his forehead on his pulled-up knees. "I don't know where Jack is, and hell only knows where Cook's gone."

"Has she ever *not* shown up before?"

"No, even if you miss her, she'll usually be waiting." The weight of Wolf's arm on his shoulder was a distraction, nearly as much as the occasional burr of his unshaven jaw against Tristan's cheek when he shifted about. "Stop moving. It's hard… to think."

"Hungover?" Wolf's snort ruffled the hair on his neck. "Mara said you didn't get… how did she put it? Ossified?"

If he'd been hungover by anything, it'd been by the uncoordinated mashing of Wolf's tongue against his lips right before the man passed out on top of him. They'd shared whiskey and the storm between them, a hot, heady pounding of damp and lightning punctuated with kisses nearly as violent. It all ended too suddenly for Tristan, a searing heat, then nothing but a slack masculine weight and not-so-delicate snores.

It was like sleeping with Boris. Except a lot less hairy.

"I'm sorry about Cook," Wolf whispered. Shifting, he stroked Tristan's cheekbone with his fingers. "I feel like I should do something."

"You should. You've brought this mess to the Grange." He tried to sound angry or at least ruffled, but it was difficult to concentrate with Wolf's feathering touch moving over his face.

"Because nothing shitty's ever happened here before?" Wolf cocked his head, and Tristan blinked, caught in the man's clear blue gaze. "Maybe it'll be like the rest of your guests? Three days and it'll be gone."

"I—" Tristan gulped, his breath mingling with the sweet heat of Wolf's exhale. "You're making me crazy. I can't think."

"Yeah, well…." Wolf trailed another long, skittering path over Tristan's cheek, ending with a press of his finger against Tristan's lower lip. "You did that to me a few days ago. Glad to see you finally caught up. Never thought you'd be the slow one."

He knew it was coming. Everything pointed to it. Hell, his *dick* pointed to it, but Tristan *still* wasn't prepared for Wolf's kiss. His mind churned with enough white noise to drown out the storm raging just beyond the library's windows, and the scent of citrus and Wolf buried the cloying sting of rain in the air. It was a sweet touching of mouths and Tristan heard himself make some little noise, muted in the rushing pound of his heart as it began to skip a beat.

That's when he found out Wolf was apparently turned on by little sounds when they became trapped between his pursed lips, because Tristan found himself pushed up against the side of the couch with one of Wolf's hands tangled in his hair while the other skimmed up under his shirt.

Throwing caution to the wind, Tristan dove in, tossing himself into the uncertain tempest brewing between them.

There was too much of everything keeping Tristan contained. His clothes twisted around his waist and chest, and his shirt pulled at his shoulders when Wolf's hand slipped over his belly and found his right nipple. With not enough room to do more than rake and pull at Tristan's nub, Wolf could only do so much, but it was enough to drive Tristan's cock to a frenzied heat.

He didn't know what to do. His hands felt like they couldn't grab enough of the other man. Their tongues dove and dipped between their pressed mouths, and when Tristan finally needed some air, Wolf's teeth joined the dance, scraping and biting at the tender spots on Tristan's throat. The light sear of Wolf's unshaven jaw prickled Tristan's skin, chafing a skittering burn Tristan knew he'd feel later.

And if he didn't, he'd feel cheated, because he wanted *something* to show from their kiss.

He got something fairly quickly. Wolf's gentle nibbles turned fierce, and Tristan writhed, arching his back when the man's bite dug in. Wolf's hands came up, capturing Tristan's wrists. Pulling Tristan's arms up over his head, Wolf imprisoned him against the couch, his long fingers wrapping around Tristan's delicate bones. He squeezed just tight enough for Tristan to know he was trapped. Then Wolf's dark head dipped again, nipping along the spot he'd bitten down on before.

When Wolf's teeth closed over his skin again, Tristan found out he really hadn't known what being on fire felt like until right then.

He liked the weight of the man on him. Wolf fit into the place he'd longed to be filled, although one part of him ached, flexed in response to the sharp scoring along his throat. His jeans were taut, pushed up from his tingling erection, his dick craving more than the rub of cotton against its tight skin. Groaning, Tristan thrust his hips up, needing something to ease the throbbing anguish building up in his belly and crotch. Wolf responded, anchoring his mouth into Tristan's throat, then grinding his hips down into Tristan's hard length.

Wolf's mouth left the stinging crease he'd made, moving back up to Tristan's mouth and finding it open, parched and dry from Tristan's mewling. More than willing to quench Tristan's thirst, Wolf took control of Tristan's mouth and filled him, pressing a skilled tongue up against the roof of his mouth, then licking at the underside of his upper lip. The sensation of the man's tongue on his palate and slick inner cheek teased, and Tristan's mind swam between being tickled and aroused.

"God, I want you," Wolf said into the gape of Tristan's panting mouth.

The man would have said more... probably even done more if the Grange hadn't suddenly rolled around them. The room creaked and rocked, shoving the couch back a few feet, slamming it into a suit of armor held together by apparently what was a few strings and a chant to Herne. The armor's antlered helm flew, striking the glass front of a long-dead aunt's mantle clock, and its arms and legs scattered, landing in different parts of the room. The stuffed crow Mara swore hated her fell straight down from its perch on a tigerwood wardrobe, the bird's lacquered beak piercing a book on Malaysian botany Tristan really hadn't intended to read. The crow's legs stuck straight out behind its rigid body, perfectly aimed to catch the curtains swaying nearby. Wrapped up in the length of fabric, the bird and book were yanked from the desk, swinging back and forth in the rippling aftermath of the house's assault.

Neither man had taken a full breath when the Grange erupted again, this time with a terrified howling loud enough to fill the manor's halls and pierce any seduction spell Wolf cast over a very disappointed Tristan.

"You okay?" Wolf asked when the couch finally settled into a corner of the room.

"Yeah," Tristan grumbled. The shrieking continued, only stopping long enough for Tristan to hope it was finally over before starting up again. "Three days, huh?"

"Maybe?" Wolf grinned sheepishly. "Hoping?"

"You better fucking hope so." Tristan worked his hands free of the man's loose hold, gingerly untangling himself from Wolf's legs and arms. "Because if it doesn't, I'm going to kill you and you're going to be the Grange's new Cook."

Chapter 8

"THEY'RE LEAVING, you know." Mara trod up behind him, a silent harbinger of common sense and doom. "The guests, I mean. They're going."

"I know." Tristan scowled at the register, glaring at the names on its yellowed, ink-stained pages. Names that were scribbled through with a rough hand, as if working a pen took great effort. He'd checked in a couple just yesterday, their smiling older faces turning younger with each step into the lobby toward the desk. By the time they'd reached Tristan, their monochromatic forms were bursting with a youth neither had seen in more than a century, if he judged their clothing right. They'd walked up the stairs, hand in hand, toward a honeymoon beyond their lifetime.

That afternoon, the day after Cook failed to ask for her job, he opened the register rand found their names crossed off and a small, unsteady *Apologies* in the margin. He rifled back and forth through the pages, his stomach sinking with each scrubbed out entry.

For the first time in his memory, the Grange was empty of guests.

Except of course for Wolf and his team of Hellsingers.

"Fucking hell." Tristan scrubbed his eyes. Blinking, he looked at the pages again, only to be disappointed once more. "*Pezzo di merda.*"

"That was nicely done. Was that last one for your Dr. Kincaid?" Mara plucked a dead leaf from the flower arrangement at the end of the reception desk. "The Italian was a good touch. He has the look of an Italiano to him. Maybe his mother? Kincaid is Scottish, I think."

"No, it was for me," Tristan sighed. "I never should have agreed to have them here. I've fucked everything up, Mara."

"No one says the Grange *has* to be a gateway for departing souls," she replied. "Other places have disappeared as well. It won't be the first."

Tristan shot her as filthy a look as he could manage. "The Grange is my legacy from Uncle Mortimer."

"Legacy." Mara couldn't have put more derision into her scoff if she'd tried. "Grab life by the balls, Tristan Pryce. Or at least grab

Kincaid. Have something they need to pry out of your cold, dead hands besides the deed to this place."

"I have a life," Tristan protested. "I write—"

"You write about silly monsters." The woman dismissed his livelihood with a wave of her hand. "You live in an old mansion filled with ghosts and scribble cute pictures of hairy boo-wigglies. That's not a life, Tristan. Those are things you're doing while you're waiting to die."

"Are you done scolding me?" He leaned across the counter, stretching his legs out behind him. "Because you know, I've got *nothing* else to do in my life besides listen to you."

"You can order more towels," Mara sniffed imperiously. "I don't know what it is about people. They *have* to steal towels. Even ghosts heading to the afterlife steal towels. I think everyone's taking Douglas Adams a bit too seriously, if you ask me."

"Towels, got it." He was debating putting them on auto-purchase as the woman stalked off. Mara was right. Even ghosts seemed to walk off with a hotel's linens. "Must have to take your own toga up with you to heaven. Thank fucking God St. Peter gives them their own halos. God knows what the hell they'd take for those."

"Did you just swear at heaven?" Wolf emerged from the shadowy hall and gave Tristan a crooked smile.

The last thing Tristan wanted at that exact moment was Wolf Kincaid walking in on his own personal breakdown.

Especially while wearing a pair of jeans so old they could qualify for a seniors' discount at any pancake house and the jeans' obviously equally ancient wife, a body-hugging thin T-shirt. If he looked hard enough, he could see the perk of Wolf's nipples under the tatty cotton. Taking a second glance, Tristan found he really didn't have to search. They were right there, lustful and beckoning, nearly begging Tristan to take a taste.

"*Culus.*" Tristan tried out the sound of the word in his mouth. "I think that's right... *culus.*"

"You're a funny little boy, Tristan Pryce." Wolf leaned on the reception counter, bringing his sensual mouth within whispering distance of Tristan's face.

Leveling a serious glare at the man, Tristan said, "I'm not a little boy, Kincaid."

Wolf gave him an impenetrable look; then his crooked smile grew wicked. "No, you're definitely not."

He was about to reply with something he hoped would be snappy and cutting, but something large and dark appeared through the misty rain outside the Grange's front doors. Mottled by the glass insets, the form lumbered, filling the slender cut panes, but Tristan could definitely make out one thing in the shapes that had his heart pounding with excitement. *Wrinkles.*

"It's an elephant!" Tristan was around the desk before he could finish exhaling the breath he'd been holding in. His bare feet caught on the polished wooden floor, and he jerked sideways when his heel found a particularly well-oiled spot. "There's an elephant outside! God, let it be an elephant. Too small for a brontosaurus, but still… an elephant?"

He felt like a little kid again, running through the lobby at the first hint of an arrival and Uncle Mortimer chuckling softly when Tristan threw open the doors to let in a new guest. He'd been so frightened during his first week at the Grange, but the soft huff of a ghostly camel plodding up to the manor changed *everything*. Majestic, proud, and shouldering the burden of a round, elaborately dressed man in a turban and jewels, the animal's appearance was so *real*. When his elderly and kind-voiced uncle described to Tristan exactly what they were seeing… and everything matched down to the off-red tassels on the camel's bridle, Tristan knew he'd found a home.

The Grange made him feel… *normal. His* kind of normal, and no one, not even the perky-nippled, charismatic Wolf Kincaid could take it away from him.

Roses from the gardens brushed his shoulder when Tristan grabbed at the center table for support as he headed to the doors. His bare feet made a *snick*ing sound as he ran, squeaking again when he paused only long enough to grab the door handles. The shapes outside the door were still moving, ponderous and lumbering by. Rattling at the latch, Tristan threw the doors open and stepped into the rain, eager to welcome his guests inside.

There was evidence.

Lots of it.

Mostly a long trail of circular footprints filling up with rain, embedded into the expanse of once pristine sod in front of the Grange's broad steps, but it was enough to cause Tristan's heart to skip more than a beat or two. That excitement soon fell to dust when he looked around and saw *nothing*.

The Grange's drive was desolately empty, with not an elephant hair in sight.

Seeing the large press of tracks in the Grange's central lawn dug deep furrows of pain into Tristan's tender soul. The depressions were round, a curious two-step gait squished into the mud, an oddly graceful line of delicate circles. They were as deep as Tristan's foot was high, almost single file, and edged up at the rim with a thick slurry. The grass suffered beneath the massive creature's weight. The lawn's lush green strands were pushed down deep into the sticky, rich mud, chunks of sod lying a few inches away where it flew off when the creature pulled its foot from the suckling ground.

But beyond that single line of depressions and the whiff of gamy flesh and damp straw in the air, Tristan saw no sign of the ectoplasmic beast. Or the ghost who rode it.

"Goddammit!" Tristan dropped to his knees, filling his hands with wet grass and mud. "Why didn't you stay? Why aren't any of you staying?"

Clenching his fingers, he drew up entire handfuls of soggy lawn and flung them as far as he could, nearly wrenching his shoulders out. The rain continued, uncaring and unabated, soaking him down to the skin. Mud crept in everywhere it could reach, its thick slurry stealing into the folds of his jeans and into the spaces between his toes. His face felt hot, stung with his tears and disappointment. Bowing his head, Tristan let his sorrow and frustration break, allowing his anguish out in shuddering, hiccuping sobs.

Despite years of Mara's teachings, he had no words for how he felt and certainly nothing other than raw emotion when Wolf put his hands on Tristan's shoulders to guide him back in.

"Don't." He jerked out of the man's grip. Refusing to meet Wolf's searching gaze, Tristan slowly got to his feet, smearing mud over his thighs in a futile attempt to clean his hands. The rain did as much as it could. As hard as it was falling, his fingers dripped with a viscous brown runoff. "Don't *fucking* touch me. You did this. To me. To the Grange."

"Tristan… wait…." Wolf turned, trying to grab at Tristan's arm as he struggled to get by. "I want to—"

"I don't care what you want," Tristan ground out. "As of right now, you and your team are not welcome here. Pack up your shit and leave. In fact, stay the fuck out of my sight. Period. I never want to see you ever again."

WOLF SPRINTED after the enraged, mud-splattered blond stalking away from him. Tristan was definitely angry. His fury rolled off of his skin in hot waves that threatened to turn the pounding rain hitting him to a bank of steamy fog. He slipped on the wet asphalt, nearly going down on his ass, but he caught himself in time, staying on his feet.

Also in time to have the Grange's front doors slammed in his face.

Hoxne Grange was definitely made in the day when pride was taken in a manor's workmanship. Some long-ago craftsman tasked with the job of creating the Grange's imposing entrance obviously took his responsibility seriously. Hand carved with swirling designs and sleek panels inset with ancient glass, the double solid wood doors dented Wolf's nose fairly dramatically when they came to a shuddering stop against his face. He felt a small crick of cartilage giving way and quickly stepped back, pressing the bridge of his nose between his fingers as he tilted his head back to stop an impending gush of blood.

He'd grown up with a vicious younger brother, and their epic battles were enough of an experience for Wolf to know he'd lost a melee with a nosebleed even before it began. Sniffing at the whiff of metal forming in his sinuses, Wolf blindly felt for the door latch, hoping Tristan was too pissed off to lock it behind him.

Luck was with him. The latch snicked, and he opened the door.

Just in time for his luck to run out and the terrified screaming to start.

Tristan hadn't made it very far into the house, so they both hit the stairs at a dead run, leaving a trail of water and mud behind them. The steps were slick, made slippery from their wet feet, but the men continued to run toward the screaming woman.

Because Wolf was pretty sure the woman yelling her head off in a frantic terror was Gidget.

Matt met them on the second-floor landing, rounding the sweep of stairs leading down from the third floor. Gidget's screams devolved into a fierce swearing, a hot spitting rage of words echoing from the elongated stretch of rooms toward the left of the Grange. Grabbing a decorative dirk from the wall, Wolf headed for the cursing with Tristan and Matt close behind.

"Don't know what you think you're going to do with that," Tristan muttered. "Not like there's anyone here but us."

"Someone could have broken in and hurt her." Wolf instantly regretted what he'd said. Matt turned pale and rushed past them, his flat sneakers flapping a hard tattoo on the hallway carpet. "Shit."

It was easy enough to find Gidget. Once they'd reached the T in the hallway between the length of the manor and its jutting wing, her screams became louder, and then she appeared out of the thin shadows, her vibrant hair streaming behind her in a flaming trail of silken curls.

Wolf didn't have much time to process anything other than Gidget's terror... and more importantly, the gray-fleshed older woman running behind her. A sour-faced woman in a long, old-fashioned dress chasing her prey with an ax circling over her head.

"Run!" Gidget screamed at the men blocking her escape. Pushing past them, she turned left instead of right, going deeper into the Grange instead of heading downstairs to the open foyer.

Startled, Matt blinked owlishly once, his mouth widening in shock. The old woman was rushing them too quickly for him to do anything other than throw his hands up to ward her off. Wolf grabbed Tristan, shoving him against the wall and putting himself between the blond and the ax. Holding the dirk out in front of him, he braced himself for the woman's assault, ready to throw her off her stride. She wasn't slowing down. If anything, her eyes grew larger and darker as she drew near, and Wolf swallowed at the sight of the double-bitted ax heading straight for his head.

Reaching up to grab its handle, he prepared himself to take her weight when she passed right through them.

It was an odd feeling. Cloying and sticky. A bit of a tugging of his skin as it was jerked out from inside of him, and for a moment, Wolf thought his heart had stopped cold, gripped in an iciness he couldn't shake off. The sensation lasted for the briefest split-second, but the prickling remained, a phantom impression of his flesh being pulled up from his bones.

As incorporeal as the woman was, the labrys she wielded definitely had some effect on the world around her. Its fore blade gleamed dully as it swiped through air next to Wolf's leg. The metal curve made a solid *thunk* into the floor, and the woman was forced to stop, pausing only long enough to jerk the ax handle back and forth until she pulled the blade free. The splinters dislodged by the ax were solid and sharp, flying up from the damaged wood to skitter across the floor nearly a foot away.

"Holy fucking shit." Wolf jerked his foot out of the way in case she swung again, but the woman was already gone, hurrying down the hall after Gidget. Stepping over the long gash in the floor, Wolf turned to Tristan. "What the hell do we do now?"

"How the hell should I know?" the blond spat back. "My *guests* don't usually try to kill me."

"Gidge," Matt stammered. "She could hurt Gidge. Come on."

Chasing after a ghost... an armed and pissed-off ghost... was certainly not how Wolf saw his career ending. After spending years studying phenomena and cracking apart frauds, he was now merrily waltzing after a Victorian woman with murder on her brain. Definitely not something he could bring up to prospective clients hoping to get a fair assessment of their spectral woes.

"Mom's going to be fucking laughing her damned ass off," he muttered as he followed the two men into the second floor's warren of rooms.

The path toward Gidget was laid out for him. Even without the swearing and screams, Wolf only had to find the line of ax cuts in the floors or walls. One painting, a heavy depiction of dogs hunting a duck pond to blood and feathered corpses, suffered as well. One of its springer spaniels had its head neatly severed in two, leaving its brain case on one side while the rest of its head was folded into a flap of cut canvas.

Running didn't seem to help. The maze of corridors on the second floor crisscrossed into other spaces, but he finally found them in an alcove in front of a rear balcony. Matt, Gidget, and Tristan looked whole and unharmed, but he couldn't say the same about the rest of the room. Or the flickering gray womanly shape in front of him.

She'd been more solid in the hall, but in the watery light coming from the balcony's french doors, her solidity suffered nearly as much as the ill-fated painted spaniel. Now Wolf could see straight through her, right to the blond man who stood between her ax and the young couple clutching one another in front of a broken wing chair.

Gidget stood trembling in Matt's arms, and they rocked back and forth amid the carnage of broken chairs and a destroyed table. Strips of wallpaper hung from the walls, the tattered fabric rippling from the cold wind coming through a cracked window. Tristan had a line of drying blood on his cheek. Since it looked more like damage from flying glass or wood, Wolf skidded to a stop and sighed with relief.

"Slattern! Whore!" The specter's ghoulish howl was a grate of noises and crackles, and Wolf strained a bit to make out what she was saying. "I will kill you before I let one of my own touch your diseased filth again! Do you think you can trap him into taking you to his bed? As his wife? I don't care if I hang for your death. Anything to protect him."

The ax rose up once more, and the seams of her dress strained with the press of her shoulders against the unyielding fabric. Taking a step forward, the woman screamed, a horrific, bone-rattling howl that dropped her jawbone down and elongated her mouth into a stark black maw.

For the first time since he'd put up his shingle as a skeptic, Wolf was terrified of a ghost.

Too many things happened at once for him to process, but he was clear on two events. The first was the wild-eyed woman plowing into a full run at his vibrantly haired technician. The second was Tristan flinging himself at the woman's trunk, hoping to stop her from reaching Gidget and Matt cowering behind him.

He was about four steps too far away to help, but Wolf lunged forward anyway, his adrenaline-hopped brain ordering him to tackle her from behind. The logical chunk of gray matter normally in charge scoffed at the nonsense flowering up from his primal fears, carelessly buffing its nails in smug arrogance as it reminded the rest of his consciousness that one did not simply tackle something that had no physical presence.

Wolf only wished that part of his overly confident, haughty brain had spoken up before he'd flung himself at Tristan's long body.

Tristan yelped when he flew through the woman's body and saw Wolf looming up in front of him. Twisting to avoid Tristan, Wolf arched badly and struck the other man in the chest. They hit hard, tumbling to the floor in a tangle of legs and arms Wolf would have been happy to be involved in but for the fact they were both fully clothed and on the far side of arousal. His elbow hit something hard, and he hoped it was the floor instead of something on Tristan's body, but his luck, already thin in places, proved to be as solid as the woman passing through the Grange's wall, her furious howling fading behind her while the very solid ax tumbled to the floor.

His elbow struck Tristan's lip, and Wolf could practically feel the man's tender flesh split beneath the solid cut of his sharp teeth. Blood gushed out from Tristan's mouth, and he rolled away, clutching at his face and spitting. Wolf's shoulder continued on its trajectory, slamming into the floor, and he lay back, stunned at the amount of places that ached on his body.

"Are you trying to fucking kill me?" Tristan muttered through a mouthful of blood and fingers. Red dripped from his palm, and he shook off Wolf's attempts to reach for him.

"What?" Wolf gaped up at the man. Tristan struggled to get up from the floor, using one hand to steady himself while the other staunched the slackening flow of blood from his face. "You tried to grab her too. We both figured we could hold on to her."

"You're holding a fucking knife, asshole!" The blond jerked his bloodied chin at Wolf's clenched hand. "That thing would have gone right through me."

He'd forgotten about the dirk, and Wolf stared at it in horror. Flinging it away, he got up and grabbed the remains of a pillow, stripping it of its filling. He pulled away Tristan's hand and pressed the fabric against the man's cut lip, murmuring his abashed apologies to what he figured were probably deaf ears.

"Whatevers." Tristan spat again, wiping at the pink spittle hanging from his split lip. "Just… can you do me a favor and check to see if she's outside? I mean, I doubt it, but…."

"Yeah, hold on." Wolf kissed the top of Tristan's head, thankful the man was okay. Grabbing the dirk off the floor, he held it up for Tristan to see. "Don't know if this will help, but maybe the whole cold iron thing works?"

"That's a reproduction," Tristan snorted at him. "It's made of stainless steel, but you just go with that."

Stepping carefully around the glass and wood shards, Wolf checked the balcony for the crazed woman. The wind bit through him, paring off any remaining adrenaline from his blood. Finding the sweeping overhang empty, he returned to the alcove. Shaking his head at Tristan, he gave Gidget and Matt a quick look over, satisfied the couple was okay except for a few shaken nerves.

Once back inside and out of the cold, he rubbed at his bare arms and laid the dirk down on the only whole piece of furniture left in the alcove, a tiny side table tucked under the scant protection of a splintered chair rail. Gidget was pacing back and forth, her arms wildly flailing about as she muttered angrily at Matt, who was stunned into silence.

"How the hell did all of this happen so fast?" Wolf surveyed the damage to the space. "She didn't have enough time."

"It just sort of happened," Tristan said softly. "She wasn't here when we got to Gidget, but things were just… exploding around us. She appeared right before you showed up. It was like a sneak attack before we could circle the wagons or something."

"Any idea who it is?" Wolf eyed a particularly heavy raking of a framed canvas. It had taken more of a beating than the hunting dogs. The woman obviously hated canines, because the oddly contorted pair of white lap dogs lying on a chaise were nearly julienned.

"I'm guessing it's Matt's granny." Tristan let Wolf grab him by the chin, moving his head when Wolf turned to inspect his lip. "And I don't think there's really a question of who that was. Let go. I'm okay. I just bit my lip."

Wolf didn't want to let go of Tristan's jaw, but there definitely was a storm brewing, and it was inside the Grange, swirling around his two young technicians. It crackled for a moment, then broke loose in a hail of angry words and spitting curses nearly as furious as the ghost they'd just encountered.

"Your grandmother!" Gidget poked Matt's chest, pushing him back a step. "Your fucking grandmother tried to kill me!"

"Hey, we don't know that." Matt held up his hands, trying to calm her down. "This place is humming with activity. It could have been anyone!"

"Really? Anyone? She had your dad's honker!" Gidget's fury turned outward, blasting the room at large. "Some crazy woman with a British accent in a long dress appeared out of nowhere and tries to kill me, but we don't think it's Matt's grandmother? You know, the serial killer?"

"Didn't she mostly poison?" Tristan sounded like he was trying to offer a reasonable doubt, but Matt shook his head, mournfully sorrowful as Gidget reared herself up for another fully steamed rant. "No?"

"No." The bookish tech twisted his mouth into an ashamed grimace. "Um, she also liked to hack up her neighbors' wives. But only one that they know of. Really."

"Just the one," Tristan repeated flatly. His hazel eyes went hard, nearly amber-yellow as they pinned a fierce glare through Wolf. "Okay.

This shit's got to stop. You two, go clean this mess up. You're the ones who tossed that ring into my pond, and you, Kincaid, since you brought this crazy into my house, you're going to have to find some way to make her leave before she kills someone."

"She didn't actually hurt anyone," Matt offered up, then withered when Tristan glanced over his shoulder at him.

"Your grandmother, assuming it's the only murderess we actually know *could* be here, just got loose. I've always been able to see the spirits visiting here, but others haven't." Tristan softened his words, but Wolf could still hear the fear cutting into the other man. "The Grange helps the departed manifest. It always has. She's starting to feed off that power. Since I think we can all say she's not going to follow the three-day rule everyone else does, she's going to build up that power. She might not have been able to hurt us now, but can we say that in a week? A few days? Tomorrow?"

"No, we can't." Wolf pursed his lips, grim with the awareness they'd brought a certain destruction into Tristan's calm and orderly world. "And we sure as hell can't wait to find that out. Let me make a few calls. I think I know someone who can help. I just need you to trust me to help, Tris."

"Do I have a choice?" Tristan answered wearily. "I don't have anyone else, remember? The world thinks I'm crazy. Now you're crazy too. Welcome to my life, Kincaid. However long I have it."

Chapter 9

"HOLY SHIT, ghosts are real," Matt said around a mouthful of Black Lager. "I mean, really, that's what this is all about. We actually *found* ghosts."

Freshly showered but still buzzing with excitement, Wolf joined his team, who'd fled to the ballroom. Once the scare had subsided, the first thing they'd all thought about was the cameras and what they'd captured on video. Tristan slunk away, shaking off Wolf's offer to join them once he'd cleaned up. The blond muttered something about needing space and possibly hard liquor. Wolf agreed with him about the booze. He'd liberated a six pack of Guinness from the walk-in as soon as he hit the first floor, snatching the lager up as well as some jerky. His two technicians were already into the chips and cookies from their snack table, and he tossed them each a small bag of dried meat, ordering them to get some protein into them.

"There's nothing on the screens," Gidget muttered from her perch in front of their monitors. Her lager sat unopened next to her, the bottle dripping its condensation onto a napkin set under it. "There's absolutely nothing but a couple of flickers. The ax shows up pretty solid. Looks like poltergeist activity, but nothing on Grandma Crazy Bitch."

"Her name's Winifred." Sniffing behind his beer bottle, Matt grinned at Wolf and put his feet up onto a crate next to him. Easing his chair back, he rocked back and forth, a silly grin on his friendly face. "Dude, a real fucking ghost. We could make millions off this shit."

"Or people are going to chase you down to put you in a straitjacket like they did Tristan," Wolf pointed out. "His uncle's the reason we're here. You don't think the guy's going to be calling for butterfly nets if we go to him and say Tristan's ghosts are real?"

"But isn't that the truth?" Gidget's voice was soft but cut through them with a sharp condemnation. "He's telling the truth. The Grange *does* have at least one ghost. We *saw* her, and we know where she came from. Shouldn't the truth set him free? Doesn't he deserve that kind of validation?"

"Yeah, he does." Matt stretched to grab Gidget's lager and popped off the cap with a twist of his hand. "Dude's not crazy. There's shit happening here. Even if we don't have proof, we saw it. Shouldn't that count for something?"

"We came here to bury Tristan, not to praise him." The day had left a harsh stamp on Gidget's face, and she slumped back into her chair, giving into her exhaustion. "Isn't that how it goes? Even if we say we're open to all possibilities, we're sitting here still looking for *some* proof of what we've lived through. So we can show who? The world? Tristan's asshat of an uncle?"

"I'd rather be Marc Antony than Brutus in this," Wolf admitted. "Let me go talk to Tristan first. He needs to know what will be in my report to his uncle—that the Grange is definitely haunted. I'll probably leave out the fact that we've brought a poltergeist to his door and chased off the other ghosts, but I don't think that's what Pryce Senior's going to be focusing on."

"I really thought Tristan was nuts." Matt frowned, then reached for his lover's hand and squeezed Gidget's fingers. "How are we going to deal with this kind of shit? She could have hurt you. Maybe? And what Tristan said? She'll grow stronger. That's insane."

There was no shared glance of amusement between them. Not on this. The appearance of the ghost was enough to rattle their carefully laid down skepticism. The existence of the ghostly woman was going to alter how they viewed every case going forward, coloring their necessary neutrality. Coming to the Grange would change all of them, and Wolf suspected most of the changes in his life rested in the hands of the blond man lurking upstairs in his ivory tower.

"Like we deal with everything we have so far," Wolf replied softly. "We go into every job with a clear mind and a need to search for the truth. That can't change. The only thing that might be different is that we'll have a better idea on what to look for. Our job here isn't done, guys. Yeah, we found a ghost, and we can tell Tristan's uncle—"

"But we brought it here," Gidget responded. "Well, I did. We've got to fix it. Somehow."

"Yeah, I've got people I can call in to help with that," he said ruefully. "But right now, time to go make my speech to the crowd and try to convince him I'm not the one holding the dagger."

HE HEARD Kincaid before he saw him. It wasn't hard to say that. Especially since Tristan was lying stomach down, on his bed with his face buried in his pillows. Boris's weight on his legs shifted as the dog slithered off the bed to greet Wolf. The dog's soft chuffing whines lowered to a few chuffs as Wolf murmured his hellos. Boris's nails snicked across the floor, and a few moments later, the sound of his dog tag hitting his metal food bowl out in the living area jingled in Tristan's ears. A few seconds later, the bed dipped down, and Tristan did his own grumbling, muttering foul things into his feather pillows when Wolf's hand skimmed across his shoulder blades.

"Hey, you," Wolf murmured. "You doing okay?"

"Go away." He didn't know if Kincaid could hear him. Hell, he could barely hear himself through the linens and down, but Tristan was pretty happy with how fierce he sounded. Not nearly as terrifying as being chased through his home with an ax, but still impressive. If he'd been standing up and frowning, he might have even gotten a derisive snort from Kincaid. He wasn't going to hope for anything more than that. The Pryces were never a warrior stock, and he certainly didn't buck the trend.

"You know you're covered in mud, right?"

Wolf didn't have to point out the obvious. He'd been flaking dirt chunks since before they'd left the alcove. Ruining the bedsheets was something that occurred to him long after he'd bounced down on the bed and hugged his pillow to his face. In fact, there was probably even evidence of his primal screaming into the pillow left behind. He only had to lift his head and pass the cotton case off as an early Munch.

"Fuck off." It seemed like a wholly appropriate response, and in a perfect world where Tristan's anger might have made the skies quiver in fear, Wolf would have fled from the room, averting his eyes from Tristan's enraged form.

Instead, Wolf's hand continued to stroke at the tense bundles of muscles along Tristan's shoulders and spine, making murmuring sounds that reminded Tristan of an enraptured guinea pig.

"Come on, get into the shower, and I'll change your sheets for you." Wolf slid his hand down to Tristan's side and gently turned him over, probably smearing more drying mud into the already filthy linens.

Tristan allowed himself to be turned over. Either he was a glutton for punishment or the subconscious part of his mind was tired of being alone in his sulk. It didn't much matter the why of it, not when Wolf's broad, warm hand on his side made him think of better ways to dirty his sheets.

"I'm really pissed off at you." It sounded weak even to him. There was no trembling rage in his voice or any towering fury. Instead, his traitorous mouth and tongue slid a husky rasp into his words, wrapping a seductive slither around them. He forged ahead anyway, trying to concentrate more on what he was saying than the long, blunt fingers seemingly counting his ribs through his shirt.

"Yeah." Wolf made a show of studying his face. "You look it. Come on, I've got to talk to you about… well, kind of everything. It's hard to do that with you cosplaying Pig Pen."

"Is Gidget okay?" That hand continued with its slow revolutions over Tristan's side, and he shivered when Wolf's fingers strayed farther down to his hip. Tristan's cock certainly took notice, sending maddening tingles of awareness to his brain.

"Yeah, she's… worried about you. Matt's kind of freaking out you're up here by yourself."

He didn't want to say it. In fact, Tristan locked his teeth over the tip of his tongue to stop himself from spilling out what was lingering on the treacherous pink muscle in his mouth, but apparently his entire mouth was in on the rebellion, because what he said next certainly was nothing he wanted Wolf to hear. He'd never flirted in his life, or if he had, it had been such a catastrophe neither he nor the guy he'd tried to chat up even realized Tristan was making the effort. Apparently now, his brain decided to kick in and give it a try, because as angry as he was at Wolf, he needed someone to touch him. To anchor him before he drowned in his uncertainty.

"And you?" His rasp grew huskier, if that was possible, and Tristan wondered if something had actually crawled into him to possess at least his voice box. "You worried too?"

The man's dark-blue eyes flickered with heat and a shadowy something Tristan badly wanted to explore. He was playing with a fire he wouldn't survive, and still his tongue and the rest of his body merrily danced onward toward his destruction. Flames were licking at his skin, and Tristan shifted on the bed, unsure how to take Wolf's silent perusal.

Lifting himself up onto his elbows, Tristan brought his face closer as Wolf bent toward him. The man's warm breath blurred away the chill on Tristan's mouth, and he licked his upper lip, suddenly nervous enough to swallow at the lump forming in his throat.

Daring himself to do something, Tristan tilted his chin up, stretching his neck out until his mouth barely stroked Wolf's lower lip. Gently, he kissed the rounded, moist skin there, pinking the underside of Wolf's lip with his warmth. Hooding his eyes, Tristan felt his tongue slip free of his lips and skim the stubble-roughened spot under Wolf's mouth, leaving a tiny damp buss behind.

"I am so not going to fucking regret this," Wolf growled. "But I *just* got clean."

Whatever thoughts Tristan had—whatever the dangerous part of his mind thought would happen—were seared away from the intensity of Wolf's response. The room darkened, either from the storm outside thickening its strength or the lights being drowned out by the sharp darkness of Wolf's answering lust. Either way, the room's thin light stole away from them, wrapping them in a dim blanket.

His legs were pressed in, shoved together by Wolf's knees, and his arms were suddenly warmed by rough hands moving up over his elbows to his shoulders. His mouth was invaded, his lips pushed open by a forceful tongue hot with promise. Tristan tried to answer Wolf's lust with as much skill as he could, but the onslaught on his senses proved to be overwhelming, and for a long moment he could only gasp and mewl, yearning to beg for more but afraid of what those words would bring him.

There was too much going on between them for Tristan to find one thing to concentrate on. Wolf's entire body lowered down on him, rubbing and smearing the mud on his clothes and skin. The other man's weight felt good, too good for him to believe he'd not had someone lie on him before. He felt Wolf everywhere, tasted him in places Tristan knew he didn't have a tongue.

But there his hands were, reveling in the flavor of the man they held close.

Wolf's tongue was exploring his mouth in long, sweeping lines. He gasped when Wolf's fingers tangled through the hair at the back of his head and pulled, forcing Tristan to bare his throat. Wolf left his mouth empty and longing, and Tristan hated the whimpering, needy sound he made when cold air rushed in to replace Wolf's heat against his lips. The mouth he needed found a new place on his throat, and the teeth that had been just nibbling on the corner of his gasping lips sunk into the curve of his neck, a spot seemingly connected to his nuts, since they pulled up in response.

The man felt so good on him. Wolf's broad chest stretched across his, and when the man moved, Tristan's shirt rubbed at his sensitive nipples, the fabric scoring his tender flesh. Arched into Wolf's hard body, Tristan moaned and clenched at whatever part of the man he could reach. His fingers roamed, unable to see the muscled landscape they explored, but there were tantalizing hints of hard bulges and slightly rough skin that could only belong to another man.

Gasping only pulled Wolf's scent into him, and Tristan inhaled entire gulps of sweat and sweet skin, tasting the citrus from the soap he'd put in the guest bathrooms as well as the burn of lager foam lingering on his tongue from their kiss. The contrast of their bodies fascinated Tristan. Wolf's bones were heavier, denser than his, or at least that's how the man's hands felt as they pressed into Tristan's body.

Letting go of Tristan's hair, Wolf worked both his hands into Tristan's shirt, yanking it up over his head and off his shoulders. Their arms tangled briefly as the shirt snagged on Tristan's elbow, but Wolf was determined. Something ripped, either fabric or thread, but Tristan was past caring. All he wanted was to be handled and coaxed by Wolf's tongue and fingers, his body eager to be touched.

His jeans were suddenly gone, stripped from him in an easy swoop of quick fingers and strength. Tristan tried to remember what pair of underwear he'd put on that morning, hoping he'd worn at least something mildly interesting. At best, they'd be black. Worst-case scenario, he'd be sporting Hello Kitty briefs, depending on how lazy he'd been with his wash.

When Wolf sat up onto his knees to peel off his own shirt, Tristan dared to peek down the length of his belly, hoping to catch a glimpse of his own briefs. He tried to ignore the contrast in their bodies. Where he was lean and pale, Wolf gleamed golden, either from the sun or some swarthy ancestor who'd left a kiss of the sun on his descendant's skin. A dark trail of hair ghosted around Wolf's navel, winding down the lower half of his muscular stomach and burrowing under Wolf's jeans.

Seeing Wolf's strong thighs straddling his crotch brought the fire in Tristan's bones up to his face, and his blush burned away nearly all of the lust he'd tangled himself into, dusting him with a fine coat of shyness like a falling ash. His arousal burst back with full force when Wolf's fingers brushed over the bulge in his underwear, coaxing a response from Tristan's cock.

His underwear was a pair of eggplant boxer briefs, freshly decanted from the packet he'd opened a few days ago. The color no longer seemed to matter, especially since it appeared to be soaking up the weep of his precome, turning the fabric nearly black where his cock head rubbed against it.

"Grape," Tristan muttered insensibly. "They're supposed to be grape."

"What?" Wolf stared down at him, shirt halfway off his shoulders and behind his neck.

The pose did everything right for the man's body, pulling out the strength of his arms and the line of his abdomen. The V cut down along his hips pushed Wolf's crotch forward, and Tristan eyed the heavy pouch of his aroused sex through Wolf's jeans. His dark-brown hair clung, its damp, mink-soft strands falling over his cheekbones and jaw, and his smile slowly turned sensual, a sly tilt to lips Tristan still could feel on his throat.

"God, you are so beautiful." Tristan was pretty sure he said those words, but strangely, the voice was Wolf's. He wasn't totally convinced until Wolf tossed aside his shirt and bent over until his nose touched the end of Tristan's. "Anyone ever told you that before? You, Pryce, are just so fucking beautiful."

He didn't feel beautiful, but there under Wolf's deep-blue gaze, an ocean of need and desire he'd put there, Tristan felt the first stirrings of being wanted.

And something inside of him opened up beneath the heat of Wolf's smile.

"Tell me you have something here." Wolf's next murmur dashed all of the warm feelings and tingling awe into a craggy iceberg he'd not seen floating there in the fog of his arousal.

"Something?"

His brain short-circuited. Something meant... *something*. Things that oiled and covered... allowing that heavy, thick meat Wolf sported between his legs to go places Tristan'd only explored tentatively with a probing finger. No, Wolf intended to go there, and Tristan wasn't sure he *had* anything to do that with.

"Yeah, because, babe, I can't wait to be deep inside...." Wolf cocked his head, and something shifted in those blues Tristan was drowning in. "You hate 'babe'? It just slipped out. I can change it."

"No one's ever called me babe before," Tristan whispered. "Or beautiful either."

"Someone should have," Wolf replied huskily. "So babe's okay?"

"I'll think about it," he grunted, still thinking about what they needed and where he could find it. Tristan was certain he actually had picked up something they could use but couldn't remember where he'd put it.

Wolf's weight still felt good, especially where his dick was pressed up against Tristan's cock. The rub of denim against precome splattered cotton was nice. Even nicer was Wolf's hand finding its way down to Tristan's balls and the rasp of his fingernail beneath the elastic on Tristan's thigh.

"You've never done this before, have you?" Wolf's soft words cut straight through Tristan's doubts and desire.

"Not everything," he confessed slowly, easing his gaze up to Wolf's handsome face. The man's hair tumbled down over his forehead, and Tristan's fingers itched to stroke it back. Or maybe just to play with it. He wasn't sure which. "Some."

"How much is some?"

"You're not the first guy I've kissed," Tristan admitted. Oh, and that was a hard admission. The few times he'd actually crossed into something more daring than a kiss, he'd pulled back, not feeling the *rightness* of the man touching him. With Kincaid it was different. There was actually a continuous tightening under his skin and the need to press into the man's hands.

"Kissed?" Wolf's frown was a small flitting crease on his forehead. "And the rest?"

"Not so much on the rest." He flung his relative virginity out there, splattering it onto the walls around them. "I want the... rest. And God help me... maybe Uncle Walter's right and I am nuts, because I want it with you, Kincaid."

There. He'd said it out loud and there was no taking it back. As much as Wolf pissed him off, and he was slowly flaking off a cake of mud from the Grange's front lawn… not to mention the aches and bruises he'd gotten from slamming into Wolf when they'd both gone through Matt's killer great-granny, he *wanted* the man.

Wolf said nothing. He stared down at Tristan, his bulging arms and spread knees supporting his weight. Studying Tristan, he must have found something promising or willing in Tristan's face because his sensual, wicked grin came back, and Wolf dipped his head to suck Tristan's lower lip into his mouth.

"Well, every guy you've met has been stupid or blind. Because, Pryce, you are fucking, deadly beautiful, and I promise I will take very good care of you." Pinching the swell of Tristan's lip between his teeth, Wolf suckled on it briefly, then let go. "So, do you have something? Or am I going to have to hit Matt up? Because that's definitely not something I want to ask for from someone who works for me."

"Oh God no, he'd… know. We…." He gulped. "Shit…."

"Yeah, I'm pretty sure they're going to know anyway. Your face is too open. You'd be a shitty poker player," Wolf broke in gently. "And there's nothing wrong with what we're doing… what you want. However far we go here, Tristan, there's nothing to be ashamed of. Okay?"

"Okay."

"Good. Now, about what you might have…?"

"Um… I think there might be…." Tristan tried to remember what his agent once shoved into his luggage during a Las Vegas convention. "There was a hotel package. It had condoms in it. I think I dumped all of it into my nightstand."

"Stay. Right. There." Wolf tweaked Tristan's right nipple. It responded hungrily, pearling up into a nub Tristan thought he could use to cut glass later. Perhaps even a steel beam if he needed one. "I'll be right back."

He missed Wolf's weight. More importantly, Tristan missed Wolf's heat and the press of the man's legs against his thighs. Still, Wolf was gorgeous to watch when he slithered off of the bed and crouched in front of the nightstand, then looked at Tristan until he nodded silently.

Tristan wasn't sure what he was agreeing to, the location of the red-foil-wrapped condoms he knew were there or if he wanted to use them.

"Yeah, they should be in there," he murmured, taking a step toward easing the hard ache of his cock and the emptiness inside of him. "I think

I came home and just dumped them in there. It was… there were people dressed in latex catsuits in the hotel lobby. They were sword-fighting with dildos. I wanted to kill my agent for booking us there."

"So no dildos, then?" Wolf laughed. "Maybe you should have grabbed one as a parting gift."

"They kept dropping them on the floor." Tristan wrinkled his nose. "I don't care how dishwasher safe they are. Do you know what kind of bacteria most hotels are crawling with? I could have gotten pregnant with an alien Elvis baby or something."

Wolf's jeans slid down to the curve of his hips. The nightstand's rails squeaked, refusing to give up its secrets, but Wolf wrestled it into submission. Turning over onto his side, Tristan studied the long line of Wolf's back, smiling at the peek of his feet from under his jeans legs.

"God, I must be horny if toes are exciting." Tristan lay back and flung an arm over his eyes. He heard Wolf whistle. Then the bed dipped once more, and he peeked out from under his forearm at Wolf sitting cross-legged on the bed next to him.

"Where did you get this shit again? Vegas?" The man had definitely found the stash he'd shoved into the drawer. There were at least seven of the hotel guest pouches. His literary agent was a tiny evil woman who felt he should experiment more with life. Having plundered a housekeeping cart, she'd shoved her booty into his suitcase, telling him to have at Vegas like the painted whore it was.

Instead he'd gone down the Strip to look at white tigers and watch a fake volcano erupt a few times. Then he'd climbed into a gondola for a couple of trips around a too clean Venetian canal. The only action the pouches saw were probably a TSA agent who searched his luggage, and considering there'd been both a furry and a sex toy convention in town, Tristan's bag was probably the tamest thing they'd seen all day.

Now he was not so sure the pouches were all that tame, especially when Wolf held up a small jar for him to see. The label was a florid pink-and-brown scrawl that left little doubt about what its contents could be used for.

"Fudge ointment, for when you need something a little dark and delicious between you and your lover," Wolf read, waggling his eyebrows at a now-blushing Tristan. "Dildos aside, exactly what hotel did you go to when you were in Vegas? The Bunny Ranch?"

"It was downtown. One of the retro hotels. They'd refurbished it or something. I don't know," Tristan protested. "I was there for a book convention. I didn't know it was Sodom and Gomorrah weekend."

"It's called Sin City for a reason, Pryce." Wolf cracked open the jar and held it up to sniff at, then passed it under Tristan's nose. "Damn, this is nice. What do you think?"

"It smells like chocolate," Tristan mumbled, sitting up. A few flakes of dirt remained on his hands, but most of the drying mud went with his discarded clothes on the floor. "Isn't that why they call it that?"

"Babe, it says for your anal pleasure on the label. Fudge… never mind. God, you're… so innocent." Wolf's finger traced under the small print below the company's logo. He put the lube aside and dug through an open pouch. Pulling out a metallic red-foil packet, Wolf winked at him. "Here we go. You sure about this, Pryce?"

"You keep asking me and I'm probably going to say no, which I don't want to do, so stop," Tristan grumbled. "And I'm still pissed off at you. Just so you know. I keep hoping if I get you out of my system, I'll be able to just kick you out and wash my hands of you."

"Yeah, you couldn't even wash your hands of the dirt you rolled in. You think you're going to be able to get rid of me?" Wolf worked the soiled quilt Tristan'd been lying on off the bed, then pushed him down onto the relatively clean sheets below. Straddling Tristan's thighs again, he stretched out on top of him, capturing Tristan's wrists with his hands. "Now, let's see where exactly on that hot body of yours I left off."

Chapter 10

"KEEP YOUR hands there," Wolf ordered Tristan and let go.

Fisting his fingers into Tristan's wealth of blond hair, Wolf bent down to softly bite the man's earlobe. Tristan was so damned responsive to his touch, writhing beneath him with every small brush of a finger or a lip ghosted across a spot of pale skin. Wolf felt Tristan tremble under his hands, a shivering ruffle of sinew and bone splaying out onto the bed in front of him. Guiding Tristan with a gentle nudge of his knee, Wolf got the man to spread his legs apart, the jut of his hips pushing Tristan's cock into the hollow of Wolf's thighs.

A virgin.

The last time he'd been with a virgin was when he *was* the virgin. Trying to remember back to the days of frustrated hard cocks and aching, clenched asses, Wolf sighed and rested his head on Tristan's shoulder. Leaving a gentle kiss on the man's collarbone, he whispered, "If something gets too much for you, you let me know, okay? This should feel good. If it doesn't, say something. All right, babe?"

"Okay. Sure." Tristan's hands clenched Wolf's shoulders, and he nodded, still caught by Wolf's fingers in his hair.

Tristan probably didn't know how sexy he sounded. A smear of posh over a tumbled amber voice did something to Wolf's innards, and every time the man opened his mouth, a pour of heady verbal liquor flowed from between his kissable lips. There was a rich smokiness to the blond's words, a slow slide of intelligence and sin, as if God took his time carving out a shard of golden moonlight and decided to use it for Tristan's voice instead.

"Hold on," Wolf murmured. "Forgot something."

"What?" Tristan frowned and looked at the condom, lube, and other sundry surprises from the hotel's packets laid out next to him. "What else do we need? What else *is* there that we need?"

"Tea parties. Wait, no, that's what life's about. Wrong answer," he said, then pulled down Tristan's body to blow a raspberry into his belly button.

He slid off the bed and closed the door before rejoining Tristan. Shoving the flyers, beads, and a couple of bottles of bubbles off of the mattress, Wolf moved the lubricant and condoms to the side so he could stretch out over Tristan without losing what they'd need later.

"Oh…." Tristan's changeable eyes were drenched in emerald, and a blush ran up his belly before staining his cheeks pink. "Boris."

"Yeah, Boris," Wolf chuckled. "Nice enough guy, but I think he can keep himself occupied in the living room for a while."

"He'll probably sleep."

"So long as he's the only one in this apartment sleeping, then I'm okay with that." Wolf hooked his fingers into the waistband of Tristan's underwear. "You ready for me, Señor Pryce?"

"That's got to be the weirdest thing someone's ever said to me." Tristan's shyness was back. Wolf could see it creeping up to smother the laughter in his gorgeous face, a somber veil to drape over any scrap of happiness Tristan might have found inside himself.

"Oh no, Tris," Wolf cautioned the other man. "No hiding away from me. Not now."

He raked away the golden strands that fell across Tristan's sharp cheekbones and firm mouth, pushing them aside so he could see the man's nearly ethereal beauty. Their differences fascinated him, and Wolf was intrigued by the creamy lengths of porcelain skin laid out for him to taste.

Tristan's cotton briefs were a slash of unexpected color across the seemingly endless stretch of ivory and gold of Tristan's body. The intense purple drew out the delicate blue veins across Tristan's hips and belly, creating a cobweb of enticement Wolf's tongue practically itched to follow. A dark damp spot marred the briefs' unyielding tint, and a whiff of bittersweet salt clung to the moistness, drawing Wolf in even more.

"I want to taste you," Wolf murmured as he kneeled down between Tristan's legs. "Will you let me do that, Tristan? Can I just spend some time seeing what you're like on my tongue? 'Cause damn, I think you're going to make me drunker than any scotch I've ever had, and I want to take my damned sweet time drinking you in."

He didn't wait to hear Tristan's response. The man was definitely reserved, and if Wolf could spare more than a thought to giving him pleasure, he knew he'd probably find an anger toward Tristan's family for hemming in his wild fey nature. There was a freedom inside of Tristan.

Wolf could feel it beating against cage walls crafted by hard, hateful words and skeptical derision.

And Wolf silently promised Tristan he'd be damned first before he helped paint those bars with any bit of gold to gild them. If anything, he'd break himself before he allowed Tristan to be held in that cage any longer. In the watery light of Tristan's bedroom, Wolf would show him the way out, hoping to show him a pleasure of being he'd not found before.

Tristan Pryce deserved that. Hell, Wolf owed him that for the stabs of criticism and doubt he'd thrust into Tristan's life. It took a fey-pretty, strong blond man to remind him of the mysteries in the world, and Wolf was not going to repay that gift by taking more of Tristan's faith.

Hell, Wolf thought, he probably was the one in the cage and Tristan was the one setting *him* free.

Staring up the length of Tristan's long, slender body, Wolf was caught by the man's hooded gaze. The duality of Tristan's soul lay bare on his face, a delicate, pure innocence striated with a weary, tattered wisdom Wolf wanted to patch together with kisses. The man's bruised beauty was enough to make him cry, especially since his mouth seemed rarely visited by an unguarded smile.

"Can I, Tristan?" Wolf nearly begged as he leaned forward to run his hands up Tristan's side. "Will you let me?"

Tristan's breath hitched when Wolf's fingers rubbed his nipples into hard points, and his eyes darkened, flushing a shade of forest that nearly matched the thickets outside the Grange's walls. A single nod would have done Wolf in. A single word would be more than Wolf could hope for.

"Please," Tristan purred, that hot slither of amber sex in his voice turning molten. "Yes, Wolf. Please."

Something in Wolf broke. Whatever held him back shattered under the hammer strokes of Tristan's erotic whisper. Suddenly his mouth was too empty of Tristan's flesh, and he needed to fill himself with anything he could have of the man lying before him.

Wolf hooked his teeth under the dark spot on Tristan's underwear, and the ghost of the man's taste lingered on his lip before he had a chance to fully suckle him in. Drawn hard by the touch, Tristan's cock danced away from Wolf's mouth, leading him on a merry chase beneath its cotton veil.

Frustrated, Wolf hooked his thumbs into the briefs' elastic and pulled them down to Tristan's thighs, binding the man's legs in. He was too impatient, and despite his promise to go slow, Wolf found himself pushing at his own control, which bowed beneath his lust. Dipping his head, he opened his mouth and lapped at the tiny bit of pearly liquid seeping from Tristan's slender, pale cock.

It was as if someone poured a drop of a silvery-lit night onto his tongue, and Wolf was afraid to swallow, in case he never had the taste of stars in his mouth ever again.

He needn't have worried. Tristan's body arched at the touch of Wolf's lips, and his hands scrambled to find something to hold onto. He first grabbed at the sheets, leaving a trail of muddy specks on the pristine cotton. Then one hand fisted Wolf's hair, pulling on the strands until they were wrapped around his hand nearly painfully tight. A leak of seed pooled over Wolf's cupped tongue, and he sipped at it, slowly letting the musky smoke of Tristan's cock fill him.

"Kincaid." The man curled up, his knees splaying out on either side of Wolf's shoulders. "No, I can't...."

"It's okay, Tris." Wolf tried to stamp down the disappointment in his voice, but it was ripe inside of him. "If you want to stop, I can—"

"I don't want to stop," Tristan panted and cupped Wolf's face in his lean hands. "I just want you in me. Please. I... want this, and I don't think I'm going to last much longer. God, just please, Wolf. *Please*."

It took Wolf only a moment to peel off the rest of his clothes. Then he had the pleasure of sliding Tristan's starkly purple briefs down the length of the man's long legs. He reached for Tristan's ankle and kissed the bone there, biting at it playfully. Tristan jerked his leg up, and Wolf followed it, holding onto Tristan's other ankle as he traversed up the other man's thigh in small, wet nibbles.

"I am going to say it again." Wolf laved at one of Tristan's plum-hued nipples. "You, Tristan Pryce, are so fucking beautiful it almost hurts my eyes to look at you. And God help me, I am *never* going to stop telling you that. Whenever I can. Maybe even after you finally believe me."

THEY WERE so different. Tristan could *feel* their differences in his bones. Wolf's cockiness, the arrogance of his spirit, and the staunch belief the world was for his taking amazed Tristan to a stunned silence.

But nothing stunned him more than hearing the gorgeous Wolf Kincaid murmur sweet nothings over his body and then telling Tristan he'd be there forever.

It was bedroom talk. Tristan knew the flimsiness of such words. They had as much substance as the ghosts who wisped into his life every few days and stole his towels, taking them to God knew where. He only hoped that when Wolf left, he'd leave his thievery to the Grange's bath linens instead of stealing Tristan's heart as well.

And if he did—Tristan closed his eyes so Wolf couldn't see the pain he knew would be filling them—at least he would have this time with the brash, piratical investigator to look back upon and say he'd brought someone incredible to his pleasure. That would have to be enough. He was a Pryce, Tristan reminded himself. Pryces didn't do happily-ever-afters. And when there was anything remotely resembling an after, it either died into a business-like relationship or crashed against the rocks in a violent demise.

There were no afters. Only nows. And Tristan was going to grab hold of the one right in front of him and let it ride him until he could only smell, taste, and feel Wolf Kincaid.

"It's enough," he murmured when he heard the lubricant jar click open and the smell of rich chocolate nearly drowned the aroma of their mingled bodies. "Take a chance. It's going to be enough."

"I don't have any on my fingers yet, so no, there's not enough." Wolf kissed the inside of Tristan's knee. Skimming his hand over Tristan's belly, he traced small circles around his navel. "Tell me you're sure, Tristan. Please… whatever you say, I'll go with you."

When he opened his eyes, Tristan was surprised to see how close Wolf was to his face. The man's eyes filled his vision, an ocean of possibilities, most of them wicked and wet.

Hooking his hands around the back of Wolf's head, Tristan pulled him in for a kiss. It was savage, brought up from someplace primal Tristan didn't even realize he had in him. At least not until he found himself delving deep into Wolf's mouth with his tongue to steal the breath from the man's body.

He pulled off, still holding Wolf firm between his spread palms, and cocked his head. "How much more are you going to make me beg, Wolf Kincaid?"

"No, babe," Wolf panted. "No need to beg. I got it."

He hit the bed again, pushed down by one of Wolf's powerful hands. The chocolate scent grew stronger; then he felt the brush of cold fingers along his taint. Tristan jerked, nearly bringing his knees up into Wolf's chin.

"Sorry," he mumbled. "I just wasn't... expecting... I thought you had... lube on your fingers."

"No, we're not quite there yet." Wolf grinned, then kissed him soundly as he lowered his knees. "I didn't realize my hands were so cold. Want me to warm them up?"

"Just on me," Tristan replied softly. "'Cause I'm a little bit too warm, I think."

"No such thing, Ace." Wolf made a face. "Okay that's worse than babe. Let's not do that again."

"Yeah, makes me think of Batman's dog."

"No, all dogs... are outside." Wolf's words were spaced out, interrupted by tiny kisses along Tristan's rib cage and then down his belly. "Okay, the ones I can see. Let's hope the other fucker has some common courtesy."

When the man's mouth reached the soft skin below his navel, Tristan sucked in as much cold, rain-scented air as he could and arched his head back into a pillow, driven half out of his mind by Wolf's slow passes over his hips and the faint scattering of hair above his cock.

Where Wolf's mouth left him wet and hot, his questing fingers found the delicious, aching spots on Tristan's body and tugged at them until Tristan's skin was tight with need. He was being played. There were strings of nerves beneath Wolf's fingertips and palms, rough, reedy cords being tuned with every long caress.

A ghosting touch of Wolf's finger at his entrance bucked Tristan into a shocking refrain of clashing cymbals and thundering heartbeats. He became a symphony of oddly synced instruments, his gasping pants setting the beat for Wolf's playing.

Then Wolf's mouth closed over the head of his cock, and Tristan lost all thoughts of fancy and music.

His body had only felt the touch of his own hand, and until that moment... until he felt the tip of Wolf's tongue along the slit of his cockhead, Tristan thought no one could know him as well as he knew himself.

Oh, how fucking wrong he was.

If he'd been driven mad before, he was surely down the rabbit hole looking to kick a lizard up through a chimney now. Wolf's fingers rolled his balls around, stroking them downward, and his thumb played first at his taint, then circled down to his ass, teasing at its entrance with gentle, insistent pushes. The tiny slurping sounds of Wolf's mouth on his length were nearly timed with his exhales, and Tristan writhed, instinctively thrusting down on Wolf's hand as it explored his body.

He wanted to feel Wolf there. Needed to feel more than the feathering kiss of his thumb and the barest snag of Wolf's fingernail on the skin beneath his tight balls. Tristan's thighs tightened, painfully so, and he forced himself to relax, afraid he'd come apart before Wolf found his pleasure.

At the very least, he didn't want to embarrass himself.

Another pass of Wolf's seemingly endless tongue along the corona of his cock and Tristan wasn't sure he'd live through the afternoon, much less not shame himself by emptying his balls into Wolf's mouth and hands.

"Wolf…." Another gasp ran through him, this one shuddering and hard. His spine hurt from its reverberations, and the small of his back itched for the press of Wolf's body against it. "I don't know if…. God…."

"You ready for me, Tris?" Wolf's guttural whisper was muted by a mouthful of Tristan's cock. "Because, God, I am *so* ready for you."

He couldn't do much more than nod, halfway aware Wolf couldn't really see him. It didn't seem to matter. The wanton spread of his raised legs and his nerveless fingers stroking at the man's broad shoulders was enough to tell the man what he needed to know.

"I'm going to warm the lube up a little bit in my hand, okay?" Wolf lifted his head from Tristan's hips and kissed his belly button, tonguing its ridge in a mimicry of his thumb's flirtatious advances on Tristan's hole. "Just a second and then I'll be right there with you."

Some part of his mind heard something tear and the snap of something against skin. A curious chemical odor joined the chocolate before disappearing beneath the drench of their musk. Then Wolf's fingers were back… and this time, they were coated slick and rimming around his entrance in a slow, lazy spiral.

He couldn't lift his knees up any farther, and for the first time in his life, Tristan wondered if he could possibly take yoga so he could learn to fold himself up for Wolf to take him.

"You okay, Tris?" Wolf's kisses were centered first on his nipples before moving up the length of Tristan's throat. He must have made some insensible "yes" noise, because Wolf's chuckle was a delightful, wicked thing, hot and sultry enough to send another wave of tingles down Tristan's spine. "Put your legs on my hips, babe, and I'll do the rest."

He struggled a bit, nearly unmanning himself, but somehow, his shins found the curve of Wolf's legs. Tristan was open, much more open and vulnerable than he'd ever been before. Even when he'd been stripped of his family's affection and left to drift about, doubting his sanity, Tristan had some small delusion he'd be okay.

With Wolf leaning over him, his weight pushing down on the bed between Tristan's knees and a line of slick running down the crease of his ass, Tristan had nothing to hold onto... no experience to tell him he'd come out the other side of what they were doing and he'd be okay.

He almost stopped Wolf right then. It would have been simple. A touch of his hand on the man's shoulder. A simple push of his palm on his chest. Even a single shaking no from his kiss-swollen lips and he knew Wolf Kincaid would stop... and probably cuddle him to tell him it was all right. That he didn't need to go anywhere he didn't feel ready to go.

Realizing that, Tristan suddenly understood he wasn't going to fall. Not if Wolf had anything to say about it. Wolf *would* take care of him. He'd hold him and guide Tristan along to where they both could be entangled in the mystery of their bodies.

Something on his face must have made Wolf curious, because the man paused, a hiccup of a breath held between them as his tumbled-sky gaze searched Tristan's face. A single dark eyebrow swooped up, a question posed to give Tristan time to sort out his thoughts. Kincaid wouldn't go any further until Tristan said the word.

He knew it. In his bones. He could trust Wolf with anything. His body. His ghosts. His soul.

Life, sex, and the messy tangle of their personalities suddenly made perfect sense, and Tristan let loose the stagnant fear he'd been holding inside of him for as long as he could remember, breaking it free with a single word.

"Yeah."

Wolf's mouth descended on his, breaching him as the man's fingers found his entrance. His tongue played at being the aggressor, pushing past Wolf's lips to tease at what he could find in the man's mouth as

Wolf's touch invaded him. The intrusion was slight at first, then grew, an almost burn of a promise along the crest of his body. He thrust his hips up, mewling with the need Wolf stroked out of him. Clutching at the man's shoulders, he pulled Wolf down as close as he could, holding him in a fierce embrace as he suckled out the man's breath.

It warmed him. The hot air tasted of sweat and man, and it burned going down like a fine whiskey. Much like the push of Wolf's fingers pulling him apart and inebriating his skin with a tantalizing bite of sensations.

The breach of his body began slowly. A nudge at the edge of his entrance followed by the soft coaxing of Wolf's fingers on his chest. Tristan wasn't prepared for the intense shove of his flesh as it contracted over the tip of Wolf's cock, refusing the man entrance. A few quick breaths and murmuring encouragements from his now-lover helped. Bearing down, Tristan felt Wolf's push again and clung to the man's shoulders as his body was pulled apart by Wolf's thick-headed cock.

"Oh fuck," Tristan panted.

"Want me to stop?" Wolf was bent over Tristan's body, his arms rigid from balancing his weight on his hands. "Anything you want, love. Talk to me."

"I never touched your dick." It was the stupidest thing to think about as the man's cock was entering him. "I didn't even see it. Fuck."

"Don't worry about that. You can look at it later. Pretty sure we'll be doing this again." His laugh teased Tristan's shock, coaxing it away into nothing. "'Sides, your hands are pretty fucking dirty. That's not something I want inside of you. Just me there, Tristan. Just me."

His hands were still dirty. Flaking from the dried mud, his fingers and forearms were leaving dusty smears on Wolf's skin. His chest bore a slash of dirt, nearly a sumi-style circle around one nipple. Emboldened, Tristan arched up and licked at the clean nub framed by the Grange's dirt.

The aroused hiss he pulled from Wolf when his teeth nipped at the tender bud was enough to drive them both over the edge of their want. Tristan pushed his hips up, some primal inkling rising up from its burrow deep under his awkwardly civilized layers. His hands couldn't get full enough of the man pushing through him. Neither could his mouth. He wanted to fill himself with Wolf. Taste every part of the man's body until he could swallow his scent and feel it seep out from his own skin.

An instant later, he was full of Wolf Kincaid, his body pierced by a hot, hard length seemingly designed by the hand of a God with intimate knowledge of Tristan's core.

Wolf fit everywhere. The burn was still there. Not quite a heat or pain but more an unfamiliar throb of his nerves suddenly raked and stroked, as if lightning had touched his pulse and sent a current through his blood. He lost touch with the world around him. There were no ghosts, no storm, and not even the worry of the Grange's now-resident serial killer crept past the muscular, golden man plunging into him. Everything stopped and started a few inches above and inside of him, becoming lengths of tanned skin, laughing blue eyes, and a wicked mouth intent on leaving its mark on Tristan's tender skin.

Then the tightening in his ass unfurled when Wolf hit a spot inside of him, and Tristan howled, clenching Wolf in a death grip as he rode out the shock wave hitting him.

There were no words for what he had searing his nerves. The man filling his ass stroked it again, and Tristan broke, trembling around Wolf's plunging cock. His heart couldn't catch up, skipping and falling over itself in an attempt to keep up with the blood shooting through his veins. He was barely aware of the ache forming in his thighs and back, his muscles worn from the adrenaline ebbing from his tissues. Then Wolf found that spot again and Tristan was riding out the tempest again.

He needed something to hold him through it. Wolf's arms were around his shoulders now, and the man's weight held him down, keeping Tristan in place as Wolf's hips snapped hard against his ass. Wolf's sac slapped at him, a flinging weight adding to the overwhelming sensations tearing him apart, and the slick of their sweat rubbed between them, capturing his aching cock in a wet clench.

Tristan found what he needed at the same moment Wolf's hand crept between them and closed over his heavily leaking cock. The curve of Wolf's neck needed to be between Tristan's teeth, and it felt delicious when he sank them into the man's flesh and dug his canines in deep.

Wolf didn't miss a stroke. Keeping up the pounding on Tristan's ass, Wolf stroked up the length of Tristan's sex, palming his hypersensitive cockhead and smearing mingled sweat and precome into his skin. The jerking thrusts grew shorter, stabbing through any meager resistance Tristan's body might have had left. Time and time again, Wolf found the nub of Tristan's nerves and slammed his cock against it, drawing out his strokes only far enough to give Tristan the briefest respite before hammering at him again.

He lost it. Plain and simple. Any fragile hold he might have had on his sanity was gone, cut loose by the keen edge of Wolf's cock running through him. The blade they'd honed with their bodies cut through the Gordian knot Wolf discovered inside of him, and Tristan broke free, snapping outward in all directions from the tension released from his coils.

Somehow, he'd grown wings and flew up into an emotional storm, driven higher by the pounding wind and the salted rain of sweat from their skin.

His cock jerked, stripped of its tight hold on his seed. Wolf's fingers gripped him, working him faster, until every bit of his release gushed free. It boiled up out of him, a virtual Alpheus harnessed by a wicked smile and gentle touch to shear the innocence from Tristan's body.

He regretted none of it. Lying in the final throes of his release, Tristan reluctantly let go of Wolf's throat and clenched down on the man's jerking cock as it pulled off its own climax. Shuddering and trembling, Wolf bowed his head and came, his shoulders locked and rigid beneath Tristan's hands.

It was over before Tristan could catch another breath, and a warm molasses lethargy crept over him, loosening his bones from their sockets and soothing his stimulated senses into a murmuring numbness. Wolf slid from him, the heaviness of his lax cock still hefty enough to leave Tristan with a gaping emptiness when he pulled free.

"I'll be right back," Wolf murmured into Tristan's ear.

He returned with a couple of washcloths and a towel. After slowly washing Tristan's hands and arms, he used the second cloth to wipe away the mess they'd made on his thighs, rubbing him dry with the hand towel. Tossing the linens somewhere onto the floor, Wolf lay down, then hooked one arm around Tristan's waist, spooning his still throbbing ass against Wolf's hips.

"Fuck." Tristan huffed his cheeks out. "No. Words."

"Never thought I'd see the day you couldn't find something to say," Wolf laughed. "You've got a mouth on you."

"Don't get too cocky, Kincaid." He snuggled back, finding an odd security in the curl of Wolf's arm. "I might still be pissed off at you. I'll have to think about it."

"You do that, Pryce. You do that, and I'll be more than happy to take the time to get you to let it go again." Wolf shifted, then hissed, and Tristan turned, looking at the man behind him.

The last thing he wanted was another visit from Matt's crazy-eyed grandmother, especially since they were both naked as the cherub statues in the garden. Frowning, Tristan asked, "You okay? She didn't come back to knife you or something, did she?"

"No, not her this time," Wolf grumbled, then held up a small red rubber ball. "You're just going to have to talk to Jack, babe. Because from now on, there's not going to be any toys in this bed but the ones I might want to use on *you*."

Chapter 11

WOLF WAS warm. Not in an overheated and need-to-let-his-skin-breathe kind of warm but the soft, toasty heat of being wrapped around a man who smelled of lemon curd soap and sex. His back ached a little bit. He halfway recalled slamming his hip into one of the faucet knobs in Tristan's multi-head shower, but at the time, he was more focused on the mouth closed over his cock than the dig of metal into his skin.

For a beginner, Tristan's tongue seemed to hit every erotic spot Wolf had on his body… including a few he hadn't even *known* would drive him insane. He'd never scratch the inside of his wrists again without thinking of Tristan's teeth nibbling along his soft skin while the man's graceful fingers stroked him to a bone-shattering spill.

They'd been at it all night. At some point… probably around three in the morning…Wolf gave half a thought to the couple he'd left downstairs, then went back to what he was doing. The virginal Tristan learned quickly, and the prickly, shy blond proved to be playful and willing to experiment… as much as their meager supply of condoms allowed. They'd both given as good as they got, and Wolf felt every inch of his body tingling with the memories of Tristan's hands and mouth on him. It was a good way to wake up.

It would have been even better if they'd not run out of supplies at five in the morning after they'd changed the sheets and crawled back into the bed's warmth, slightly damp from a hot shower and contentedly aroused from a kiss-and-tug under the spray.

From the way he felt, his bones were still off someplace besides holding up his flesh. Groaning softly at the light creeping in from the outer room, Wolf closed his eyes and snuffled against Tristan's neck, blowing away the man's hair to get to his skin. The light grew stronger, brightening up the darkness behind Wolf's eyelids.

Mumbling into his lover's hair, Wolf tried to bury himself further into the shadows of Tristan's back. "Tris, tell me that's a UFO come to probe us and not someone waking us up."

"I'm sorry, but there is a problem, and I need you two sex monkeys to get out of bed and downstairs," Mara proclaimed through Wolf's contented lethargy. "Your boy's grandmother is back, and she's off killing her husbands in the lobby. Can't you hear them screaming?"

"Shit." Tristan punched the bed. The loose and cuddly man beneath him tightened up immediately and slid out from under Wolf's embrace. "Okay, I'm up. Shit… why now?"

"Really, she's already dead. Just make sure she doesn't have any weapons," Wolf grumbled. "We can go salt her bones. Or maybe salt Matt's bones. That might work. He's related."

Taking a brief moment to look up the length of Tristan's legs, Wolf settled on the tight clench of the man's ass as he pulled on a pair of cotton pants. He was about to object to the loss of his pillow when his underwear hit him full in the face. They still smelled freshly laundered, and Wolf did a quick tally in his head. He'd had them on for maybe an hour tops. He could wear them long enough to check on Lady Belladonna's Manor Tour before heading to his own room for a change of clothes.

"Get dressed, Kincaid." Tristan tugged a T-shirt over his shoulders. "Did she do anything, Mara? I mean to anyone?"

"No. The men are screaming that she's killing them, but she's scaring the hell out of the lovebirds downstairs." The woman shook her head, then sniffed at the air. "It smells like a barnyard in here. Not that I'm a prude, but really, both of you need to put some clothes on and deal with this. She's rattling everyone's nerves."

"Yeah, mine aren't doing too well right now either," Tristan muttered. "I've got to go brush my teeth. They feel all furry."

"If that's a crack at my name…." Wolf paused when Mara's narrowed gaze settled on his naked body. "Hey, Mara… mind turning around a bit?" Wolf made a little circling motion with his finger.

"If you are ashamed, I would suggest pulling the sheet over you and putting your knickers on under them." The older woman gave Wolf a withering look hot enough to sear his balls off. "Yours is not the first dick I've seen, Dr. Kincaid. And it certainly isn't the best."

"Quit looking at Wolf's dick, Mara, and tell me what's going on." Tristan stalked to the bathroom, and Wolf heard the sound of water being turned on.

"She's into everything. Moving things. Destroying things. The mint vase in the lobby is broken. I tried to clean it up, but there's too much…

she's too much to bear. All of the moaning and crying. I can't be here with this, Tristan Pryce." Mara's face was strained and her mouth tight with fret. "If you don't mind, I might go stay with my… sister in town. Or stay in the carriage house until she's gone. Anywhere but here."

"Your sister hasn't lived in town for like… centuries, but yeah, I don't mind. I just want you to be safe." The blond returned to the bedroom, a speck of toothpaste on his chin, and patted Mara on the shoulder. Glancing at Wolf, he frowned. "How come you're not dressed?"

"So much for the afterglow and cuddle," Wolf muttered under his breath. His jeans going up his hips hurt as much as his back did. Tristan Pryce had very sharp teeth and seemed to like to chew. Mara stomped out, and he was left standing there, his fly undone and his shirt half-on. Reaching out, he snagged Tristan's arm and pulled the man closer. "Hold on there, Pryce. Let's take a second here."

The last time he'd been that close to Tristan's face, Wolf had taken his time licking at the faint freckles on the man's nose, then lost himself counting the amber flecks in Tristan's seafoam irises. The burnt gold was bled down to a thin-hammered bronze, and his pupils were blown out from the fear he was keeping inside of him. Pulling Tristan closer, Wolf wrapped his arms around the man's body, holding him tight until he felt Tristan relax in his embrace.

"No matter what's downstairs, Pryce," Wolf murmured into his lover's hair. "I'm going to be here with you. We'll take care of this. I'm going to make this right."

"Can you?" The man's shaky whisper was so very different from the husky, purring moans Wolf had pulled out of him last night. "Fix this?"

"Believe it or not, yeah," he reassured. "I can. Now, do I have time to brush *my* teeth, and can I borrow a toothbrush?"

IT WAS a scene out of an old movie or a child's ride gone wrong.

A haunting had come to Hoxne Grange, and whoever set up the attraction had left out all of the fun bits and only brought a scattering of broken filmy toys.

Tristan stepped out of his suite and immediately wished he hadn't.

The Grange felt like it was pushing back at him, squeezing something inside of his soul until it whimpered from the pressure. Something dark and cold crept through the familiar aroma of old paint, lemon polish, and old books, a slithering tendril of sharp bitterness that left a sting on the back of Tristan's tongue when he gasped.

If Wolf hadn't been at his back, there was a good chance he'd have gone back inside and joined Boris in his hiding place beneath the large table in his library. He had enough food in his kitchen to last him at least a week. Three weeks if he wanted to break into the dried food stash he'd stored in the pantry. If he was feeling generous, he might even let Wolf join him.

A nudge at his lower back reminded him why he couldn't do that. The long night they'd had left more than a few bruises and strained muscles in spots he'd never thought about having to work out. Between those aches and the gentle throb deep inside of him, he didn't know if he could survive a couple of weeks barricaded with Wolf Kincaid.

"That and we're out of condoms," Tristan reminded himself with an angry mutter.

After more than two decades of virginity, he hadn't exactly planned for a hot-mouthed, wicked-eyed man to pry him open until he lost his mind from the pleasure. If he had, there'd have been more than the dated Vegas dregs in his nightstand. He'd been about to slide into Wolf's primed body when the sole remaining condom they'd freed from its sticky foil prison split down the side, and he didn't know who'd been more frustrated. Wolf certainly was disappointed, but Tristan was left aching and hard.

Until Wolf's mouth and prying fingers took their sweet time, and Tristan was left panting and dazed, sticky from his own seed and the spray of Wolf's release on his thighs.

The incessant sensation in his ass throbbed again, and Tristan sighed. No, they definitely could stand to go a few hours without having one part or another inside the other, and he really didn't have enough food for Boris to last those two weeks. Dealing with the wispy, horrified men running through the Grange was something that definitely had to be handled first.

Besides, he really didn't know if he could sit down long enough to drive into town and get anything from the drugstore.

The third floor seemed mostly empty, but they passed a scrawny man cowering against the banister sweep, his eyes bled white and his skeletal hands working through the tatters of clothing hanging from his thin frame. Plumes of dust wisped up from his thighs when he slapped at his legs and arms, but Tristan couldn't tell if he was trying to keep warm or brushing something off. There wasn't much left of his face other than bone and skin. The droop of his nose hooked down over his nearly invisible lips, and his tongue moved thick and sluglike around the edges of his mouth, leaving behind a glistening shine so bright Tristan could see it on his gray, translucent skin. Crouched over, his body ended at his knees, misting off into nothingness below the joint, and he hung in midair, his sightless eyes wide with fear and poised to flee if anyone came near.

He neither saw nor heard them, and Tristan gave him a wide berth, edging as close to the wall as possible.

"Tell me you see him," Wolf said softly. "That man there. With no legs."

"I see him." Tristan reached for Wolf's hand. The man's warmth felt as good on his skin as it did inside of him, and the ravenous butterflies in Tristan's stomach calmed.

He hadn't been around an oblivious specter in years. Not since he was a teenager and decided to walk across the Golden Gate Bridge. He'd made it only a few feet before the people began flinging themselves off the edge, and he'd crumbled into a heap, a chittering mess that had to be led home like an insensible child. All his ghosts since then had been guests at the Grange, spirits looking for one last glimpse of the mortal world before leaving to sights unseen.

Something startled the man, something unknown and terrifying, because his body jerked, pulled up tight as if yanked on by strings, and he flailed about, howling soundlessly at the ceiling. Wolf hooked his arm around Tristan and pushed him back, edging between Tristan and the ghost.

If he hadn't been so unsettled, Tristan would have taken Wolf's head off, but protesting seemed stupid, especially since Wolf was only playing knight errant.

There wasn't much time to protest anything. Tristan blinked, and the man flew up, his missing legs apparently strong enough to hurtle him into the air. Both men moved to the rail, and Wolf's arm snapped out, creating a ripple through the man's bony arm. The thin ghost tumbled, his arms and thighs cartwheeling uncontrollably for a long, agonizing second before he splattered onto the lobby floor below.

Peering over the banister, Tristan saw there was nothing left of the specter. No body. No blood. Nothing but a wide ring of dust where his twitching, skinny body hit.

"Why do they always jump?" Shivering, Tristan stepped back, bumping into Wolf's chest.

"Because it's the easiest thing to do. People are driven by flight or fight. Biologically, it's our only choice when confronted with fear. I think we've worked hard to try to talk things out, but deep down inside, it'll always be *jump away or jump on*," Wolf whispered as he rubbed Tristan's chilled, bare arms. "Come on."

There were others on the way down. The stairs were littered with victims. Most were men, although a few were shivering women, their filmy skin darkened and punctured from blows and knives. But all were screaming.

Some Tristan could hear. A whispering, high-pitched wheeze that cut through his ears and burrowed down into his brain. The cold of the storm had somehow gotten into the Grange, eating away at its delicious heat and frosting over its many-paned windows. Invisible hands clawed at the glass from the inside, scraping through the winter glaze and littering the manor's parquet floor with icy shavings.

"It's okay." Wolf squeezed his hand, and Tristan's heart began to skip again. "I'm here, Tris."

"You're going to take the ax for me, is that it?" He squeezed back, raking his fingernails over Wolf's wrist. "'Cause it seems like she likes weapons now. Of course, I guess it's harder to poison people when you're dead."

"Well, if I *had* to take an ax for you, I would, but really, it'd be a pretty shitty thing for me to do." The man turned, walking across the lower landing backward until he got to the next flight of stairs down. "I've ruined you for all other men, remember? You said that last night. Without me, you're going to die only knowing heaven once."

"Glad the lobby's open all the way to the top floor so there's room for your ego there, Kincaid." Tristan snorted, but the shivers were gone. "Okay. Let's do this. Don't you have a photon pack or something?"

"Nah, spent my cereal box tops on those damned sea monkeys." The waggle of Wolf's eyebrows turned lascivious. "Oh, and X-ray glasses. Those are going to come in handy now that I've got something hot to look at."

FROM THE upper landings, the lobby hadn't looked that bad, but once they hit the main floor, things went to shit pretty quickly. Wolf's bare foot hit the parquet, and it seemed like all hell came out to play.

Mara told them the giant vase on the round table had been broken, but she hadn't quite explained it was as much of a pile of dust as the hapless suicidal ghost on the third floor. A broad ring of faint green and white powder surrounded the lobby's grand table, remnants of the porcelain monstrosity he'd last seen loaded with cabbage roses and some frilly yellow flower he couldn't put a name to.

The flowers hadn't fared much better. Torn into shreds, they were reduced to a layer of brightly colored, aromatic confetti, a sunset-hued stratum thick enough to hide the wooden surface they lay on. Tristan's fingers left a streak in the scattered remains, and the blond who'd warmed Wolf's body stood stock still as they drank in the carnage before them.

Granny certainly had been busy. The already dead lay about the fringes of the grand hall, caught in the throes of either their previous demise or the one newly created by their murderer. To the left of them, a rotund man wobbled on his bloated stomach, his torso stripped of a shirt. Something was trying to work its way out of his body, stretching the man's mottled skin along his ribs and distorting the man's already deformed body. His face was slack, and his tongue lolled back and forth as his body rocked from its parasite's efforts to break free.

"Shittiest version of a black cat clock I've ever seen," Wolf joked to ease the tension he saw building up in Tristan's slender body. When Tristan turned to stare at him, he offered a weak smile. "You know, those kitschy plastic cat clocks where the eyes move back and forth?"

"I don't have any idea what you're talking about," the man sighed, looking at the remains of his lobby. "How the hell are we going to fix this?"

The other victims were in various states of distress, equally as disturbing as the fat man rolling around in his own juices. A woman's skin and flesh lay on the reception desk, her bones piled up neatly in a stack next to her. She moaned as they walked by, her eyes rolling about in the sagging gaps of her former sockets. Her dress was a pristine white and covered with rows of pressed ruffles along its skirt. A pair of sturdy boots lay on the floor, arranged as if she were about to step into them.

Others were searching for their heads or trying to keep their innards from sliding out onto the floor. Another was a child, unmarked by any violence, but his enormous eyes were a stygian black and bulging and they followed Wolf and Tristan as they walked toward the end of the hallway to the ballroom's entrance.

It was there they found the older woman they'd seen chasing Gidget, her fingers hooked into talons and scraping at the ballroom's thick double doors.

She was nearly solid, so very different from the moonglow-clear ghosts they'd left behind in the lobby.

And unlike the others, she also seemed *quite* aware of them standing around her.

Time flowed differently for enraged phantoms, or so it appeared to Wolf, because one moment, the dead woman was clawing apart the doors, and the next, she had her hands latched over Tristan's shoulders. Shocked, the blond stumbled back, slamming into Wolf, and they both went down, taking her with them.

A marrow-shattering chill cut into Wolf's belly when the ghost's knee pierced through his body and pinned him to the floor. An intense agony crept out from above his navel, a barbed-wire cobweb spinning out faster than he could absorb the pain. Next to him, Tristan writhed and fought to dislodge the woman, but his hands passed through her, his fists thrusting out through the jutting pricks of her bony shoulder blades.

While they couldn't touch her, she didn't seem to have the same problem. Her hands were pushing down into Tristan's chest, rippling his shirt. As Wolf fought to pull free from her torturing pain, he could see fractal shadows beginning to flow up from Tristan's exposed collarbone, a crinkled ebony-and-azure pattern spreading up his bared throat and down his long arms. His breath began to mist in the air above him, his chest heaving with the effort to breathe, and Tristan's eyes caught Wolf's, brimming with terror and pain.

Help me, the man mouthed once. Then he shuddered, his body convulsing in waves of violent spasms.

It was enough incentive to break free. Tearing himself loose of the woman's ethereal grip nearly ripped his insides apart, and Wolf could barely stand, his feet unwilling or unable to support his weight.

He reached for the first thing he knew would help. It'd been too long since he'd been in the kind of life the rest of his family lived, but he'd sat through enough lessons and more than enough exercises to know what would work.

And the banquet table the house staff had set up for the Hellsingers outside the ballroom door had enough ammunition to help him loosen the ghost's hold on his lover.

The creamer set was sitting where he'd last seen it, edged up against a trio of coffee decanters they'd long ago emptied and washed out. While the creamer was bare, its companion was still full, and Wolf grabbed at it, turning on his heel to lurch back to where Tristan fought off his ghostly attacker.

Wolf's mind scrambled for any word he could use to trigger the will to send the woman away. Stumbling through the language bits floating through his brain, he plucked out the first thing that seemed even remotely useful—a spell of any kind, even if it were ludicrously stupid. His mind responded, grabbing at a single word, and Wolf flung the silver dish of sugar, spraying its sweet crystals over the wildly screaming woman covering Tristan's body.

"*Hanareru*!"

He didn't really know what to expect—especially since he didn't know if he even got the word right. Certainly not a howling steam of smoke and dust shooting up to the ceiling in a twisting line and disappearing into the hall's etched tin above them, leaving behind a stain of black ichors that slowly began to drip down to the floor below.

"Tris... babe...." Wolf kneeled down and slid his arm under the blond's shoulders, lifting him up from the floor. "Talk to me."

"Was... that Japanese?" Tristan gasped, coughing out a mouthful of sugar.

"Yeah, um... sorry. It was the only thing that popped up." Wolf kissed the man's forehead, relief flooding through him. "It doesn't matter what the language is; you just need to be firm about the intent."

"And the sugar?" The blond struggled to sit up, and Wolf cradled him closer, patting his back as he caught his breath.

"Yeah, you hear everyone screaming about rock salt and shit like that, but really, sugar will work too. Anything granular and mirrorlike. I've got a cousin who uses ground-up mica, but he's fucking insane." Crossing his legs, Wolf slid down to the floor next to Tristan and pulled the man into his lap, ignoring the blond's feeble protests. "Shush and just... try to breathe. I've got to make a phone call."

His cell was in his pocket. Surprisingly. Digging out the thin metal device with one hand, he kept his other arm around Tristan's waist, holding the man to him. Thumbing the screen on, he hit the first number in his contact list, then tucked the phone into the crook of his neck and looped his other arm around Tristan's body. Caught in his embrace, the slender man sagged against Wolf's chest and exhaled hard, his breath ragged and thin.

The phone rang in Wolf's ear, once, then twice, before a lilting, floral-pretty voice answered. Smiling despite himself, Wolf kissed the back of Tristan's sweaty head and nearly lost the phone before he could slide his shoulder up to catch it.

"Hey, Mom. You busy? I need some help." He paused, listening to the worried but excited ramble start up on the line. Taking his own deep breath, he whispered into the receiver when she stopped long enough to be heard. "And, um… can you bring a few boxes of condoms with you when you come up?"

Chapter 12

THEY FOUND Gidget and Matt huddled together in the ballroom, sitting cross-legged inside an unevenly laid circle of white powder. Dozens of empty sweetener packets were strewn on the floor around them, and they both look startled when Wolf swung open the ballroom doors. Their faces were flushed, but there was a definite bleached-out fear beneath the pink of their skin.

Shaking his head, he stalked in, approaching their dubious sanctuary. "Ah, there are the two lovebirds now. Tris, come in and let me take a look at your chest."

"I'm fine. I just need something hot to drink." Tristan shuffled in after him, rubbing at the spots where he swore he could still feel the ghost's clammy fingers digging into his flesh.

There were pockets of chill left under his skin, but the mottling she'd caused was gone, leaving his skin as pale as it'd been before she touched him. His heart, however, was still skipping a few beats, and his lungs hurt from trying to suck in enough air to sustain him.

But what really pissed him off was the growing suspicion that Dr. Wolf Kincaid knew a hell of a lot more about getting rid of ghosts than anyone else in the damned place, and it was about time he spilled his guts.

Or Tristan was going to spill them for him.

"Equal?" Wolf picked up one of the packets off the ballroom floor. "Don't know if that works, but hey, there's enough sugar and saccharine to make up the difference. Now here comes the big question. Why didn't the two of you just put a line across the door and call my cell phone? What's with this whole fucking circle nonsense? Trying to summon Houdini? Get up. She's gone."

Tristan staggered over to a wing chair near the Hellsingers' equipment and fell into its stuffed comfort with a weary sigh. As Gidget and Matt sheepishly stood up and brushed away the sweetener, Tristan took inventory of his body's aches, sorting out which were Wolf's doing and what he could put down to his ghostly attacker.

A new, pulsating pain on his tailbone was definitely from Granny. He'd hit the floor hard, and his ass now hurt on the outside and down his spine, an alternating beat to the once pleasant, faint sensation of Wolf's lovemaking. The pains in his shoulders and chest were definitely from their enraged dead serial killer, but he couldn't decide if the twinge at the crook of his throat was from her nails or a remnant of his lover's ravenous biting during their shower.

Either way, he narrowed his eyes as he spied Wolf sweeping up the floor, then spreading the sweetener on the floor in front of the closed ballroom doors. He really could blame every single ache and pain he was feeling on the three people in the enormous chamber with him.

Tristan waited, a patiently simmering bundle of nerves stroked to a fury so very different from the floating, contented state he'd woken up in. Wolf checked a few things at their equipment bank, turning knobs and murmuring complicated things at squiggly jumping lights on gauges Tristan couldn't make heads or tails out of. Gidget and Matt rushed about as well, and Tristan sat, slowly notching every second that passed into the fucking-pissed-off ledger he was holding against Wolf.

"Here, drink this. It'll help with the shakes." Wolf handed him a cup of steaming coffee Matt had brewed for the team. "There's… um… no sugar because well…."

"Yeah, because it's all over the floor by the door, but no worries, maybe I can shake some out of my armpit hair from the time you threw the salver over me," Tristan snarled, unleashing everything he'd been percolating inside of him. "How about if you sit your damned ass down and tell me what the hell I'm in the middle of, because it sure looks like you know a fuck of a lot more than you've let on."

The look Wolf gave him was priceless. Nearly as embarrassed as the one exchanged by the couple working behind him. Pointing to a folding metal chair, Tristan raised his eyebrows at his lover until the man lowered himself into it. Taking the paper cup from Wolf's hands, he grunted at Gidget and Matt.

"Both of you too. You started this shit here," he growled. "Pull up a fucking chair, and let's all play *Catch Tristan Up On The Fucking Shit* game."

He had to give them some credit. They moved quickly when motivated. Chairs scraped, and his coffee was still steaming by the time he had his meager audience gathered around him. Leaning back in his chair, Tristan winced at the stretching ache along his thighs as he pulled his knees up, but he waved off Wolf's concerned hands reaching for him.

"No, no touching me. Not until I find out exactly who *you* are." Tristan shook his head at the man he'd sucked to a shivering, boneless heap a few hours before. "Start talking, Kincaid, and don't give me any of the what-do-you-want-to-know shit."

Wolf ran his hands over his head, pulling spikes of dark hair. He stared up at the ceiling for a bit, as if to gather his thoughts. Beside him, Gidget fussed a bit with her nails, shooting her love a look every once in a while from under her lashes. She and Matt seemed to be having some sort of silent conversation between them, a mute language evolved from years of being together. Tristan would have been envious of that bond if he hadn't been hurting in places Wolf hadn't gotten to, and he was about to rap the man in question across the knees when Wolf began to speak.

"Let me start by saying I never lied to you, Tris." This time, he let Wolf's hand skim over his knee and rest on his thigh. The fan of the man's fingers was familiar but still made Tristan's insides clench with the want of him. "I want you to know that."

"Okay," he replied softly. "So… what?"

"I *am* in the business of disproving hauntings. It's what I do for a living." Wolf cocked his head, his lush-blue eyes sharp and focused on Tristan's face. "It's just not… what my family does for a living."

"Um, do we need to be here?" Matt interrupted. "'Cause I'd really like to do some readings outside now that… *she*'s gone."

Wolf looked over at the couple, and Gidget nodded toward the ballroom doors. "Really, Kincaid, I think we're okay now. And we can always leave the sugar trail up in case we run into trouble."

"Sure. Go on. But take your cells with you and call if you run into any shit," Wolf replied softly. He waited as they gathered up their things, halfway listening to their subdued chatter as they exited the ballroom, leaving the doors open behind them. When their voices had faded off into the echoing halls beyond, Wolf turned back to look at Tristan.

"You know… stuff about ghosts." Tristan tried not to sound as if he was accusing Wolf of something, but the edge of it was there.

"You do too," his lover pointed out.

"No, I just accept them… see them," Tristan replied sharply. "You *know* shit like sugar and salt and words. Who the hell knows those kinds of things and *still* doubts ghosts exist?"

"Because they… don't always exist!" Wolf exhaled sharply, forcing his words out between his teeth. "Because there are people out *there*… in that world you're avoiding… who con and trick others into believing things that aren't real. Are there such things as ghosts? Maybe. Yes. In this place… with you… I can say, yeah. They do exist. But it's rare, and even in this crazy hotel you've got, I'm not so fucking sure that what we're seeing is—"

"Real?" Tristan pulled at the collar of his shirt, exposing the tiny bruises he'd found from the specter's grasp. "What the fuck was that out there if it wasn't real? I was hallucinating some crazy woman trying to push into me? That I *imagined* you throwing a sugar bowl at her and she flew away screaming? That I'm *crazy*?"

"No, you're not crazy." Wolf pulled up and leaned closer to wrap his arms around a resisting Tristan.

"No… you're going to make me… do something stupid like forgive you and stop being pissed off. Cough up the information, Kincaid. Before this… us… goes any further."

The house moved around them, breathing in its own sanity for a moment before Wolf broke its silence with the slow rumble of his deep voice.

"My family's… different from other families. Kind of… weird, if you want to go that far." Wolf's hands rested on the small of Tristan's back, his knees settling on either side of his lover's until they were close. "My mom… she'll be here soon. She'll be able to help us. She's a… I guess you could call her a medium. She and my sister, Ophelia Sunday, own a crystal shop and um…."

"She sees ghosts. Like I do," Tristan whispered. "You *knew* I wasn't crazy before you got here."

"I didn't know anything. I didn't know you, but no, I never thought you were crazy," Wolf admitted. "I just didn't know if you were…. Hell, Tris, I'm not even sure my *mother* actually talks to ghosts. She's five ways of insane herself, but things *happen* around her. Things I can't explain. Hell, I've spent my whole life trying to explain away the things that go bump in the night, but my family… all of my family, not just my mother… believes in the supernatural. We cut our teeth on herbal remedies and candle colors.

"For the Kincaids, Samhain was our biggest holiday, and attending school is kind of optional. Hell, going on a spirit quest could be your entire fucking freshman project and the family would be okay with it." Wolf's hands kept moving, warming small circles on Tristan's chilled skin. "I have cousins who hunt out hauntings, hoping to... shit, I don't know what they think they're doing. My mother... my aunts... hell, even Ophelia Sunday... put people in touch with their deceased. My grandmother's eyes used to turn white, and she'd start rattling off about where someone could find their watch. It was... hard to grow up in. For me, anyway. Everyone else, it was natural, but for me... it was hard. Sometimes I think it's a lie, but then... they say things... things they wouldn't know, and I've seen the relief on these people's faces. I just needed more... *proof.*"

"So that's how you knew about the sugar? Because they taught you?" Tristan's head was reeling. While his own family had a few screws loose—most notably his Uncle Mortimer—Tristan always felt they were *normal.* What Wolf was describing seemed like a trip through a cracked mirror.

"Sugar... salt... really anything granular and faceted at some level would work. I told you my cousin uses mica. I think one of them likes ground quartz, but shit, that's expensive. Mirrors would work too. The surfaces... their reflective nature... repel spirits. I can't remember if they're afraid they'll be trapped or if it turns them away." Wolf shrugged. "Either way, it works."

"Anything else you need to let me know?" Tristan's own voice sounded shaky in his ears but the downcast sweep of Wolf's eyes concerned him more. "Anything? Should I be worried about you growing fangs on the full moon or something?"

"No, babe. At least that would be useful." Wolf's mouth quirked to a silly grin. "The only thing I've got to tell you, Pryce, is that I don't know what the fuck to do in all of this. I never wanted to be... a Kincaid. Not like the rest of them. I went to school. Actual school. With books and homework. Instead of memorizing what kind of rock formation I could find hematite in, I was learning how to do advanced calculus. I'm shit at this ghost stuff. I *look* for them. I *prove* they're not there. So now, in this crappy duck shoot we're in, I'm fucking useless. I only hope my mother's got something to help us out, or I'm afraid you're going to have to give up the Grange, and I know... deep inside of me... that'll straight-out kill you."

THE REST of the night was spent in Tristan's apartment with Wolf prowling the doors' line of rock salt and sugar every few hours. Settling Gidget and Matt into the library on a Murphy bed hidden in one of the walls, he'd paced off the time, waiting and watching for any sign of the ghost. By the time a waterlogged sun rose to cut through the drizzle outside, he'd collapsed into a nerveless heap on the bed beside his lover, too exhausted to do more than wrap an arm around Tristan's waist and snore into the hollow of the man's shoulder blades.

And when he finally woke, his arms were empty, his bladder was full, and there was an enormous furry weight sprawled out over his back and legs.

"Boris, get off." The dog couldn't possibly have heard him. Not through its own sonorous gurgles, although it was more likely because Wolf's face was pressed down into a pillow.

The dog ignored him, and if anything, his snuffling growls grew louder, and one of his paws dug into Wolf's shin in an act of canine defiance.

"Great."

It took him nearly five minutes to get out from under the slumbering Irish wolfhound, and by the time he tumbled to the floor, Wolf was soaked with sweat. That was how Tristan found him, stretched out on an area rug and panting heavily with a glee that could only come from having space in his lungs for air.

"Why are you on the floor?" The furrow between Tristan's brows angled his eyes up at the edges.

"Your dog was using me to practice for his *luche libre* career," he replied in a coughing fit. "I think he's got the pinning part down, but he's shit on the acrobatics."

"I see." Tristan's words rolled with mocking humor. "Your phone rang, so I answered it. Your mother said she's going to be here in about twenty minutes and for you to get your ass in gear so you'll be ready to help her out."

"Ah, the maternal element of my DNA." Wolf heard his hips pop as he stood, and the crick in his neck flared up, throbbing to remind him he'd slept funny. "Let me take a shower. What time is it?"

"It's the middle of the afternoon. The children are downstairs playing with their electronics. Something about capturing waves of light on video. They're very excited." Tristan shrugged. "I'm not sure how I feel about that. What are you guys going to do with all of that? Because I don't want—"

"You don't want any of that published for people to see," Wolf finished for him. "You'll have ghost hunters parked out on your lawn and pissing on your life. None of that's going to happen, Pryce. I'm going to give your uncle his money back, and when that's done, you're going to give me a dollar for our work here. That way, you'll own everything we've got in the can. I can't promise you I'm not going to study it, but it'll be confidential. It won't ever leave Hellsinger's. Okay?"

His blond nearly sagged in relief, and Tristan's face softened with a sweet smile. "Thanks."

"Good." Wolf stretched and yawned. "Let me scrape off my filth and maybe run a razor over my face. I want to look good when my crazy mother gets here. Just a word of warning, okay? Don't let her near the kitchen, and sure as fuck don't eat anything she cooks. I'm pretty sure I had an older brother or sister and her turnip casserole killed it off. Made me glad I found out she couldn't breast-feed, and we all had to survive on formula. The woman's a menace."

WOLF WOULDN'T have admitted he missed his mother. Certainly not since she lived only a relatively short distance away, as far as Californians measured distance. But there was something odd fluttering in his belly when he heard the familiar cough and rattle of a VW bus trundling up the Grange's long driveway, and he couldn't fight the smile creeping over his face as he headed to the front door.

"What's she like?" he heard Tristan whisper over to Gidget and Matt.

"Like Willy Wonka and Gaia fucked and had a kid," his technician murmured back, her voice tinted with awe. "But in a good way."

The skies must have been kinder to his mother than they were for him, because the rain had dialed itself down to a drizzle by the time her exhaust-popping sleeper-bus crested the final rise. It lumbered, rolling back and forth on its suspension, but its familiar rounded shape brought with it a burst of rainbow colors to the dreary gray day. Standing under one of the Grange's side porticos, Wolf noted the bus sported a new paint job, a blend of dragonflies and flowers over a base coat of night-sky blue and deep purples. The sleeper top looked as if it had been replaced as well. Probably something his brother, Bach, insisted she do since the old one leaked.

It was a piece of his childhood arriving to save the day.

And while he hated having to call her to help clean up his mess, Wolf was damned glad to see the lushly curved woman who crawled out of the VW bus and threw her arms open for a hug.

Somewhere in Haight-Ashbury there was a portrait of an eighteen-year-old woman with a toddler on her hip and her belly rounded with another life. Wolf was certain it was there—in that painting or photo—that his mother aged, because other than a few lines at the edges of her enormous blue eyes, she looked exactly the same as she did the day he graduated from high school.

"Wolfgang Starfox!" His mom's voice was a trilling rumble of high notes and baritone dips, curling around his name in a joyous dance, and he took the stairs two at a time, catching up her full-figured body in his arms so he could spin her around a few times in a tight embrace before setting her back down on the wet driveway. Taking a step back, she studied him carefully, taking in any minute changes since she'd seen him last. "Stand there. Let me take a look at you."

"Mom—"

"Hush and let me see you." Her eyes grew unfocused, and Wolf grinned, knowing his mother was dropping into a semitrance to feel out the edges of her son's aura. "Ahhhhh."

Like the van, she'd gotten a small paint job. Her long, curly hair had been dyed a vibrant merlot, so very different from the sun-sparkled chestnut he'd seen her with the last time, but other than that, she looked achingly, familiarly Meegan Ocean-Kincaid.

Her feet were bare because she hated driving with shoes, and her toes bristled with silver and gold rings, each dotted with gems or embellished with carvings. A pair of loose red harem pants hung low on her broad hips, and she wore a gold-and-green belly dancer's vest over a buttercup T-shirt that strained to hold in her generous chest. Her hands were as decorated as her toes, sparkling with metal and stones, and a single pendant hung from her neck, a leather thong strung with rows of glass beads he'd made when he was six at a commune they'd traveled to.

She was nearly too bright to look at, iced with a brilliant-white smile made imperfect by a small chip in her front tooth and a spray of freckles over her snub nose, but she was definitely and most emphatically his mother.

And he smiled when she shook her head at him and sighed heavily.

"Oh, you are in love."

"Like you couldn't have guessed that from me asking you to bring condoms?" He snorted. "Or maybe when Tristan answered my phone and you grilled him?"

"I did *not* grill him." She lifted her chin and looked down at him, an impressive feat since she only came up to his shoulder. "I merely spoke to him about the haunting. I can't trust you to be objective."

"I am the most objective person you know," Wolf pointed out, turning to reach into the bus to get her things. As usual, she'd packed up a steamer truck of clothes and supplies, another relic from his younger days of tramping through the wilds of America's highways.

"You are the most cynical person I know," she corrected with a laugh. "I swear, even covered in my blood, you took one look at me and harrumphed."

"I was probably trying to get the taste out of my mouth." The trunk luckily had wheels, and he was wise to the wonky nature of the upper left caster. Mounting the stairs, he looked up and found Tristan standing at the Grange's threshold, his changeable gaze wary at the sight of the woman standing barefooted in the rain.

Reaching Tristan's side, he gave the man a kiss, then turned, watching his mother come up behind him. Meegan took one look at Tristan and squealed, running up the rest of the way to launch herself at the slender artist. Wrapping her arms around him, she squeezed, and Wolf heard Tristan grunt in shock at her strength.

"Tris, meet my mother, Meegan Ocean-Kincaid, medium and bane of grilled cheese sandwiches everywhere." Wolf pronounced his mother's name carefully, emphasizing its *mee* syllable. "Mom, the man you're assaulting is Tristan Pryce, owner and resident proprietor of Hoxne Grange, an inn for passing spirits."

"And your lover," Meegan gushed. "Oh, Wolf. He is so beautiful. I am so happy for you. Oh, the things he can *see*. It's like he's a Kincaid already."

Another gushing squeeze and Tristan nearly turned blue from her embrace. Wild-eyed, he struggled against the small woman's hold, but she held fast, her face buried into his chest, and Wolf heard her taking a deep sniff of Tristan's scent, anchoring him to her senses as she'd done to nearly every friend he'd ever dragged home to meet the circus he'd grown up in.

"Wolf, tell her to let me go," Tristan gulped as he wormed in his mother's grasp. "I think you've got Rainsong from the Wolfriders for a mother. I can't—"

"Yeah, whatever that means." Wolf shrugged and grabbed the trunk's one remaining leather handle. Wheeling it around his lover and mother, he called out behind him, "I'll be waiting in the ballroom with the others. When the two of you are done getting acquainted, we can talk about how to get rid of this bitch that's moved in. That is if you can separate yourself from your new son there, Mom."

Chapter 13

MEEGAN OCEAN-KINCAID took one look at the bank of beeping panels and flickering monitors set up in the Grange's ballroom and sniffed.

Loudly.

Tristan wasn't certain exactly what flavor her sniff would be defined as. He was leaning toward derision when Wolf cleared his throat.

"Mom, science isn't evil. Technology is our friend. Don't go hating on my job." Wolf clasped his hands on his mother's shoulders and led her away from his equipment, aiming toward the set of comfortable furniture Matt had arranged around a low table. "Here, have a seat and I'll get you some tea. Then we can get started."

It was surreal sitting around one of his tables and being served a mug of coffee by a grinning Gidget. Boris flopped down on his feet, letting out a sigh of contentment when Meegan leaned over and scratched his belly, his left leg thumping on the area rug Matt spread out to warm up the floor. Gidget and Matt returned to their equipment, seemingly recording a few findings on a laptop as they shut off a noisy array of sensors. Caught between Wolf and his mother, Tristan wasn't sure who he should be paying more attention to, Meegan or her son.

Even more bizarre was the woman next to him and her touch on his arm. He couldn't recall his own mother touching him as often in one lifetime as Meegan brushed his hand with hers and pressed her arm on his shoulders when she sat down on the loveseat next to him.

"Wolf, why don't you go into the kitchen and see if you can't find us something to eat?" Meegan grinned up at her son. "I want to take some time and get to know Tristan here."

"You're going to shake him down for information." Wolf's answering smirk did little to ease Tristan's nerves, but the soft, lingering kiss the man left on his lips did its job. He relaxed into the kiss, leaning his head back against the rise of the loveseat when Wolf pressed his fingers on the curve of Tristan's jaw. "Don't worry. She likes you. She won't bite. Hell, this might even be a month she isn't eating meat."

"Bach assures me that bacon is considered a vegetable in some cultures." Meegan drew her bare feet up onto the loveseat and tucked them under her. "I also discovered a fondness for rare ahi, but no, I haven't quite moved yet to cannibalism, Mr. Wolf."

"Bachman will tell you anything you want if it lets you eat the all sacred crisped pork strips," Wolf teased.

"You named your son Bachman?" Tristan eyed the woman. "Like Bachman-Turner Overdrive?"

"No, his name is Bach. Bach Mystery Moon Ocean-Kincaid. Wolfgang just likes to call him that to irritate me." Meegan looked anything but annoyed, scooting around until she faced Tristan, yet Wolf grimaced at her as he left. "Go get me some food, spawn of my loins, and let me talk to your boyfriend."

He took a moment to drink in the rainbow of a woman sitting next to him, searching her face for any sign of the familiar mockery he'd seen in others… in his own parents' faces, but there was nothing there. Just a simmering, cinnamon-warm sweet look of acceptance and a fierce fire in her too-much-like-Wolf eyes.

"Tell me about your home, Tristan," Meegan prodded gently. "And tell me about your gift. Wolf tells me you see spirits. Tell me about that."

"My *gift*?" Tristan trumped Meegan's earlier derision of Wolf's tech with a sarcasm-laden grunt. "It's not a… people think… my family thinks I'm crazy. I didn't *want* to see ghosts. I didn't *want* to talk them. I'd just rather have been… normal."

"There is no such thing as normal, Tristan." The woman reached for his hands, pulling them into her lap in a tight, warm clasp. "What you have in you is an ability. It's no different than Wolf's skill with beeping gadgety things or Bach's ability to know what flavors go with one another. There are things in all of us that are innate. And some of those things are so rare… so spectacular… that others who aren't as fortunate can't comprehend those gifts. People, at the very base of their being, aren't as evolved as we would like."

"Wolf said something like that." He inched closer, scooting across the loveseat until his crossed knees touched hers. "Fight or flight."

"And sometimes fight includes attacking things or people we don't understand," Meegan whispered conspiratorially. "But I'm here now. And so is Wolf. We'll stand with you. No matter what. Now, talk to me about what you see, and maybe I can give you some answers to questions lurking somewhere inside of that sweet poet heart of yours."

Sitting amid the flood of color, Tristan found himself opening to the woman holding his hands. He started slow, his eyes drifting off to stare at the ballroom's wallpaper, searching for the dappled dog shape he'd discovered in its pattern when he was a young boy. He told her of his Uncle Mortimer, a man who'd been more mad scientist than mentor but provided him with welcome sanctuary when his world closed in on him too tightly. There were moments he'd forgotten, but there in Meegan's warmth, he found them again, pouring out his sorrow about his parents' death and how he'd never felt a part of their close-knit family of two.

Only then did he speak of the ghosts.

"They come in, usually in the morning for some reason." Another dog shape, the third he'd found in the silk paper panels, hung upside down, a curious aberration he'd not noticed before. "Most of the time, it's a single person, but sometimes a couple comes. Once when I was fourteen, there was an entire family. Parents and three children soaked down to the bone, but they were laughing as if death didn't matter. I think that was the first time I realized I didn't have my parents' love. Not like... those children did. The mother kept straightening their jackets and telling me about their schoolwork. Even in death, she was proud of them. I don't think my mother ever said something like that about me. I remember wishing for so much then."

"Some parents don't know how to show their love, Tristan," Meegan murmured. "It doesn't mean they didn't love you. It just means that they didn't know how to show it. Perhaps even they were confused about what you needed. You did nothing wrong. You were a child, a much deeper soul than they were prepared to have. Sometimes people are just at a loss as to what to do with a child like that, but that doesn't mean you weren't loved."

As he looked back at his parents, their shadowy presence in the vibrant flow of specters and phantoms around him, Tristan struggled to see their affection in the perplexed looks they'd given him.

"I don't know," he admitted slowly. "Maybe. They were... gone before I was ready. I feel like if I'd just had more time... if we'd had more time, I could have made them understand. Everything was just so confusing, you know? I couldn't tell the difference between the living and the dead when I was young. My mom thought I'd eaten bad mushrooms from the garden once because I kept seeing men riding horses through the street."

"And your Uncle Mortimer was like you?" Wolf's mother reached for their mugs and pressed his into his hand before sipping at her tea. "Did he see the Grange's spirits?"

"Yeah, sorta. He didn't… they weren't as solid for him. Or at least that's what he told me." Tristan snorted with a sip of coffee on his tongue. "Sometimes I think he said that just so it would make me feel like I was… better than him at seeing ghosts. To give me confidence. I'm not sure. I know they spoke to me and that they came here for one last taste of being human before going away."

"Tell me about that. Is that what they tell you?"

"Sometimes. If they feel like talking. Most of them are just… too happy to be here. It's like they know they're heading someplace wonderful and this is their going away party." He nodded, grateful for her hand on his leg. Meegan helped anchor him, taking his mind off of the wandering memories flitting through his mind. "I can remember the first time I saw a guest come through the door. He was an older man, older than my father. Very distinguished and dressed in a very long coat. He took off his top hat and smiled at me. I think I was maybe… ten? Eleven.

"He told me he was there to check into the hotel. To have one last fling at life before he moved on to the next world." Tristan laughed softly. "I didn't know if he was a really a ghost. He was so solid. I'd seen Uncle Morty fill out the register before, but usually it was afterward… or so he told me. I hadn't believed him, but then here was this man in a superfine suit and gloves, asking me if the best room in the house was available. So I checked him in and told him his room number. He tossed me a coin, but it disappeared before it hit my hand. The ghost's items don't always, you know, disappear. Sometimes things appear here in the Grange, like tips they leave behind for us. If it's something expensive, I try to find a family member and return it. But sometimes the ghosts are too… dated. From a time I can't track down easily enough. It's not always possible."

"So they're from different times?" Meegan cocked her head, her long wine-hued hair spilling over her shoulder. "Not everyone is from our time? Some are from other centuries?"

"Yeah, it's always a mix. Some are older. Some don't even speak English. Once there was a very old man wearing only a fur around his hips. He was covered with thick hair, and his teeth were ground down to his gums. He wandered around the Grange, but he never really saw me. He was gone on the third day, just like the rest."

"And they only stay three days?"

"Yeah, fish and ghosts. Both stink after three days." He laughed, hearing his uncle's age-crumbled voice in his head. "I never see them again after that. I'll find their names or marks crossed out of the register, and the beds are usually unmade. That's when we find trinkets left behind, in the rooms. And sometimes the towels are gone too. That's the worst of it. No matter what, living or dead, some of the guests will steal an inn's towels. Pisses me off but I'm used to it."

"And this woman… the one we think is Matty's great-grandmother… she's been here longer than three days? Troublesome. That break in the pattern." Tristan nodded, and Meegan sat back, shifting her foot when her rings chimed against the silver band on Tristan's toe. "Look, we have the same ring. Ah, I knew you had good taste, and not just because you love my son."

The word *love* hovered in the front of Tristan's mind, and a part of him ran screaming to hide behind a nest of cobwebs he'd stored bad ideas behind. Swallowing hard, he was about to deny… something… anything when Wolf came up behind him with a plate of sandwiches.

"Mom, don't scare him. We haven't gotten to the picking-out-a-china-pattern stage." The man sat down in the chair nearest Tristan and called Gidget and Matt over for food. Passing Tristan a paper plate with a roast beef sandwich on it, Wolf whispered. "We can… *talk* later, okay?"

"Okay," Tristan murmured back. He picked a piece of meat out of his sandwich and held it out for Boris, patting the dog when he slurped up the treat with a thump of his long tail. "Oh, wait… some ghosts stay. Like Heather, our cook. She comes every Tuesday to be hired, except this past week. I think Matt's grandmother kept her away."

"Her name's Winifred," Matt piped up around a mouthful of bread and meat. "Winifred Culpepper. Well, that was the last surname she had. She had a lot of them."

"How much do you know about her?" Meegan asked. "Give me some idea about why she's come here."

"She really liked killing her husbands," Matt replied, pursing his lips as he thought. "Maybe a few other people who pissed her off too. We don't know for sure."

"She's here because Gidget tossed her ring into the pond out in the garden." Tristan tried not to narrow his eyes at the couple, but he couldn't help himself. Catching their ashamed faces, he exhaled slowly. "The folly's pond is where I've seen some of the ghosts... I don't know... leave? They turn... um... I've seen a few brighten like light is filling them and then disappear when they cross over the water. It happens a couple of places here on the Grange grounds, but the lily pond's where I've seen it happen the most."

"And the ring you threw in the water was one of her wedding rings?" Meegan sighed heavily when the couple nodded. "Ah, so you were fighting and then threw out a symbol of her murderous love. That definitely would summon a foul spirit."

"I sort of cursed at him too," Gidget offered hesitantly.

"Not at... you just plain cursed me," Matt retorted. "You said something like you hope my dick rots off so I could see how much I hurt you."

"As curses go, that's pretty weak," Wolf slid in. "But hey, apparently it was enough for Winifred the Serial Killer to come over."

Tristan ate as Matt delved into his great-grandmother's history, including the supposition she'd murdered more people than she'd been given credit for. Tucked in between Meegan and Wolf, he listened with half an ear to the now familiar tale, caught up more in the sensation of Wolf's fingers making tiny circles on the inside of his wrist than anything else.

He touched Wolf's fingers, tracing the edges of his nails and exploring the lines on his palm. At some point in the man's life, he'd earned himself a Y-shaped scar on his thumb's webbing, and Tristan rubbed at the spot, wondering what he'd done to himself.

"Bach stabbed me with a knife," Wolf whispered into Tristan's ear, then licked at his earlobe. "My younger brother's a vicious little bitch."

"You probably deserved it," he murmured back, scratching Boris's side with his foot.

"It was a crab fork, and it was an accident." Meegan shot her son a look. "Now stop telling lies about your brother, and let's talk about what we need to do. Tristan, was your Uncle Mortimer the only one in your family to see the Grange's spirits, or was there someone before him?"

"I think he was the first." Tristan shrugged. "I don't know. The Pryces actually lived here before Uncle Mortimer inherited the house, but everyone moved to the city afterward. It was too far out for most of the family back then."

"Something draws them here." Meegan tapped her chin in thought. "I just wish I knew more about your uncle. He might have actually been the one to open the Grange to the spirits."

"There might be something in his library." He shifted on the seat. "I don't know. He never really talked about it… hosting the ghosts. It was just a thing he did, and then… it became what *I* did."

"So something in your rooms might help us out?" Wolf cocked his head.

"Um, no, not my rooms. His. The door right off the third landing? In front of the lift? That goes to his suite. That's where Uncle Mortimer's library is." Tristan bit his lip, recalling the day he'd last closed his uncle's door behind him. "But I haven't been in there since I found him. Not since the day he died."

HIS HAND was shaking when Tristan closed his fingers over the crystal doorknob to his uncle's rooms. It rattled a bit against his palm as it always did, a faint, familiar brassy scent coming from the latch as he turned the faceted ball and opened the door.

And let go of the shuddering, frozen breath he'd been holding in his lungs.

The room was as he'd left it. Stagnant and trapped in a slice of time he'd rather have never looked at again. Yet as he stood in the doorway, Tristan couldn't help but smile, thinking of the man who'd raised him and the nights they'd spent watching the moon rise over the mountains, sipping coffee and talking of nonsense only they could see.

Like all the family suites, the main room was a long rectangle, its outer wall lined with arched windows covered with heavy tapestry drapes. Wolf threw back one of the curtains, letting the remains of the sun into the room. The fading light caught at the dust motes swirling around in the air, glittery streams fed by benign neglect.

"When you said you hadn't been up here since, I thought it would be more… Addams family-ish. You know, cobwebs and stuff," Gidget murmured, slipping past him to get into the room.

"No, remember? I have staff that comes and dusts once in a while."
He felt as if he was caught in a trance, moving slowly through a space he
knew intimately where everything seemed achingly unfamiliar. "Mara
comes in here and sits sometimes. They were together for a long time. I
think she misses him too."

"Mara?" Meegan looked up from her perusal of a large tome his
uncle had been reading the week he'd died. Nearly the size of a toddler,
its thick pages were yellowed, but their gilt edging was still bright and
glowing with a metallic sheen.

"The housekeeper," Wolf answered from his spot by the windows.
"Really nice woman. Sweet."

"She lives in the carriage house." Another few steps in and Tristan
was struck by how still the room was, empty of the man who'd filled it
with his quiet presence. "Matt's grandmother... Winifred... scares her.
She said she was going to stay, but I think the attack on me changed her
mind. She'll be at her sister's or something until this blows over."

"Damn, I'll miss those scones she makes," Matt grumbled.

"I make those scones," Tristan said absently, running his fingers
over the back of the studded leather chair his uncle had often fallen
asleep in. "Mara doesn't cook. It's better that way."

"Ah, so she and my mother have a lot in common," Wolf muttered,
crossing over to Tristan's side. Ducking Meegan's teasing slap, he
touched Tristan's face with a delicate skim of his fingers. "You don't
have to be here, Pryce. Not if it's too much for you."

"No, the Grange is mine. I should be a part of this. What kind
of coward doesn't defend his own home?" He smiled, catching Wolf's
cocky smirk. "And if your mom is right, my uncle created this... portal...
for the spirits to come through. If that's true, then I should know about
it. I've kind of just been operating on faith and blind luck up until now.
I'm lucky something like Winifred the Crazy hasn't happened before."

"Well, not everyone carries around a serial killer's ring on their
finger and then tosses it into a pathway for spirits to leave the earth."
Wolf kissed his neck lightly, and Tristan smiled, feeling the tip of his
lover's tongue dab at his skin. "So this is where your uncle—"

"Passed." Tristan murmured. "This is where I found him."

"I was going to say *lived*." His arms snuck up around Tristan's
waist, a band of warm comfort. "It's a nice place. Kind of looks like you,

actually. A little bit. Without all the grinning, happy monsters but still, a bit of you."

He'd spent so many months, years really, sitting with his uncle in the tome-packed room. Tristan could name off each of the vintage pinned butterflies trapped beneath their glass panes above the enormous fireplace. He knew the location of each hand-spun marble he'd pressed into the mortar between the river-tumbled stones when his uncle had the facing redone. His feet had scuffed at a row of faded violet tulips on the long rug under the room's cluster of mismatched chairs, rubbing at the nap while Mortimer went over his finished lesson before his tutors saw it the next morning. The room's walls had seen him take his first sip of whiskey, a coughing, smoky affair that burned his nose hairs more than warmed his belly.

It was also the room where he'd haltingly confessed his attraction to men to the stoop-shouldered man who'd offered him a place to live, only to be told it was about time he realized it for himself.

"Yeah, this is where he lived." Tristan leaned back into his lover's embrace and closed his eyes, drawing in the scent of the man and the sweet tang of the old books surrounding them.

"He died doing what he loved," Meegan murmured happily. "Like your dad did, Wolfgang."

"Mom, my father was eaten by a polar bear." Wolf's exasperated breath ruffled Tristan's hair, and he opened his eyes to give the man a curious look. Kissing the end of Tristan's nose, he sighed heavily. "I was eight. I think I'd seen him maybe three times in my whole life."

"Tristan, don't listen to him. Ocean was a visionary. He went to the Arctic circle to protest the encroachment of the polar bear's natural environment." Meegan squared her shoulders, tossing back a length of her hair with a smug expression. "Besides, he froze to death on the ice floes. It was a sacrifice he chose to make to highlight their plight. Very romantic."

"He got lost going out to take a piss and couldn't find his way back into camp. That isn't romantic. It was stupid." Wolf sighed. "Either the ice or the bears got him. Neither of which would be a way I'd want to go out. I'd take Uncle Morty's sitting back in a chair and sipping good whiskey. 'Course, a hot blond named Tristan in my lap wouldn't be too bad."

Wolf squeezed Tristan once before letting him go. Gidget and Matt shared a laugh before moving to the bookshelves to investigate the antiques crammed in between volumes of mythology and fairy tales.

"What are you hoping to find here, Mrs....?" Tristan paused when Meegan shot him a warning look.

"Either Meegan or Mom," she said, padding over to the wide table nearly covered with stacks of books. "I have a good feeling about this room. About you."

"Meegan, then," Tristan murmured softly. "What do you want us to do?"

"First we're going to go dredge that pool. Wolf and Matt, you two go suit up and see if you can find rakes or something. How deep is the water, Tristan?" Meegan frowned, spotting the folly at the end of the garden. "Can they get in it without drowning? Wolf will haunt me for the rest of my days if he dies suffocating on a lily pad or something."

"Maybe four feet in the middle?" Tristan guessed. "Maybe deeper now that it rained so much. We can drain it off. It's man-made. It might take a bit, but it'll help. The release valve is right next to the path. You can't miss it."

"Draining would make it easier," Wolf agreed. "Especially if I'm going to be wading into freezing water to look for this thing."

"Go get that started, Wolfgang." Meegan rubbed her hands, her rings chiming as they struck one another. "Tristan, Gidget, and I will be going through Uncle Mortimer's books. I have a feeling that somewhere in this room we'll find the Grange's secrets and maybe even a way to get rid of that Winifred bitch."

Chapter 14

"THE DAMNED thing nearly bit my balls off!"

Wolf could hear Matt going on about the turtle to Gidget in Tristan's library and smirked, shaking his head at his mother, sitting on a couch in the main room.

"It nibbled his ankle. And I told him *not* to take off his shoes," Wolf shouted toward the library's open door. Making a face at his mother, he shook his head. "We started draining the pond, but the rain's probably filling it up as fast as the water's going out. It'll take a bit."

"Every little bit will help." Meegan gestured over to the stacks of books and papers piled high on the coffee table in front of her. "You can help me read some of this. My Greek isn't as good as yours."

"I'll be right there." Taking Jack's ball from his pocket, he bounced it on the floor a few times, then launched it down the hall. Tristan's eyes followed the red streak for a moment before drifting back to Wolf, his eyebrows raised in a silent question. "I'm going to salt the door so Winifred can't come in. I just want to make sure Jack's here first."

"Ah, good plan. Thanks." The blond stood up from the couch and stretched, his back popping loudly. "I'm going to throw a frozen lasagna in the oven and then get back to Uncle Morty's books."

"Did you guys find anything?" He snagged Tristan before the man could sneak past him, drawing him into an embrace. Tristan ducked his head, shy at showing affection in front of Wolf's mother, but he didn't let the blond pull away. It was too important to hold him, especially after he'd been in the maelstrom of one Meegan Ocean-Kincaid. "Don't you go anywhere until I get a kiss. I braved an angry terrapin for you. He could have ravaged me."

"You *like* getting ravaged," Tristan whispered, but his lips pressed against Wolf's in a delicate kiss. "There."

"*So* not good enough. Jaws that could cut steel. His claws were rakes, sharp enough to cut through skin and down to bone." Wolf grinned.

"We barely escaped with our lives and I get a little peck? What am I? Your elderberry-perfumed aunt?"

He didn't quite dip Tristan. The man wasn't that much in need of romance, but it was close. Curling one arm around Tristan's waist, Wolf slung him back, enough to rock him on his heels and tilt his head a bit. Gasping slightly in shock, Tristan's mouth parted, and the small puff of air escaping his lips was enough to pucker them into a willing shape Wolf recalled from the time they'd spent in bed. His cock ached from the memory of that mouth and what the man's tongue could do to Wolf's body, but for now he would have to be satisfied with a simple kiss.

Tristan's mouth became a silken trap his tongue would gladly have been caught in. Just beyond the faint burr of his lips lay a smooth slickness Wolf sought out with an exploring jab. Teasing the man's jaw with his fingers, Wolf coaxed Tristan open, then plunged in, pulling out a long, simmering moan from deep within the blond's warm chest. A brush of his fingers at the start of the sound was enough to draw Tristan's nipple to a hard peak, and Wolf returned to it, plucking at the nub until it was rigid beneath Tristan's cotton shirt.

He only pulled back when he felt the force of Tristan's breath in his mouth, the man struggling to inhale while not breaking their kiss. Drawing away only enough to give his lover air, Wolf murmured, "*That* was much better."

"Your mother's right here," Tris muttered back.

"She's had three kids," he mumbled against Tristan's throat, eager to feel the man's Adam's apple jump beneath his lips. Tristan gulped again, and Wolf straightened him up, setting Tristan back onto his feet. "Pretty sure she knows what kissing is, and I'm really certain she knows I'm not going to get you pregnant, although I sure as fuck would like to try. Need help with the lasagna?"

"No, I'll...." Tristan shook his head, stepping away from Wolf's arms. "You, Kincaid, are very dangerous for my blood pressure. Go sit by your mom and help her. I need to learn how to breathe again."

"Anytime, babe." Wolf shot him a lascivious wink, liking the faint pink he could pull out of Tristan's fair skin.

Spotting the red ball on the living room floor, he laughed and threw it again, waiting for it to bounce someplace off the hallway wall. After grabbing an open box of rock salt he'd left by the door, Wolf lay down a thick line of it near the door seam, sealing the apartment off from unwelcome spirits. Dusting off his hands, he sauntered over and flopped down on the couch next to his mother and gave her a foolish grin.

"I like what he does for you. He makes you a little silly." Meegan patted her son's leg. "Silly looks good on you."

"I thought I was being romantic." He sniffed, picking up one of the dusty books they'd dragged in from Mortimer's library. Crossing his eyes at the scrawl of Latin on its pages, he sighed and settled in to read.

"Romantic isn't dipping him for a kiss before he goes to pop a frozen meal into the oven," she teased him with a bubbling laugh. "It's taking him to an Italian dinner and sharing a spaghetti noodle with him."

"And rolling a meatball over with my nose?"

"Only if you really love him," Meegan replied tartly, tapping his nose with her fingertip. "And it should have a ring in it for him to find."

"He'd probably end up choking on it. Or I would." Wolf scanned the page, trying to find the beginning of the passage. "We're not at any rings yet, Mom. Hell, I'm just glad I can make him smile. We started out kind of rough."

"That's your way, Wolfgang." She pursed her lips in mock disgust. "You're not happy until you press everyone's buttons and set them off. I'm surprised Tristan even puts up with you."

"Trust me, he gave as good as he got," he grumbled under his breath, then leaned over to his mother. "And he bites too."

"Good," she whispered back, nudging him with her elbow. "Maybe you'll learn to be nicer once in a while. Honey versus vinegar, you know."

"Yeah, I know." He was flipping forward a page when he felt something hit his bare foot. Looking down, he spied the red rubber ball rolling slowly toward his heel.

"You have to have more faith in yourself, Wolf," his mother continued. "And faith in Tristan. I feel good about the two of you. I really do."

"Mom, I'm playing ball with a dog I can't see." Picking up the ball, he winged it again toward the end of the hall, hooking it around the corner. "How much more fucking faith can I have?"

The evening passed slowly. From beyond the apartment door, howls and rattles shook the Grange, and the night was pierced once by a shrill keening that whispered away into the storm's winds as they picked up once again. By ten, the rains were pounding against the manor's outer walls, rattling at its windows as if furious at the lack of entry, and periodic flashes of lightning crackled above them, bleaching the room with a drowning light.

Sitting three across on the sofa, Wolf let his bare foot stray over Tristan's, winking at the man when they happened to exchange glances. Next to him, his mother scribbled in a notebook, passing papers and notations to Tristan over Wolf's lap to verify something she found in Mortimer Pryce's writing. Across from them, the loveseat bristled with more books as Gidget ran through them, looking for something interesting to hand off to Meegan. Beside her on the floor, Matt fiddled with one of the Hellsinger sensors, working to fine-tune its range to pick up his great-grandmother's signature.

"Ah, see here! I was right. Your uncle laid out the six points for the Grange." Meegan turned her book around for Tristan to see. Wolf stared at the diagram she pointed out, catching flashes of Greek mingled in with Gaelic before his mother righted it in her lap again. "There's three points of entry leading to the front door and three exits for the spirits to leave to their afterlife. The largest of which is centered right in the middle of that pond."

"Six points?" Wolf wrinkled his nose. "Six-pointed star. Old school, then. Damn. Okay, something to go on then at least."

"What does that mean? Entries and exits?" Tristan brushed his hair out of his face, and Wolf caught himself before he kissed the slight frown on the man's forehead.

"It means that he mapped out fey lines along the property and found six nexus points to anchor his spell on," Wolf explained. "Spell's kind of a loose term. It's not like tossing newts into a cauldron or anything. More like a psychic thingy."

"Is that a technical term? Thingy?" The blond's slow drawl teased a snort out of Wolf.

"My son's inelegance is an embarrassment to the family. I would call it more of an arcane procedure." Meegan flicked her son on the knee. He made a great show of rubbing at the spot, widening his eyes in mock sorrow until she huffed back at him and kissed his cheek. "There. That's as good as you're going to get. I'm not bending over. I'll fall out of my shirt, and as magnificent as my breasts are, I don't think this is the right audience."

"I'd appreciate it." Gidget looked down at her chest. "I don't even fall out when I'm taking my bra off."

"Okay, less talk about girlie bits." Wolf held up his hands in surrender to his mother and Gidget. "More focus on the crazy ghost and what we've got to do to get rid of her."

"So Uncle Morty basically *made* the Grange as a place for ghosts to… leave?" Tristan circled the conversation back. "How does someone do that? And why?"

"It's a very nice thing, really," Meegan assured Tristan. "He must have been worried about someone not finding their way out of this life and into the next. He did a lot of research on it, and voila, the Grange became a threshold of sorts. Much like Stonehenge or Kawaiha'o. For a layman, he was surprisingly thorough. I mean, the place works. That's quite significant."

"Great." Tristan's lower lip edged forward, and Wolf rubbed at his thigh, hoping to ease the blond's pique. "Why didn't he tell me any of this? It's not like he didn't have any time. We were *always* here."

"He probably hadn't counted on anyone breaking it. From what I can tell, it's keyed to draw in spirits who are tired of haunting and need a way out." She reached for Tristan's hand, stretching over Wolf's legs to touch him. "It's not very complicated, really. The Grange seems perfect for it. Out of the way and surrounded by forest so there's not a lot of outside interference like cell phone towers or cable lines. It looks like he hoped to provide a way for trapped spirits to find a way to peace. That's an extraordinary legacy."

"So how do we fix it? This incredible legacy I've somehow fucked up." Tristan tangled his Meegan-warmed fingers into Wolf's when the woman let go. "Draining the pond is probably going to take hours, maybe even days. What do we do with her before then?"

"I don't know yet, sweetie," Meegan murmured. "I wish we could send her away, but honestly, right now I think she's trapped here and can't get out. It's probably safer for everyone else that she's here. For all we know, she's been terrorizing people for years."

"Shit, she probably *did* come from someplace else." Matt whistled under his breath. "People there must be dancing a happy jig."

"I'd rather be dancing too." Gidget looked up from the papers she'd gathered and glanced nervously at the door. "Think she's done for the night?"

"At the very least, the salt will keep her out, but most spirits don't like electrical storms so I think we're okay," Meegan pronounced with a yawn. "It plays havoc with their ability to sustain themselves. There's a lot of electromagnetic interference in the air. It's probably why Wolf can't see Tristan's dog, Jack."

"None of us can see Jack," Matt quipped. "But Wolf keeps tossing the ball away and it keeps showing back up."

"I see Jack just fine." Tristan shrugged. "Well, not now but usually. I told Wolf not to pick up that ball. He'll bring it back constantly if he's bored."

"So you did, and I didn't listen." Wolf lobbed the red sphere again, bouncing it toward the kitchen. He yawned, catching the motion from his mother and scowled. "You're jinxing me."

"If I could do that, you'd be working for me, not against me," she pointed out, jotting down a few notes.

"I'm just an observer, Mom. People pay me to find out the truth. That's all." He sighed, edging Tristan with his elbow. "Tell her I readily admitted there were ghosts once I had proof."

"Really?" Tristan cocked his head. "I can't remember you actually saying, 'Tristan, I believe you've got ghosts.'"

"Trust me, I've said it. Probably in between swearing at Matt's insane granny," he muttered darkly. "Mom, how about we get an idea of what we're doing here? So far I've found seven recipes for butterscotch brownies right alongside a chant used to ward off purple toads."

"Are they decent brownies?" Meegan peered over his shoulder, leaning into her son. "Because one can really never have too many good recipes for butterscotch brownies."

"Uncle Mort made really good ones. I'll give you the instructions before you leave," Tristan replied from the other side of Wolf as he shifted on the couch.

"Mom, forget the brownies. You'll just kill someone with them. What are we going to do here? Now?" Wolf gritted between his teeth, bringing them back on track. The last time he'd picked up one of his mother's baked treats, it was a fruitcake they eventually used as a doorstop. If he could somehow work out a way to use Meegan's failed meals to ward off Winifred, he'd be the first one to tie an apron on her and wear an asbestos suit for protection. "Let's focus on the task at hand, okay?"

"Well, I have a plan of sorts," Meegan said, closing the heavy book she'd been reading. "I actually think we need to do a séance. It'll be the easiest way to get a hold of Tristan's uncle. If you're okay with that, Tris.

I've found his notes on how he created the portals to the afterlife but nothing on how he warded it from malevolent spirits. I think Gidget and Matt broke those wards when that ring flew into the pond."

"Shit, that was on us. Because the pond is one of the spell's anchors, huh?" Matt interjected. "I swear to God, we didn't know."

"Last fucking time I wear something from your family." Gidget rubbed at her face, smearing the edges of her eyeliner. "From now on, everything I buy is new. I'm swearing off estate sales and thrift stores."

"Is a séance going to hurt? I mean Uncle Morty. I don't want to call him here if it's going to be painful," Tristan murmured under a roll of thunder. "And I sure as hell don't want him where Winifred can reach him. Bad enough we have to deal with her. I can't have her touch him. Not now."

"I won't be calling him here." Meegan pressed her hand on the book, spreading her fingers out over its leather binding. "That's more than I can do. What I can do is punch through the curtain separating the mortal world from the beyond. I can talk to him through that. He won't be in any danger. He can maybe tell us how he set up the wards so I can replicate them. It might even be easier if I teach you how since you're related to him. In case something like this happens again."

"Okay." Tristan nodded, and Wolf felt the man's fingers grow cold in his grasp. "So long as... he's safe."

"It'll be fine." Wolf hooked his arm around Tristan's shoulders, holding him close. "Mom knows what she's doing. I think. Not that I've really documented—"

"For once, Wolfgang, don't make this about science," Meegan interrupted. "Let's just try trusting your mother, okay?"

"I trust you," he conceded. It was a long-standing argument. He defied his family's trust in the occult and arcane, wanting more solid proof than feelings and intuitions, while they looked on in amused sorrow at his skepticism. "So long as you're not in the kitchen or trying to do any plumbing. Other than that, we're good."

"Plumbing? Really?" Tristan eyed the woman sitting next to Wolf.

"She blew up a toilet. At a national park. We had to decamp in the middle of the night before they hunted us down for destroying federal property," he whispered into his lover's ear. "And she's a really fucking shitty cook. I am *not* lying. Bach became a chef just so we could survive childhood. Do not put anything she's made into your mouth. You'll regret it until the day you die."

"You sucked out any cooking skills I had when you were in my womb," Meegan shot back. "I could cook entire four-course dinners before you came along."

"Mom, I can barely grill a steak without setting my hair on fire, so it wasn't me," he replied. "I learned how to read so I could figure out how to make blue box mac and cheese until Bach could reach the stove. Thank God for ramen and peanut butter."

"Bah, your aunts helped with the food. I had other things to do." She yawned again, exposing the silver stud in her tongue. "Okay, I'm going to crash on the couch. No arguments. The children have the library and you two can go off to Tristan's room. Boris and I will be fine."

"You sure?" Tristan leaned forward, his shirt riding up his back and exposing the dip of his spine. Wolf let his fingers roam over the line, stroking at the soft skin until Tristan smacked his leg. "We can sleep out here. I've got sleeping bags someplace."

"No, I didn't stop at the drugstore and pick up three dozen condoms and a quart of lube for you two to sleep out here." Meegan shooed them with a flick of her hand. "Go on. Pretend you can give me grandbabies, but for God's sake, keep it down, Wolf. I know how noisy you get. I don't want to wake up thinking you've been possessed or something."

"GOD... I...." Tristan fell onto the bed, burying his face into the pillows. "Just kill me. Now. Please."

Despite the coolness of the sheets, his face burned hot from embarrassment. A plastic bag sat empty on the bed next to him, its contents laid out in mute evidence of Meegan's claim she'd emptied the store of prophylactics and lubricant. With the door closed, he wondered if she was a heavy sleeper and if he could sneak out to drown himself in the pond some time when no one was looking.

"Hey, what's the matter?" The bed dipped down near his hip, and he felt Wolf's hand touch his bare back, his fingers skimming along the edge of Tristan's briefs. "Honey, your shoulders are turning pink."

"I want to die." He didn't know if he could be heard through the linens and pillows, but he did his best. "You'll take care of Boris, right? Sure he eats a lot, but...."

"You're not going to die," Wolf laughed, pressing his lips on the small of Tristan's back. "This isn't a dying kind of thing. Mom and I have a... special kind of relationship. Our family's kind of open about things like sex and... brownies."

Wolf's mouth traced the path started by his fingers, and Tristan turned his head, looking over his shoulder at the man bent over him. His skin prickled, and a shiver began down his arms and legs. Despite his mortification, his cock was responding to Wolf's touch, thickening enough to push at the bed beneath him.

"Shit, you're driving me... crazy, Wolf." He gripped the sheets in his fingers, panting when Wolf's teeth began a lazy gnaw down the back of his leg. His ass twitched, and his skin shivered again when some primal part of his brain recalled the feel of Wolf piercing through him.

"How about if you turn over, baby?" Wolf licked his way up Tristan's back to nibble at the spot between his shoulder blades. "And we can take turns working our way through these condoms my mom brought us."

Chapter 15

TRISTAN FUMBLED, struggling to open the foil packet Wolf pressed into his hand, and it slipped away, tumbling to the floor and wholly out of reach. Swearing, he dove after it, only to be caught about the waist by his lover's strong arms.

"Leave it, babe," Wolf whispered into his shoulder. "We've got lots more."

The *more* was what worried him. It was a mocking of his sexuality and prowess. He'd only had one night with another man—a hot, sexy man—and he was already wondering about his ability to bring the man off like he'd done before. When Wolf pressed him down onto the bed to kiss him, Tristan hooked his arms around the man's neck.

"I'm not sure I can...." He took a shuddering breath, hoping to calm his nerves. "I don't know how to do this."

"Tristan, we were born knowing how to do this." Wolf rolled over onto his side and propped himself up on his elbow to stare down into Tristan's face. "Do what you know feels good for you, and I'll show you what I like. We'll learn about each other as we go. Just... relax, Tris. Relax."

There was so much he wanted to tell Wolf. Of the times he'd tried to reach out to another gay man in the hopes of finding pleasure when in fact he'd been looking for solace. How he'd searched for something in a man's face, anything warm and welcoming, but the smiles he got were sly and predatory. How he'd often left when he felt someone's hands on him, searching through his clothes for a bit of skin or his ass.

With Wolf it was different. There was something between them, a spark he'd been afraid to blow on in case it became a fire he couldn't control... an inferno that would consume him and leave nothing behind but the ashes of what he once was. Meeting Meegan... having Wolf by his side as he read through his uncle's books... even the bounce of Jack's ball against the familiar walls of his apartment was so... intimate. He ached with the thought of losing that warmth.

But his soul cried when he debated pushing Wolf away. It was a risk, letting the man into his heart.

And when was the last time he'd truly taken a risk? Tristan thought, staring up into Wolf's smoky-blue gaze. Never. And if not now, when? And if not this man, would he ever find someone else who just got him like Wolf did?

"Now, Tris," he murmured to himself. "Before you die alone and surrounded by books like Uncle Morty."

"You okay?" Wolf cocked his head. "Babe, if you don't want to—"

"Can I… explore? You, I mean?" Tristan felt his cheeks fire up, but he no longer cared. He needed to start someplace, and that place was definitely Wolf.

"Yeah." Wolf's husky voice softened to a whisper. "Please."

When Wolf lay on his back and lifted his knees, Tristan lost his breath, a tightness moving into his chest at the sight of the man displayed before him.

They were so different. Wolf's skin was rougher in places, certainly darker from being in the sun, but the paler area at his hips where his swim trunks covered still gleamed golden in the bedroom's soft, low lights. Tristan's fingers trembled when he pressed his hands onto Wolf's chest and his lover's nipples pearled immediately under his palms, scratching at his love lines. Smiling shyly, Tristan allowed himself to roam over the man's torso, investigating every inch of skin before leaning over to touch his tongue to one of Wolf's still-hard nipples.

He tasted of lemon, soap, and salt. He tasted *damned* good. Almost as good as the dab of Wolf's seed Tristan caught on his tongue when they'd fooled around in the shower.

There were textures to Wolf's body he'd not really known existed before. The last time he'd been against the man's body, he'd been stripped bare of anything but nerves and want. Now, taking his time, he discovered planes and dips of Wolf's he could take hours exploring.

The soft burr of hair on the man's navel entranced him, and Tristan licked through the trail, circling the dip of Wolf's belly, laughing when he made the man's stomach muscles jump. He left him wet, pulling back to blow on the damp spots to watch Wolf's skin prickle with goose bumps.

"You having fun down there?" Wolf reached for Tristan, threading his fingers into his hair. The touch felt good, especially when Wolf began to rub at the tense spots along his nape.

"Yeah," he replied softly. He brushed his palm against the rosy head of Wolf's cock, just enough of a touch to let the man know he was aware of it pressing up against his leg. "I'll get to that soon."

It was powerful to have the man trembling underneath him. His own cock was hard, painfully throbbing whenever it brushed the sheets or Wolf's skin. He'd left a smear of his own seed along Wolf's ribs, and he studied the silvery translucence, pondering its glisten.

"Try it, love." Wolf stroked his neck, then moved his hand down to Tristan's shoulders. Wolf's eyes were blown out black with desire, and Tristan moved closer to the smear he'd left. "Let me see you taste yourself."

He closed his eyes.

Licked.

And held himself and Wolf in the depths of his throat before he swallowed.

Opening his eyes, he found himself reflected back in Wolf's dark gaze, and he smiled, emboldened by the encouragement he saw in his lover's face.

Tristan reveled in the shivers he pulled out of Wolf. His mouth on the man's inner thighs ground out tiny gasping mewls, and when he stroked his fingers over Wolf's taint, his lover's hands pulled and tugged at the fitted sheet, gripping the linens tightly enough to white his knuckles. He played at Wolf's cock head, lapping at the slit welling up with come and ignoring the concerned mumbles coming from Wolf's open mouth.

"Let me. I needed to taste you," Tristan shushed the man's faint objections. "You say you're clean, and we both know you're my... first. I want you in my mouth. Just a bit of you."

Wolf bloomed there. On his tongue. In full glory and sweetness. And like bitters.

Wolf was there.

He swallowed, needing more. Needing something to wrap himself in, and in that moment, he knew that something was the man he savored in his mouth.

Tristan found the curve of Wolf's cock with his lips. His lover's sac weighed heavily on his palm when he took hold of it, the crinkle of hair along its velvety texture tickling his hand. The skin there smelled of man and a faint powdery sweetness, a secret fragrance Tristan drew in, hoping to engrave it somewhere in his memories. Wolf's powerful thighs spread easily, his knees nearly touching the mattress, and his ass parted, welcoming Tristan's explorations.

He'd never been this close to another man's entrance. Hell, he'd barely brushed against his own. Even in the darkness when he touched his own body to bring himself off, Tristan blushed at the idea of sliding his fingers into himself. With Wolf, the thought of it was not just welcome but necessary.

Especially when he heard the man growling with need and felt him shifting against the mattress, anticipating Tristan's touch.

A dollop of lube slickened Tristan's fingers, and he pressed gently on the plum-ringed hole, letting the clench of his lover's muscles resist him for a moment before sliding his fingertip in. Wolf arched, his ass tightening for a moment around Tristan's invasion, and the sheets moved, wrapped tightly in Wolf's fingers. Then the man forced himself down, hissing and moaning when Tristan drew back out.

"No, babe," Wolf growled. "Keep going. God, you feel so... fucking good. Don't stop."

Tristan was unprepared for the man's heat. It surrounded his fingers when he braved another finger against the tight ring. Sleek with oil, they slid in, fighting the instinctive push of Wolf's body. Then, once past his clench, he easily breached Wolf's defenses and the man's legs trembled with the effort to stay still. He leaned forward and grasped Wolf's cock by its base, licking at its head until it flushed a hot red with his want.

"Can't hold off, Tris." Heaving breaths shook Wolf's chest, and Tristan suckled at the man's dewy slit, playing with its sensitive skin as Wolf writhed with the pain-pleasure of his touch. "God, just fuck me. Please."

There was something erotically charged about hearing the man beg, especially when Tristan twisted his fingers around, then spread them apart. The hissing from Wolf's parted lips grew intense, and his own cock began to throb again, a painful reminder it was being left out of the fun.

Having given up the first foil packet he'd tried to open as lost, he reached for another, tearing it open with a twist of his hand and the edge of his canines. The condom slid out, landing on his thigh, and Tristan chuckled softly.

"You laughing at me over there, Pryce?" Wolf shifted, clenching his ass around Tristan's fingers, trapping them in his heat.

"The condom plopped out. I thought it would have been funny if it'd actually landed on my dick." He moved, sliding his fingers from Wolf's tight ring. His lover moaned when he pulled free, and he stopped to kiss Wolf's knee. "Stop making noises for a bit. You're going to make me come before I even get near you."

Wolf groaned louder, modulating his tones into a slow yodel. Tristan buried his face against the man's belly, laughing as he bit around Wolf's navel.

"Stop, your mom's going to hear us." He was having problems with the condom. It slid around his head and moved about too much when he tried to roll it down. Tucking his fingers around its thick latex rim, Tristan finally got it down, sheathing his cock. A coat of lubricant made his shaft glisten, and he frowned at the shine. "I think Meegan bought us stuff that glitters or something. My dick looks like a unicorn horn."

"If you don't hurry up, I'm going to turn into a virgin, and then there really will be unicorns in here. Get over here, Pryce." Wolf leaned forward and grasped Tristan's hips in his strong hands, pulling him up between his knees. "You are taking way too fucking long over there."

"I'm new at this. You're going to make me lose my place." Tristan smeared the rest of the lubricant from his hand around Wolf's entrance. Looking down into his lover's eyes, he adjusted the man's legs until they rested on his hips. "Tell me… talk me through this, Kincaid. Please."

"You're going to rock this, babe." Wolf ran his hand down Tristan's chest, tweaking one of his nipples. "You'll be fine."

Tristan nodded, took a deep breath, then pushed in, seating himself into Wolf's hot, tight body.

And it was like winging up into heaven.

FUCKING HELL, the man felt good. Tristan's cock was wide enough to stretch him out to a slow burn and long enough to hit his center in the first thrust. Wolf's belly tightened, readying for the pull out of his body, but the man inside of him seemed more intent on staying deep instead of hammering at him.

Tristan was… cute, Wolf decided. Supporting his weight on those long, graceful hands and slender legs, Tristan was bent slightly over him, his choppy blond hair falling about his impossibly high cheekbones and patrician nose. The look on the man's face was studious in its seriousness, as if every move he made would be graded and judged. Too much of Tristan's life was a careful placement of each foot… of every word… and Wolf loved that he could drive the man crazy enough to just… be.

It was what Tristan truly needed. Above everything else, he needed to let himself go and enjoy life.

And Wolf was so looking forward to showing him exactly how to do that.

He rocked his hips, mostly to jump-start the man poised against him. The movement was enough for Tristan's primal urges to take over, and he followed, a look of sweet innocence still plastered on his face. A few strokes and his kaleidoscope eyes bled gold, narrowing with the pleasure he was finding in Wolf's body.

They were lost in the start of their bodies moving. Tristan's head bowed, and his hair brushed over Wolf's belly, caressing his skin every time he pushed into another stroke. The man took his sweet time with Wolf's pleasure, seemingly more entranced with the feel of Wolf's ass around him than anything else. When Wolf's hand came up to stroke his cock, Tristan's eyes flew open, and Wolf found himself caught in the man's heated-brandy stare.

"Let me." Tristan's hand closed over his own, and Wolf couldn't help groaning when the man's fingernails raked over his sensitive head. The blond stroked up over his slit, smearing the seed already pooling at his cock's tip.

It was a delicate dance. Their bodies moved in small circles, Tristan's cock piercing down into his core to slide over his nerves, and Wolf's balls sang with glee with every glide. Most of his encounters were quick affairs, hot flashes of passion meant to shatter any control either man had left inside of him after a long foreplay, but Tristan obviously had other things in mind.

Especially when he seated himself firmly into Wolf's ass and rocked his hips up against Wolf's body, plunging far deeper than anyone else had ever been.

Tristan had a hell of a lot more to teach Wolf about sensuality than he'd ever imagined, and he couldn't contain himself. Clutching at the base of his cock, Wolf tried to stop himself from coming, drawing Tristan's hand away with a whispering pant.

"Damn, you are so…." Wolf couldn't come up with a word to describe what he was seeing in the man's angelic face and long body. "Don't want this to end."

"Me neither," Tristan whispered back, hidden once again behind his hair. "Want to do this… with you… in you… you in me… forever. Please."

Wolf lost track of time. With the lightning pouring itself into the sky, the night was punctured with sparks, filling the room with glowing bursts. The storm rolled over them, seemingly matching their moving bodies stroke for stroke, murmuring its thunder across the horizon before moving in closer when Wolf's body finally gave into Tristan's slow caress. Their skin rubbed and sweated until they slid easily against one another. He alternated between clutching at Tristan's ass, kneading and fondling the man's tight rear, then returning to skate his palm over his own shaft.

Tristan's hands were busy, playing in Wolf's hair or at his nipples, plucking them in time with his hips. Their mouths were a lazy glide of kisses, their lips often skimming over the other's jaw or throat in a soft, affectionate slither. Just when he thought they would go on forever, Tristan's shoulders began to shake, and his hips snapped forward in a hard rhythm, drawing Wolf even closer to his own climax.

Their slow buildup came crashing over them in an unexpected wash of furious passion. One moment Wolf was sitting on simmer, and the next his balls were tangled up into his hollow, bursting with the need to spill. Tristan's thrusts turned erratic, his thighs smacking against Wolf's legs. The wet between them pulled the soft sound of rain into the room, and Wolf's gasps were nearly lost in a paint-shaking clap of thunder when a strike opened up above them.

The walls turned white from the storm's light, and Wolf blinked, catching the edge of a corona forming around his lover's body just as his cock jerked and let loose, splashing his hot release into the tight space between their sex-slicked torsos.

He felt Tristan's desire give way, first in the shuddering twists of the man's hips, then by the faint hint of hot filling his tight channel as his lover's seeds were caught behind their latex sheath. Wolf mourned the loss of Tristan's fill. Something within him *wanted* that. It was an intimacy he'd never wanted from another man, but here, in the curiosity of a manor haunted by passing spirits, he'd found a man he wanted to fill with his own release, and he was eager to have the same done to him.

Tristan collapsed next to him, too exhausted to do much more than protest feebly when Wolf tugged the condom off his softening cock. They were both too sensitive, and the rub of Tristan's soft T-shirt over their cocks was painful, but Wolf carefully cleaned up as much as he could of their mess.

"There we go. One condom down." Tossing the shirt someplace where it could keep the condom packet company, he pulled a very sleepy Tristan into his arms and kissed his nose. Wolf did a quick calculation and mumbled. "And sixty more to go. I think. Plus or minus that one you lost if we ever find it."

"You like noses," Tristan mumbled. "You keep kissing mine."

"I like your nose," Wolf agreed. Their legs tangled, a seemingly effortless braid of their limbs, and Tristan sighed, relaxing in a boneless slump on Wolf's chest. "It's a pretty nose. You're pretty. Shit, right now I'm happy enough to think Boris is pretty. But not in a want-to-love-Boris kind of way. Not like how I think about you. Shit, I'm babbling. You've done fucked me senseless, Pryce."

"I didn't... hurt you, did I?" The blond blinked, focusing on Wolf's face, searching for reassurance. "I wanted it to be good for you."

"Tris, you... made me *fly*." There was no other way to say it. Tristan reached into him and squeezed out every bit of want Wolf had. "Damn. I am *never* going to let you go if you do this to me."

"Don't say things you don't mean," Tristan murmured. "I know this has been... nice—"

"It's been more than nice," Wolf cut him off. "I'm serious. You and I... fit. There's something between us. Even in this crazy nuthouse you've got going on, I feel like... it fits. *You* fit. Just... think about it, okay? You and me. Is that such a bad thing? Can you see *us*?"

Tristan was silent for so long Wolf wondered if he'd actually fallen asleep, but a hitch in his breathing told Wolf otherwise, and after a sigh, the man settled in and murmured his reply against Wolf's throat.

"Yeah, I can see *us*." It was a sweet whisper, nearly as climactic as the release they'd both shared. "I can totally see an *us*."

Chapter 16

A LIGHT drizzle left cobwebs of water drops in Wolf's dark hair, and Tristan became fascinated by a single bead soaking up the others around it until it swelled large enough to fall from its spiky perch. It followed the curve of the man's cheek, then ghosted around his mouth, touching on a spot Tristan knew drove Wolf insane when he nibbled on it. From there it fell from grace, landing in a soundless plop into the murky shallow pond below.

The same murky, smelly pond that was also home to a man-eating turtle with flesh-rending jaws of steel, a beast so fierce and deadly Wolf needed Tristan to stand guard with a pole to fend it off as Wolf skimmed the mostly drained pool for Winifred's lost wedding ring.

So far, Tristan not only saw no sight of the rabid terrapin, he was also beginning to suspect a medium-size, hump-shaped rock near the edge of the pond was what Matt had scraped his ankle against when he'd fallen into the water.

Still, spending the morning with a cup of hot, steaming coffee and watching a damp Wolf stretch his body out to squeegee a length of the pond wasn't a bad thing. Especially since the drizzle plastered the man's thin T-shirt and cotton shorts to his hard body, and the rise of Wolf's tight ass was something to behold as he moved about.

The ass he'd been buried in only a few hours before.

Tristan was pretty sure his face was now hot enough to turn any of the misting rain into waves of steam. He shifted on the patio cushion he'd dragged down with him, feeling a bit of a tug on his ass from times he and Wolf switched things up. The ache in his knees was different, as well as the pull along the inside of his thighs, a reminder of the first time he rode Wolf's thick cock and nearly fell backward when trying to shift his rhythm.

"What are you thinking about?" The man's rumbling voice broke Tristan from his cataloguing of aches and burning muscles.

"Nothing." He poked at a particularly turtle-like clump of lily roots, finding nothing beneath the pad other than a scatter of mosquito fish.

"First off, you're a shitty liar, and you've got that contemplating-the-depth-of-my-navel look on your face that tells me you're about to stab your finger into something to try things out." Wolf arched out again, dragging up another line of thick algae and mud to go through. "I am amazed you didn't electrocute yourself licking light sockets when you were a kid."

"Fuck you. I only did that once," Tristan growled at his lover, then paused. "Wait, I never told you that."

"Nope. Didn't have to. You look like the kind of guy who spent a lot of his childhood in the ER trying to explain why you thought sticking your hand into a wasp nest seemed like a good idea."

"Okay, *that* I didn't do."

Wolf lay down the squeegee he'd been using and picked up a metal detector they'd found in Uncle Morty's workroom. Stashed among the strange devices and objects his uncle had stored away in the garage, it proved to still be in working order, beeping furiously when they'd tested it out on different metals. Wolf moved smoothly, without a hint of discomfort, and Tristan shifted on his slightly sore ass, mildly resentful of the continuing ache there.

Pulling up his knees, Tristan rested his cheek on his thigh, listening to the scanner's faint beeping. "Can I ask you something?"

Wolf waggled his eyebrows at him. "How do I make this mud look so sexy?"

"No, that's a given." Tristan smiled at Wolf's scoffing guffaw. "I want to know...." He bit his lip, unsure on what to say. "Is it normal to kind of... for my body to ache a little bit after... um... you know?"

"Sex?" Wolf's eyes flicked up from his study of mud and searched Tristan's face. "Are you in pain?"

"No, just...." He sighed. "Sometimes it's like I can still... feel you. Inside I mean. Or like, there's a kind of... not burn but... a throb? I don't know what to call it. Something anyway."

"Yeah, I know that feeling. Kind of right now, as a matter of fact. You know, from what you did to me last night."

Tristan was sorry there wasn't enough water left in the pond to drown himself in. Or at the very least, put out the fire eating at his skin when Wolf's cocky glance burned his cheeks up with embarrassment.

Maybe in the winter when the pond iced over a bit. He was pretty sure his face would still be red by then.

"There's nothing wrong with you," Wolf said quietly. "Or me for that matter. You're new to this. To sex. To being with someone. I know that, babe. And it's okay. I want you to ask questions. Don't be scared to open up to me. I'm here to take care of you. Okay?"

"Okay." Tristan nodded. "It's just... weird talking about stuff like this out in the open."

"Well shit, remind me to keep you away from our family reunions," the man snorted. "Those fucking people pry you open like they're gynecologists looking for teeth. If ever we go to a Kincaid dinner, hide behind me and I'll fight them off, but between you and me, you're safe to ask me anything you want."

The beeping grew furious, and Wolf bent over to dig through the muck with a stick to loosen up what he'd found from the mud. Sighing, he tossed a metal toy soldier toward Tristan's feet, then picked up the detector again, resuming his sweep.

"Your family sure likes to toss its toys in here," Wolf said above the dancing sounds. "That's like the seventh soldier we found in here. Of course, little boys like doing shit like that, so maybe it's normal."

"The Pryces only have boys. I don't think we've had a girl born into the family in forever." Tristan watched Wolf work. "What about your family? I mean, there's Ophelia...."

"It's Ophelia Sunday," Wolf murmured with a shake of his head. "My mom let me and Bach name her. Crazy shit, but there you go. It's *always* Ophelia Sunday. No Opie or Sunny. She said it made her feel like she was choosing between her brothers. She was a very serious kid. Probably like you were."

"So it's just the three of you? In your family?"

"Yeah, about my family." The sexy look was replaced with one Tristan had begun to think of as Wolf's apologetic little boy with puppy dog eyes. "I haven't been... I'm not going to say I've lied, but there are probably a few things you should know."

"They're all ax murderers, and your mom's really upstairs chopping up Gidget and Matt for stew tonight?"

"God, no." Wolf looked horrified. "Did you miss the part where I said not to eat her cooking? Murdering them would be the nicest thing she could do to them so they wouldn't have to eat her stew. No, nothing that bad. Shit. I wish it was that simple."

"I see ghosts. How fucking bad can *your* family be?"

"They… um… hunt them," Wolf mumbled down into the mud, scraping at a pile of gunk with his foot when the detector began beeping again.

"They hunt them? Like…." Tristan tried to make sense of the images in his head. "Like they catch them in… a muon trap?"

"I'm kind of scared you know the name for that thing." Wolf eyed him from across the edge of the pond.

"I'm not surprised *you* know what I'm talking about," Tristan replied. "So do they?"

"No, nothing like that." Wolf frowned as he thought. "I don't know if that's actually possible. I mean, you'd have to quantify what type of energy, and really, there's no way to register an apparition showing up on that broad of a spectrum, much less somehow contain it into a—"

"Can we get off of the science and back to the family thing? What do you mean they hunt ghosts?"

"Not just ghosts. Kind of… anything funky." He stopped sweeping and put the device down. Once free of the muck, Wolf shook off the wellies he'd found in the manor's garage, then plopped down next to Tristan. "Now, you're going to think this is nuts—"

"Have you been missing the whole sees dead people thing I've got going on?" Tristan shot back.

"Okay, fair enough," Wolf acknowledged. "My family… the Kincaids… make their living hunting ghosts. Well, and doing things like reading tarot cards, séances… kind of anything to do with the supernatural. Some of them are like my cousin, Cin. People hire him to rid themselves of infestations or hauntings. Or… other stuff."

"What kind of other stuff is there?" Tristan's mind reeled. "Like what? Vampires?"

"Vampires aren't real. Do you have any idea how impossible it would be for an undead to function? The sheer generation of energy to move a large mass of dead cells would be incredible. There's no possible way for that to happen. Not really. And the whole drink-blood-to-survive thing wouldn't work. You'd have to drain someone dry every few hours just to walk across the street. Not to mention decay—"

"I now understand why your brother beat you when you were kids." Tristan rubbed at his eyes in frustration. "Wolf, finish what you're saying, and we can get back to the why vampires can't exist later."

"Well, they can't. Even with a supposedly magical element powering their existence, the drain of energy would be too great." Wolf snuck in the last word as he scraped bits of drying mud from his fingers. "Some people think they're being visited by cryptics or maybe being possessed by a spirit. Cin and a few others handle those kinds of things. We've been doing this for centuries. We're descendants of the Van Helsing family. Well, the Kincaids are the American branch. It's where the word Hellsinger comes from. It's what the family calls someone like Cin."

"And you," Tristan whispered. "Because you *do* hunt them even if you don't do anything about them."

"Yeah, me too," Wolf admitted slowly. "It's why I chose it for my business. Kind of a shout-out to the family, even if I'm not knocking down walls to draw out bones or spirits. The others… they *believe*. Me? I don't know. I mean, I see them. Shit, here at the Grange is the closest I've come to actual activity on a large scale, but is it recordable? So far we haven't documented enough to prove anything other than electrical fluctuations and possible video anomalies, even if we've seen the shit Winifred's done."

"Is it so important to prove to the world that ghosts exist?" There was a bit of sadness on the edges of Wolf's mouth, and Tristan leaned over to kiss it away, taking long enough to draw a growling moan from the man's throat.

"Yeah, it is," Wolf said when they came up for air. "If I can prove ghosts exist… I feel like I can prove my family's legacy, I guess. I hate that we operate in the shadows. People think we're nuts until they're scared shitless, and even then, when everything's over, they still begin to explain things away with excuses like infected rye bread or poisonous gas coming up from a nearby swimming pool. I guess I kind of want to shove it into every skeptic's face and say… fuck you from the Kincaids. From all Hellsingers. You can all go suck my dick."

"Even if you don't believe?" Tristan asked softly. "Because you don't."

"I didn't," he replied. "Not really. This place… fuck, this place changed so much of how I thought. I never really *knew*, but now, it's like I've got to work harder. Maybe even come up with a way to really identify spectral analysis. I'm tired of my family hiding behind crystal shops and gypsy tents. Cin's good at what he does, but people look at him and think, shit, there's a grifter. Even when they're handing him money to take care of their problems, some part of their brains doesn't *believe* what's going on. I want to prove that the bumps in the night actually aren't just in our heads."

"I'd like to meet Cin. Maybe if we can't get Winifred out of the Grange, we can get him to come in and kick her out?"

"First, he's on the East Coast working or I would have called him." Wolf stood up and reached for the detector again. Bending over, he nipped sharply at Tristan's neck, hard enough to leave a stinging mark. "Secondly, I saw you first. Last thing I want is for you to fall for the hot, bad-boy thing he's got going on and toss me aside. So, Tristan Pryce, you're stuck with the Hellsinger you were dealt. Now let me find this fucking ring so I can take you back into bed and show you just how nice it is to walk around with that throb going on inside of you."

"IT'S SO small." Tristan held the ring up and examined it, turning it around as he blew off any remaining drops of water from its curlicue embellishments. "Who'd have thought it would cause us so much fucking trouble?"

Wolf couldn't begin to answer the blond. Not while Tristan's lips were pursed and blowing off specks of liquid from the stones. The motion reminded him of the agonizing minutes Tristan blew warm air over Wolf's spit-wet cock, his changeable green-gold gaze going dark while he watched Wolf's head respond to his breath. The memory seemed to make it impossible for Wolf to walk, but he forced himself to cross the room, heading to the fridge to grab something cold to drink. If the juice bottle's mouth had been wide enough to dip his dick in, Wolf would have doused the heat of his cock in the liquid. With his luck, his cock would get caught and he'd have to explain to his mother what the hell he was doing when he tried to yank himself free.

He'd heard about a guy getting his dick stuck in a bottle once. From what he remembered of the story, it didn't work out well for the guy, his dick, or the bottle.

Drinking the juice didn't seem to do enough to calm his raging hard-on, but it was just going to have to do. Especially since Meegan sat down next to Tristan on the couch to examine the ring. If he wasn't careful, she'd be knitting the blond one of her crazy-quilt scarves to keep him warm when *she* felt cold. He had about seventeen of the things and hated each of them. Tristan, however, would wear them around the manor proudly, and Wolf didn't think he could stand to be around that much acrylic.

"Wolf, come over here so I can tell you what I think we should do with this ring." Meegan waved him over. "I think I know of a way to get rid of Tristan's problem."

"She's not *my* problem," the man exclaimed. "It wasn't like she was one of the guests."

"Okay, so she's like termites, but still, we need to get her out of here. Wolf, come on!"

"Well, so much for grabbing him and tossing him onto the bed," Wolf muttered through a mouthful of sweet guava juice. Clearing his throat, he joined his mother and Tristan on the couch, nestling up to his lover's side. "So what's the plan, then? We're going to dredge up Winnie, then go out for Chinese?"

"We'll have to go into the city for Chinese. There's nothing good around here." Tristan looked up at Wolf from under his bangs.

"That was a joke, dear." Meegan patted Tristan's knee. "My son has a horrible sense of humor. I blame his father's genetics. The man's family is very uptight."

"They paid for my college," Wolf reminded her. "And for Ophelia Sunday's braces. For Bach's training in Europe too."

"Ophelia Sunday did not need braces." His mother's nose inched upward, a sure sign of her growing repugnance. "She was pretty as she was."

"Her family nickname was Piranha."

"Kids can be mean." Her nose ratcheted up another notch.

"Mom, *Grandma* gave her that nickname."

"I am so glad I'm an only child," Wolf heard Tristan mutter under his breath.

"Yeah, I tried to be, but Mom kept catching me trying to murder my siblings." Wolf slung his arm over Tristan's shoulders. He got a tingle in his belly when the blond scooted closer. "Mom, focus. What are we going to do about Winifred now that we've got her bubble-gum-machine ring? You said something about a séance?"

"Not here," Tristan declared loudly and Boris looked up briefly from his spot on the floor. "Not in my apartment."

"No, we've safeguarded this space. It would have to be downstairs. Perhaps in the lobby. She manifested there before. It'll be easier to call her up." Meegan patted Tristan again, rubbing at his knee absently. "And there's a table down there already. Gidget and Matt are down in the ballroom doing whatever they like to do with those machines of yours, but they can help. I've got everything I need in the van, so we can do it before dinner."

"So, Chinese really isn't out," Wolf mused. "Okay, but promise me one thing, Mom. If shit starts to get scary, you shut it down. Deal?"

"How scary can she get? A few broken vases. Some wind. We can work around that." Meegan's nose was practically high enough up in the air for her to drown if she were a turkey outside in the rain. "She's just a little ghost."

"She tried to grab my insides," Tristan pointed out. "It was pretty fucking scary."

"We'll all be there with you," she reassured him. "Nothing can happen if we're all there. And Wolf knows what to do if she gets too close to you now. It shouldn't be a problem."

"That's what you said after the Brickyard job, remember?" Wolf's eyebrows still twitched in fear when he thought back on *that* disaster. "I still can't eat lamb because of what happened there."

"We can do this, Wolfgang." She leaned forward to stare her son down. "If you don't have faith in my abilities...."

"I have faith. Faith. Acceptance. Love." Wolf shook off her subtle accusation of betrayal. "I just want Tristan to have a house to live in when you're done. Sure, let's go drag Winifred up from the pits of hell and banish her from this plane of existence, but I'm holding you to your promise, Mom. One glitch, even a small one, and we're pulling the plug."

"Deal. You two meet me downstairs. I'm going to get my things out of the van." Meegan was up off the couch before Wolf could say anything. "We might want to leave Boris up here. He's a very sensitive soul. The séance might disturb him."

Wolf took a good hard look at the sleeping wolfhound, his long gray body stretched out as much as his limbs allowed. His mother was as much of a ghost as Winifred, leaving a trace of glitter and confusion behind. Boris didn't so much as flinch as the woman danced over him, her long skirt trailing over his face and shoulders.

"That dog is about as sensitive as the rocks I found on the bottom of the pond," Wolf scoffed. "And about as intelligent as the algae growing on them."

"I got him because he needed a home." Tristan shrugged helplessly. "It's okay he's not smart. It's not like I need him to play Scrabble with."

"No, you don't." Wolf pushed him down onto the sofa, trapping Tristan's legs between his. "From now on, I'm the only one you're going to play word games with."

"I don't think what we do can be called… a word game." Tristan was getting bolder. His hands were warm as they slid up inside of Wolf's shirt, and he purred under Wolf's questing mouth.

"Really?" Wolf grinned down at him. "Let me show you how to spell… suckle."

Chapter 17

AS SÉANCES went, Wolf had certainly attended some in worse places and with odder participants, most notably a yak with a sour stomach, a penchant to vomit, and fantastic aim for any human head within horking range.

The lobby with its polished lemony-scented floors and enormous high ceilings was a damned welcome change compared to most of the places his mother insisted were good to call up the spirits. The fact it was dry put it miles above some of the places they'd lived when his family took it into their heads to wander the countryside.

No, Hoxne Grange really only had one drawback—Winifred, great-grandmother of Matt. And as drawbacks went, it was a fucking doozy.

He also preferred the company.

Especially the long-legged hot blond dressed in old jeans and a tight T-shirt currently helping his mother spread a tablecloth over the enormous round table in the middle of the lobby.

A table big enough to make Tristan bend over its edge as much as he could to get the wrinkles out of the cloth.

Wolf was just about reaching a nirvana point in examining Tristan's ass when a small red ball hit his bare foot, bouncing a few times before rolling up against the chair leg. They'd lined up the formal dining room chairs against a wall to give Meegan space to arrange her ritual, and Wolf thought he'd have enough time to really study his lover's butt before he had to do anything remotely resembling spectral interaction.

Apparently, he was mistaken.

Looking down, Wolf found himself staring into the earnest light-blue eyes of a translucent cyan Jack Russell terrier. The dog grinned up at him, his preternaturally elongated tongue stretching down the front of his furry chest. The slender pale ribbon rolled up like a window shade every time the dog inhaled, an odd thing considering the canine didn't actually need air. But there he was, breathing, panting, and nudging the ball against Wolf's naked toes.

"Look, dog." Wolf paused when the terrier cocked his head. "Okay… Jack. Thing is, we're kind of busy right now and—"

Jack stood up and nudged the ball again, leaving a cold, damp spot on the top of Wolf's foot.

"Jesus. Fine. But once the oooo-eeeee-aaaaah and smudging starts, you're out of here. Got it?" He reached for the ball, then tossed it down the length of the lobby. Jack took off, a streak of light in the dark.

He kept the pseudo-dog busy for a few minutes, only stopping long enough to kiss Tristan on the mouth when the man collapsed into the chair next to him. His mother was gone, lost in the depths of her Volkswagen bus, leaving the lobby strangely quiet except for the squeak of the rubber ball hitting its slick floors.

"How much stuff does someone *need* for a séance?" Tristan shook his arms out. "I thought all you needed was a crystal ball and some candles. Maybe an Ouija board?"

"No Ouija board. That kind of shit is not what you want knocking at your door," Wolf replied.

Wolf studied the table, taking in the crystals arranged around a large geode bristling with clear amethyst spires. There were only a few candles, really not enough to do more than provide light. His mother probably would be emptying out not only her van but also the manor's supply closets, looking for pure beeswax if there was any to be found.

"Nope. It's not done yet. Mom's got to lay out a circle and probably a few runes or ghost traps." He hefted the ball again, following the dog's run down the long hall. "And a few more candles wouldn't hurt. The clearer the light, the better."

"There's chandeliers." Tristan pointed up at the high ceiling where several crystal monstrosities hung on long chains. "And lamps."

"Nope on that too. The lights have to be off, and the curtains can't be open. Electricity disturbs a ghost's resonance so they can't manifest as easily. Same thing with sunlight, even if it's overcast. There's still sunlight coming in. Sure, ultraviolet doesn't penetrate the glass, but the rays usually are still strong enough to ripple the visible spectrum. Might not be enough to bother something on the spectral scale, but we don't know. Not enough science to back it up, so it's better to be safe than sorry." Wolf stopped himself before he started rambling about visible light versus phantom energies. "It's actually a science thing. Amid all the other craziness, there's some solid foundation for the candles."

"It's just so… insane," Tristan sighed heavily. "Okay, but if she catches anything on fire, save Boris. Okay?"

"What are you going to be doing while I do that?"

"I'm either going to be beating your mother or the flames out. Depends on which one I'm angrier at."

Tristan intercepted the ball from Jack when the dog dropped it. Arching his arm back, he tossed it expertly against the far wall, bouncing it against a piece of trim. The ball skewed to the side and shot down the hall toward the ballroom with Jack in close pursuit.

"That was seriously impressive." Wolf whistled.

"Yeah, I've had practice. I can't tell you how many times I've thrown that ball since I've moved in here. Or how glad I am that you're throwing it now. I was beginning to get worried if my right arm was getting larger than my left and people would think I masturbated too much."

"One can really never masturbate too much," Wolf whispered into his lover's ear and chuckled at the stain of red on Tristan's cheeks. "Of course, hopefully now, that won't be as necessary as it was in the past. You might even have to give it up."

Tristan rolled his eyes at Wolf, but the deepening green in their depths was enough to let him know he'd tickled Tristan's arousal. Jack either couldn't find the ball or he grew bored because the terrier ambled through the lobby to flop down under the table, his small body wiggling into a curl before he closed his eyes.

"So, ghosts kind of provide their own… electricity?" Tristan cocked his head and looked around the lobby. "Or something? How does that work?"

"They generate an energy." He thought for a second, trying to figure out how to lay his theories out for Tristan to understand. "I don't think I've got any piece of equipment that can truly register the spectrum they exist on. I'm going to have to work on that. Basically, ghosts are like infrasound, a thrum existing in a slice of sound and light humans really can't pinpoint until the ghost bleeds into the visible or audible spectrum. That's when you see them, or in your case, interact with them."

"Because I needed to be weirder than everyone else," Tristan grumbled softly.

"No weird, just different," Wolf corrected. "There's something different in your DNA that allows you to see through those layers. You're able to pick up their vibrations. It's innate in you. Like someone with fine-tuned taste buds or hearing. You're just tuned into ghosts."

"But you see them too." Tristan nodded his chin toward the sleeping dog. "You just played catch for half an hour with a dead dog."

"I've got a theory for that too. Most people in my family are sensitive to spectral resonance on some level... just not at your scale. You're kind of off the charts, but see, it also has to do with the location of the haunting." Wolf warmed up to the subject, leaning forward in his chair. "Places... some places... amplify the spectral resonance. I just need to find a way to identify those places and how that works. Think of the places that people feel are... haunted or holy. I think it's that amplification they're feeling. You're more sensitive to it, but someone like you is probably a receiver of some kind. Or that's what I'm working on proving."

"And you want to prove this why again?" Tristan frowned at him, slightly wary. "You said it was for your family, but... you're kind of an asshole about ghosts."

"Okay, in the beginning, yeah. I usually am, but that's because there's so many people just trying to lie about shit to gain something. And really, it is about my family." He rubbed his hands together to warm them up. The lobby was taking on a slight chill from the cold storm outside, and they'd turned the heat off to keep the ambient noise down. "And it's kind of about me. I want to be able to prove the spectral spectrum exists."

"But you're in the business of disproving ghosts."

"No, I'm in the business of proving people are faking it," Wolf corrected. "It pisses me off when people try to lie to the world about a ghost bleeding through. I'm always skeptical, but I have to be. It's what I'm good at. I'm going to poke at anything unusual until I can't eliminate a ghostly presence. I've dedicated my life to finding a way to quantify a haunting because I've got relatives who spend their lives trying to exorcise a destructive spirit, and wouldn't it be nice for them to know going in what they're dealing with? The rest of it... the fakers? All they do is fuck up what everyone else is trying to do... fuck up what you do."

"I don't do anything," Tristan said with a frown. "I just write their names down in a book, then ask Mara to make the beds after a few days. Oh, and I hire Heather when she shows up looking for a job. That'll be nice to go back to."

"You want to hear my theory? Well, Mom's too." He smiled at Tristan's suspicious nod. "Your Uncle Mortimer only built on what was already here. The Grange is a natural gateway to… well, wherever spirits go to once they're done here. I think the ghosts that come here to stay are coming from their hauntings and this is their final destination. They get one final respite from their stressful existence, then head off into the light… or whatever is there. It's why you see them disappearing into those points on your uncle's star. You… the Grange… help those souls move on. I think if you weren't here, there'd be a lot more troubled spirits roaming the earth."

"But we knew they were leaving. We know those things."

"I think you and your uncle are a large part of them being able to leave. You're like a beacon. Your presence in this place calls them to their salvation when they're ready to go. And your uncle somehow found a way to lower the resistance between our world and what's beyond, but only for ghosts. At their level of energy and existence."

"Huh." From Tristan's tone, Wolf couldn't figure out what the other man was thinking, but still, he was pleasantly surprised when Tristan continued. "So you'd want to come back to the Grange when this is all over. To study it. The ghosts and stuff."

"No," Wolf replied softly. He lifted his hand up to Tristan's crestfallen face and cupped the man's cheek. "I want to be at the Grange because you're here. Even if I never see another ghost here, I'll still be coming back for as long as you let me. Hell, I might even spend a lot of time trying to convince you to let me rent a room here."

"Really? A room?" Tristan's eyes widened dramatically. "Rooms are hard to come by. We usually have so many guests. You might have to share with someone."

"I'm good with sharing a bed. As long as it's someone I really, really like. I prefer long-legged blonds," Wolf murmured against Tristan's mouth, licking at the seam until the man parted his lips for him. "Especially ones with stormy-green eyes and lazy wolfhounds."

"I might be able to find you a space, then." Tristan opened up for him, leaning into the crook of Wolf's arm when he pressed Tristan into the chair's firm back. "Something to match your specific… needs."

Tristan's skin was cool against the warmth of his palms, and Wolf took great delight in rubbing some heat into the man's back and sides. Nearly purring, Tristan curved eagerly into Wolf's embrace, sliding sideways to let

Wolf ravage his mouth. It would be hours before Wolf would get a chance to be alone with the man again, so he delighted in slowly exploring the hot damp of Tristan's mouth, stroking at the man's tongue and lips with his before capturing Tristan's chin in his hand to hold him still.

Next time, Wolf thought, I'm just going to pull him into my lap.

His cock scoffed at the thought. Next time they did this, it warned, there better be enough space to lay Tristan out so he could fuck him until they were both mewling, boneless messes.

"Just so you know, my dick has excellent ideas." Wolf licked the rim of Tristan's ear, an echo of what he'd done to Tristan's ass a few hours before.

"I like your dick." Tristan bent his head back to let Wolf bite down his neck. "It seems to know what I like before I even know."

"Good, it looks forward to your continued patronage." He was getting harder than he'd wanted, but the man tasted too damned good to let go, especially since Tristan's shyness melted away under Wolf's exploring kisses.

"You two can do that later." Meegan's cheery voice was a dash of ice cold water on Wolf's libido, and he groaned, feeling his cock soften and Tristan stiffen in his arms. "Right now, we're going to do some house cleaning!"

"God, I hate her," Wolf whimpered into Tristan's hair. "Really, five minutes. Would it have been asking too much for five more minutes?"

"Gidget and Matt are carrying in the last of it so we can get going. I'm going to lay down a circle using the powders I got from that swami. I've been waiting for something this powerful to use them all. Don't want them going to waste on something as silly as a door-knocker or moaner. Nothing but a full poltergeist for these babies." Meegan paused only long enough to shoot her son a mildly annoyed glance. "Hurry up, Wolf. I'm going to need you to help me scribe out the arcs. Your arms are longer than mine. And where'd that ball come from? Tristan, can you get it out from under the table? The red will attract hangers-on, and we certainly don't want that."

She pushed at both of them as she walked by, her long skirts swirling about her ankles. Reaching the table, Meegan dropped a small box down on the cloth and began unpacking yet more candles and jars of colored sand Wolf thought looked suspiciously like what tourists bought on the pier as souvenirs.

Sighing, Tristan gave Wolf a quick peck on his cheek, then moved to get off his lap. "Come on."

"I swear to God, babe, I have no fucking idea what Oedipus was thinking," Wolf grumbled, but he reluctantly let Tristan go. "In fact, if I wasn't sure about my dad delivering takeout to those polar bears, I'd have probably gone all Orestes by now."

"You know, Wolf… you are all kinds of weird." Tristan brushed his hand off on his jeans and stood up. "I think I could get used to that."

"Enough so you'd consider renting me half of that bed you were talking about?" Wolf stood behind Tristan and wrapped his arms around the man's waist before he could get too far away.

"Yeah." Tristan pressed back against Wolf's chest before pulling free. "Boris can find someplace else to sleep. Consider half of that bed yours."

HE COULDN'T believe he'd just probably agreed to have Wolf move in. It was insane. Especially since they'd known each for what was probably only a week and most of that time was spent either arguing or fucking. They'd had… moments. Long moments of talking and sharing if Tristan was being honest with himself, but honesty was the last thing he was looking for.

Honesty wasn't helping the panic threatening to choke him to death as he lowered himself into the chair next to Wolf and reached out to grasp his lover's hand. Wolf rubbed at his fingers, trying to chase away the chill on Tristan's skin, then brought Tristan's hand up to his lips and kissed his palm.

"It'll be okay, babe." Wolf winked at him. "Mom's crazy, but she's really good at this kind of thing. Really."

Wolf's touch on his skin calmed his nerves, and suddenly the potential roommate coming into his life didn't seem so odd.

"Especially since I'm not even sure I'm going to live through this," Tristan muttered to himself.

Gidget slowly pulled out a chair, wincing when its legs squeaked across the wooden floor. Sitting down, she puffed her lips out and frowned. "Wolf, I think being here is a really bad idea. I could be in the ballroom monitoring any activity."

"Meegan says we need five people. Something about points on a star or something." Matt settled down in the chair next to her, nearly knocking over a candle in the process. He and Gidget had a frantic moment of grabbing the wax column before it could fall over. Gidget righted the candle, slapping her boyfriend's hand away before he could do any more damage.

"Great, like your grandmother isn't already trying to kill us," she hissed at him.

"Sorry," Matt whispered.

"It's not a church. You don't have to whisper." Gidget rolled her eyes.

"You know, it's not too late to call a priest." Matt sighed. "My mom's always screaming at the television during those fake possession shows that they should have called in the Catholics. Really, lots of churches in the city. I'm sure someone down there with a collar and rosary would pop on up here."

"Shush." Meegan frowned at the technician. "If this doesn't work, then we'll just wait for Cin to get here, but we're not calling any fish-on-Friday ghoul. They get all uppity when you point out their rituals are as borrowed as their holidays. Now let me smudge the space clean and we can start."

Trying to ignore the sensual waves of want Wolf's fingers were stroking up along his skin, Tristan studied the table's contents, briefly wondering if the Grange would combust just from the sheer amount of candles Meegan crammed onto the flat surface.

In the center of the table, she'd created an intricate pattern of spirals and paisley from the sands she'd brought in. Small ceramic rice bowls of rock salt sat in front of everyone, along with what looked to be a handful of Tootsie Roll Pops. Curious, Tristan leaned over to sniff at the sands, then stifled a sneeze when he caught wind of the strong perfumes permeating the grains.

"Don't ask." Wolf shook his head. "The closest that sand has ever gotten to a swami was the tell-your-fortune gypsy mannequin at the end of the pier."

"Is that the ring in the middle of the sand?" Tristan didn't dare a closer look, not with the tickle of floral still lingering in his nose. "Why did your mom put it there? Aren't we calling my uncle to ask for help?"

"Um, good question." Wolf cleared his throat loudly, but his mother ignored him in favor of setting a sage stick on fire with a butane salamander. "Mom! Shit. There's enough candles to get the sage smoking. What the hell are you using?"

"I borrowed it from your brother. He was using it to char sugar and salmon skin." She waved the torch about before turning it off. "It's too cool to be used for *food*."

"My mother, liberator of household appliances." Wolf squeezed Tristan's hand. "Next question, what's the ring doing here?"

"Oh, change of plans. Didn't I tell you?" Meegan paced around the table, waving the smoking bundle of sage about their heads. "I talked to your Aunt Passarabi, and she said Mortimer's ritual probably is fine, but we just need to get rid of Winifred. So we'll be calling her instead. When she arrives, you all will toss the salt at her while I invoke her dismissal. Then we'll have some dinner. Someplace nice. With tablecloths. We could even go down to Union Square and see if Bach has his little place open yet."

"Wait, back that up." Gidget held up a hand. "You're calling Winifred? What happened to calling up happy, loving Uncle Morty? When did the plan change?"

"Plans are fluid, dear." Meegan whooshed by in another dancing sweep. "Like the universe. One must learn to bend to its flow. It's better for the soul and spirit. Builds character."

"Welcome to my childhood," Wolf muttered and held on when Tristan tried to pull away. "Don't go anywhere. I'm here. I'll take care of you."

Panic was too mealy of a word to explain the anxiety erupting in Tristan's chest. His throat began to ache as if remembering the last time he'd been in Winifred's angry presence, and if he'd been cold before, he was downright chilled to the bone now.

"No... no... no." He tried to stand up, but his legs weren't responding. "I did not sign up for this. She tried to fist me... and it was someplace I don't even have any *holes*! We aren't even sure this is going to work!"

Meegan was too caught up in what she was doing, but Wolf was there, pulling Tristan in. Turning his chair sideways, he reached for Tristan's hands. Wolf's knees bumped against his legs, and Tristan gulped in some air to chase away the frantic sparks threatening to send his fear into a full inferno blaze.

"Mom, stop with the smudging for a fucking minute," Wolf said calmly over his shoulder. "And come over here and talk to Tris about what the hell you're up to. Are you sure about Winifred?"

To her credit, Meegan doused the sage in a cup of water she'd left on the reception counter and hurried over to Tristan's side. Crouching down between him and her son, she closed her hands over their clasped fingers, adding her warmth to their touch. The cheerful, fluttering woman faded, and a seriousness settled over her pretty face, giving it a stern expression reminiscent of her son's face when he spoke about his work.

"I should have told you what I was planning, Tristan." Meegan brushed a strand of hair from Tristan's cheek, tucking it behind his ear. "I'm sorry. I get so wrapped up in what I'm doing… and I guess I already think of you as one of my kids… like you already know what I'm doing because you've grown up with it."

"But I haven't," he pleaded softly. "I just thought I was weird. Maybe even nuts. How was I supposed to know you all were crazy out there with me? I've never met anyone like me before."

"Babe, there's *no one* like you." Wolf kissed the edge of his mouth. "And yeah, Mom gets a bit crazy sometimes, but I *trust* her to know what she's doing, even if I don't always believe in *what* she's doing."

"I'm asking you to trust me, then." Meegan looked up him. "If you decide against this, then we stop. We'll all go to a hotel that takes dogs and wait for Cin to de-ghost this place. But it might be a couple of weeks until that happens."

"I don't want her in here that long," Tristan admitted slowly. "I want her gone. I want the Grange back to how it used to be. I want my home back. I know that sounds boring—"

"Trust me when I tell you that wanting your home to be a home is *not* boring," Wolf said with a grin. "She's outstayed her welcome. How does it go? Fish and guests stink after three days?"

"And ghosts. Them too. Mostly." Tristan smiled, unable to stop himself from responding to his lover's slow molasses smirk. Taking a deep breath, he nodded at Meegan. "Okay. Yeah, let's see if we can get her out. I'm just… fucking scared as shit about what she can do to us."

"That's why we're all here. Together. Wolf and I will keep you safe." Meegan's pixyish face brightened. "And I've got about ten pounds of salt under the table. We'll brine that bitch if we have to, but she's going to be gone. I promise you that, Tristan, if it's the last thing I ever do."

"Don't say that, Mom," Wolf hissed. "Really. Bad enough he's got Winnie the Terrible, he doesn't need you haunting this place up too. He'll never get any sleep from the guilt, and I'll never get any sex because you'll never leave me alone. So yeah, if we fuck this up, Cin's already on my speed dial."

"Hah, it's a pity I didn't breed a funnier son. Thankfully, you've gotten me a new one so I don't have to put up with the original model's crap anymore." Patting Tristan's leg one last time, Meegan stood up and walked over to the remaining empty chair at the table. Easing into the seat, she reached for Tristan's hand, clasping it firmly before taking Gidget's in her other hand. "Okay, kiddies. Let's rock this down to Electric Avenue."

Chapter 18

TRISTAN HAD to admit, he was rather disappointed there wasn't any chanting. At the very least, he'd expected some mystical sounding noises or words. No, instead what he got was Meegan sounding more like she was coaxing a very naughty child to come take a bath with an underscore of Gidget hiccupping loudly because she'd drank her Coke too quickly.

The hiccups were much more entertaining than the beguiling. Gidget had the unfortunate luck of sounding like a pissed off baby pterodactyl when she let loose, and her whole body jerked upward as if she were about to take flight.

Despite the periodic screeching and Wolf's bemused chuckles, Meegan soldiered on.

After an hour had passed, Tristan's stomach began to growl nearly as loudly as Gidget's lovesick Hatzegopteryx calls, and nothing he did shut it up.

His butt was numb, and not in a good way, and when he stole a peek at Matt, he could have sworn the tech was dead asleep with his eyes partially open. Only Wolf's fingers around Tristan's hand kept him mostly awake. Well, aroused was more like it, but awake worked too.

When the hell would Wolf touching him *not* make him hard?

Tristan was shifting in his seat, trying to get feeling back into the meat of his ass, when the table jolted slightly.

"You okay?" Wolf whispered under his mother's pleading.

"Yeah, my ass is just falling asleep." Tristan frowned. "Why?"

"Felt like you hit the table with your knee or something." The man's eyebrows came together when Tristan shook his head. "Maybe it was Gidget. Or Matt kicking in his sleep."

"That's not possible. It's got a thick pedestal leg in the—" Tristan never got to finish explaining how the table couldn't have been kicked hard enough to move it because he was violently flung back from the wooden edge, his fingers tearing from Wolf's grasp.

From there, things went blurry for a minute, mostly due to the fact that he was upside down with his cheek to the floor and his ass plastered against the lobby's curved reception desk. Meegan's cajoling sounded far away, a fuzzy, distant scolding much like the too-gentle remonstrations his own mother used on a household staff member who'd disappointed her.

Somewhere close by, something wet trickled onto his face, and Tristan sniffed, suddenly realizing he couldn't quite breathe out of his left nostril. Even more alarming, the something wet appeared to be coming out of his nose and tasted more like blood than the salty, viscous fluid of an overworked sinus.

There also seemed to be a very concerned Wolf crouching over him and trying to straighten him up. Ever helpful, Tristan did what he could, which mainly entailed falling over onto his side like a piece of too-wet fish on a piece of nigiri. The floor was colder than he'd remembered, but it felt good considering his face was too warm from the blood leaking out of it.

"Just let me lie here a bit. I'll get up later." He was pretty certain he'd have remembered getting his tongue pierced, but apparently something had happened in between the pterodactyl cries and the table suddenly throwing a fit because his tongue no longer seemed to fit in his mouth properly.

"No, babe. Now." Wolf was unfairly stronger than he was, especially since Tristan had just committed to lying on the floor when he was summarily lifted up to his feet like a sack of slithering beans. "Come on. Get up. Winifred's coming."

The peaceful droning of Meegan's calm, soothing voice had gone the way of the dodo if the raspy screeching coming from her mouth was any indication of how the séance was going. Winds whipped through the lobby, and Tristan battled to keep on his feet when a gust nearly knocked him back into Wolf.

When he finally stood up, Tristan was horrified at what he saw. The Hoxne Grange he'd loved and dedicated his life to was gone, and in its place a mouth to some sort of hell had opened, allowing a host of fanged and winged shadows to pour out of its inky depths and into the heart of the manor.

Right in the middle of it, a partially formed Winifred stood with her arms up and her lips peeled back in a keening wail, exhorting the shadows to rise up as if she were a three-foot-tall mouse in a star-embellished magician's hat and the darkness were her brooms.

And Winifred looked a damned sight more scary than anything the Kingdom of the Mouse could *ever* have come up with. Especially when she turned her soulless gaze at them and scowled.

It was difficult to reconcile the slightly moon-faced technician as having come from the skeletal from filling out in front of him, especially when the flickering candlelight seemed to be swallowed up by her shape, sucking away any bit of glow from the air around her. Nothing of Matt's nearly constantly smiling face showed in the woman's thickening features, her skin forming slowly around her long, crooked teeth.

The sands scattered about the floor seemed to be feeding her manifestation. The grains were caught in swirling devils, adding to Winifred's long body, and she stretched out, her heavy, rough skirts flowing down her hips and dragging on the floor. Tristan blinked, trying to shake off the fuzziness in his vision, but it was doing him no good.

Gone was the see-through essence of the transient spirits he'd known all of his life. While she was definitely less alive-looking than the guests arriving at the Grange, their faded blue-gray forms solid to his vision but elusive to the touch, Winifred was certainly solid enough. Or would be once the sands and debris in the lobby were sucked up into her presence.

There was no mistaking the ghost for a living woman. All signs of life were bleached from her skin, and her flesh hung sloppily from her bones, waves of nearly translucent folds swaying to and fro every time she moved. Her jaw worked back and forth as she turned, misshapen either by time or circumstance, but the bone didn't appear to be solid enough to keep her tongue in because it slithered up and around her lips, sliding out to dangle over her chin until she pulled it back in with a slurping curl.

A stench preceded Winifred's form, something dark and musty layered with a tart foulness, more regurgitated spoiled milk than anything sulfurous. Her feet were bare, gnarled, stick-like things she toddled on as she took her first step into the human world in what must have been over a hundred years.

Her head hung at an odd angle, as if the weight were too unfamiliar, too unwieldy for her neck to handle, and the specter jerked as she took another step, her joints clattering with the effort to coordinate her movements. There was something odd about her limbs, and Tristan wondered how hard he'd hit the desk, because they seemed to… move… undulate, really, a fluid motion at total odds with the twitch and shudder of her knees and elbows.

"Shit, this is the last time I agree to call up a ghost," Tristan muttered, grateful for Wolf's hands on his hips. "Her arms… they keep bobbing up and down. Like she's Doc Reed or something."

"Yeah, Mom and I are going to have a fucking discussion once we get out of this shit," Wolf agreed. "Now come on, babe. Move."

For some reason, the pounding at the back of his head began to really catch his attention. His eyes felt like they were about to pop out from the throbbing behind them, but still, he couldn't really close them. He needed his eyes if he was going to see what Winifred was up to.

"Can't move, Wolf," he blurted out. "If we move, she'll see us. Don't they hunt by sight?"

It was nonsense, but it was all he could find operating in his brain at the moment, and it was enough to make Wolf smile.

Apparently, Winifred disapproved of humor, because the black orbs in her eye sockets latched onto them, and suddenly Tristan wondered if the woman was actually descended from a T-Rex.

Catching the dead woman's attention was possibly the worst thing he'd ever imagined could happen to him, because the instant her eyes found him, every speck of smoky, howling shadow in the Grange's lobby came gunning straight for him. There was nowhere to run, certainly nowhere to hide, despite Wolf's insistence that he somehow curl up behind the man's large body. Winifred had Tristan in her sights, and she wasn't going to let him slip away.

The misting shadows buffeted him, pushing him into the side of the reception desk, and Tristan fought to keep his ground. Grabbing at Wolf's arm, he used the man's larger body to steady himself. He'd taken a few steps along the curve of the desk when Wolf started shouting something at him, something he couldn't hear through the whooshing of the shadows pushing past them. The ghost was a few yards away and moving slowly. They had to get out of the lobby, or at least take some shelter and regroup.

Looking around, he spotted Gidget and Matt cowering behind the upended massive table. A small trickle of blood spackled Gidget's forehead, but for the most part, other than fear, they seemed to be fine. Meegan, however, was a different story. She stood in the middle of it, an avenging paisley and brightly hued angel, chanting through the screaming winds to extol the ghost to behave.

Winifred just didn't seem to be cooperating.

"Tris! Duck!" Wolf yelled at him, but the words were muffled, the sound of the man's voice barely breaking through the cotton in Tristan's head. "Get. Down!"

"What?" Tristan had turned to see what Wolf was talking about when Winifred's arm elongated out of her body, snapping toward him in a slithering wave of pale mist and dead flesh.

He couldn't move fast enough to block Winifred's attack, and she struck hard. Wolf proved to be no obstacle for the ghost's nearly solid form. Her rubbery appendage smacked Wolf aside, sending him flying back over the reception counter. Tristan ducked, hoping to roll out of the way or at least hide behind something until he could figure out a way to stop her, but she found him.

And sank her fingers down through his shirt and into his chest.

Pain. It was all he could feel. It overwhelmed him in its intensity, and Tristan wasn't certain he could find its beginning, even though the specter's fingers were clearly diving down into his sternum, past the bone and into his soft tissue. She worked through him, and Tristan lost the air in his lungs when her hand passed straight through him to pop out of his back.

He tried to pull away, but the woman's arm held him fast. A torrential fire burned inside of his lungs, flickers of its heat spreading outward to touch at the twisting ache of his muscles and nerves. Tristan tried to catch his breath, taking in small jerks of air only to find he couldn't pull in much more than a huff or two before the pain began anew. Stumbling back, he slammed into the reception desk, Winifred's hand clenched into a tight fist between his shoulder blades.

Her corporeal flesh gave somewhat against the wooden counter, and Tristan slammed back again. Some small part of his consciousness warned him against the lingering presence in his body, even if he couldn't form a coherent thought. He lost everything to the pain, especially when it ratcheted up another notch and a soothing darkness began to creep up around the edges of his mind.

It would be so easy to give into the darkness, especially with its promise of peace and surcease.

Easy enough until Tristan heard Wolf calling out to him through the crackling noise of his body cooking around Winifred's arm.

He pushed back again, forcing his hands up to close around the ghost's flesh, then pulling away as hard as he could, using the countertop behind him to leverage the woman out of him. Wedging her hand against the wood seemed to help. Whatever powers the ghost had now, they didn't include passing through walls or wood, because her hand was a solid lump against the desk's side.

He'd gotten her to withdraw a few inches when she flew toward him, bringing her decayed form up against his, smearing a shadowy, inky grime over Tristan's skin and clothes.

The dead woman's mouth hadn't quite kicked into a working model, and her chin slid around as she tried to form a sound, but her face certainly worked well enough to make out what she was trying to say.

"Diiiiiie."

She wasn't real, Tristan reminded himself, but it was hard to believe that when the stench of her breath was burning his nostril hairs.

"You first, bitch." Wolf appeared behind Winifred, rising up over her shoulder.

His cupped hands were full of shards of salt that sparkled in the dim light, the thick grains' surfaces catching the flames of the remaining banks of candles. Wolf slammed his palms into the dead woman's sunken cheeks and growled something Tristan couldn't quite catch.

Whatever he said… whatever its meaning was… it was enough to burn through Winifred's hold, and she fell away, screaming in a shuddering agony as she pawed at the dripping remains of her face.

A face that really was made of nothing but shadows and sand.

Fine grains dribbled out of the thready dregs of Winifred's cheeks. The tautly stretched skin over her skull was burning where the salt touched it, turning to ash and crumbling off the shadowy construct below. Her tongue lashed about in the emptying space along her jaw, anchored to something Tristan couldn't quite see, but it was obvious by the murky plumes now pouring out of the smoking ruins of her face, her tongue wasn't going to stay hidden much longer.

No sooner did he have that thought than the sand-and-smoke-formed organ convulsed violently. Spurting out of a hole in the side of Winifred's face, it struck the floor with a solid, moist-sounding thump.

Once there, it twitched and writhed for a few seconds, an angry gray slug furious at being ejected from its den.

Amid the howling, Tristan and Wolf skirted around the desk, crunching through specks of fallen salt, sand, and broken candles as they hunted for some cover. The table was too far away to be useful. Too small, really, since Gidget and Matt took up refuge behind its wide circular top, and the reception area was too open, despite the pigeonholed demi-wall built up behind it.

It was the best they could do, and Tristan dove behind its somewhat useless shelter, the winds cutting through the lobby dampened slightly by the counter's high rise.

Winifred's tongue did its best to follow them, a tripe-like skinned golem intent on its prey. It humped along the floor, undulating its unwieldy mass through the debris to reach Tristan's hiding place, and he watched in sheer horror as the thing flopped around, inching closer with each screech Winifred let loose from her now denuded skull.

"I need to grab some more salt," Wolf practically screamed into Tristan's ear. "Stay here."

"What about that?" he asked, pointing to the determined tongue heaving its bloated mass across the parquet.

"I don't know. Make a sandwich? Maybe with a nice golden mustard?" Wolf kissed the corner of his mouth, and Tristan was left with the taste of the cinnamon candy he'd sucked on during the séance mingled with the smokiness of Wolf's natural flavor. "Hold our position, Pryce. I'm going in for reinforcements."

"Be careful. Apparently we're supposed to be going for Chinese after this," Tristan replied. "I want to read what my fortune cookie will say. Should be interesting."

"Deal." Wolf got to his feet and took a look around. "I'll be right back."

The other man sprinted across the lobby toward his mother, leaving Tristan behind. Another peek at the tongue startled Tristan into action. It had gotten much closer, wiggling and flopping nearly six inches while Wolf kissed him.

As he ran, Wolf's foot passed over the muscular organ, and it arched up, a moment too late in its attempt to touch Wolf. Denied its new prey, it resumed its slow sea-cucumber flailing dance. As Tristan watched its uncoordinated crawl, it lurched another few inches, rapidly closing the distance between its initial landing place and the reception desk. A smoking trail of gunk curled up in its path, its pseudo-flesh smearing ichors on the wood and pieces of its form falling off where it made contact with any of the spilled salt.

"If I'm going to die by anyone's tongue, it's going to be Wolf's." Tristan ducked back behind the desk as Winifred's arm swooped out and nearly struck his head. "Shit, this is like a game of Whack-A-Mole."

He spotted a silver letter opener he'd left on one of the desk's shelves. Originally from a writing set his uncle insisted once belonged to Elizabeth I, the piece was heavy and sharp enough Tristan often used it to carve apples as he waited for guests to arrive during the morning hours.

"That'll work. Silver is good." He couldn't remember if silver actually worked for anything other than werewolves, and even then, there wasn't any guarantee. Despite his connection to the Grange, Tristan knew he was woefully uninformed about the supernatural, and if it hadn't been for a cheesy George Hamilton movie, he'd have thought silver would work on vampires too.

Hefting the letter opener, he steadied himself with a long, hard breath. "Okay, tongue. Now we do battle."

It was much larger than he expected. So much bigger than it had been a few feet away, because when Tristan peeked around the side again, the smoldering organ was nearly the size of a gorged, legless Chihuahua, and from the way it was flailing, about as pleasant.

Tristan leapt around the corner, arms stretched out and makeshift dirk at the ready. His aim was slightly off, but it was keen enough to plunge the letter opener through the bulbous tip of the tongue's end. Pinned to the floor, it began to struggle violently against its capture, its flesh tearing slightly from the silver opener's sharpened edges.

The tongue leaked something black and sticky from its flesh, and wherever Tristan got it on his skin, it burned slightly, pocking up the area with small red spots. Despite the blade plunged through it, the tongue refused to give up its hunt and struggled to break free by dragging its end against the sharp edges to split its own flesh.

"Fucking hell." Tristan ducked another fling of Winifred's arm, her fingers narrowly missing his explosion-mussed hair. A few feet away, Wolf flung something into the ghost's face, and she retaliated, screaming her defiance in a garbled mess of sound.

The salt under his hands and knees was uncomfortable, and he sat back on his haunches, feeling the crunch of the crushed grains under his shins. Staring at his hands, a small light bulb—probably not much brighter than one of Meegan's candles—went off in his head.

"Fuck. Salt." He frantically looked around, spotting the small sweeps of grains around him. "Wolf *just* used it. God, Tristan. Think sometimes."

It took him longer than he'd hoped to gather enough of the salt from the floor to make a decent-size pile, and by the time he had a handful, Winifred's tongue had worked its way free of the letter opener. With its back end spread apart much like a dissected fluke worm, it was turning over to begin its slog when Tristan scooped up his ammunition and jumped the unsuspecting tongue.

The handful of salt he'd gotten off the floor proved to be enough. He plunged his cupped hands over the squirming pseudo-meat, driving the chunky grains deep into the tongue's severed flesh. Trapped between Tristan's salty skin and the grain-covered floor, the tongue thrashed about, struggling to free itself from the burning torment capturing it.

Using all of his weight, Tristan pressed down, smashing as much of the salt as he could get into the tongue's surface, pausing long enough to scoop more on before leaning on it again. Thick smoke began to swirl up from the tongue's flat, rough surface, and the familiar burn of the thing's odd sticky core began to eat at Tristan's palms.

Unable to stand the scorch any longer, he yanked his hands away and skittered back, just in time to see the tongue burst outward, its fleshy bits sparking in the air before falling to the floor in drifting specks of burnt sand.

Relieved at the tongue's demise, he got to his knees and turned, hoping to find out where Wolf had gotten to amid the craziness of Winifred's detached body parts, when the ghost struck again, this time slamming him across the head with a winding snake of her shin. He toppled back, falling into the tongue's remains and the piles of salt-speckled sand around him.

The shock of hitting the ground forced the air from his lungs, and for a brief moment, Tristan wondered if the tongue was having its final revenge as he saw Winifred rise up over his sprawled-out body with her fingers wiggling out of her hands and pushing into the startled O of his opened mouth.

Chapter 19

LEAVING TRISTAN by the desk was hard. Fucking difficult was really what Wolf was thinking, but he was going to go with hard. Especially with Winifred lurking over them.

The haunting was bigger than any he'd ever seen before. Whatever his mother had done, she'd broken through to something stronger than she could control, and he'd be damned if Tristan would pay for their mistakes. Sprinting across the lobby, he avoided Winifred's detached tongue as it squirmed about on the floor and reached his mother's side in a few strides. Meegan was still chanting or cajoling, her arms raised over her head as she beseeched the angry ghost to join them to work things out.

Or at least that was what Wolf thought she was saying. At some point his mother had left her Latin behind and seemed to be working through what sounded like fractured Bengali, not a language she was good with even without a furious poltergeist hammering at their heads.

"Mom! Put your hands down!" Wolf grabbed at Meegan's arm as she began to drone out a recipe for *basanti pulao*, wrenching her hand down from above her head. "And stop with the chanting. You're making things worse. What the fuck's in that sand?"

"Just the usual." His mother finally put her arms down, and the winds died to a whimpering breeze, an occasional gust picking up the feed into Winifred's growing bulk. "The sand I got from the holy men down the street. Oh, and some ground chicken bones. It keeps better than the whole ones. Really, I got tired of eating two pounds of hot wings before a séance. It was giving me indigestion."

"Shit, Mom." Wolf chewed the inside of his cheek, trying to remember the lessons he'd gotten from one of the many older Hellsingers who'd raised him.

He'd been a better student with traditional subjects. Somehow, he hadn't seen himself following the family business, paying more attention to the reason Diet Coke exploded when a Mentos was dropped into it than whether or not four naturally claimed butterfly wings were necessary for a love potion. Still, something of a warning tingled at the empty recesses of his brain where he'd shoved his childhood. Something about porous organic material becoming a vessel for a ghost's energy. It came to him in a snap… just as Tristan plunged a silver letter opener into Winifred's wiggling tongue.

The blond stopped the tongue dead in its slug-like tracks.

Winifred, however, was a whole different kettle of snails.

"Mom, you used organic grains for the summoning." Wolf turned his mother around. "Ground chicken bone. You spread it on the sand circle."

"Fuck, you're right." Meegan paled. "I put the chicken grit where I'd put the bones. Right on top of the sands."

"Yeah, and when you called her up, you gave her something organic to pour into. Mom, that's why you're supposed to use the whole bone. A ghost can't animate something that large. The ground-up dried bone you laid down? She can *use* that. That's why she's here. Smoke, bone, and mirror, Mom. That's what keeps a ghost contained in the circle. You *broke* the circle."

What little he'd retained as a kid, Wolf couldn't forget about the big three in summoning: smoke, bone, and mirror. Like the holy trinity of Creole cooking, nothing good could come out of altering the basics. The hint of smoke from a candle was enough to break down the light spectrum so a ghost could cross over, and the salt acted as the mirror, its tiny fractal surfaces shiny enough to trap a spirit from wandering, but it was the bone that drew the spirit. A representation of life, the bone was meant to be used as lure to draw the ghost's attention but it needed to be fairly large too heavy for the malevolent spirit to possess and move about.

Much like Winifred was doing right now with the chicken bone grit sliding over the floor and up into the body she was building with her willpower and hatred.

It was one of the major tenets drilled into every Hellsinger since they were able to hold their first salver of salt. Never ever give a ghost a chance to grab hold of the physical world or you'd have a shit of a time getting it to leave. From the way Winifred was cackling from her tongueless maw, Wolf had to wage a battle he was ill-prepared to fight.

"Fucking shit damn it to hell," Meegan swore. "I am *so* stupid! What was I thinking?"

"Yeah, let's have that conversation later. I've got to get Tristan out of her way."

Tristan was out in the open, and the ghost had him in her crosshairs. Before Wolf could detach himself from his mother, Winifred was on his lover, her fingers snaking out from her hands to press at the lips he'd just kissed. Black goop dripped from the ghost's torn-apart cheeks, and the slime splashed onto Tristan's bare arms, leaving red welts where it hit.

There wasn't much mistaking Winifred's intent. For all of Tristan's ignorance about ghosts and Wolf's fuzzy awareness of the supernatural, they both knew there was something paranormally attuned about Tristan, and from where Wolf stood, Winifred's assault was less about revenge and murder and more about gaining control of Tristan's body.

"Yeah, I never really liked sharing." Wolf grabbed at one of the fallen boxes of salt his mother had left under the now-upended table. "And I sure as fuck ain't going to share him."

The red cardboard box was battered, and Wolf had to cup his hand over a tear on its side or he'd have lost all of it in the dash to reach the reception desk. Yelling over his shoulder at his mother, he began to fill a coffee cup with some of the salt.

"Mom! Blow all the candles out." He caught a stir of bright hair from under the table. "Gidget, get out from under there and give us a hand. Drag Matt with you. Mom, figure something so we can fix this. We've got to send this bitch back to where she came from."

He didn't stop to see if the others were moving. Wolf was focused on one thing… stopping Winifred from crawling inside of Tristan's body and doing God knows what with it.

If there was any time he regretted not listening to the complicated "lessons" his older relatives ran him and his cousins through, it certainly was now. Okay, maybe when Winifred first appeared ranked up there in regretting his inattention, but the stakes were higher now.

The thought of losing Tristan—any part of Tristan—made something inside of him curl up and die. Painfully.

Suddenly the few pounds of salt he was holding didn't seem enough. He'd need an entire salt mine to bury Winifred so deep she couldn't resurface, but what he had would hopefully be enough to get her off of Tristan.

The pinned tongue was slowly dissolving into sand and grit, its twisting remains oozing out a thin black trickle of gore onto the lobby floor.

The inky smears on the opener were drying, the stains slowly turning to a wispy smoke, leaving the blade in soft gray plumes.

"Open the curtains! We need to get this place lit up." If blocking the light gave Winifred an advantage to rise, flooding the lobby with it could only help Wolf's cause. Not stopping to see if Meegan was listening to him, he launched himself at Winifred, armed only with a cup of rock salt and a feeble hope it was enough to push her back. "Come on, bitch. Let him go."

Her fingers were pushing Tristan's lips apart, invading him in a grotesque mockery of the pleasures he and Wolf shared in Tristan's bed. That had to be taken care of first. Aiming for Winifred's wriggling appendages, Wolf dumped the cup of salt over Tristan's mouth, hoping the sear of the salt would be enough for the ghost to let him go.

Her high-pitched screams were definitely a good sign the salt was working.

Too bad he hadn't thought about the salt dissolving her flesh and filling Tristan's gullet with burnt grind and inky slime.

Winifred flew off of Tristan, her ruined hands smoking and sizzling as she waved her arms around in agony. Pushing in between the ghost and his lover, Wolf turned Tristan over and pounded his back to clear his airways. The blond spat out wet mouthfuls of sand, gagging on the gore he couldn't get off his tongue, and his accusing eyes were a stormy green when he straightened up to look up at Wolf.

"Are you trying to kill me?" Tristan cleaned his tongue with his nails, flicking off a thin layer of moist grit.

"No, I'm trying to save you." If Tristan was grumpy, it was a good sign he wasn't too injured, and Wolf gave him a quick hug, then began to brush away as much of the sand and salt as he could see. "Okay, now to find a way to get rid of her once and for all. Can you stand up?"

"Yeah." Tristan let Wolf hoist him up. Peeking around his lover's shoulders, he frowned. "Shit, she's coming back."

"Grab the box and throw salt at her. We've got to disrupt her—" Wolf didn't get much further when the lobby flared with light. It poured in from the windows and from the old-fashioned bulbs above them as Meegan and Gidget threw back heavy curtains and turned on the chandeliers.

Winifred's mouth peeled back from her uneven teeth, crackling her already damaged cheeks. Her lips stretched up over her purplish gums, her skin mottled with uneven black and pink. Her arms hung loose from her shoulders, her wrists nearly at her knees, but her nests of serpentine fingers were gone, seared away from the dense coating of rock salt still clinging to her burnt stumps.

Matt dragged himself closer to Wolf, clutching a couple of salt boxes to his chest. His jeans were wet with blood, the denim soaked black around a nasty looking tear on his thigh. His hands shook violently when he passed one of the boxes over to Wolf, and either fear or blood loss stole the color from his face.

"Go hide behind the desk. If she can't see you, she'll leave you alone. I've got this." Tristan took the other box from Wolf's trembling technician. Matt looked at Wolf for reassurance, and Wolf nodded, urging his assistant to take cover.

"I dropped my cell phone back there someplace." Wolf had to shout to be heard through Winifred's increasingly frantic shrieks. "Call my cousin Cin. See if he can't get someone here. We're going to need backup if we can't drive her out."

Matt looked like he was about to protest, and Tristan shoved his shoulder, pushing him toward the reception desk. Stumbling, the young man ducked down behind the mahogany swerve, and Wolf could only hope he found the dropped phone to call in reinforcements.

Gidget was now throwing as much of the sand and salt as she could gather from the floor at Winifred as Meegan circled the ghost, her fractured Latin exhorting the ghost to leave the premises. Despite the chanting and splashes of toxic grains, the phantom stood fast, flailing at the women with her truncated limbs.

"Take the salt." Tristan shoved his box into Wolf's hands. "I've got an idea. Keep her here. Don't let her leave. I'll be right back."

"Yeah, I think leaving's the last thing on her mind." Wolf glanced at the ghost doing battle with his mother. "Where are you going?"

"You'll see. Let's hope this works."

Meegan had found a fireplace poker and was coating it with cooling wax from the candles. Dipping the poker's end into the wax, she packed salt into the slick and stepped in, swinging her crusted-over weapon at the ghost, beating Winifred about the head. It was effective enough to sting at least, because when the cold-iron-and-salt hook struck Winifred's forehead, sparks flew, and a thick gash opened up above her eyebrow, sending speckles of grit tumbling down the front of her dress.

Tristan bolted off toward the ballroom, leaving Wolf holding both boxes of salt.

"Fuck, well at least he'll be safe," Wolf muttered to himself.

The boxes were both half-full, and he needed to find a way to cover Winifred with as much of it as possible. She was hard to get close to. Her spinning about made her dangerous, and Gidget's face and bare arms were welting up where she'd been hit.

Handing the younger woman a box, Wolf yelled, "Get as much on her as you can. Like you're spreading chicken feed."

"I have never fed a chicken in my fucking life!" Gidget screamed back. "Chicken comes on Styrofoam trays or in little white globes."

"Fucking hell, just watch." Wolf poured some salt into his hand and flung the grains out, scattering it over Winifred's back.

The ghost's reaction was immediate—a screech of pain—and the buttoned-up back of her dress began to dissolve, peeling down into crumbling trickles. A thin cobweb sheath of shadows peeked out from between the tears in her outer layer, and Wolf hit her again, aiming for the viscous dark threads.

The salt hit the strands and passed through the holes between the lines. Smoke began to pour out of the holes, tearing the edges further. Wolf scattered another handful, aiming for the same spot, but the ghost turned, slapping at him with her fingerless hand, and he reeled back, a sharp pain creeping across his right cheek.

Gidget screamed when Winifred advanced on her, and the young woman flung out handfuls of salt crystals at the ghost, her thick mascara running down her cheeks from the tears on her lashes. Meegan wound up and struck again, catching the poker hook into Winifred's neck.

"Wolf, I'm stuck!" Meegan called out as he was shaking off the hit. "I can't get it loose."

He had to step quick to avoid the ghost's rubbery arms, but Wolf scrambled over the messy floor to grab at the poker's wooden handle. Meegan released her hold and snatched up the box of salt he'd abandoned, filling her hand to strike Winifred down again.

Then the music hit them in its full discordant fury, and Wolf was nearly dropped to his knees by the rolling bass coming from the corners of the room.

"What the fuck?" Clapping his hands over his ears, Wolf tried to keep most of the cacophony out of his eardrums, but the screech of guitar stripped right through his fingers. The noise settled down, an undertone of thundering beats layered with a bluesy melody and the roil of a liquid-smoke voice.

I took his hand, ran to temptation and sin
Drowned in song, ink on a pin
Dusted off the rust, let go of my pain
Best thing I did, was come out of the rain

Wolf recognized the song. It was a few years old and still coming up on rotation whenever he shared a car with Cin. A chorus followed, something about pretty boys, stolen kisses, and fire escapes. Then the music shifted, toning-down distortion was gone, and the piercing pain in his ears had subsided.

Winifred, however, didn't appreciate the music, even after it leveled out. Her shrieks of outrage and pain turned to a nearly soundless keening, but the edge of her voice lingered at the edge of Wolf's hearing, drilling through his skull. If anything, the noise coming from the specter was harder on his ears than the music's initial dissonance.

He also couldn't yank the poker out of the back of her head, no matter how hard he tugged, and Winifred twisted around, lifting Wolf off of his feet as he clung on for dear life to the poker's wooden handle. She spun again, her arms a whirligig of motion around her, and one truncated hand flew up, striking Wolf across the mouth.

Spitting blood, he did the sensible thing and let go.

Halfway through the flying arc through the wide lobby, he belatedly realized he should have been closer to the floor before he released the handle.

Wolf hit the floor hard enough to rattle his brain… or what little he had left. Tucking his elbows in did nothing other than making it easier for the parquet to find his funny bone, and he rolled somewhat, slamming his knees against the floor in an awkward attempt to come to a stop. The waxy sheen on the parquet definitely was thicker in places, and he hit a slick patch, scooting farther down the walk and tumbling against the lobby's antique wainscoting before coming to a shuddering stop.

Right at Tristan's bare feet.

His lover jumped out of the way, a thoughtful gesture until Wolf realized he probably moved so he wouldn't be mowed down by Wolf's legs and arms. Amid the tumbling and flying, the song played on, a rough growl of music guaranteed to make a long stretch of highway a little more interesting and a lot less lonely.

I came on down, fell from the sky
So fucking glad the Devil stopped by
Tears wiped dry, bruises faded from skin
Made whole and loved, drunk off Sinner's Gin.

"It looks like it's working!" Tristan shouted through a stretch of guitar licks.

"What the fuck are you doing?" Wolf yelled back, his voice suddenly too loud in a drop of chords and words.

"You said ghosts are like infrasound," Tristan explained hastily. "They're on a spectrum, right? Well, so is music. I figured if she's physical, she wouldn't be able to stand something audio in her physical spectrum. So, music!"

"God, I love you. That's fucking brilliant." He cupped Tristan's face and gave the man a deep kiss. "I'll thank you better later. Right now...."

"Get rid of her." The blond nodded, his eyes bright. "Got it."

Behind him, Winifred continued to scream and wail, turning Wolf back around in alarm. His mother was flinging as much of the salt she could on the ghost, the white specks turning Winifred a mottled black where they struck. More and more of the woman's dress flowed from her form, leaving small dunes on the floor as she struggled to get free of the salt-encrusted poker stuck in her ravaged head.

The music was relentless, hammering at the specter as she continued her macabre dance, but Wolf wasn't leaving anything to chance. Winifred was spotty in places, and he could see her disintegrating right in front of them.

Motioning to the mess on the floor, he shouted at Gidget and Tristan, "Find the ring! It's probably anchoring her here."

"That ring's a family heirloom," Matt yelled out from behind the desk.

"So's this fucking ghost, and we're going to get rid of her too," Gidget screamed back, flinging her hair away from her face. "When this is done, we are going to have a serious talk about your priorities!"

"I'm running out of salt, Wolf!" Meegan warned.

"Go look for the ring," Tristan said, patting Wolf on the shoulder. "I'll grab salt off the floor and help your mom."

The table had landed on its side a few feet away from where it started, tossing the candles and sand everywhere. A few of the salt salvers survived the toss, their contents mingling in with sand and ground bone, but thankfully, the candles guttered out before their flames could catch on anything nearby. The sand was lumpy with wax and crystals his mother had set into her mandala, so Wolf dropped to his knees and frantically dug through the mess, hoping to find the jeweled monstrosity that brought the howling nightmare to the Grange.

A second later, his heart leaped when Gidget sat up suddenly, brandishing the ring. Shoving it under Wolf's nose, she squealed, "I found it!"

"Smash it!" he ordered, handing her one of the heavy candle bases his mother had dragged in from her van. "They've got her cornered. Sort of."

Tristan was doing his best, going toe-to-toe with the phantom who'd spent a good part of her corporeal existence trying to crawl down his gullet. Her wobbly stumps were withered cobweb shapes flapping about helplessly as Winifred tried to escape. His mother had grabbed the poker and wedged herself against the curve of the desk, anchoring herself against Winifred's now desperately churning form.

The ghost's once horrifying visage was now a shredded mass of black slime and sand flecks, her jaw ruined and her eye sockets now a dull matte, the light gleaming from their empty holes fading rapidly. The sand coming off of her dress was now pouring from her where they'd done the most damage, creating an oddly disjointed sand painting beneath her disintegrating feet.

"I can't," Gidget said tearfully.

"What?" Wolf's breath caught, and he nearly choked on his tongue. "Are you fucking crazy?"

"I can't do it!" Gidget wailed. "Matt gave it to me, and...."

"Fuck that. Give it to me." He reached for the ring and tore it from her hands. "I'll buy you a new one. Whatever you want. But that fucking thing goes."

He wasn't sure what the candle holder was made of, but it was large, heavy, and definitely up to the task. He cleared a space on the floor, put the ring down, and raised the holder over his head. Taking a deep breath, Wolf slammed the base down, smashing the ring beneath its cumbrous weight.

The ring shattered.

And so did the woman tied to it.

Winifred went out loudly, her body exploding into bits, leaving nothing behind but the splatter of fading wet shadows, sand, and bits of cobwebs floating in the air. The poker clattered to the floor, and Meegan tumbled back, landing on her ass as the ghost's resistance was suddenly taken away, leaving her nothing to leverage herself against.

Tristan leaned over, supporting himself with his hands on his knees, and panted to catch his breath. His blond hair was tangled, wild around his patrician face, and a small smear of blood marred the length of his straight nose. Grit speckled his mouth, remnants of the salt Wolf poured over Winifred's prehensile fingers, and his clothes were filthy, but to Wolf, he'd never looked sexier.

Wolf spat out a piece of cobweb and grinned up at his lover. "So, still up for Chinese? 'Cause you know, this whole thing can count as our first date. Shitty horror movie and dinner."

"Sure," Tristan muttered as the music slid over to something softer. "Chinese sounds great, but next time, I'm picking the fucking movie. Yours sucked."

Epilogue

WOLF SHOULDN'T have been able to see her. If see was the word for the barely there whisper of a woman standing across from Tristan on the other side of the reception desk. The filmy specter grew stronger as he came down the stairs, her dress swaying with fringe and beads when she brought her hand up to pat down an errant curl of her short bob. He could almost make out the feathers of her spangled headband, but her legs were still amorphous, although there was a strong hint of a pair of Mary Jane heels tapping soundlessly at the floor. The ostrich feathers on her headband danced in time with her feet as she cocked her head, listening carefully to his lover as he registered the Grange's first spectral guest since they'd turned Winifred into a pile of smoking sand.

Tristan was practically beaming as he leaned in to talk to the glossy shadow across the counter from him.

Wolf had to give the cleaning crew credit. The lobby sparkled, and the floors were spotless, returned to their glossy, overwaxed state. The past few days had been hectic, a beehive of activity and flawed explanation about how the lobby got to be the mess the crew found it in. Tristan had hemmed and hawed a bit, running off into stories before Wolf finally shoved him aside, wrote a blank check, and told them to make the place look good.

The table was back up with a new vase, a shallow, wide affair in a translucent cerulean blue. The sprays of lavender, cabbage roses, and some white fluffy flowers Wolf couldn't identify were less fussy than the lobby's previous arrangement, but the same could be said about the blond man he was coming downstairs to see.

Or maybe, Wolf thought, he didn't have his knickers in a twist anymore about ghosts and their existence. They certainly were present at the Grange. The rest of the world, however, was still suspect.

"Thank you, Miss White." Tristan scribbled something on a line in the register. As difficult as it was to see the lithe woman's shape, there was no mistaking the flirtatious cant of her head and the bright flash of her broad smile. Tristan's answering murmur was a soft acknowledgement of the woman's teasing jibe, his cheeks flushing with a slight pink glow at something she said. "Meg, then. Thank you. You can call me Tristan."

Wolf stood on the landing halfway up the first-floor stairs, leaning on the banister as Tristan finished up with his guest. The light on his right shoulder went dark for a moment, and he glanced behind him, a part of him still a bit on edge.

"I'm not going to knife you." Mara rolled her words, her face smug with satisfaction. If he didn't know better, Wolf would have said she made a game of sneaking up on him and scaring the shit out of him. But then, he thought, he really *didn't* know any better. For all he knew, it was how the housekeeper got her jollies. Between that and counting the linens, the Grange didn't offer up much for entertainment.

For Mara, anyway. Wolf was entertained just fine. Especially by the long-legged, green-eyed blond artist standing a few feet below him.

Mara returned the day after Winifred exploded, and the Grange and its occupants settled into a lazy routine, mostly centered around cleaning and, for Tristan and Wolf, sex. Gidget and Matt periodically dropped by, and his mother had left a day ago, her brightly painted VW van bumbling down the driveway to take her back to her life at the crystal shop and dealing with Hellsingers looking for supplies.

"It's good to be home, Mara?" he asked the older woman.

Smoothing down the front of her housekeeper's uniform, she quirked a saucy grin at him. "You tell me, Dr. Kincaid. Is it good to be home?"

He caught her meaning as she glanced at the stairs below. Nodding, he thought of the craziness over the past weeks and the blond man he'd found living in his heart.

"Yeah, Mara. It's damned good to finally be home."

The shadowy figure was gone by the time Wolf looked again, but Mara was turning, as if to greet someone coming up the stairs. She smiled warmly at Wolf, then patted his arm. "You go to your man. I'll see our guest to her room. She looks to be a pistol."

"See you later, Mara." He didn't question the woman being able to see the flapper. Wolf was pretty sure, after a few months of staying at the Grange, he'd pick up on the boo-wigglies as much as she did. "Try not to get into too much trouble."

"Oh, little boy, I've caused more trouble than you've ever imagined," the housekeeper scoffed. "Go on. I've got to work to do."

He couldn't see the ghost coming up the stairs, and other than a brief hope he hadn't run right through her, Wolf hit the lobby with a cocky swagger. Tristan watched him cross the space between them, his expression bemused when Wolf gathered him up in his arms and swung him about in a rocking hug.

"Missed me?" Wolf murmured into his lover's ear.

"We've only been apart for twenty minutes."

"So you were *dying* with longing, then?"

"Devastated," Tristan drawled. "Nearly suicidal. Thank God I have Boris to stop me from leaping off the desk to my certain death."

"Yeah, I can see you wasting away."

He stopped rocking the man and trapped Tristan against the wooden counter. Capturing the man's lips in a fierce kiss, Wolf explored the warm depths of Tristan's mouth, sucking on the tip of his tongue, then teasing him with a nipping bite at the end of his nose. He left Tristan panting, and from the thickening of the man's cock beneath his jeans, Wolf guessed he'd also left him wanting more.

Rubbing his nose on the wet spot he'd left behind, Wolf whispered, "So are you done here? Can I take you upstairs and ravage you?"

"Actually, I've got to go pee. Ravaging is going to have to wait," Tristan teased, and Wolf dropped his head in mock exasperation. "Can you watch the lobby for me? It's Tuesday. I keep hoping Cook will come back."

"You're assuming I can see her," he pointed out.

"I have faith. You see Jack. Maybe you just need to be tuned." Tristan suckled on Wolf's lower lip and let his hands drop down to cup Wolf's ass. "Besides, you only have to watch out for wet footprints on the floor."

"She'll wait, right?"

"Maybe. Once it hits noon, the ghosts usually stop coming. Cook's different, but I just… don't want her to come in and not find anyone here." Tristan's guileless pout nearly broke Wolf's heart. "I don't want her to think she's alone. She might not talk to you, but she'll see you and wait."

"Don't worry, babe. I'll be here." He'd come a long way in believing the Grange held ghosts, but the skeptic in him still picked and prodded at the mysteries left to be uncovered. "You have any idea why she comes back over and over and the others leave?"

"I don't know," Tristan replied softly. "There's a lot of things I don't know. Like how come most of the guests aren't old. Why people show up looking younger than when they probably died. They're always cheerful, or at least pleasant."

"Maybe they come here looking like when they were the happiest," Wolf mused. "Of course I guess that means I'm never going to leave this place 'cause I'm pretty happy right here... right now, Pryce. With your fucking obsessive ghost dog and his red ball."

"You're kind of nuts, Kincaid." Tristan studied him, his eyes going gold in the late morning light.

"You're supposed to think that was romantic," Wolf sighed heavily. "And say something like, 'Yes, Wolf, and I'll be right here with you. Forever. At the Grange. Like Heather the Cook, except without the coming in every Tuesday to ask after a job.'"

"See? There's the nuts part, right there."

"Yes, Wolf." He rolled his eyes. "I'll be right—"

"Yes, Wolf. You're right. I'll be right here. You, Jack, and the fucking ball...," Tristan parroted back. "Which I *told* you not to pick up."

"Yeah, you love me." Wolf grinned. He was being silly, but he didn't care. If anything, for the first time in his life, he finally understood the insanity his mother seemed to thrive in. It was a grabbing of his gums and brain in the tight grip of *happy*. "Go pee. The romance between us is just killing me."

"Don't... break anything," Tristan warned him, sliding away from Wolf's embrace. "I'll be right back."

"It's a desk. What can I break?" He watched Tristan disappear into the side hallway, then looked down when he heard a thumping near his feet. Boris's eyes slit open wide enough for Wolf to imagine the dog was rolling his eyes at him, just like his master did a few seconds ago. "Furball, you with us on this madcap adventure into eternity?"

If a long-suffering sigh was any indication of agreement, then the wolfhound was going to be their bosom companion until the sun burned from the sky.

The door creaked open and Wolf looked up, but no one appeared on the threshold. A second later, a small puddle appeared on the lobby floor, then another a few inches away, until a clear path of wet footprints made their way to the curved desk.

A sunbeam filtered down from one of the high windows, and the shadows around it caught on the partially formed woman's face, her wide eyes bruised with fatigue. Her hands trembled when she removed the lace cap from her upswept hair, the loose strands about her face dripping from a storm raging somewhere in the past.

"Pardon me, sir," she murmured, keeping her eyes partially down. "But I'm here about the cook's job. I would have gone around to the servants' door, but I couldn't find one marked. I've got no references, as the Lady turned me out for what the Lord was doing, but—"

"It's okay," Wolf interrupted. "We don't need references. I don't know what Tristan pays you, but you're hired. Um… kitchens are over that way. Through the door and down the hall. If there's anything in the fridge, toss it out. Chances are something my mother made is plotting to take over the universe."

The ghost gave him a curious look, then pointed toward the rear of the manor. "That way, sir?"

"Yeah, sure." Wolf winced. "You probably have no idea what a fridge is."

"No, sir, but I'll do my best." Her fading voice lightly mocked Wolf as she headed off to her duties, leaving a trail of damp footprints behind to show she'd been there.

"It's all we can do, cupcake," he murmured as she wisped out of his sight. "Now, where the hell did Mara put that mop?"

TRISTAN HAD never imagined seeing water on the lobby floor would make him happy. Even better was the view of Wolf's ass as he bent over to wipe away the last of the footprints left behind by his Victorian London cook. Boris was up and out from behind the reception area, trailing after Wolf as he moved about the lobby.

Any thoughts of drawing that afternoon crept away under the heat of the need to strip his lover down and swallow as much of Wolf as he could get into his mouth. He was about to suggest that when Wolf looked up and winked at him.

"Your cook's here," Wolf growled at him with his whiskey-tough voice. "I told her she could clean out the fridge, but she looked at me funny. I guess they don't have Maytag where she comes from."

"No, not so much," Tristan chuckled. "Hopefully, she won't figure out what you were talking about. I think your mom's leftover casserole has started to summon forth Zuul. We might have to just set the whole thing on fire."

"I love that you know Zuul." Wolf stood and wiped his damp hands on his jeans. "The fire will come in handy for the marshmallow man who'll be by later. I saw the chocolate and graham crackers up in your apartment. We can make a night of it."

"I was hoping to make an afternoon of it. If you want to lock the front door, I want to head up and start a pot of spaghetti sauce." Tristan cocked his head and tried to look as sexy as he could. He didn't have much experience at it, but Wolf didn't seem to mind. "It can simmer in the Crock-Pot for a few hours, and—"

"Hell, it can simmer overnight if you want, Pryce." Wolf hooked his fingers into Tristan's waistband and pulled him in for a kiss. "But yeah, I think I can come up with something for us to do until the sauce is done."

Their mouths touched, a light sizzling brush of their lips, and Tristan fought not to let himself fall into Wolf's kiss. The last thing he needed was to have sex on the lobby floor. Not when there was a comfortable bed waiting for them. Pulling away, he shook his head at Wolf.

"Nope, not doing this. The last time I let you con me into someplace other than the bedroom, I ended up with carpet burns on my ass."

"I kissed and made them better."

"You kissed and made some more," Tristan accused. "Lock the door and meet me upstairs."

He was almost to the first landing when Wolf called out to him. "Hey, Tris!"

"What?" Bending over the railing, he yelled back, feeling stupidly daring for screaming across the lobby. After years of being… sedate, it felt good to let loose.

"How about when the spaghetti is done… simmering, we invite Mara to eat with us. She's got to be sick of her own cooking, right?" Wolf leaned back, staring up at him with his arrogant smirk. "Don't you think she gets lonely at dinner-time?"

He couldn't stop the laughter burbling up inside of him, and a fit of giggles broke free from his belly, the sound clearly insulting Wolf down below. It was going to break Wolf's heart to realize he'd steeped in the Grange's stew even before Winifred's arrival. The blow to the man's ego was going to be huge, and Tristan allowed himself a small bit of glee over Wolf's continuing downfall.

"What's so funny? I thought it was a nice idea."

"She can't eat with us, Wolf," he called back down. "She's been dead for over seventy-five years. It's why she goes back to the carriage house in the afternoons. It's where she haunts. Didn't you figure that out when no one else saw or spoke to her?"

"What the fuck? Are you kidding me?" Wolf's shout followed him upstairs, and Tristan shook his head at the outrage in his lover's voice. "I thought it was just because we were... shit, fucking hell."

"No, I'm not kidding you!" Tristan called down from the second-floor turn. "And don't forget to lock the door before you come up."

"Just tell me one thing," Wolf yelled back. "Tell me this dog here is real. Right? Boris? He's real, right?"

"Lock the door, Wolf!"

"Fucking hell," Tristan heard Wolf mutter at the enormous shaggy dog angling for a head scratch. "Let me go lock the door. Then me, you, and your daddy are going to have a long, serious talk. But maybe after that spaghetti finishes simmering."

Stay tuned for an Excerpt from

Sequel to *Fish and Ghosts*
Hellsinger: Book Two

Paranormal investigator Wolf Kincaid knows what his foot tastes like.

Mostly because he stuck it firmly in his mouth when his lover, Tristan Pryce, accidentally drugged him with a batch of psychotropic baklava. Needing to patch things up between them, Wolf drags Tristan to San Luis Obispo, hoping Tristan's medium ability can help evict a troublesome spirit haunting an old farmhouse.

With Wolf's sister handling Hoxne Grange's spectral visitors, Tristan finds himself in the unique position of being able to leave home for the first time in forever, but Wolf's roughshod treatment is the least of his worries. Tristan's ad-hoc portal for passing spirits seems to be getting fewer and fewer guests, and despite his concern he's broken his home, Tristan agrees to help Wolf's cousin, Sey, kick her poltergeist to the proverbial curb.

San Luis Obispo brings its own bushel of troubles. Tristan's ghost whispering skill is challenged not only by a terrorizing haunting but also by Wolf's skeptical older cousin, Cin. Bookended by a pair of aggressive Kincaids, Tristan soon finds himself in a spectral battle that threatens not only his sanity but also his relationship with Wolf, the first man he's ever loved.

Chapter 1

THE SMELL of rot permeated the air.

It was a foul smell. A blackness to it Wolf would never get used to. With the proximity of the Florida swamp and Atlantic, there was a faint hint of stagnancy as well, with an overlay of brackish algae just for good measure. He couldn't imagine living in its stink every day. Like cigarette smoke, it would flavor everything he touched, breathed, or ate.

He'd expected some dampness, especially in the lower jut of an ill-advised half basement below the church turned hostel, but when his sneaker sloshed through an actual puddle in the kitchen, Wolf wondered if the owners had less of a ghost problem and were more in need of a home demolition.

The basement seemed to be where most of the noises were coming from. At least from what Wolf could figure out. Creaky, eerie sounds wafted through the sprawling hostel, carried through the antique ductwork set into heavily built walls, and they certainly appeared to be originating from underneath the first floor. Tapping at the plaster, Wolf frowned, wondering what the builders had been thinking when they'd put in so many tight hallways and corners. The maze made it difficult to find the source of the hostel's supposed haunting, but it apparently helped keep the place cool when it got too hot.

"It's like they got paid by the fucking corner," he grumbled. "Every single damned old house has a million stupid little corners."

An undulating groan drifted through the hostel, and a screeching wail followed close on its heels. A startled yelp nearly broke Wolf's eardrum, and he stopped for a moment with his foot on the second step down to the basement.

"Jesus, you trying to get me killed?" Wolf muttered, flipping the light switch at the top of the stairs one more time. "I could have fallen down this death trap and broken my neck."

Much like the other five times he'd clicked it, the light stayed off, and he glanced up, fumbling in his pocket for his flashlight. After finding it, Wolf turned the torch on and splashed the beam up along the ceiling, not surprised to find a pair of dangling capped-off wires where a light fixture should have been.

A woman's voice tickled Wolf's ear as he crept down along a tight spiral staircase. "I'm not exactly sure what I'm supposed to be doing here, Dr. Kincaid."

Wolf sighed and leaned his head against the cramped interior stairwell. Cupping his mouth over the wireless headset he wore to keep in contact with his intern, he counted to three, then said, "You're supposed to keep up with me."

"I'm trying to, Dr. Kincaid." The young woman sounded exasperated. "But your legs are too long. I can't keep up. I lost you back in the hallway. The lights aren't working in this end of the house. Everything went black."

"Where are you, Trixie?" he growled into his mic. "And more importantly, how soon can you get to the basement stairs?"

"Shit, you're going to go down there? Why? Can't we just use something to see underneath the house? Like they do for dinosaurs. What is that? Sonar? Can't we use that?"

Biting back a sarcastic reply, Wolf reminded himself that soon-to-be-Doctor Trixie Huff was his only staff on the hostel job, so snarling at her probably wouldn't necessarily endear him to her.

Initially, he'd agreed to use the headsets because he wanted to keep his communication to a whisper so as not to telegraph where they were in the building's labyrinth of cellar space and servants' quarters. Now Wolf was partially glad he had it on because he kept losing his damned intern.

It wasn't Trixie's fault.

Wolf was just too used to working with his team, and the intern, while highly intelligent and sharp, hadn't planned on spending her summer vacation hunting ghosts in tourist-infested St. Augustine, Florida. Instead of lounging about the pool—or beach—being brought drinks by hot cabana boys in tight, skimpy shorts, she was tromping behind a grumpy parapsychologist in cobweb-cluttered mazes while rats and spiders dropped down on her like turtle shells in a game of Mario Kart.

When Hellsinger Investigations agreed to take on a pair of summer interns from Berkeley, it sounded like a perfect solution to his staffing woes. His techs, Matt and Gidget, longed to explore the Welsh countryside with its rambling hills and ghostly apparitions, while his office manager,

Nahryn, planned on having a three-week visit with her grandparents in Los Angeles.

Trixie'd been a godsend. Especially since she was enthusiastic and, more importantly, a bit of a skeptic about paranormal activity.

If there was one thing Wolf needed in his life at the moment—it was a skeptic.

No, he wouldn't think about Tristan. Not while he stood halfway down a flight of stairs with one wet foot waiting for an intern he was probably abusing by dragging her off to Florida so she could record his progress through a haunted hostel.

Something dropped onto him from above and skittered across his neck. Wolf resisted the urge to slap at it. He'd done that piece of stupid when he was younger and bore a half-moon scar on his shoulder from the very pissed-off centipede he'd slammed his hand over.

A strong beam of light cut over him, and Wolf grinned, glancing up at Trixie as she aimed the shoulder camera down the stairs. At some point, she'd dragged her glossy brown hair back and pulled a ponytail through a Hellsinger Investigations ball cap. Having abandoned her contacts for a sturdy pair of glasses to protect her eyes against the hostel's dirt and cobwebs, Trixie's eyes glittered with excitement behind her clear lenses.

"You ready, Huff?" Wolf grinned in the bright light.

"Sneakers on, boss," she retorted saucily.

"Good, because we're going in."

They went down the stairs together, Trixie's camera beam lighting up Wolf's shoulders. It actually wasn't a bad thing, because in the dank darkness, any light was welcome. Aiming his own smaller flashlight up, Wolf trudged through the tiny rooms built into the hill under the hostel, noticing the damp air thickened into an almost mist as they drew closer to the outer wall.

"Isn't a basement in Florida kind of stupid?" Trixie asked above their squeaky footsteps.

"Yeah, not exactly the smartest thing. Whoever built this place made the hill first. It's called a berm. It's a smart thing to do to get your property above the flood line, but instead the asshole dug in and put half of the house into it. I'm surprised this place hasn't come tumbling down on their—" A hissing noise made Wolf pause, and he turned, holding up his hand to stop Trixie from going any farther into the dark.

"What was that?" She kept her voice as steady as she could. Wolf gave her that. Even with the tremble in her throat, she held the camera steady, trained just beyond Wolf's shoulder as he'd instructed her. "Oh God, something's over there."

Wolf's beam was too weak to do anything but catch a sliver of movement beyond a turn in the hall. He took a few steps forward, but the camera's light didn't follow him, so he turned around, staring into the beam at the silhouette behind it.

"Come on, almost-Doctor Huff. Time to chase our ghosts," he urged her on. The light bobbed once, and Trixie moved in step behind him, but he could still hear her mutter under her breath at his back.

"You are certifiable. No college credit is worth this."

The thick rough walls under the old church must have been the only thing shoring up the foundation, but Wolf had to acknowledge the builder might have had something going. Lifted up off the ground, the airspace below would keep the building's lower level cooler during the hot summer months, but he'd have been more scared of wood rot than a high air-conditioning bill.

Especially when his foot went through one of the floorboards, and his leg dropped out from under him, slamming his crotch into the rotted wooden planks.

Wolf grunted from the pain of getting his balls shoved up into his rib cage, but he stopped himself from whimpering out loud. Huffing to maintain his composure, he shouted back, "Trix, stay back there. The floor's gone here."

"Oh God, are you okay?" The large light bobbled and then dropped low when Trixie set the camera on the floor next to her. "Do you want me to go get someone?"

"Let me see if I can get out of this hole." Wolf hissed when he leaned back. Massive splinters from the rough floorboards drove into his palms, and for once he was glad Nahryn insisted they all were current on their tetanus shots. "Okay, I'm going to rock back and pull my leg out. Be careful in case the boards go down behind me. I don't know how big this hole in the ground is."

"Why would someone dig a hole in the basement, then cover it with boards?" Trixie scooted forward a bit. "Do you want me to grab you and help?"

"No," Wolf said with a shake of his head. "Our weight might bring the whole thing down. Stay back where we know it's solid."

Wolf gritted past the pain and pushed himself up, leveraging his weight back until he got his knee clear of the hole. His jeans were shot, torn along his thigh and flecked with blood where broken wood scratched into his skin. Another heave, and he cleared the hole up to his calf. Then the deep shadows beyond the camera's powerful beam moved, and a low hiss echoed through the confined space.

The movement was slow, nearly graceful, and Wolf froze, trying to see into the darkness.

Then he realized what he was looking at, and his stomach crawled up to lodge itself into his throat.

"Trixie, I need you to move slowly back and go up the stairs. Now."

"And leave you here?" she scoffed. "That makes—"

"Leave the camera and get the hell out of here. Use the flashlight I gave you." Wolf kept his voice low, not wanting to spook the young woman. "Like right—"

The gator lunged out of the shadows, its teeth flashing a sickly yellow in the light beam. The reptile was nearly as wide across as Wolf's hips, its quick legs whipping its long body back and forth as it moved across the floor. Its long tail slapped into one of the walls, making a wet sound on the hard surface.

Trixie screamed and fled, her cries for help seemingly coming from all directions as she ran out of the space. Wolf jerked himself free of the hole, rolling to the side as he tried to scramble to his feet. The alligator made another lunge, throwing its body up a few inches, and his sneaker sole caught in its teeth, ripping from the bottom of his shoe as the gator twisted its head.

"Fuck!" Wolf dodged the camera, catching his nearly bare foot in its harness.

The gator went after him again, the floors creaking under the reptile's enormous weight. The boards bounced, and Wolf heard them cracking under him as he ran toward the room's entrance. Trixie's anxious screaming continued to bounce about the basement, a high-pitched wail loud enough to drown out the gator's aggressive hissing.

His own flashlight flickered woefully when Wolf tried to aim it down the hallway outside the room. A fragmented beam warned him he'd probably broken the lens, but it still gave off enough light for him to see his way out. Something heavy slammed into his side, and Wolf's heart jerked in fear until he realized it was Trixie running out from another room.

"I can't find my way out!" she wailed, grabbing at his arm. "Oh God, it's right there!"

Wolf chanced a glance back, and the gator grumbled with a menacing roar. Nudging the discarded equipment, the gator made the camera's light flash and tilt against its hide, illuminating its variegated skin. Wolf grabbed Trixie's arm and dragged her with him, urging her to run. A loud cracking sound came from the room behind them, and some small part of Wolf's brain wondered if the gator would be trapped in the hole he'd almost fallen into.

The larger part of his brain shoved that thought down, intent on escaping the seemingly pissed-off reptile rather than pondering if the rot would give before the gator could catch up with them or if gators could climb stairs. They hit the steps at a run, and Wolf pushed Trixie up ahead of him. Her sneakers pounded up the staircase, and he followed close behind, his hands pressed on the small of her back.

All around them, they heard the hissing and screaming wails of the gator thrashing its way through the basement. Its vocalizations echoed through the ductwork, and somewhere in the hostel, someone else started screaming, matching Trixie and the gator in volume.

Voices called out from various rooms, but Wolf didn't have the breath to answer. He shoved the intern through the open door at the top of the stairs, flung himself through, and kicked the door closed behind him with a mighty thump.

He lay on the floor, panting as people poured into the kitchen. Trixie lay on her stomach next to him, her body heaving from the sprint up the tight staircase. Someone sounded alarmed at the sight of his leg, but Wolf didn't care about the pain. From what he could tell, he was still intact, if just a little bit winded.

The owner, a long-haired older woman, leaned over him, her bright blue eyes blinking in surprise at his bloodied and mud-caked body. Patting him on the shoulder, she asked someone to call 911 before Wolf could stop her.

"Oh my, Doctor Kincaid. Are you all right?" she murmured in her soft butterfly voice. "What happened?"

"Found your ghost," Wolf gasped, fighting to push words out as he sucked in clean air. "And it's big enough to make a whole set of luggage."

"THEY ARE never going to give you another intern," Nahryn, his girl Friday, complained loudly as Wolf came through the front door of Hellsinger Investigations. "You keep breaking them!"

"Hey, I returned that last one in perfect working order!" he shot back, dropping a bag of donuts on her desk as he hobbled by. They were damned good donuts, hot and yeasty malasadas from a nearby Portuguese bakery. Good enough to ward off a scolding from a girl ten years his junior, but Nahryn wasn't having any of it, judging by the look on her face. "I'm the one who got fucked up."

"Yeah, well, death by gator isn't something a lot of people want to put on their résumé." She sniffed at him and opened the bag. The pretty Armenian girl eyed him, as if searching for sugar around his mouth. "Did you already eat one?"

"Yeah, on the way in." He winced at the steady ache along his thigh. Eight dissolvable stitches and a few shots later, his leg was patched up, but he was reminded constantly of his refusal to take any of the painkillers the doctors shoved at him. A few ibuprofens would do the trick, he promised his leg, along with a very nice hot cup of coffee.

"Well, take one in with you. Meegan's here." His office manager stepped in behind him before Wolf could turn around and drag himself out of the office. "Oh no you don't, Kincaid. She's your mother, and she's here to ask you something."

"I'd rather be eaten alive by the gator," Wolf muttered darkly. "Go get me coffee, and if I buzz you in ten minutes, I expect you to come rescue me."

"You'll be lucky if I even answer," Nahryn shot back with a Cheshire cat smile. "But I'll bring you some coffee, you big baby."

His mother was standing at the wraparound glass window of his office, her hands cradling a large cup of fragrant jasmine tea and her eyes dreamy as she stared out at San Francisco's bay. Ferries jetted from shore to shore, carrying tourists and locals alike. The morning fog kept a light grip on the shoreline, but it was a weak one, with a lemony sun pushing its way through the watery mist.

The faint sunlight shone around the older woman, outlining her long, curly bright auburn hair and crazy-quilt peasant dress. Large chandelier earrings made of tiny bells and beads tinkled when she cocked her head, her eyes following the activity on the pier below. She'd lost her sandals somewhere in the office, her bare toes spread over the office's wooden floors, and she shifted slightly, adjusting her black cobweb lace shawl over her pale arms.

His coffee arrived with a filthy look, both courtesy of Nahryn, and Wolf nodded pleasantly at her, then shooed the young Armenian woman out. Meegan Ocean-Kincaid turned and caught her son's eye, but instead of the beatific, motherly smile she normally gave him, her mouth was set into a neutral straight line.

From his hippie-gypsy mother, this was tantamount to a scowl.

"Hello, Mom." Wolf leaned in to give his mother a kiss, but she tilted her head back to stare up at him. Sighing, he rolled his eyes and said, "What?"

"What now, you mean?" Meegan sniffed.

It was a mighty sniff. Possibly one of the greatest she'd ever given him. It rivaled the one she'd aimed at him and Bach when they'd shaved Ophelia Sunday's head with their Uncle Stavros's clippers, but he still thought the time he'd dumped an entire load of horse manure on their living room floor because he was looking for gold coins held the top spot.

Another sniff, and the Horse Manure Incident sadly dropped to second place.

"I take it this is about Tristan?" He wondered if he could bribe Nahryn to go to the corner store and grab him whiskey so he could doctor his coffee or if it was still too early to start some serious drinking. "Have you talked to him?"

Her arched eyebrow lift was pointed enough he could hang a Christmas ornament on it, and Wolf took a gulp of his coffee, wincing at its sugary taste.

"Great, now even my office manager is trying to poison me," he muttered, setting the mug down. "Okay, get it out of your system, Mom. Go on and scream at my head."

"I don't scream, Wolfgang," Meegan informed him smoothly. "What I am going to do is tell you how disappointed I am in you. You have a chance at so much happiness, and you're letting your pigheaded stubbornness get in the way."

So yes, his mother had spoken to Tristan, and knowing his reclusive lover, he'd probably been nudged, bothered, and poked at until he spilled every last detail of their argument.

He didn't need his mother to tell him he'd fucked up. He screwed up by starting up a fight with Tristan Pryce, owner and proprietor of Hoxne Grange, a spiritual hub for ghosts passing on to the afterlife, then walking out on Tris. The gorgeous blond man was reserved, quirky, and more importantly, willing to shove back at Wolf's strong personality—and damn it, if Wolf didn't miss the hell out of him.

Tristan ended up under Wolf's skin, and part of the argument—most of the argument, if Wolf was really honest—was that he was scared. He was frightened by how quickly Tristan hooked his soul and pulled in Wolf's heart. He hadn't been looking for love when he went to debunk Tristan's ghost-hosting inn, but that's what he found—and he didn't want to ever let him go.

And that scared Wolf most of all....

"We had a fight, Mom," Wolf protested. "Things like that happen—"

"You accused him of hallucinating everything the two of you went through!" She turned on him, setting her cup down. Jasmine tea sloshed over the cup's rim, leaving a small amber puddle on his desk. "What happened at the Grange was—"

"Mom, the iced tea you gave us to drink had euphoric honey in it, and then you left a quart of it in his kitchen cabinet!"

"How was I supposed to know he'd make baklava with it?" She waved off his disgusted look. "Really? Does he look like he's the type to bake homemade anything? Does one even bake baklava?"

"He could have poisoned us with it! Honey's a major ingredient in that."

"No, really, how do you make baklava? Does it really go into the oven?" Meegan's attention had obviously wandered off into the intricacies of Greek pastries.

"Jesus, Mom. That stuff was potent. Hell, no wonder we ate ten pizzas after that damned séance. We had the raging munchies. What were you thinking?"

"Just to calm everyone down after the haunting!" Meegan protested. "I'll even bet you the baklava was good. It was premium honey. So what if it was a bit hallucinogenic? Some of my best memories were when I was a bit baked. Hell, you're here because of a bit of that honey."

"That's not the point." He rubbed at his face, then dropped his hands to his hips. "And I didn't say what happened that day wasn't real. I just—"

"You accused him of drugging you and said the whole experience was a mass hallucination!"

"I did not say that." Wolf kept his voice as even as he could. "When I was done tripping along the Timothy Leary Highway—"

"Something that wasn't his fault—"

"Mom, will you let me finish one sentence?" Wolf gritted his teeth and took a long breath to steady himself. "Please?"

"Fine, go ahead." Meegan threw her hands up. "Talk, but nothing you say to me is going to fix what you messed up. So you got a little bit stoned. It's just a relaxer—"

"It wasn't the five minutes of fun-house-mirror world, it was the hour and a half of me living in the bathroom, wondering if I was going to have to reel my guts back in, after the two hours of trying to talk to Tristan's monster illustrations," he insisted. "I might have said a few things I wasn't proud of, but I never accused him of drugging us that day. You did that."

"Afterwards!"

"I told him I loved him and I'd call him in a bit. Did he tell you that?"

"I didn't actually talk to him about afterwards. He's very close-lipped," his mother hedged. "But I definitely got the feeling things went a bit haywire. Then you hied off to God knows where."

"Florida. I had a job in St. Augustine, and I couldn't cancel. I was going to call him this morning." Suddenly tired, he sat on the edge of his desk, wincing when his leg reminded him of his stitches and bruises. "I just needed to think of what I was going to say."

"I'm sorry is a good place to start," Meegan replied tartly. "Then I'm sorry again. Maybe even I love you? You do love him, don't you?"

"It's complicated." The weariness of dealing with his mother set in, and he rubbed at his leg. "But yeah, I love him. It's crazy because I've known him for what? A month? And it's not like he's totally normal. We're going to have to come to some kind of middle ground."

"Well, it's time to uncomplicate it," his mother ordered. "And I have just the thing for that. Something you both can do together."

"Why does that scare the shit out of me?" Wolf picked up his coffee and took another sip. The sugar in it hadn't magically evaporated. "God,

I'm going to kill Nahryn. This is like hummingbird food. I did text him while I was in Florida."

"And what did you say? That you were sorry?"

"That we needed to talk." Admittedly, his messages had gotten more and more insistent with each unanswered text. He hated being ignored, and Tristan could ostrich with the best of them. "And I was an asshole. He didn't text me back."

"You should have called. It's been over a week, Wolf," Meegan huffed. "Okay, we can fix this. I have just the thing."

"I'm already going to go up there, Mom. I don't think I need—" He intercepted her simmering glare. "Fine, what is it?"

"Do you remember Sey? Your second cousin from your Great-Aunt Natty?" Meegan frowned at Wolf's clueless look. "The one in San Luis Obispo."

"Sey with the toys? Yeah, I love her. We've kept in touch." A slender, brash woman known for her boisterous laugh and nearly endless energy, Sey was one of the few relatives he positively adored. He'd spent more than a couple of summers as his older cousin's satellite, a tall lanky girl with sharp elbows and freckles. She'd been the one who'd taught him how to shoot a crossbow… and more importantly, how to run away from a charging bull when he'd accidentally fallen into the temperamental bovine's corral. "Why? What's up with Sey?"

"Funny you should ask that," Meegan practically cackled as she rubbed her hands together. "Because she's got a problem, and it's one that is totally up your alley."

RHYS FORD is an award-winning author with several long-running LGBT+ mystery, thriller, paranormal, and urban fantasy series and was a 2016 LAMBDA finalist with her novel, *Murder and Mayhem*. She is published by Dreamspinner Press and DSP Publications.

She's also quite skeptical about bios without a dash of something personal, and really, who doesn't mention their cats, dog, and cars in a bio? She shares the house with Yoshi, a grumpy tuxedo cat, and Tam, a diabetic black pygmy panther, as well as a ginger cairn terrorist named Gus. Rhys is also enslaved to the upkeep a 1979 Pontiac Firebird and enjoys murdering make-believe people.

Rhys can be found at the following locations:

Blog: www.rhysford.com
Facebook: www.facebook.com/rhys.ford.author
Twitter: @Rhys_Ford

THERE'S THIS GUY

Sometimes all a broken man needs is a bit of light and love.

RHYS FORD

How do you save a drowning man when that drowning man is you?

Jake Moore's world fits too tightly around him. Every penny he makes as a welder goes to care for his dying father, an abusive, controlling man who's the only family Jake has left. Because of a promise to his dead mother, Jake resists his desire for other men, but it leaves him consumed by darkness.

It takes all of Dallas Yates's imagination to see the possibilities in the fatigued art deco building on WeHo's outskirts, but what seals the deal is a shy smile from the handsome metal worker across the street. Their friendship deepens while Dallas peels back the hardened layers strangling Jake's soul. It's easy to love the sweet, artistic man hidden behind Jake's shattered exterior, but Dallas knows Jake needs to first learn to love himself.

When Jake's world crumbles, he reaches for Dallas, the man he's learned to lean on. It's only a matter of time before he's left to drift in a life he never wanted to lead and while he wants more, Jake's past haunts him, making him doubt he's worth the love Dallas is so desperate to give him.

www.dreamspinnerpress.com

A HALF MOON BAY MYSTERY

FISH STICK FRIDAYS

RHYS FORD

Half Moon Bay: Book One

Deacon Reid was born bad to the bone with no intention of changing. A lifetime of law-bending and living on the edge suits him just fine—until his baby sister dies and he finds himself raising her little girl.

Staring down a family history of bad decisions and reaped consequences, Deacon cashes in everything he owns, purchases an auto shop in Half Moon Bay, and takes his niece, Zig, far away from the drug dens and murderous streets they grew up on. Zig deserves a better life than what he had, and Deacon is determined to give it to her.

Lang Harris is stunned when Zig, a little girl in combat boots and a purple tutu, blows into his bookstore, and then he's left speechless when her uncle, Deacon Reid, walks in hot on her heels. Lang always played it safe, but Deacon tempts him to step over the line… just a little bit.

More than a little bit. And Lang is willing to be tempted.

Unfortunately, Zig isn't the only bit of chaos dropped into Half Moon Bay. Violence and death strike, leaving Deacon scrambling to fight off a killer before he loses not only Zig but Lang too.

www.dreamspinnerpress.com

A HALF MOON BAY MYSTERY

HANGING THE STARS

RHYS FORD

Half Moon Bay: Book Two

Angel Daniels grew up hard, one step ahead of the law and always looking over his shoulder. A grifter's son, he'd learned every con and trick in the book but ached for a normal life. Once out on his own, Angel returns to Half Moon Bay where he once found… and then lost… love.

Now, Angel's life is a frantic mess of schedules and chaos. Between running his bakery and raising his troubled eleven-year-old half brother, Roman, Angel has a hectic but happy life. Then West Harris returns to Half Moon Bay and threatens to break Angel all over again by taking away the only home he and Rome ever had.

When they were young, Angel taught West how to love and laugh, but when Angel moved on, West locked his heart up and threw away the key. Older and hardened, West returns to Half Moon Bay and finds himself face-to-face with the man he'd lost. Now West is torn between killing Angel or holding him tight.

But rekindling their passionate relationship is jeopardized as someone wants one or both of them dead, and as the terrifying danger mounts, neither man knows if the menace will bring them together or forever tear them apart.

www.dreamspinnerpress.com

www.ingramcontent.com/pod-product-compliance
Lightning Source LLC
Chambersburg PA
CBHW051642260626
47170CB00004B/1284